By the same author

The Ex-Wife's Survival Guide
Annie May's Black Book

About the author

Debby Holt was a shambolic supply teacher until she (and her pupils) were saved by her writing. She has five grown-up children and lives in Bath with her nice husband and her horrid mortgage.

Visit www.debbyholt.co.uk

The Trouble With Marriage

Debby Holt

POCKET
BOOKS

LONDON • SYDNEY • NEW YORK • TORONTO

First published in Great Britain by
Simon & Schuster UK Ltd, 2008
An imprint of Simon & Schuster UK
A CBS COMPANY

3 5 7 9 10 8 6 4 2

Simon & Schuster UK Ltd
Africa House
64–78 Kingsway
London WC2B 6AH

www.simonsays.co.uk

Simon & Schuster Australia
Sydney

A CIP catalogue record for this book
is available from the British Library

ISBN-13: 978-1-4165-2676-6

Typeset in Plantin by M Rules
Printed and bound in Great Britain by
Cox & Wyman Ltd, Reading, Berks

For David

Acknowledgements

As always, my editor, Kate Lyall Grant, and my agent, Teresa Chris, have been invaluable. Thanks to Alex Ryan who sorted out my computer. Sally Moon stopped me from making too many mistakes when I was a classroom assistant. Doctor Audrey Sawdy provided me with contraceptive advice which I used in the novel despite the fact that Audrey had just given birth to her fourth child. Emily Gerrard and Jill Miller gave me invaluable suggestions and Crysse Morrison told me to write this book. Finally, I would like to give heartfelt thanks to my lovely children, Ben, James, Sara, Rosie and Charlie who provide me with constant inspiration.

CHAPTER ONE: Past

'Oh, what a dear ravishing thing is the beginning of an Amour!'

APHRA BEHN

Tilly met Robin in her first year and second term at university. She had recently broken up with a boy who liked to clamp his arm round her neck whenever she was talking to anyone else. Someone invited her to a party on the other side of town and, with some trepidation, she went.

It was the first party she'd been to on her own since she'd arrived at Exeter. Hitherto she'd always had the safety net of boyfriend or flatmate. But her boyfriend was history and her flatmate had fallen in love with a wild-eyed anarchist who preferred pubs to parties.

So Tilly was nervous and tried too hard with her appearance. As soon as she entered the smoky living room she knew she'd overdone it. She was wearing too much make-up and the tight-fitting shirt with the straining buttons that seemed so sexy in her bedroom mirror felt absurdly out of place here. Most of the guests were terrifying third years who glanced at her with only fleeting interest before returning to their riveting conversations.

Glancing around the room with rising panic, Tilly spied her lifeboat: Steve, the tousle-haired boy who had invited her with such flattering enthusiasm the day before.

'Hi, Steve!' It was a welcome of desperate enthusiasm. 'I'm sorry I'm so late . . .'

'Are you?' His response denoted a dispiriting lack of interest. 'I don't think you are. Shall I take your coat? I'm going upstairs, so I might as well.' He sighed and waved a hand. 'The drinks are in the kitchen. Help yourself and have a good time.'

She watched him take her coat upstairs and, with it, her chance of escape. Don't panic, Tilly; enjoy the party, Tilly; get some alcohol and forget you're surrounded by strangers. She made for the kitchen and fought her way through to the bottles then helped herself to a very large glass of cheap white wine. The small room was packed tight with people and Tilly found herself wedged between the fridge and an immovable phalanx of drinkers. Since she couldn't move, she sipped her drink and tried to look as if she liked nothing better than to stand in a small, sweaty space watching everyone else being fascinating to each other.

A hand tapped her shoulder and a voice said, 'Hello. Are you a friend of Luke?'

Her saviour was overweight, with a white T-shirt that did him no favours. He had a few wisps of hair on his chin and damp patches under his arms. He was also rather short, which was possibly why he had made for Tilly; at five foot two inches, she was the only person in the room who could make him feel tall.

She rewarded him with a grateful smile. 'No . . . no, I don't know anyone here really. I'm Tilly.'

'I'm Mikey.' He took her hand, clasped it warmly and then turned it palm-side up. 'That,' he declared, 'is a good hand.'

His own was moist. 'Thank you,' said Tilly.

2

'You're welcome. What do you think of the party?'

Tilly nodded, saying, 'It's great!' and swallowed another large gulp of wine.

'I'm sure I haven't seen you around before. And I rather think,' Mikey stared at the over-stretched buttons on her chest, 'that I'd remember. Who invited you here?'

'Do you know Steve Richardson? He's a friend of mine.' Damn it, she couldn't lie even to someone with damp hands and moist armpits. 'Well, he's a friend of my flatmate's boyfriend. In fact I only met him for the first time yesterday. He asked me if I'd like to come along, though actually –' Tilly tried a laugh, an isn't-he-a-one sort of laugh – 'I think he's forgotten who I am!'

'Oh, you don't want to worry about Steve, he's out of his head half the time.' Mikey took a hefty swig from his bottle of beer. Tilly wondered if she should tell him his flies were half undone. 'Yeah, they're a pretty good bunch of people here. Stay with me and I'll introduce you to some of the crowd. Are you in your first year?'

'Yes,' said Tilly, mortified it was so obvious. 'I really like it here,' she added just in case he thought she was a pathetic loner. 'Exeter's a great place.'

'Yeah, I remember thinking that.' Mikey laughed, though not unkindly. 'It has its good points, I suppose: nice campus, good pubs near the sea.' He was pulling at the hairs on his chin. Tilly finished her drink and looked at her glass wistfully. Mikey instantly dived into the wall of backs and reappeared seconds later with a bottle of wine. 'Here,' he said, 'let me fill your glass. That's it. Yeah, I used to share a house with Max and Luke but I found I needed my own space, know what I mean? Sometimes you just need to be quiet to sort out all the noise in your head. All those hassles about who cleans the bath and who lets the kettle boil dry – I mean, who needs it? There are more important things to think about. You know what I mean?'

In front of her a voice was emanating from the largest back. 'It's not just sex, you know. I mean, it wouldn't be anything without the sex but that's not what it's all about, though she is something else in bed, I tell you, you have no idea . . .'

'It's funny,' Mikey said. 'I feel like I can really talk to you, like you understand. It's all about empathy, isn't it? Last year I sort of freaked out. I was reading *The Fall* by Albert Camus, great little book, do you know it? It said it all, you know? I mean, I thought: what's it all about?'

He looked at Tilly hopefully, so she murmured, 'Right!' and nodded furiously.

'Are you a Capricorn?' Mikey asked suddenly.

'No.' Tilly was apologetic. 'I'm a Pisces.'

'Of course, I can see that now, I should have known. Look, it's getting pretty crowded in here. Why don't you come up with me to Luke's room? There are some pretty good people in there and we can talk without shouting.'

The big back in front of her was becoming increasingly animated. 'It's incredible,' he was saying. 'I just lay there on the bed and she took out this pot of clotted cream and you won't believe what she did . . .'

'Let's go,' Tilly said, and she followed Mikey out of the kitchen.

Luke's room was large and cavernous, lit only by candles and thick with a pungently sweet aroma of incense. In the background, Alannah Miles was singing 'Black Velvet'. Tilly blinked and gradually identified a group of individuals sitting cross-legged in a circle.

'Hi, folks,' Mikey said. 'This is Tilly.' He laid a proprietorial hand on the small of her back which Tilly itched to shake off.

One of the group glanced up at her. 'Hello, Tilly. I'm Guy. Want to sit down?' Guy shifted his bottom and patted a place beside him. Tilly joined him on the floor and Mikey hastily squeezed himself into the circle so that he was on her other side.

Her new friend held out the fattest joint she'd ever seen. 'Want some?'

Until now, Tilly had steered clear of drugs. She didn't quite see the point of them since they seemed to reduce even the most fascinating person to a state of mind-numbing dullness. Tonight, however, surrounded by strangers and with Mikey breathing down her neck, a mind-numbing condition seemed pretty alluring.

'Thanks,' she said, took a puff and coughed violently as the combination of hash and tobacco hit her throat.

'You're not supposed to swallow it. Try again.'

This time she did not cough. She was at last beginning to relax. She felt a little light-headed but that was probably the wine. Mikey rested his hand on her thigh and when she let it remain there he looked like someone who's just scaled Mount Everest. She laughed and Mikey did too, which made her laugh even more. Then she noticed that her new friend had put his hand on her other thigh and she laughed again. She was enjoying herself. Sitting here with nice people who were relaxed and friendly, sharing a joint, drinking wine, listening to music: this was fun. She could have spent the entire evening in this warm, twilight room. But she stood up at last and told her new friends, 'I need the bathroom.'

'First left,' Mikey told her. 'Do you want me to come with you?'

'No!' Tilly giggled. 'Thank you very much!'

In the bathroom she gazed at her reflection in the mirror. 'I love you!' she said. 'You're beautiful!' She came out with a smile on her face and sailed straight into someone's chest.

Tilly looked up into warm, brown eyes fringed with thick, dark lashes. Below the eyes there was a straight nose and a delectable mouth with a slightly protuberant top lip. It was a beautiful face, instantly recognizable. It belonged to Robin Taylor. Tilly had bumped into Robin Taylor! She had never talked to him but she knew who he was. Everyone did. He and his girlfriend, Louise, were one of those golden couples other students regarded with wistful envy. Both of them were tall, gorgeous, supremely assured third years who strode round the university as if they owned it. Their break-up, just before the end of the autumn term, had been the talk of the campus.

Robin Taylor put his hand on her arm. 'Are you all right?' he asked.

In the face of such exquisite magnificence, Tilly would normally have stammered a few strangulated words of apology and fled. But tonight she stood free and unfettered, she was beautiful, she was funny and, most important of all, Robin Taylor was the most stunning man she'd ever met. She could hear EMF singing 'You're Unbelievable' in Luke's room. Such uncannily appropriate music surely had to be a sign of something.

'It was my fault,' she said. 'I wasn't looking where I was going. I hope your chest will recover!'

'My chest rather liked it.'

'Really?'

'Really. Why are you smiling like that?'

'I don't know. I didn't know I was. I suppose I just like looking at you.'

He laughed and took her hand. 'Come and dance with me,' he said. He led her downstairs and she was aware of people, especially female people, looking at them. She was Cinderella to Robin's Prince Charming, and when he slipped his arm round her waist she let her body sway close against his. Oh, the gorgeous agony of dancing with a man whose every touch seemed to set her body alight! They were dancing to the most romantic single of all time: 'Unchained Melody' by the Righteous Brothers. How wonderful, how extraordinary that she and Robin should be dancing to the very record that summed up the power and beauty of love better than any other song!

Now Prince was singing 'U Got the Look' on the stereo and the words were uncannily, amazingly appropriate. Tilly looked up into Robin Taylor's face and she ached to kiss those beautiful lips, and then – it had to be telepathy, there was no other explanation – he bent to kiss her and Tilly knew she finally understood why all Prince's songs were about the joy of sex. Robin's kiss was the most natural and the most exciting sensation in the world, and when he stopped she flung her arms round his neck and kissed him again.

'Look,' he said at last. 'What's your name?'

'My name is Tilly.' Tilly stopped swaying to the music and looked around the room, outraged. 'I don't believe it! I hate this song! Why have they put on Phil Collins?'

'I can't think. It's definitely time to leave. Do you have a coat?'

'Yes,' Tilly said. 'I do. I'll get it. Am I coming home with you?'

'Do you want to come home with me?'

'Yes,' said Tilly. 'I want to come home with you very much.' She giggled. 'Do you want me to come home with you?'

'Yes. Now, get your coat.'

'Right,' Tilly said. She walked carefully up the stairs, holding on to the banister because she felt as light as a feather and didn't want to float away without Robin. There was a dense pile of coats on the landing and Tilly methodically peeled them off, one by one, until she found her own.

Mikey came out of the bathroom. 'Hello,' he said. 'I wondered what happened to you. Do you want to go home? I'll come with you. You look like you could do with some company.'

Tilly smiled radiantly at him. 'I have some company! I'm going home with Robin Taylor!'

'Robin?' Mikey regarded her gravely. 'Tilly, I know Robin, he's a great guy, don't get me wrong, but he's getting through a lot of women at the moment, if you know what I mean, and I don't think it's a good idea for you to go back with him. Tilly, you're a lovely girl . . .'

'I know I am!' Tilly laughed and kissed Mikey on the cheek. 'And so are you! Though of course you're not a girl! Goodbye, Mikey!'

Robin was standing at the bottom of the stairs. He was talking to two men and a girl. They were laughing and when Tilly joined them they laughed some more, and she thought how wonderful it was that everyone was so happy.

Robin helped her into her coat. 'Adam's giving us a lift back,' he said. 'Let's go.'

Now Tilly was in a car, perched on Robin's lap in the back, squashed against two other passengers, all laughing and talking at the tops of their voices. Robin's arms encircled her waist and when she felt one of his hands steal inside her shirt she could barely wait to be on her own with him.

The car stopped to let them out. 'Have a good time!' shouted Adam, and one of the girls in the back giggled and added, 'Be good, Robin, and if you can't be good, be careful!' More giggles and then they were gone.

Now they were walking up some stairs and Tilly was glad that Robin was leading her by the hand because the stairs were melting around her and the walls weren't too fixed either.

Robin opened a door. 'Welcome to my home,' he said and helped her take off her coat. He switched on a lamp. It had a red lampshade and gave off an inviting glow next to the bed. The bed looked very comfortable. Tilly sat down on it and watched Robin crouch down to light the gas fire. She wished he would come over to her and touch her again. He glanced up at her and smiled. 'Do you want a drink? Are you all right?'

'I'm very all right,' Tilly assured him, 'and I don't want a drink.' She kicked off her shoes. 'Do you want anything?'

'That,' Robin murmured, 'is a very silly question.' He came and sat beside her and kissed her lightly. Then he kissed her again and this time his kiss was so strong and so passionate she felt she could drown in his embrace. He undid one, then two, then all of the buttons on her shirt. Now he was pulling her shirt off her and she gasped with delight as he unfastened her bra. Oh, but she revelled in her beautiful breasts spilling out just for him! He lay back on the bed, pulling her down above him, cupping her breasts with his hands, then gently teasing up her skirt.

And that was it. Tilly had no idea what happened after that. When she woke it was dark. She moved her leg and froze in horror as it brushed against something. Another leg, a long and hairy leg, a leg that quite definitely did not belong to her, was lying next to her own.

Tentatively, Tilly put out a hand and then withdrew it quickly. The leg belonged to a body, a naked male body next to her naked female body.

Tilly remained motionless, thinking furiously. She was in someone's bed. She tried desperately to recall the events of last night. She remembered smiling at herself in the bathroom mirror and she remembered the miracle that was Robin Taylor. She was in Robin Taylor's bed.

She was wearing no clothes, neither was Robin, and they were in bed together. So, presumably, obviously, they had made love. Had it been good, bad or indifferent? Typical, Tilly thought, absolutely typical: trust her to literally lose her virginity. All those years of speculation with girlfriends, all those temptations withstood, only to have not the faintest recollection of the actual act.

She moved her head up a fraction. The clock on the mantelpiece had luminous hands which revealed that it was ten minutes past five. The thought of Robin waking up and seeing her was unbearable. She could imagine only too well the studied politeness in his voice failing to disguise his impatience to be shot of her. Far better to escape now and retain a few illusions.

Tilly held her breath and slowly, very slowly, rose and slithered out of his bed. He stirred slightly and she bit her lip in silent panic until he was still again. She groped around for her clothes, hit her shin on something very hard and very painful, screeched soundlessly and tiptoed out of the room into the corridor. The landing light, harsh and unforgiving, had been left on and she dressed as fast as she could with fingers that had changed into blocks of wood.

She was about to leave when she realized she'd left her coat and bag in Robin's room. With a heart careering like a loose cannon in her chest, she tiptoed back in and crawled around the floor. This time, her knee made an extremely unpleasant connection with a chair and she sucked her lips together in pain. At least she'd found her things. She collected them from the chair and made her way on all fours towards the door.

The sheets stirred and a sleepy voice murmured, 'Are you going?'

'Yes,' Tilly whispered. 'Go back to sleep.'

'Goodbye.' Pause. 'Thanks for everything. You were great.'

'Was I?' Tilly asked doubtfully, but Robin turned his back on her and she heard his breathing lapse back into the rhythms of the unconscious. Hugging her coat to her chest, she slipped out of his room, crept down the stairs, let herself out of the front door and stood on the pavement, breathing in the early morning air.

The street was empty. Everyone was asleep. The city belonged to her. Tilly felt an unexpected rush of euphoria as she walked. She ought to be feeling ashamed of herself but she couldn't help it; little bubbles of joy kept intruding into her brain, banishing all attempts at sobriety. A milk cart trundled by and the milkman shouted, 'Had a good night, darling?' and she shouted back, 'Yes, I have!' and laughed. She felt a million miles from her previous safe and steady life in Somerset. Who would have thought that she, Tilly

Treadwell, would be creeping out of a gorgeous man's house before daylight? It was ridiculous, it was exciting, it was living!

She had spent a night with Robin Taylor and he had said she was great. She was glad about that, at least. She wished she could remember what had happened. She did remember him kissing her and the very thought of that kiss made her weak with longing. He was utterly beautiful, so beautiful he had spoilt any other man for her. But if she could end up in bed with Robin Taylor then anything was possible. She could climb mountains, she could take on the world, she could even, just possibly, see him again.

Her euphoria lasted until 11.35. At 11.34 she walked to the university and wandered into Devonshire House. At 11.35 she spotted one of the girls who had been in Adam's car, and waved cheerfully at her. The girl gave a brief nod and then turned to the man at her side. Tilly saw the man glance at her curiously for a moment before whispering to the girl. The two of them laughed. They were laughing at her.

Tilly knew her cheeks were flaming red. She remembered the knowing grins of Robin's friends at the party, she remembered the way she draped herself all over him within moments of their meeting, she remembered the disapproval on Mikey's face just before she floated down the stairs to where Robin and his friends were waiting. She recalled the journey back to Robin's flat, the laughter and the jokes of Adam and his passengers. She'd assumed they were laughing with her, a cosy conspiracy of irresponsible youth, when in fact they'd been laughing at her, a lovesick idiot who couldn't wait to take her clothes off for a stranger.

And Robin! He'd cared so little he had hardly stirred when she told him she was going. In fact, given her behaviour towards him, his casual dismissal of her was very under-standable. As far as he was concerned, she was a randy little slag who'd done all but lie down before him, saying, 'Take me, please!' He had simply given her what she wanted.

If Tilly hadn't been meeting her flatmate, she would have fled the building. As it was she walked through the coffee bar, dragging her worthlessness behind her. Kathy was waiting for her at a table by the window.

'I've bought you some coffee,' Kathy said. 'How was last night?'

Tilly took a gulp of the hot liquid and proceeded to tell her. Then she told her about the smirks she'd received a few minutes earlier.

'I think you're being paranoid,' Kathy said. 'So you get stoned and go to bed with Robin Taylor. Lucky you! I grant you, it's a pity you can't remember it but still . . .'

'Kathy, I met him for the first time last night and must have exchanged about five words with him before I had my tongue down his throat! Another five words and I was tearing all my clothes off. Or perhaps he was tearing my clothes off, I don't know. The fact remains that he must think, along with all his horrible cronies, that I'm the easiest lay in the entire univer-sity – no, the entire world. Oh, God, Kathy, don't turn round, don't look out of the window . . .'

Kathy turned round and looked out of the window. Robin Taylor was sitting on the balcony steps. Beside him, talking intently and stroking his arm was the beautiful, the desirable Louise Honeytree.

'Great,' Tilly muttered. 'He spends one night with me and it's enough to make him rush back to his ex-girlfriend.' For one ghastly moment Robin's eyes met her own and she saw him stare blankly at her. Tilly looked away quickly. 'I hate this,' she said. 'I'm off to my lecture.'

'It's not for another fifteen minutes. You can't keep hiding every time you see him.'

'Watch me. I'll see you later. Are you going out this evening?'

'No. Tom's going to a meeting and I want an early night. Stop looking like you lost a leg. You got laid. It's no big deal. It happens all the time, so cheer up!'

'I'll try,' Tilly said.

At least she found the lecture productive. She might not have taken in anything about the 1832 Reform Act but she did decide that the best way to salvage what dignity she still possessed was to ignore the whole incident. If she saw Robin again, or rather *when* she saw Robin again, she would act as if she didn't know him. Which, Tilly thought forlornly, was only the truth.

For the rest of the afternoon she hid herself in the library, failing to concentrate on the ramifications of nineteenth-century electoral reform. Images of Robin and Louise kept popping into her head. If she and Louise were animals, Louise would be a sleek, thoroughbred racehorse and she would be a donkey. Louise had shining blonde hair. Tilly's pale brown mop had spent its whole life unable to decide whether it was curly or straight. There was no point in comparing herself to Louise. Women like Louise were put on earth to make women like Tilly learn how to embrace humility.

Hunger pangs at last drove her back to Devonshire House. She hovered in front of the fruit and decided she'd made enough good resolutions for one day. In a spirit of reckless defiance she bought a Mars Bar.

Someone was shouting her name. Startled, she turned round.

Robin Taylor – languid, heroic, unassailable, handsome Robin Taylor, love-object of half the women on the campus, possessor of the sexiest mouth in the world, erstwhile and possibly current companion of the divine Louise Honeytree – Robin Taylor was shouting her name from the other end of Devonshire House. Robin Taylor ran across the vast expanse of floor and, ignoring a hundred curious eyes, took Tilly Treadwell in his arms. It was the most romantic moment of her life.

CHAPTER TWO: Present

*'Courtship to marriage is as a very witty prologue to a
very dull play.'*

WILLIAM CONGREVE

In some ways, Tilly and her daughter, Lucy, were very similar. Tilly, for example, was not a bad cook. She was not a
great cook either. She had never been one of those people
who could chuck things together and somehow produce the
perfect couscous salad. (Anyone who could cook couscous
without transforming it into cotton wool had Tilly's undying
respect.) Nevertheless, she knew how to follow a Delia Smith
recipe and her stews and pasta bakes were always good. Yet
every time she entertained her in-laws, she somehow produced a culinary disaster.

Lucy was a spectacularly healthy child. In her entire school
career, which admittedly had started only a year ago, she had
never missed a day. Yet every time they visited Robin's parents
or Robin's parents visited them, she managed to acquire a
vomit-making physical ailment.

Last time the conjunctivitis had made her look like a
Spielberg alien. The time before that, there had been the gargantuan wart on her left thumb. Her grandmother had been
horrified. 'Tilly,' she had said, 'you must take Lucy to the
doctor at once.' Tilly had promised Anne she would certainly

do so if the current treatment didn't work. Lucy had nodded eagerly. 'We rubbed it with raw steak and buried the meat in the garden. Mummy's friend says it will soon disappear.' Anne had opened her mouth and then shut it again. (The steak did indeed prove victorious. Tilly had enjoyed giving Anne the good news.)

Tilly was brushing Sam's hair when she heard the now familiar yelp. She went through to the bathroom and found Lucy sitting on the lavatory seat, her hands clenched grimly on the wooden seat, on her face an expression of weary pain. 'Stupid bottom!' she whimpered.

'Luce, I'm so sorry.' Tilly picked up a damp towel from the floor and returned it to the rail. 'I know it's horrid and you're being very brave. I've got you an appointment straight after school. Dr Sheldon will sort you out. Try not to be too long. We don't want to be late for the first day of term.'

Back in her bedroom, Sam's hair looked wild and unbrushed, probably because he had hurled himself over his father's shoulders. Robin unclamped Sam's hands, threw him back against the pillows and tried once more to put on his shoes. 'Poor old Lucy,' he said. 'I'm glad you're taking her to the doctor. It's like listening to a horror film every time she goes to the loo.'

Sam fought his way up from the pillows and nodded wisely. 'Lucy has a weally stupid bottom.'

'Yes, well, she won't for much longer,' Tilly said. She gathered Sam up and took him down to the kitchen where they were given the usual sleepy welcome by Horace, who unwrapped himself from his basket and padded amiably towards them.

Tilly set Sam down and gave Horace an affectionate pat

before opening the back door for him. She watched him run across the drive and onto the small, square lawn where he would, she knew, spend at least five minutes inspecting various possible locations before selecting the one on which he would empty his bowels. Tilly mentally added the task of turd removal to her list of pressing assignments. The last time her in-laws had visited, Anne had given her a mildly reproachful lecture on the dangers of dog-turd-induced blindness.

Tilly was not the only member of the family to be preoccupied by the evening ahead. Over breakfast, Robin bemoaned the fact that he hadn't cut the lawn at the weekend.

'It looks fine,' Tilly said. She was proud of their garden. As she had told Robin more than once, it might not be tidy but at least it was natural, the variety of weeds only adding to its charm. Tilly saw herself as a liberator of plant life, letting flora and fauna grow where they would, untroubled by forks or trowels.

'When I'm rich,' Robin said, 'I'll employ Garden Maids to do the lawn.'

Robin had discovered Garden Maids when he'd walked past the big house at the bottom of the lane three weeks ago. He'd spotted a white van bearing the eponymous legend, fetchingly painted in pink. Intrigued, he and Horace had peered through the big gates and observed a pneumatic blonde in skin-tight dungarees, wielding a spade with great enthusiasm. Robin had been very impressed and had even suggested that Tilly would look good in a similar outfit.

This morning, his mind was on more important matters. 'I'll try to get home early tonight,' he said. 'Dad said they'd be here about eight.' He downed his coffee and picked up his jacket from the back of his chair. 'I'm late already.' He kissed the top of his daughter's head. 'Have a good time at school, sweetheart.'

'I will,' Lucy said. 'I'm in Year Two now. I get to play in the front playground and I'm in Mrs Dawes's class this year and—'

'I want to hear all about it this evening,' Robin said hastily. 'And, Luce, when you get back home, tidy your room a bit, will you? Goodbye, Sam, be a good boy and help your mother.'

'Bye, Daddy!' Sam puckered his lips and raised his yolk-covered face. Tilly raised her face too. Horace, not to be outdone, positioned himself between Robin's legs.

'Out of the way, Horace, there's a good boy!' Robin grabbed his car keys from the dresser and disappeared through the back door.

Tilly lowered her face. 'Never mind,' she told Sam. 'My mouth didn't even have egg on it.'

'Daddy,' Lucy stated, speaking for them all, 'can be very annoying.'

Tilly stared at Lucy's mass of tangled curls without enthusiasm. 'I ought to do your hair. Will you go and bring your brush down?'

Lucy slipped off her chair. 'I'll do my teeth,' she countered.

Tilly began to clear the breakfast away, mentally shuffling the day's chores. The floor must be restored to its original colour, the fridge required a wholesale decontamination and the dresser was a heap of unpaid bills, premature seasonal charity catalogues and various notes and reminders that no longer made sense. Next door, the sitting room waited its turn, awash with dog hairs, dirty windows and drooping pot plants, while upstairs . . . upstairs could wait its turn.

'Howace!' Sam chortled. 'You tickling me!'

'Sam!' Tilly protested. 'Take your fingers out of Horace's mouth!'

Sam duly extricated his fingers and sat with resigned stillness while Tilly cleaned his face and hands. Horace, deprived of Sam's hand, began hoovering the crumbs around the chair.

Lucy clattered downstairs, her school rucksack on her back, her blonde hair fanning out around her like Frankenstein's monster bride. She took her lunch box from the fridge and eyed it with suspicion. 'I hope you haven't put too much butter in my sandwiches. You always put too much butter in my sandwiches.'

Tilly lifted Sam from his chair and was intrigued to find that egg yolk had found its way onto his bottom. 'How did it get there?' she mused and then, remembering it was dangerously time-consuming to pose rhetorical questions in front of Lucy, said quickly, 'Never mind! Let's go to school!'

This time last year, they had stood in fearful solidarity among the massed hordes of tall and terrifying children. Today Lucy disappeared seamlessly into a cluster of classmates. Tilly, spotting a friend by the hopscotch squares, clasped Sam's hand and made her way across the playground.

Tilly had met Amy three years ago. She had deposited a tearful Lucy at her playgroup – her first full morning – and was hovering unhappily on the pavement, unable to decide whether to go back in. The door had opened and a tall, big-boned woman came out. She had shoulder-length red hair, black leather trousers and a crimson T-shirt. 'Hi,' she had said. 'I'm Amy. And this,' she'd added, pulling from behind her a freckle-faced toddler, 'is Edward. I saw you in there. Your little girl is fine. Come and have a coffee.'

While two-year-old Edward entertained baby Sam with an astonishing variety of facial expressions, Amy had made coffee and aired her views on sex, love, politics and playgroups. She was confident, efficient, dynamic and dogmatic, without a hint of romance in her soul. Since that first meeting, Tilly had often thought they had nothing in common. Yet Amy was one of her most treasured friends.

'Where's Edward?' Tilly asked now. 'Is he nervous?'

Amy grinned. 'Not him! Ever since Luke started, he's been counting the days . . . him and me both!'

Tilly let go of Sam's hand and watched him walk carefully round the hopscotch squares. 'No small lump in your throat now your baby's starting school?'

'Will you cry when Sam starts?'

'Yes,' said Tilly. 'I'll no longer have any excuse not to work full-time.'

Amy snorted. 'You know your problem? You should have been a mother fifty years ago. You could have spent your days going into tea rooms and taking library books back, like Celia Johnson in *Brief Encounter*.'

'Celia Johnson went off with Trevor Howard in *Brief Encounter*.'

'So would I if I did nothing but drink tea and exchange library books.'

'I wouldn't.'

'No,' Amy sighed. 'You probably wouldn't.' She paused to check that her sons were only pretending to strangle each other in the far corner of the playground. 'I'm going to

21

Frederick's this morning. I'm fed up with my hair. I want a dynamic new look.'

'You ought to have Kirsty,' Tilly said. 'She's ever so nice and she comes to your house.'

'Tilly,' Amy said, 'do you *know* that one side of your hair is longer than the other?'

'She's cheap,' said Tilly defensively.

'So is my husband. I still wouldn't let him near my hair.'

'Never mind about your hair, I want some advice. You know my in-laws are moving down to Somerset? Today's the big day and they're having supper with us. What do you give a brilliant cook that won't go wrong when I make it?'

'Do that casserole thing you gave me and Derek last month. I loved that.'

'Chicken in barbecue sauce? I did that for them last time they came. I thought I should try something new.'

'Stick to what you're good at. Or you could just make spaghetti Bolognese and let your mother-in-law enjoy feeling superior.'

'I feel I ought to make more of an effort. I think Anne would expect it.'

'Really? Is she a dragon? I thought you liked her.'

'I do. I like them both. They're very nice.'

'Oh, dear.'

'No, I mean it. They're both charming.'

Amy grinned. 'What's wrong with them?'

'Nothing's wrong with them. I'm just not sure I want them living only four miles away from us, that's all. And then there's the fact that . . . oh, it's nothing, I'm probably being silly . . .'

'Silly about what?'

'In their London home, they had a framed photo on the

wall of Robin and an old girlfriend. She and Robin went out with each other for two years before he met me. She was seriously beautiful and brilliant with it. I sort of thought that when Robin and I got married, they'd take it down and replace it with one of our wedding photos, but they never did.'

'You don't want to read anything into that,' Amy said confidently. 'Perhaps Robin doesn't look very good in the wedding pictures.'

'He looks gorgeous in all of them!'

'You're biased. He might look extra scrummy in the one with the ex-girlfriend . . . I say!' Amy clutched Tilly's arm. 'Look at those two! Not your usual Lockwood School parents!'

Tilly picked out the couple at once. Amid the sea of jeans and anoraks they looked like alien birds in a field of sparrows. In fact the woman resembled a stick insect rather than a bird. Her angular little face was shrouded in dark curls and her short, black leather jacket was worn over tight, black leather trousers. Tiny and thin, her hunched shoulders minimized what inches she possessed.

Her partner, a blond, blue-eyed Adonis in matching leather uniform, towered above her while between them stood their son, a pint-sized replica of his father, unconsciously aping his pose, hands in pockets, eyes straight ahead, apparently oblivious to his surroundings.

The headmaster blew his whistle and Lucy ran up to kiss her mother quickly, before running off to join the queue with all the aplomb of a seasoned apprentice.

A few of the new children were crying, reluctant to leave the shelter of their parents. Tilly saw the stick insect yawn with luxurious, rather shocking abandon. The Adonis gently pushed his son. With a studied jauntiness that Tilly found touching in one so young, the little boy approached the line of children, hands still thrust firmly in his pockets.

'Right!' said Amy. 'I'm off. And don't worry about your meal tonight. I'm sure it will be fine. Just remember, your in-laws would hardly choose to retire to their son's neighbourhood if they didn't love their son's wife. I must go. Did I tell you I have an interview for a very exciting job this afternoon? I'll tell you all later. Bye now!'

'Sam,' Tilly said, 'do you think I'll ever have an interview for a very exciting job?'

Sam smiled sweetly. 'Silly Mummy!' he said.

'Silly Mummy!' Tilly agreed. 'Let's go to playgroup.'

Robin's mother was drunk the first time Tilly met her. His parents were celebrating their silver wedding anniversary. Robin and Tilly travelled up from university and on the way Robin's car broke down, which was not surprising because Robin's car was always breaking down. By the time they arrived in London the party was almost over.

The house was extraordinary, like Dr Who's Tardis. It resided in an unremarkable street in Kennington, flanked on either side by unremarkable shops. Robin opened the unremarkable door to reveal a small hall filled with photos on one side and coat-hooks on the other. From there they stepped into a huge, brightly lit room dominated by a shiny baby grand piano and two vast pale cream sofas, on one of which sprawled the fattest woman Tilly had ever seen. She was dressed from head to foot in black and purple taffeta and was snoring.

Tilly had never seen such an elegant room. There seemed to be two of everything. At the other end from the piano there was a double door between two alcoves. Inside each one stood a glass-fronted china cabinet with a decorative black lacquer tray perched on top. Above the large fireplace there were two ornate mirrors and double candlesticks at either end of the mantelpiece. Tilly felt she had strayed into *Ideal Home*.

A man detached himself from a trio of laughing women who all seemed to be wearing identical little black dresses. Even before Robin introduced him to Tilly, she knew at once he must be Robin's father. He had the same dark eyes, the same cleft chin, a little less hair and a little more stomach. Tilly noticed that without his presence the three women were laughing a lot less.

He brushed away Robin's apologies with genuine good humour. 'You're here now, that's all that matters. Come and get some champagne!' He led them through the double doors into a dining room of faded terracotta, soft grey and green.

Tilly was grateful for the generous glass that was given to her. Her words of thanks were abruptly interrupted by the sudden approach of a small, slim woman who fell into Robin's arms with an extravagant shriek of 'My lovely boy! My darling!' She seemed to be far too young and glamorous to be Robin's mother. She was wearing a shocking-pink dress that displayed her fatless figure to perfection and a sleek silver choker that made Tilly's necklace of glass beads look suddenly silly.

'Mum!' Robin said. 'Happy anniversary! Can I introduce you to Tilly?'

'Tilly!' Anne Taylor repeated the word carefully. 'It's wonderful to meet you, Tilly, quite wonderful! Robin, you are horribly late. You're a very naughty boy and I want a full explanation! But first I am going to take this young lady,' Anne patted Tilly's shoulder archly, 'and have a heart-to-heart with her. Now, Tilly, you come and sit with me and we'll get to know each other, woman to woman. Shall we do that? Won't that be nice? Come along then.' She put a hand on Tilly's arm, led her back to the sitting room and stopped in front of the somnolent fat woman. 'Well, she's no fun! Let's sit over here. The trouble with Imogen is she drinks too much!'

Tilly, gripping her glass as if it were the Holy Grail, sank down beside Anne on one end of the sofa. She found herself looking straight into Anne's eyes, which were moist and shining with sincere sentiment.

Anne spoke with care and deliberation as if she were weighing up the importance of every word. 'I have been longing to meet you! I can see that you are pretty and sweet and kind. Which is good because I love my son with a passion. With a *passion*! Do you love my son?'

Anne's head was veering perilously close to Tilly's shoulder. Tilly, intent on not spilling her drink, said awkwardly, 'It's difficult not to love Robin.'

'It is,' Anne agreed, nodding her head up and down, up and down. 'You are right, you are so right! He's my only child, you know, my only precious child. Tell me, have you been to the family planning clinic?'

Tilly took a large gulp of champagne and nodded mutely.

'Sensible girl! Good girl! I think you're so sweet! Motherhood is everything to me, Tilly, absolutely everything.'

Anne's eyes were sparkling with tears. 'Do you love your mother, Tilly?'

'Very much.'

'Then you are lucky. I have never known what it is to love one's mother. I never loved my mother. My mother was not a nice woman. My mother was a horrid woman. My mother was actually an evil woman. That's a terrible thing to say, Tilly, but it's the truth. There! Have I shocked you? I can see that I've shocked you.'

'No, not at all. I mean, it's very sad but—'

'It *is* very sad. Do you know what she did when I met Peter? She said I wasn't fit to be a wife. She told Peter to stay away from me. She did everything she could to turn him against me, and when that didn't work she said she never wanted to see me again. And she never did.'

'That's terrible!'

'So that is why,' Anne accompanied each syllable with a jab of her finger on her knee, 'I decided I'd be the best mother in the world. I have always worked but I have always put my boy first!'

'And he loves you very much.'

'Yes, he does and I'm a very lucky woman because he's a wonderful son. And you're a wonderful girl. You and I will *always* be friends! Tell me, Tilly, is Tilly a nickname or what?'

'It's short for Matilda. I prefer to be called Tilly.'

Anne narrowed her eyes and sighed. For almost half a minute she said nothing and then patted Tilly's leg gently. 'Very wise,' she said. 'Very wise.'

When Tilly and Robin came downstairs late the next morning they found the fat woman eating scrambled egg and Robin's parents about to leave for a weekend in Paris. Anne was wearing a little grey suit that accentuated her tiny waist. She embraced Robin tightly, kissed the fat woman's cheek and smiled radiantly at Tilly. 'Goodbye, dear. I don't expect we'll see you again. It's been such fun to meet you.'

Years later, Tilly was still not sure whether Anne had been trying to be rude or polite.

Tilly unlocked the front door and staggered through the sitting room and into the kitchen with three very full shopping bags. She set them carefully on the floor in order to greet Horace, who welcomed her and Sam with exuberant warmth, barking joyfully and jumping on half a dozen eggs as he did so. Sometimes, Tilly felt as if she were living her life amid a never-ending whirl of chaos in a house where the taps were forever leaking, the chairs were constantly falling apart and Horace was always, catastrophically, Horace.

Her sister once told her that the secret of a tidy house was to clear things away immediately after using them. Tilly had related this fact to her husband and children, who'd signally failed to find it interesting or relevant or, evidently, memorable. Now, having given Sam a drink and promised Horace a walk before lunch she wandered among the domestic debris and realized it was time to have another talk with her family.

Every room was a mess and every room must be tidied because the Taylors would want what Anne liked to call the Grand Tour. They always wanted a Grand Tour, however often they visited, presumably because they could not believe Robin and Tilly could bear to live in their house without changing it.

So Tilly cleaned the bath and the loo, made the beds, vac-

uumed everywhere, washed the kitchen floor and threw away
the more repellent items in the fridge. At half past three she
stood in the school playground waiting for Lucy and feeling as
if she'd run the marathon.

Amy arrived looking shorn and chic and a little bit smug.
'What do you think?' she asked. 'Do you like it?'

'It's great!' Tilly said. 'I can't think of anyone else who
could get away with so little hair. You look wonderful.'

'I told Frederick I wanted to have a Demi Moore in her
butch phase. It took him an hour and a half but I think it's
worth it. What about you? Had a good day?'

'Perfect. Cleaning the loo was a particular highlight. Tell
me about this interview.'

'It's for the Curved Wheel. They're looking for a new
administrator. I think I'm in with a chance. I'm sure my haircut helped and I went on for ages about that art exhibition I
organized last year.'

'The one where seven people turned up, three of whom
were Robin, Derek and me?'

'Tilly, in this world you have to sell yourself. Everyone
does. Oh, look, here come the kids. Edward looks quite
happy, don't you think?'

Lucy ran like an avenging angel towards her mother. 'You
did put too much butter in my sandwiches!' she said.

Dr Sheldon, as usual, was running late and they had to wait
forty minutes before they could see him. Then, when they
went to the pharmacist, there was another long queue.
Consequently, Tilly was in a general state of panic when she
finally got home and set to work on her chosen pudding, a
new recipe with the enticing name of Lemon Fluff. She

should never have tried to be so ambitious. As long as she stuck to her repertoire of foolproof recipes she could produce a perfectly satisfactory meal. One thing was for sure: she would never make Lemon Fluff again.

At six, her mother-in-law rang. 'Darling, it's me! We're here! I can't believe it, it's so exciting! It is *so* kind of you to entertain us and you are *not* to go to any special trouble. We're too exhausted to be hungry!' Which was just as well because Tilly's Lemon Fluff looked about as fluffy as a scalded cat.

Tilly was bathing the children when Robin came home. He put his head round the bathroom door. 'I've put some wine in the fridge. Hi, kids! How's the bottom, Luce?'

'Lucy has a worm,' Sam told him.

'I have a threadworm!' Lucy said.

'A threadworm?' Robin grimaced. 'Isn't that one of those parasites that grow up to twenty metres?'

'No,' said Tilly quickly, 'that's a tapeworm. Threadworms are very common in children, Dr Sheldon says—'

'I've got some medicine,' Lucy said. 'We all have to take it. And Dr Sheldon says if you look at my pooh, you might see the worm swimming around in it.'

'That sounds like fun. How was school?'

'I did a painting of a cat,' Lucy informed him carelessly. 'Mrs Dawes put it on the Excellence board. Kevin did a picture of a dog with pooh coming out of his bottom and Mrs Dawes said he was a silly little boy.'

'Pooh, pooh, yucky pooh!' Sam crowed.

'Sam,' Lucy said sternly, 'there is nothing funny about pooh. Mrs Dawes says pooh is simply the waste from our bodies.'

Tilly turned to glance at Robin and told him in sepulchral

tones that his parents wanted an early supper and would be arriving at seven.

Robin glanced at his watch. 'Oh, lord,' he said, 'I'd better get a move on. Poor Tilly! I'll get changed and then I'll do anything you want me to.' His face disappeared from the door.

Tilly picked up the sponge and began to scrub Sam's back. Lucy returned to the subject she had been covering before Robin's interruption, an exhaustive explanation as to why she should stay up to say hello to her grandparents. Tilly pointed out that she had school the next morning, a reason that might be pretty feeble but it was all she could think of, since she could hardly admit that she did not want her mother-in-law to hear about the parasite currently residing in her granddaughter's alimentary canal. She was almost relieved when a shout from Robin, demanding to know where his grey jumper was, halted her in her tracks.

'I'll be right back,' Tilly said and went through to the bedroom where Robin was rummaging through the chest of drawers. 'It's in the airing cupboard,' she said. 'You could have worn something else.'

'I know,' Robin said. 'I'm being a dutiful son. I want to show Mum I do wear her birthday presents.'

Tilly sighed. 'Is it going to be like this every time they come over?' she asked. 'You promised me—'

'I promised you their moving here wouldn't change our life,' Robin said, 'and it won't. I just want their first evening in Somerset to be special.'

'Fine,' said Tilly, 'just so long as you know that I'm not cooking a three-course meal for them every time they come over.'

'You're a star,' Robin said warmly. 'I'm sorry you've had to work so hard.'

When Robin's parents had first unveiled their idea of moving down to spend their twilight years in Somerset, Tilly had experienced a sickening lurch of the stomach and it wasn't just because of the effect they had on her. Robin, normally so easy-going and tolerant, revealed a side of himself that she didn't like at all when his parents were around. Edgy, earnest, talking too much about his work and constantly seeking their approbation, he made her feel that both of them were on trial. Her only hope was that close and constant proximity would render them less awe-inspiring.

A howl of rage from Lucy made Tilly double back to the bathroom. Both children stared guiltily at her while she stared in horror at the pool of water on the previously pristine floor.

In the next forty minutes Robin put the children to bed and fed Horace while Tilly cleared up the mess in the bathroom, put the finishing touches to her barbecue sauce and wasted ten minutes failing to find candles for the table. She went upstairs and changed into her velvet trousers and long silk jumper (a present from Anne: Robin wasn't the only one who could be a creep), and was about to put on some make-up when she heard the car arrive. She hastily checked her appearance in the mirror, which revealed that her nose was shiny and her hair was a mess.

Anne Taylor swept into the sitting room, swathed in expensive scent, elegant brown silk and pearls. 'Hello, my darlings! Isn't this fun? We've brought champagne to celebrate!'

'You look wonderful,' Tilly said. Her mother-in-law was amazing. Who else could leave a home of many years, travel down from London, organize the removal men and still turn up looking like a million dollars? The woman was a walking miracle.

Peter came in behind her, clasping two bottles and looking tired. 'Are the children still awake?' he asked. 'Can we say hello?'

'Of course.' Robin took their coats and slung them over the banisters. 'I'll take you both up.'

Tilly listened to the sounds of the three voices as they went up the stairs. Anne was laughing gaily while her menfolk's deeper tones seemed to reverberate in unison: the perfect backing group. Tilly went through to the kitchen, put the champagne in the fridge, washed the rice, prepared the courgettes and wished she felt better-tempered.

They were taking a very long time. Either the visitors were still talking to their grandchildren, in which case said grandchildren would be dangerously overexcited, or else an extremely detailed Grand Tour was being carried out, in which case every cobweb would be receiving the third degree.

It wasn't as if there was a lot to see. The Small Cottage, named by some past occupant with more regard for veracity than originality, was long and narrow. Downstairs, there were three rooms: a small playroom with a window that overlooked the lane, a sitting room into which the front door opened, and a generous-sized kitchen. The sitting room had a bare wooden staircase at one end and a fireplace at the other. It had an ancient sofa, above which hung a framed print of Monet's *Poppies*, two armchairs, a television and a tea chest, next to which stood a large brass standard lamp. The beige carpet boasted a variety of interesting patterns, of which the two most striking were, respectively, a long, dark oval near the sofa (the result of a three-foot novelty bottle of Chianti, opened by

Tilly and tipped over by a newly walking Lucy), and a dull orange circle near the playroom, eternal evidence of Sam's former fanatical adherence to his bottle of juice.

The kitchen was Tilly's favourite room. In an ideal world she would get rid of the elderly cooker, the cheap plywood units and the chairs that kept shedding their legs. In an ideal world she would continue to be fiercely proud of the round kitchen table, the big pine dresser and, best of all, the Belfast sink. In an ideal world she would definitely do something about the draughty back door, which she opened and shut a hundred times a day owing to the fact that Horace was an indecisive hound.

Upstairs, there were four modestly sized bedrooms, all linked by a narrow corridor that ended with a small squashed bathroom. Tilly could just imagine her parents-in-law, wedged tightly between the loo and the basin, gravely examining the limescale round the taps.

'Oh, hell!' she muttered and thought longingly of the champagne.

She had just put the rice on when they reappeared, singing the praises of the children and making Tilly feel churlish. Glasses were found, filled and raised. Peter gave a small cough. 'I would just like to say that at a time when Anne and I are entering a new stage in our lives, it is a great pleasure to be able to share it with you and the children.'

'To the darling children!' Anne exclaimed and took a sip of champagne.

From upstairs, an ominous thud and a furious wail suggested that the darling children were having a disagreement. Tilly attempted a tolerant laugh. 'I'll be right back!' she said.

★

The rice was overcooked and the courgettes had the consistency of a wet flannel. Peter said encouragingly, 'The chicken is marvellous!'

'Absolutely,' Anne smiled. 'Even better than last time!'

'Thank you!' Tilly said with commendable brightness. 'How's the unpacking going? Have you masses to do?'

'Everywhere's a mess except for the kitchen and our bedroom,' Anne said, 'but then I always say they are the only important rooms in a marriage! Don't you agree, Tilly?'

'Absolutely!' said Tilly, resolutely censoring an immediate and unwelcome image of her parents-in-law in bed together.

'There's no way we'll fit everything into the cottage,' Peter said. 'We thought you might like one of our sofas.'

Anne clapped her hands together. 'Why don't you all come to lunch on Sunday? Our garage is full of furniture we can't use. You can see if there's anything you like. We thought we'd buy a climbing frame for the children so they won't mind visiting their boring old grandparents!'

'You don't need to do that,' said Robin. 'They're so excited that you've moved down here. Aren't they, Tilly?'

'We all are,' said Tilly. Listen to me, she thought. I'm as creepy as Robin is. She smiled at her guests. 'Anyone for more chicken?'

Anne pressed a hand against her non-existent stomach. 'Not for me. I've eaten too much as it is! Now, Tilly, I want to talk to you about your teaching job. It occurred to us that we could relieve your *poor* mother of some of her babysitting.'

'That's very kind of you,' Tilly said, inwardly noting the ability of one small adjective to insult both her and her mother. 'But Mum only has to look after Sam twice a week now that he's at playgroup and her house is just down the

35

road from my school. Besides, she enjoys having Sam. I wouldn't dream of inflicting him on her otherwise.'

'We must invite Harry and Margot over once we've settled in,' Anne said, 'and in the meantime, do remember: if you're offered more hours or promotion, don't turn them down. We're here and we're happy to help!'

'There won't be any promotion.' Tilly felt a perverse satisfaction in disappointing Anne's expectations. 'I'm not a teacher, you know. I'm only a part-time classroom assistant.'

'I know, dear,' Anne said, 'and I will never understand why you're happy with that when you have a perfectly satisfactory teaching qualification. It seems such a waste of your hard work and your expertise.'

'I taught for one year,' Tilly said. 'I was an appalling teacher.'

'You can't have been that bad,' Anne said gently. 'They asked you to stay on.'

'The headmistress was so desperate she'd have asked Little Bo Peep to stay on. It was a huge mistake. If I'd stayed any longer, I'd have gone mad and so would my pupils. I'm much better as a classroom assistant.'

Robin pushed his chair back and folded his arms. 'I'm thinking of starting a new campaign,' he said. 'More money for classroom assistants. Heaven knows, we need every penny we can get now we've moved to the Radstock premises. We've had to invest far more money than we planned. I do sometimes wonder if Tilly was right.'

Peter filled Tilly's glass and glanced at her quizzically. 'You don't think they should have expanded?'

Tilly hesitated. 'I thought it all happened too quickly. Garden Magic had only just begun to make any money.

Robin works such long hours and now they've borrowed even more money to buy the new place. I don't see why they couldn't have waited a little longer.'

'Because,' Robin said, 'the premises were a fantastic bargain. It was a once in a lifetime opportunity.' He gave a short laugh. 'At least I think it was.'

'That's the nature of business,' Anne said. 'You have to move on.'

'You see, I don't understand that,' Tilly said. 'I never have. Why do you always have to climb to the top of a mountain? Why can't you walk up to a nice plateau, take out a picnic and enjoy the view from there? If people had been content to stay on the plateau, we'd never have invented nuclear weapons.'

'If people had stayed on the plateau,' Robin retorted, 'we'd never have invented the wheel.'

'Exactly!' crowed Tilly. 'We wouldn't have gridlock on the motorways.'

'We wouldn't *have* motorways.'

'It seems to me—' Peter began.

'And I'll tell you something else,' said Tilly. 'We'd still have individual little shops instead of gargantuan supermarkets. We'd have small schools with creative teachers instead of enormous comprehensives where the staff can only teach their pupils how to pass spirit-crushing exams. We wouldn't have food stuffed with additives that make people fat and children hyperactive. And look at the water! Have you noticed how much water we drink nowadays? All the pupils at school have bottles on their desks. We need more water because the water itself is less satisfying than it used to be. That's what progress has done.'

'Tilly,' said Anne, 'you can't stop people pushing themselves. It's human nature. I think it's lovely that you don't care about money or promotion but you can't expect other people to be like that. Robin has always been ambitious.'

Tilly stiffened. 'I have never tried to stop Robin pursuing his ambitions. I've always believed in Garden Magic . . . I'm simply saying that—'

A sudden blood-curdling scream stopped her in her tracks. Tilly dashed upstairs, followed quickly by Robin and his parents.

They found Lucy standing by the lavatory, her pyjama bottoms lying round her ankles. 'Come and see!' she told them. 'There's a little white worm in my pooh!'

No one really felt like pudding after that. It didn't help that the Lemon Fluff was disgusting. Underneath the foaming surface, the egg yolks arose like blubbery sea monsters from a mustard-coloured sea. Tilly swept the bowls away as soon as she could and made coffee at breakneck speed. She was deeply grateful when Peter at last stood up and said, 'I hate to end the party but it's been a long day and tomorrow we're going to be busy.'

Robin pushed back his chair and stretched his arms. 'You must let us know if we can be any help. It's so good to have you here. It's going to be wonderful.' The worst of it was, thought Tilly, he really meant it. She could almost hear the bells of doom clanging above her head.

Anne left the table to give Robin a swift embrace. 'Thank you, darling, it's sweet of you to say so. Now we're retired we want you to use us as much as possible. That's why we're here.' Her eyes rested briefly on a large piece of Blu-tack on the wall opposite and then she put her hands to her face. 'Oh, but this is terrible! Here am I wittering on about how helpful we intend to be and now we're preparing to slink off without so much as clearing a plate! We must stay and do our bit!'

'Absolutely not!' Tilly protested a little too vehemently. 'We wouldn't hear of it. You must be exhausted.'

'Well, if you're quite sure . . .' Anne allowed herself to be helped into her coat. 'Now, remember you're coming to us on Sunday. I know how Robin loves his Sunday roast! And, Tilly, I'll give you a ring tomorrow. I want to hear more about this threadworm of poor little Lucy. It sounds horrendous. I don't understand how she could get such a thing—'

It seemed to take an eternity for them to go. Anne kissed Tilly at least twice. At last Robin ushered his parents out to their car, leaving Tilly in blissful solitude. Anne's perfume lingered in the air like a reproach. Tilly was tempted to throw open the windows but instead she rolled back her sleeves and squirted washing-up liquid into the sink.

Robin came in and yawned. 'That went very well,' he said. 'Thank you, Tilly. You were great.' He began to clear the coffee cups and glasses from the table. He looked like someone who's just passed an exam. He beamed at his wife, wanting her to share in his good humour. 'What do you think? Did you enjoy the evening?'

'Very nice,' Tilly lied, 'once I stopped worrying about the food and Lucy's threadworm.'

Robin put his arms round her waist but Tilly continued to scrub doggedly at the casserole dish. She was annoyed that he could ask such a wilfully obtuse question.

Robin withdrew his arms. 'I know why you're upset.'

'You do?'

'Listen, that pudding was incredible! It will be one of those puddings that pass into family folklore, it will be the stuff of legend: *Lemon Fluff . . . How We Lived to Tell the Tale*! If I were an artist, I'd have wanted to paint it. The striking brightness of the egg yolks . . .' He stopped, aware that Tilly was in no mood for teasing. 'Seriously, it didn't matter. Mum and Dad had a great evening.'

He extracted a cloth from behind the taps and began to wipe the table. 'I don't know why you get so nervous about entertaining them. They're very fond of you and they only want to be treated as part of the family. They don't need any special treatment.'

'Right,' said Tilly. 'So I don't need to spring-clean the house every time they visit?'

'Absolutely not. Cross my heart. Now they live near us, they have to take us as they find us. They know that.' He gave one last wipe to the table and whistled to Horace. 'Come on, boy. Let's take you out.'

Once, long ago, Tilly sat on a beach with Robin. They skimmed pebbles and watched the sea fold gently onto the shore. They talked for hours about anything and everything: families, friends, religion, *Dr Who* (which they had both loved) and Blue Peter (which they had both hated).

'What makes you cry?' Robin asked and Tilly sucked in her bottom lip and swivelled her eyes as she always did when she was thinking hard.

'Thomas Hardy novels,' she said, 'old black and white films, especially *It's a Wonderful Life* . . . You know the bit where James Stewart discovers that everyone loves him and his face breaks into that lovely slow smile and you think he's going to cry! "Hey Jude" makes me cry, and that story in the papers about the three giant turtles found alive in New York City's sewage system . . .'

Robin grinned. '*That* made you cry?'

'Yes. Do you know they were probably flushed down the loo by their owners when they got too big?'

'Unbelievable!'

'Isn't it? What about you? What makes you cry?'

Robin frowned and said simply, 'Staring at you when you're asleep. That can make me cry.'

Robin came back in from the garden and rummaged in the cupboard for a dog biscuit. 'There we are, Horace! Good boy! Basket!' He patted Horace's rump and then came over and did the same to Tilly. 'Do you mind if I go to bed? I've a couple of big meetings tomorrow.'

'No, that's fine, you go. I'm nearly finished anyway.'

'Good.' He kissed her lightly on the cheek. 'Thanks for tonight. It was fun. Wasn't it fun?'

'Yes,' said Tilly, 'it was fun.'

Later, as the sun went down and after they had put the world to rights, Tilly and Robin had wandered along the sea front. They found a pub and sat beside a couple who were eating pie and chips.

'How are your chips?' the husband had enquired.

'Very nice,' said his wife. 'How are yours?'

'Very nice, thank you.'

In thirty minutes that was all they said to each other. Such a sad couple, though at the time both Robin and Tilly had found them hilarious.

'How do people get like that?' Tilly had asked.

Perhaps, she thought now, this was how it began, with one partner choosing not to express unpalatable opinions and the other partner choosing not to hear the silences. Perhaps, as year follows year, it becomes easier to say nothing at all until one day all that is left is to ask about the chips.

CHAPTER THREE

'The universe is change; life is what thinking makes of it.'
MARCUS AURELIUS

Tilly's parents lived at the end of a row of nineteenth-century terraced houses in a cul-de-sac on the edge of town. Since they had moved there, a year after Tilly went to university, Margot Treadwell had designed a garden that was much like herself: quiet, gentle and unassuming. She had the true gardener's knack of creating an illusion of delightfully haphazard colour in which shrubs and flowers blended together in strictly democratic harmony.

This morning Tilly had little time to admire anything but her mother's promptness in opening the door. 'I'm horribly late, Mum, so I've got to rush. Sam, be good and listen to your gran!'

Sam waved an airy hand, gave an ambiguous smile and scuttled into the house.

'When you come back, can you stay for lunch?' Margot asked.

'Yes, please!' Tilly raised her voice, 'Goodbye, Sam!' She grinned at her mother. 'Nice to know he misses me so much! See you later!' She sped back down the path, dived into her car and glanced at her watch. Cursing with luxurious abandon in the absence of her son, she crashed the gears before hurtling away.

Hurstfield Middle School had been built in the sixties. The combination of concrete and glass had risen proudly among verdant lawns and generous playing fields. At the time, the building had been celebrated for its vision and originality and was regarded with envy by other schools in the county. Now it stood like a beached whale, surrounded by an ever-increasing cluster of mobile classrooms that swallowed the lawns and edged perilously close to the playing fields.

Pupils arrived at the age of nine in spotless white shirts and neat blue sweatshirts. Most of them were as enthusiastic and energetic as puppies. When they left at thirteen they were lumbering, uncoordinated adolescents who swaggered with an endearing lack of conviction in over-large shirts worn outside threadbare trousers.

Tilly bumped into one of them as she careered through the front entrance. 'Sorry, Kelvin!'

'Any time, miss!'

Tilly smiled doubtfully. (Should she tell him off? Too late and anyway he was being rather sweet.) She raced on, weaving her way through the flood of children.

'Hi, miss!' . . . 'Hello, Mrs Taylor!' . . . 'You're not supposed to run, miss!'

Tilly acknowledged all greetings and admonitions with a cheerful nod. She climbed up the stairs, turned left at the top and 'Arthur, have you started the meeting yet? I'm sorry I'm so late!'

'Ah, Tilly!' Arthur smiled. 'It's good to know some things never change!'

Tilly smiled back, hoping the remark was motivated by affection rather than by irritation. It was difficult to tell with Arthur since he expended much energy in convincing himself and others that he was deeply mellow. He liked to describe himself as a natural rebel and sported a natty little beard, an ancient CND badge and a short ponytail as proof of his radical credentials. He was excellent with children and charming with parents. Most of the time Tilly liked him very much.

Tilly squeezed in between Pam and Rhona and mouthed to Rhona, 'How are you?' and Rhona mouthed back, 'Don't ask!' which meant that break would be fun. Rhona's life, as narrated by Rhona, was an intriguing procession of dilemmas and disasters. She had a true gift, like Rumpelstiltskin, only Rumpelstiltskin turned straw into gold while Rhona turned life into drama. This was particularly impressive since Rhona had led a celibate life since her divorce three years earlier and faced no more than the usual tribulations with daughter and finances. Yet Rhona's life was fascinating while that of Tilly's next-door neighbour but one, who would try to discuss her many love affairs with anyone who'd listen, was totally tedious. What was it that made one person fascinating and another deadly dull? A tone of voice, maybe, an attitude to others? If one could analyse charm then a fortune could be made . . .

'Tilly?' Arthur's voice brought her back to the meeting. 'What do you think? Are you happy with the new Year Five schedule?'

'I think so, Arthur.' Tilly nodded thoughtfully. 'Yes, I'm quite happy.'

'That's cool. Now, before we go on to individual kids I have an idea I want to run past you all. As you know, we are the Department of Special Needs and Learning Support. Cumbersome, isn't it? Off-putting, pompous, sets up unnecessary barriers. So I thought: why not change our name to the

Extra Aid Department? To the point, short, snappy and simple. What do you think?'

Tilly glanced at Rhona and as quickly glanced away again. Pam, who adored Arthur, said doubtfully, 'It has a certain ring to it.'

Margaret, who prided herself on being a plain-speaking sort of girl, said, 'No way. It would only confuse people. It sounds like First Aid.'

'Or Live Aid,' said Tilly.

'Perhaps,' Rhona concluded gently, 'we could mull it over for a while.'

Arthur raised his hands in the air like a priest blessing his flock. 'Fine, that's fine by me. I run a democratic ship here; we're a team. So, we'll leave it for now and of course if you have any ideas of your own, let me hear them. Good. Before you rush off to your classes, a brief word about some of our charges. If you help Doug Skinner in 6E, go easy on him. He's likely to be difficult and needs a lot of understanding. Trouble at home, I'm afraid. Kylie Jeans in 5F has a bladder problem so let her go to the toilet whenever she wants. And if any of you help Jamie Ross in 8N, keep a note of everything you do with him. His mother wants to see me next week about his progress.'

Tilly frowned. 'He hasn't made any progress.'

Arthur put a hand to his forehead. 'That's why she wants to see me,' he said.

At the end of the meeting, Tilly charged down the stairs and along the corridor to Room 10 where she was supposed to be supporting Matthew Archer in his maths lesson. Since Tilly's knowledge of maths was about as extensive as her knowledge of the new Year Five schedule, this was no easy task.

She slipped in next to Matthew, who whispered gloomily, 'We're doing fractions, miss.'

'Right!' Tilly focused with determined concentration on the matter in hand and spent the next fifteen minutes desperately trying to understand the plague of figures with which the maths teacher was covering the blackboard. He was a very good maths teacher, patient and lucid, which made Tilly's failure to understand him even more galling. By the end of the lesson she wasn't sure who was the more confused, herself or Matthew. Fortunately, this was the only maths lesson she covered and at the end of it she always felt she should hand in her notice forthwith.

At break she confessed her ineptitude to Rhona. Rhona grinned. 'Don't be silly! It does Matthew good to realize he's not the only one to find maths difficult.'

'You mean it helps him to know I'm as stupid as he is?'

'Yes, of course. It's all about confidence, isn't it?' Rhona unscrewed the top of her flask and poured black coffee into her cup. 'You'll never guess what!'

'Tell me,' Tilly breathed, her failure forgotten.

'Chloe's gone back to Martin!'

'No!'

Rhona's thirteen-year-old daughter had the body of a *Playboy* centrefold. Rhona's endless ejection of boys from Chloe's bedroom was, in her own words, like bailing water from a sinking ship. Chloe had started seeing Martin in January and no one had been more pleased than Rhona when the relationship floundered and fell twelve weeks later.

'I mean, what can I do?' Rhona demanded. 'Martin's been seeing a twenty-two-year-old in the last few months so he's hardly going to be happy with a few cuddles. Chloe swears they're not sleeping together but she's crazy about him. I can't think why; he has a horrible haircut and the only things he gets excited about are beer and cars.'

'And, presumably, Chloe?'

'Exactly. So should I march her down to the family planning clinic or what? If I force-feed her with the pill it looks as if I expect her to sleep with him, but if I don't . . . well, it doesn't bear thinking about. You see my problem? What do I do?'

Tilly frowned. 'I don't think you should have to deal with this on your own. Have you talked to her father?'

'Mark and I aren't talking at the moment. He was supposed to be taking Chloe to Majorca in August and at the last moment he backed out, saying he couldn't afford it. Apparently, he'd had to buy a new bed. It was while Chloe wasn't in Majorca that she met up with Martin again.'

'So there you are!' Tilly said triumphantly. 'It's all Mark's fault! Since he's responsible, he should jolly well be the one to give Chloe a lecture on the perils of testosterone-packed males with dodgy haircuts. And in the meantime perhaps you should talk to Chloe about the whole sex thing, if only to reassure yourself.'

Rhona sighed. 'I did start stuttering about the possibility of getting carried away in a moment of passion and Chloe just looked at me and said she was surprised I could still remember.'

'Oh,' Tilly said, and silently thanked God that Lucy was only six. The bell terminated further discussion and Tilly went into 7B's double period of English, hoping fervently that Lucy would never develop big breasts.

English was fun because Tilly could do English. She was

supposed to be helping a trio of girls: Kitty, Jodie and Emma. In practice, this involved acting as referee since one of them was usually not speaking to the other two. They greeted her warmly and she pulled up a chair close to Kitty, ready for ninety minutes of creative writing. Then she noticed something moving in Kitty's hair and spent the rest of the lesson trying not to look as if she would rather be sitting anywhere than where she was.

It was a relief to walk up her mother's garden path at ten minutes to one and enter a home that was clean and tidy without being oppressively immaculate. A delicious smell of home-made bread permeated the kitchen. A vase of chrysanthemums stood on the table and a National Trust calendar on the wall displayed a stunning photograph of the garden at Stourhead. The problems of head lice and pubescent sexuality seemed a million miles away.

Tilly went over to Sam, who was sitting at the table eating a carrot. 'Hello, darling!' she cried, giving him an extravagant embrace. 'How's my gorgeous boy?'

'We went to the playgwound,' Sam said. 'Me fell off the swing and me didn't cwy.'

'Good for you!' Tilly said. 'Mum, can I help at all?'

'Me fell off the swing,' Sam repeated doggedly, 'and me didn't cwy.'

'You are a brave boy,' Tilly said. 'Mum, how can I help?'

Margot set a jug of water on the table. 'It's only soup and cheese. How was school?'

'Fine, apart from the maths. That bread looks delicious!'

Sam held out his hand for inspection. 'Me hurt myself. See?'

Tilly searched for and found an infinitesimal pink line on the palm of his hand. 'Poor old boy,' she said. 'You've been very brave.'

'Me know,' Sam conceded graciously. 'Gwanny and me came home and played on the computer.'

'You did what?' If Sam had said they'd been sky-diving she'd have been less surprised. 'Mum, since when have you gone within half a mile of Dad's computer?'

Margot handed Tilly a bowl of soup. 'I started a Computer Literacy course last week.' The carelessness with which she imparted this information seemed to suggest both pride and defensiveness.

'Why? Whatever for?'

'Have some bread. I don't know why you're so surprised. I'm not completely past it.'

'Of course not. But you loathe computers!'

'I know I do. Your father says I'll never get the hang of them in a million years!'

Tilly bridled. 'I seem to remember he said the same thing when you learnt to drive.'

'Well, I did have to take my test three times.'

'And now you're a better driver than he is! But I still don't understand why you want to learn about computers.'

'Me like computers,' Sam said. 'Gwanny, this soup is hot!'

'I'll add some milk to it,' Tilly told him. She pushed her chair back and went to the fridge. 'So tell me, Mum, why do you want to love computers?'

'I'm not sure.' Margot poured herself some water and took a sip. 'I suppose I've been thinking about it for some time. I'm fifty-five. Everyone in the world seems to know about fax machines and email and the Internet and programming video recorders and DVD recorders and computer technology, and I don't. A huge chunk of the world is completely beyond my comprehension. I'm out of touch. It's not healthy. It's like admitting that I'm too old.'

'Rubbish! It's nothing to do with being old. I've only just got to grips with the school photocopier. I have no idea what spreadsheets are and I'm probably one of the few women alive who don't have an email address!'

'Well, perhaps you should get one. But at least you've plenty of time. I've been scanning the jobs pages for months and it's impossible to find anything that doesn't require a basic knowledge of word processing.'

'What do you want a job for?' Tilly protested. 'You do masses of things. You help at the Day Centre and the WI and the Oxfam shop . . . you don't need a job!'

Margot shrugged. 'I don't know,' she said. 'I'd like my own money and I suppose I'd like the challenge. I'm stuck in a rut and I'd like to get out of it. How is the soup?'

'The soup is very good.'

'And you needn't worry about Sam. I can still look after him. By the time I'm qualified to do anything even vaguely sensible he'll be doing his A levels!'

'I wasn't worried about that. Anyway, if you were busy, my mother-in-law would be more than willing to step in. Anne says she and Peter want to help as much as possible.'

'Oh,' Margot said carefully, 'that's kind.'

'Isn't it just.'

'By the way,' Margot said, 'I'm going to visit Mummy on Saturday morning. Any chance of you coming?'

'Yes, I haven't seen her for ages. I'll check that Robin's around for the kids and get back to you.' Depression was seeping through Tilly's veins. Her mother's new interest in technology, coupled with the arrival of her in-laws, was further indication that everything was changing. Worse, Tilly was forced to contemplate the possibility that her mother, a constant source of support and calm, and a loyal recipient of all Tilly's confidences, had preoccupations of her own.

Ashamed of her own self-absorption, Tilly set about diverting Margot with an unexpurgated account of the true horrors of the Lemon Fluff. Margot laughed and offered to supply a couple of foolproof recipes, including one called Balkan Syllabub (one large carton of fruit yogurt, half a pint of whipped cream, juice of half a lemon and a sprinkling of flaked almonds). By the time she and Sam left, Tilly could almost feel that everything was as it had been. The fact that both she and her mother had been equally uncomfortable about discussing Margot's new ambitions was something she preferred not to examine.

Back at home, Horace offered a frenzied welcome and Tilly realized guiltily that she could give him only a short walk if she were to collect Lucy in time.

Usually, Tilly would have gone up the road and into the field behind the house. However, the village was temporarily blighted by the presence of Mary Rafferty's red-faced brother-in-law, who possessed an equally ferocious Alsatian. On the last two occasions that Tilly had ventured out, she and Horace had been forced to make a hasty retreat after short but dramatic encounters with them. Tytherington could hardly be called a village since it could boast only a few houses, a telephone box and a pub. Certainly, it was not big enough to absorb a dog with anger issues and his foul-mouthed, besotted master.

Tilly bundled Horace into the car, threw his lead onto Sam's lap and drove straight to the show field near Lucy's school. She pulled up opposite the entrance and thought: twenty minutes.

Horace had never quite understood the concept of a lead and Tilly's right arm was in constant danger of coming out of its socket. 'Heel, Horace,' she said hopelessly, 'heel!' Her left arm was desperately trying to maintain its tenuous control of Sam's hand. As Tilly entered the show field she nearly collided with an incongruous-looking couple in matching leather jackets. 'Heel,' she repeated faintly, 'heel!'

It wasn't necessary to see their faces: she knew they were smirking. It was definitely time to take Horace to dog-training classes. It had *always* been time to take Horace to dog-training classes. She released her son and her dog, who both bounded off in joyful comradeship across the grass. Glancing furtively behind her, she saw the odd couple disappear round the corner. The man was a giant and the girl was even smaller than Tilly. Tilly wondered why they were familiar and almost immediately remembered that Amy had pointed them out in the school playground the day before. She wondered what sort of lives they led. Perhaps they were hopeful musicians or actors, or perhaps they'd dropped out and lived in some bedsit, counting the pennies. On the other hand, leather jackets weren't exactly cheap, though it was possible they could have found them in some charity shop.

Tilly glanced around for Sam and Horace and discovered she could not see Horace's head. 'Horace!' she shouted. 'Get out of that rabbit hole!' Sam was pelting Horace's bottom with rabbit droppings. On a scale of one to ten, this walk was turning out to be a minus two.

By the time Tilly arrived at school, the place was deserted save for Amy and three decidedly grumpy children.

'Amy, I'm *so* sorry,' Tilly breathed.

'You are *very* late,' Lucy said.

Amy smiled. 'It doesn't matter at all.'

Edward regarded his mother reproachfully. 'Yes, it does. We'll miss our programmes.'

Tilly smiled ingratiatingly at him and Luke. 'Thank you so much for staying to look after Lucy.'

'They weren't looking after me,' Lucy said indignantly. 'Amy was. *They* wanted to leave me on my own.'

Tilly turned to Amy. 'I owe you! Turn up late whenever you like and I'll wait!'

'Then we'll miss our programmes again,' Edward pointed out.

'Shut up about your programmes,' Amy said calmly. 'Tilly, if you could take the boys home next Tuesday, I would be ever so grateful. I've been asked to go back for another interview!'

'Brilliant! That's fantastic! Take as long as you like!' Tilly could see Edward pulling at his mother's sleeve and said briskly, 'Come on, then, Lucy, into the car!'

Lucy climbed into the back seat next to Sam and Horace. 'Mummy,' she sighed, 'Horace smells!'

When they arrived home, the telephone was ringing. Lucy picked up the receiver. 'Hello? . . . Hello, Grandpa! . . . I'm very well, thank you, except that Mummy forgot to come and pick me up from school and the car smells and I feel sick.'

There was a long hiatus during which, thought Tilly bitterly, Peter Taylor was probably giving his granddaughter the number of ChildLine. 'We can't wait to come,' Lucy said at last. 'Have you bought the climbing frame yet? ... All right ... Yes ... Yes ... I'll go and get Mummy.'

'Hello, Peter,' Tilly said in what she hoped was a suitably relaxed and lightly amused tone of voice. 'How's the house coming along? Are you still knee-deep in packing cases?'

Peter chuckled. 'You know what Anne's like. She wants to have everything ready immediately. Rather like your daughter! We're getting there. Thank you for last night. It was just what we needed. We were far too tired to cook for ourselves.'

'It was a pleasure. Are you sure you want us to come round on Sunday? You must have so much to do.'

'Nonsense, we're looking forward to having you. And bring Horace with you.'

'Are you sure?'

'Of course I am! In fact Horace is why I'm ringing. It was Anne's idea. She keeps telling me I need to get some fresh air but I suspect she just wants me out of the house.'

'Sorry?'

'Horace. Would you like me to come over tomorrow afternoon and walk him for you? Be good for Horace and me, and perhaps I can help you out at the same time.'

'Well ...' Tilly hesitated. 'Thank you, that's very kind of you.'

'Not at all. I'm extremely fond of the old boy. And it will be good to see you. Shall we say half past two?'

'Fine,' Tilly said. 'Peter, I have to go, I've got something boiling over.' She put down the receiver and looked irritably at Lucy. 'What?'

Lucy raised her eyebrows. 'You haven't got anything boiling over.'

'Don't you believe it,' Tilly muttered. It was happening just as she feared. They'd hardly arrived and already they were organizing her life.

Horace, of course, was delighted. When he and Peter returned from their two-hour marathon the next day, he lapped up an entire bowl of water before falling into his basket and sinking into instant, blissful oblivion. Peter allowed Tilly to make him a cup of tea and brushed aside her thanks. 'I loved it. We drove to Cley Hill. What an extraordinary place it is! Strange, irregular mounds all over the place. Quite fascinating. I met a chap who told me it's a magnet for UFOs and I can almost believe it. This is a marvellous area. We're lucky to live here.'

Tilly laughed. 'Horace is very lucky you live here!' She watched her father-in-law as Lucy proceeded to tell him everything she knew about UFOs. Peter, unlike herself or Robin, was listening with genuine interest, asking pertinent questions, contributing snippets of information. It was clear that his presence could only enrich the lives of dog and children. In which case, Tilly decided, it was time to dismiss all her misgivings about their move. Everything was going to be fine.

Tilly's grandma was a victim of love. So Tilly's sister said, and if Charlotte, a woman who never read novels, could make such a statement it must be true. Tilly had always disliked the way in which married people were described as 'couples' as if implying some sinister surgical union. But if ever two people deserved the epithet it was her grandma and grandpa. Both of them discovered their reason for living in the existence of the other.

Grandpa had married his wife when she was eighteen and

still living at home. He was twelve years older and had seen active service in the war. He became her guide and protector through the complexities of adult life. She provided him with a solid, secure, deliciously comfortable base from which he could sally forth and take on the world.

She was a consummate cook and spent hours preparing meals. She liked to spread toasted breadcrumbs over vegetables that were never overcooked. She enjoyed making up recipes. A favourite pudding was Boulevard Slice: raspberries spread between two layers of crumble topping. 'So simple!' she'd crow. 'But isn't it good? Have some more!'

A meal with Grandma was always fun and invariably noisy. She loved to argue about politics, religion, books and television. Only the royal family were sacrosanct and if any mischievous soul should question their credentials she would stand up, wave her hands and say, 'No, no, no. No republicanism here! I won't have it!'

Now Grandpa was dead and Grandma was living near Trowbridge in Seaview House, an improbably named nursing home, improbable because as far as Tilly knew no sea had ever been sighted near Trowbridge.

Grandma was sitting in the lounge when they arrived, a pristine *Daily Telegraph* resting on her knees. Margot greeted her with a kiss. 'Look, Mummy, I've brought Tilly to see you! Hello, Dinah, how are you?'

Dinah was Grandma's friend. She had once been a poet and, apparently, a great beauty. 'Well,' she exclaimed, holding out her hands to welcome them, 'this is a treat to see you both! Isn't it lovely to see them, Mary?'

'Oh, yes,' Grandma responded. 'A treat indeed.'

'I thought you'd be wearing your new skirt, Mummy,'

Margot said. 'We spent such a long time choosing it last week and you look so nice in it. I thought that's what you'd be wearing.'

'Oh,' Grandma sighed thoughtfully. 'I'm wearing this skirt today.'

'I know, Mummy, but it's too tight for you. I think you'd be more comfortable in your new skirt.'

'Yes.' Grandma nodded. 'It hurts a bit.' She patted her waist. 'It hurts here.'

'It would do,' Margot acknowledged. 'It's too tight for you.'

'You're too fat, Mary,' Dinah told her friend. 'You're too fat and I'm too thin!'

'Well, you shouldn't be wearing that skirt, Mummy,' Margot said. 'I won't be a minute. I'll go and have a look at your wardrobe and see if I can find your new skirt.'

Left alone with the two women, Tilly smiled brightly. 'So!' she exclaimed. 'How are you, Grandma? You're looking well.'

'I've been very busy,' said Grandma. 'I've been all over the place. I'm going away tomorrow. I have to pack my case.'

'Really?'

'I've been very busy. I'm a finance director, you know. I work very hard.'

'Mr Potter!' Dinah shouted. 'Stop that at once! I can see you!' She turned to Tilly and spoke in a theatrical whisper, her emaciated fingers gripping Tilly's wrist like a claw. 'You see Mr Potter in the corner? It's disgusting! He plays with himself. Look at him! He's pretending he hasn't heard me! I'm sorry, dear. Let's just not look at him, it will only encourage him. Turn your chair this way. What were you saying, Mary?'

'I was saying I'm going home tomorrow.'

Dinah let out a cackle of laughter. 'Mary, you're not going home. You're barmy! We're all barmy in here! They won't let us out! We've got Alzheimer's Disease!'

'Oh, yes, that's right.' Grandma smiled benignly. 'We have Alzheimer's Disease.'

Dinah leant forward and rested a skeletal hand on Tilly's knee. 'You see the woman asleep over there? Don't you wish she'd shut her mouth? Well, yesterday she walked into my room, naked as a baby, and climbed into the wardrobe! It took two nurses to get her out! She's bonkers, isn't she, Mary? She's even more bonkers than we are!'

'She is,' Grandma agreed. 'She's quite bonkers.'

'Well!' Tilly said. 'Well!' She glanced out of the window for inspiration. 'Isn't it a lovely day? Robin's taking the children for a walk this morning. Do you know, Grandma, Lucy is in her second year at school? She thinks she's very grown-up!'

'Fancy!' Grandma said politely. She began rubbing a small stain on the edge of her cardigan.

'Your great-granddaughter's very funny,' Tilly said, maintaining a determined cheerfulness in the face of her grandmother's complete lack of interest. 'She tells us all what to do! She's only six and is convinced she knows everything. She looks very like Grandpa, I think. Don't you think so, Grandma?'

'Yes,' Grandma said. 'I expect so.'

Driving home, Margot raged about her mother's clothes. 'I told the staff to ditch her old ones. It's not good enough. She looked terrible this morning and there's no need. Mind you, if she keeps putting on all this weight, I'll need to buy her a whole new wardrobe in a few months. They hadn't even brushed her hair. It's not good enough.'

'I mentioned Grandpa,' Tilly said. 'She didn't have a clue who I was talking about. She never does. Isn't it weird? The most important person in her entire life and she has no idea he ever existed.'

'She remembers her early childhood. Sometimes, when I'm feeling sorry for myself, I wish she'd remember *my* early childhood. That would be interesting!'

'She told me she was a finance director today.'

'When credit cards first came out,' Margot said, 'she got one. But she ran up such bills that she and Daddy decided she was safer without one.'

One month after her husband died, Grandma had driven to Margot's house for lunch. Margot opened the car door and was almost overpowered by the smell of rancid milk. A carton had broken open and emptied itself over the back seat. Grandma, whose fastidious nose was a legend in the family, hadn't noticed. Three weeks after that, Grandma's neighbour rang to say she'd discovered Grandma wandering round the lane in her nightie at ten o'clock at night. Grandma had told her she was looking for her mother. Two months after that, with a mixture of cajolery and deceit, Margot had installed her in the home. She had been there for twenty-eight months now. As Charlotte said, she was a victim of love.

CHAPTER FOUR: Past

'No, there's nothing half so sweet in life as love's young dream.'
THOMAS MOORE

After Robin's gloriously flamboyant embrace in Devonshire House, he assumed Tilly would come back and stay the night with him. She surprised them both by countering his blithe assumption with a flat refusal. She continued to uphold this stance for the next three weeks. This was due to a combination of fear, apprehension and an uneasy feeling that she would disappoint him. For all she knew, in her drugged and drunken state she might have metamorphosed into a wild, outrageous nymphomaniac. Hadn't Robin said she was great? He was probably expecting an acrobatic tigress, certainly not a frightened mouse.

As it turned out, when the momentous coupling finally took place, both she and Robin were equally bewildered. Afterwards, Tilly made straight for the bathroom and when she came back, her arms wrapped tightly round Robin's towel, she found Robin sitting up in bed. He'd switched on the bedside light and was smoking a cigarette. He looked rather shell-shocked.

'You were a virgin!' he exclaimed.

Tilly glared at him accusingly. 'I was a virgin,' she hissed, 'and you never told me!'

Robin scratched his head. 'You mean you didn't know?'

61

'Of course I didn't!' Tilly glanced around furiously for something to wear and, grabbing Robin's T-shirt, achieved the difficult feat of pulling it over her head before letting his towel drop to the floor.

Robin blinked. 'I don't understand. I've never heard of such a thing. How could you not know you were a virgin?'

Tilly was cross but she was also cold. She climbed back into his bed and said through gritted teeth, 'I thought you . . . you did *it* on the night of that stupid party.'

'What? After you crashed out? Thanks, Tilly, but I'm not into necrophilia.'

'Oh, right,' Tilly said with a sarcastic grimace and then, curiosity getting the better of her, asked sulkily, 'What's necrophilia?'

'Making love to a corpse.'

'Oh.' Tilly frowned. 'Are you saying you are quite sure you did not make love to me that night?'

'To my great disappointment, I did not make love to you that night, no.'

'Well, that's just marvellous!' Tilly declared. 'So now I've lost my virginity twice!'

Robin sucked in his mouth and looked away from her. He stubbed out his cigarette and buried his face in his pillow, from which emanated a series of muffled sounds.

Tilly regarded him with suspicion. 'Have you just been taking me out the last few weeks so you could finish what you started? Robin, it's *not funny*! *Stop laughing!* For all I know, now you've had your wicked way you'll stop . . . Robin, STOP LAUGHING!'

'Tilly,' Robin said at last. 'Darling Tilly! Will you do me a very great favour and go and put yourself on the pill?'

So Tilly did. She made an appointment to see the university doctor who turned out to be a large, jolly Father Christmas. By dint of appearing completely oblivious to her transparent awkwardness he managed to put her totally at ease and she found herself able to respond quite naturally to even his most intimate questions.

'Fine,' he said. 'Everything seems to be in order.' He wrote her out a prescription and beamed at her over his glasses. 'You're obviously very smitten with your young man!'

'Robin? Yes, I am rather. Very, very smitten!'

'Good for you! Young love! Nothing like it!' He pushed back his chair, stood up and checked his watch. 'Yes, I think we have time. Now, Tilly, I want you to step up onto my desk before you go. It won't take a moment. Let me clear away these papers and my pen.'

'Sorry?' She was sure she'd misheard him. 'What did you say?'

The doctor took off his glasses and placed them carefully on his bookcase before giving Tilly a reassuring smile. 'Don't worry, it's quite easy. I want you to climb onto my desk, and when you've done that you are going to jump off it and land on my stomach.'

Tilly did not have a clue what the man was talking about. She knew exactly what Alice must have felt like when she disappeared down the rabbit hole. She watched her doctor's face redden alarmingly as he eased himself onto the floor in front of the desk. He lay stretched out with his stomach heaving hopefully in front of her.

'I'm sorry,' Tilly said. 'I know I'm being stupid but I don't understand what you want me to do.'

'Jump!' The doctor patted his stomach. 'Jump onto me!'

'I can't!' Tilly stuttered, aghast at the very idea. 'I'll hurt you! I don't understand! Why do you want me to jump on you?'

Father Christmas chuckled, his stomach rising up and down as he did so. 'Don't look so alarmed, Tilly, I promise you won't hurt me! I have extremely well-developed stomach muscles. Now let me explain. There is a reason for this madness!' He rested his hands behind his head and crossed his legs. 'It is very obvious to me, Tilly, that there are inner tensions within you. I would go so far as to suggest you are suffering from strongly repressed aggression. You aren't sure of Robin's feelings for you, are you?'

'Well, no, that's true, I suppose. I mean, I think—'

'You are concerned, worried, anxious to please. And you're jealous of other women, even perhaps of one in particular . . .'

The man was incredible. 'How did you know?' Tilly gasped. 'I mean, I'm not jealous exactly but then it's difficult not to be jealous where Robin is concerned. He's the sort of man that every woman wants to be with and there's this girl, Louise, and she's the sort of girl every man wants to be with. They used to go out with each other and she's very beautiful and they're still friends and I can't help worrying how long he'll be satisfied with me when he knows . . . it's silly, I know—'

'Very silly and very destructive,' the doctor said, staring up at Tilly with unblinking eyes. 'You need to dispel all these doubts before they destroy you and your relationship with Robin. By jumping on my stomach you will be releasing all your negative emotions and freeing yourself from their poisonous embrace. So. There you are! Climb up on my desk. Go ahead! Good girl . . . don't bother to take off those nice leather boots you're wearing. My stomach is made of strong stuff and my stomach is waiting for you!'

In later years, Tilly would look back at her young self and wonder how she could have been so preposterously naive. At the time, the doctor's matter-of-fact tone and calm air of authority had the effect of making her feel that *she* was at fault for being embarrassed by his instructions. Consequently, she struggled up onto his desk, something she found pretty difficult to do in the skirt she was wearing. She straightened herself, looked down at her doctor and wished she were somewhere else.

'Come on, Tilly!' bellowed Father Christmas. 'Get on with it! Jump! Let yourself go!'

'Are you sure I won't hurt you?'

'I'm sure. Now do it, do it now!'

'If you're sure . . .'

'I'm sure.' Father Christmas looked up at her impatiently. 'Go on!'

'If you're sure, then.' Tilly shut her eyes and jumped.

When she opened them again, the doctor was patting her leg. 'There!' he said. 'That wasn't so bad, was it?'

Tilly clambered to her feet. 'Are you all right?' she asked. His complexion was now a perfect puce and he was breathing in short, alarming puffs.

'Fine, I'm fine! Now do it again! Quickly! Up you go!'

Tilly had to jump on the doctor's stomach three times before he agreed that perhaps she had done enough jumping now. He stood up, dusted himself down and returned to his chair. 'Tell me,' he said, 'do you feel different? How do you feel?'

Innate good manners triumphed over honesty. It was very

sweet of him to be so concerned. 'A little better, I think,' she murmured.

The doctor retrieved his glasses and began to wipe them with his handkerchief. 'Yes, I'm afraid it will take a while to destroy all these feelings of worthlessness and distrust within you. We have a lot of work to do yet. Shall we make an appointment for the same time next week?'

Tilly looked at him blankly. 'Why? What for?'

Father Christmas smiled. 'To continue the treatment, of course. Another few weeks and you'll begin to be aware of a real difference in your inner self. Now don't look so worried, I promise I'm quite unscathed! See?' He stood up and guided her hand over his stomach. 'Feel how hard it is? Firm as this table! And you have good athletic thighs, you know. Perfect for jumping! You should be proud of them. Goodbye, Tilly. See you next week.'

'All right,' Tilly said doubtfully. She picked up her prescription and made for the door.

'Oh, Tilly!' Father Christmas put down his pen. 'One more thing before you go. Wear the same clothes: that skirt and that top and those boots. It may sound silly but if you wear the same clothes it will help you to see this as a ritual, an official exorcism of all your uncertainties. Good girl! Until next week, then!'

After the third session, when Tilly realized that her inner uncertainties seemed to be as rampant as ever, she knew she really didn't want to go any more. She decided to consult Robin.

'You do *what*?' Robin asked.

'I jump on him,' Tilly confessed. 'I'm terrified I might hurt him. It's supposed to give me confidence, I think. But, Robin,

I hate doing it. I feel so silly. It might be easier if he let me wear trousers but I have to wear my skirt. Do you think I'd be ungrateful if I told him I wanted to stop? I don't want to hurt his feelings but . . .'

'Tilly, you jump on him? How do you jump on him? Where do you jump on him?'

'In his surgery, of course. I climb on his desk and he lies down and I jump on his stomach.'

Robin stared at her blankly for a few seconds. 'Your doctor's a pervert,' he said, 'and you are mad. Did he *tell* you why he wanted you to jump on him?'

'He said it would release all my inner tensions.'

Robin grinned. 'I bet it releases his! Has he asked you about your sex life yet?'

'No, of course not. Well, not exactly.'

'You mean he has.'

'He did ask me if I have any sexual fantasies I was too shy to tell you about. I couldn't think of any. Robin, don't smile at me like that. Robin!'

Robin took Tilly's face in his hands and kissed her mouth. 'I love you,' he said.

Tilly could feel herself smiling foolishly. 'Do you?' she asked. 'Really?'

'Really,' he said. 'I do.'

'It's very odd,' said Tilly, 'but I can feel all my inner tensions fly away.'

'Hey, Tilly,' Robin said, 'do you want to try jumping on *my* stomach?'

After that, Tilly felt able, with perfect honesty, to write to her doctor and tell him she had definitely resolved all her personal problems and would no longer need his treatment. He wrote back a charming letter, assuring her his stomach would always be there for her if she needed it and that if she ever needed any private counselling he would be happy to provide it.

CHAPTER FIVE: Present

'One should never know too precisely whom one has married.'
                                        FRIEDRICH NIETZSCHE

Horace was missing. He had gone AWOL before but the fact that they were due at Robin's parents in under an hour lent an increased urgency to the search. Reluctantly, Tilly put down the rapturous profile of Nicole Kidman she was reading. It dealt at length with her level-headed charm: I don't think my personal life is that exciting, declared the stunning beauty. I'm an ordinary person, I like to sit in the park and talk to ordinary people.

Robin was standing in a corner of the garden. He glared at Tilly like a Monsieur Poirot who's found his murderer. 'Have you seen this? I thought you were going to check the fence after the last time.'

'I did!' Tilly protested, which was true enough since she had indeed begun an inspection a few days ago. She had been diverted by a phone call from her sister that had irritated her so much she'd been forced to soothe her nerves by watching *The Little Mermaid* with the children.

'Well, you didn't do a very good job. An elephant could get through this. You know what Horace is like. He'd make Houdini look like an amateur . . . I mean, for heaven's sake!'

'If you're going to do your for heaven's sake routine, I'm

going,' Tilly said. 'I'll take the car and drive around and you ring the neighbours, especially the Sellars. Horace loves going there. Mr Sellars *will* keep giving him digestive biscuits.'

Robin checked his watch. 'I'll mend the fence. If you haven't found him in half an hour, come back and we'll just have to go without him. You know what Mum's like; she'll have timed everything down to the last second. We can't be late on our first visit there.'

'Fine, fine,' said Tilly airily, sweeping back into the kitchen. So much for not standing on ceremony with his parents. Huh! She couldn't stand Robin when he was in his time-keeping mood and she resented the Taylors for transforming her usual blissful, slow-motion Sunday into a morning of adrenalin-fuelled angst.

She drove up the road and onto the by-pass. When they'd first arrived here seven years ago, they'd fondly imagined they were buying into a quiet, rural idyll. The arrival of an out-of-town supermarket just a mile and a half away, while crippling Frome's retailers, had led to an explosion of housing estates that lapped ever closer to the edges of their home.

Tilly drove through one of them now, looking first one way, then another. She felt like a kerb-crawler. Everywhere she went, her exhaust pipe, which was hanging by a thread, her-alded her arrival with a ghastly shriek.

She spotted a familiar figure emerging from a newsagent's with a pile of Sunday papers. Tilly pulled up beside him. 'Excuse me,' she said with an ingratiating smile. 'I don't suppose you've seen a big yellow dog, have you?'

'The one you were walking the other day?' The leather-clad Adonis did not bend down. Tilly found herself staring at his crotch.

'Yes,' she said. 'He's called Horace.'

'No, I haven't. Isn't it time you learnt how to look after him?'

'I don't know . . . I . . .' But the crotch had moved on, leaving Tilly alone and stunned by his gratuitous rudeness. She drove off with flaming cheeks and turned into another new housing estate. As she wove in and out of the maze of roads her mind threw up various devastating ripostes like, 'Isn't it time you learnt some manners?' or 'So you know all about dogs, do you?' Knowing her luck, he'd probably turn out to be an RSPCA inspector.

She arrived home in a filthy mood to find the children watching television and Robin stretched out on the sofa reading the colour supplement, with Horace spilt across his legs. Robin gave her an apologetic smile. 'Tilly, I'm sorry!' he said. 'Guess who came back a few minutes after you left?'

The Taylors had bought a small cottage in Nunney, just down the road from the ruined castle. It had a thatched roof, yellow walls and a garden that ran down to the stream. It was often seen on postcards and was generally regarded as the perfect country cottage.

The last time Tilly had come here was when she'd gone round it with Anne, after an exhaustive trawl of prospective houses. Then, it had been empty and naked, waiting for someone to breathe life into it. Little did it know, Tilly thought with a twinge of pity, that in its new owner it had the most ruthless house-surgeon in the business.

Anne greeted them with her usual shower of compliments. 'Darlings, how wonderful to see you! Tilly, what a sweet little jumper! Robin, you didn't have to bring a bottle with you, you are *too* naughty! Come in and welcome to our little home!' She was wearing blue denim jeans and a wine-coloured twinset. Her sleek, silvery blonde hair was tucked behind her ears. It seemed preposterous that she'd never see her sixtieth birthday again. As always she made Tilly feel like a badly dressed slob.

They trailed after her into the kitchen and Tilly exclaimed impulsively, 'Oh, Anne, this is beautiful!' The old cream Aga still dominated the kitchen but the linoleum floor had been replaced with mixed tiles in varying shades of warm amber, and the units were made of the palest ash. The table was already laid for lunch and the centrepiece was a glorious arrangement of gypsophila and red roses.

The back door was wide open, providing a compelling invitation to Horace and the children. In front of the beech tree, the old grey hut of indeterminate character was now a freshly painted Wendy house, complete with gingham curtains and imposing brass door knocker. Lucy and Sam were enchanted and ran outside, squealing with delight.

Peter emerged from the dining room with a tray of glasses. He glanced towards the children and smiled. 'What do you think?' he asked Tilly. 'Do they approve?'

Tilly laughed. 'You'll have them living here if you're not careful! It looks fantastic! Like the gingerbread house in Hansel and Gretel!'

'Without the witch, I hope!' Anne said. For a moment Tilly wondered if Anne could read her mind, but no, she serenely took a tray of roast potatoes from the oven and began basting them.

Robin put an arm round his mother's shoulders. 'No one makes roast potatoes like you do,' he said. 'You have no idea how much I miss your Sunday lunches!'

'Nonsense,' Anne said, and though she had her back to them Tilly knew she was smirking like a cat with a pond full of cream. 'I'm sure Tilly makes excellent Sunday roasts.'

Tilly decided that submission was the best form of defence. 'To be honest, I usually make a casserole. The trouble with Sunday lunch is you have to cook so many different things at the same time. And I can never make gravy like you do.'

'There's nothing to it, really.' Anne was positively purring with pleasure. 'As long as you follow simple rules.'

Robin grinned. 'You must teach them to Tilly!'

Anne received a glass of wine from her husband. 'I'd love to. You must come round one day, Tilly, and we'll cook a meal together.'

Tilly had an instant, horrible vision of herself standing humbly to attention while her mother-in-law showed her how to crumble a stock cube. Diversion was clearly necessary. 'I think I'd better see what the children are doing. It's a little too quiet!' She went out into the garden. Horace was going round and round in circles on the trail of some scent. In the Wendy house, Sam was sitting at a red plastic table, alternately eating crisps and sucking from a carton of apple juice.

'I'm looking after Sam,' Lucy said. 'I've been giving him a meal. Look, I can cook just like you.'

'Just like me!' Tilly agreed. She was impressed and touched by the thought that had been put into the children's entertainment. A plate of drinks and snacks rested on top of a white-painted cupboard whose open door revealed a set of toy pans and bowls.

Lucy wore a Mickey Mouse apron and brandished a wooden spoon. 'Would you like to join us?' she asked. 'Do sit down.'

Tilly sat next to Sam. She felt humbled and chastened by her in-laws' kindness.

'Would you like some fish fingers, Mummy?' Lucy enquired. 'With baked beans?'

'Yes, please,' Tilly said and watched as her daughter, face stiff with concentration, served out an imaginary meal. 'Lucy, these are wonderful. Thank you.'

'If you like,' Lucy said carelessly, 'I'll show you how I made them.'

Anne's lunch, predictably, was terrific: roast pork with crispy crackling, apple sauce, the perfect roast potatoes, mouthwatering gravy and tender runner beans. Tilly, newly determined to get on with her hostess, praised her extravagantly and raised her glass, saying, 'To my mother-in-law and her wonderful meal!'

Anne lowered her eyes modestly while everyone drank her health. 'You're very sweet! We are thrilled to be so near you all. It's made our retirement very exciting.'

'It must be so odd for you,' Tilly said. 'You and Peter have always worked so hard and now you have endless leisure: lovely but quite scary, I should think.'

'Scary? Oh, Tilly, you have no idea at all!' Anne shook her head in apparent amusement. 'We have longed to get off the treadmill! And I don't think you'll find Peter and I are the sort of people who find our time difficult to fill!'

'No, of course not,' said Tilly quickly, wondering why she always got things wrong with her mother-in-law. 'I wasn't implying that at all . . .'

'Knowing you,' Robin leant forward and smiled affectionately at his mother, 'you'll be running this village in a few months!'

Anne gave a little shrug. 'There is so much I want to do! Of course I want to get involved in our local community but I also want to join pottery classes, learn Italian at last, redesign the garden, decorate the house. I'm no good at being idle!'

'I am!' said Tilly.

'I'm sure that's not true,' Anne said without a great deal of conviction. 'Sam, dear, use your knife and fork.'

'You see,' Sam explained with a sweet smile, 'me can't.'

'Liar!' Tilly said. 'Of course you can. Put the potato back on your plate and I'll cut it up for you.'

'Sam's disgusting,' Lucy said. 'He did a wee on the lawn after breakfast.'

'So did Howace!' Sam protested.

Peter chuckled. 'Not quite the same, old chap! Horace can't go to the bathroom!'

'Neither can Sam,' said Lucy. 'He always does it in the garden.'

Forestalling one of Anne's anecdotes on how she had potty-trained Robin before he could crawl, Tilly turned to Peter. 'Horace slept like a baby for hours after your walk with him. You were so kind to take him out.'

'I enjoyed it. I'll do it again this week. He could do with losing a little weight and so could I. And I'd welcome the chance to explore the area. I thought I'd try Longleat Woods next.'

'Sounds great. Give me a ring the night before and if I'm out I'll leave the key under the pot for you.'

'How's your sister, Tilly?' Anne asked. 'Is she still working in that publishing company? The one that brings out academic books?'

'That's the one,' Tilly said brightly. 'She's very busy at the

75

moment. Apparently, she's nursing a brilliant new history book that is going to revolutionize the teaching of Tudor England.'

'She is so clever,' Anne said. 'Your parents must be very proud of her.' She paused to take a sip of wine. 'And what about *your* job? You're not finding it too exhausting?'

'No,' said Tilly, 'not at all.'

Anne began to clear away the plates. 'Of course you'll be able to spread your wings when Sam goes to school. I read a fascinating article just this morning about classroom assistants. I cut it out for you. It seems there are all sorts of opportunities nowadays. There are the most exciting courses you can do. You could end up being a virtual teacher.'

Tilly put Sam's plate on top of her own, carefully concealing his potato under the cutlery. 'I have a friend whose youngest has started school this term. She has an interview at the Curved Wheel on Tuesday.'

'What fun! Is that the sweet little arts and crafts place on the bridge?'

Tilly tried to conceal her irritation. 'It's not that little. In fact it holds fantastic exhibitions. You should go and have a look when you have a moment.'

Robin frowned. 'Which friend are you talking about?'

'Amy.'

'You didn't tell me.'

Oh, brilliant, Tilly thought, now they'll assume we never talk to each other. 'I must have forgotten,' she said lightly. 'Yes, Amy's very excited.' She reached across for Lucy's plate and stood up.

'Tilly, sit down,' Anne said. 'Give Peter those plates. We want you to relax.' Tilly sat down again quickly and wondered why being told to relax was an inevitable precursor to stress. In the same way, if ever someone told her she should be enjoying herself, she instantly succumbed to depression. What it amounted to was that no one, especially friends and mothers-in-law, should try to dictate or second-guess one's emotional state. How contrary human beings were! If someone said to Tilly, 'I'm in such a bad mood!' Tilly found her own disposition inexplicably lightened. She felt she'd stumbled on an interesting revelation about the human condition and in different company would certainly have shared her discovery.

'Nothing special for pudding, I'm afraid,' Anne said. 'Apple crumble for us and home-made ice cream for the children.'

'Can grown-ups have ice cream too?' asked Robin.

Anne rewarded him with a large helping of both. 'I hope your friend gets her job,' she said to Tilly. 'My friend Rebecca runs an art gallery in London and adores it. She discovered a brilliant young artist in Rouen recently . . . so thrilling!'

Robin raised his eyebrows. 'I can't quite see Amy scouring the towns of Europe for talent.'

'We're doing Europe at school,' said Lucy.

'Tell us all you know about Europe,' Tilly said. 'And be sure not to leave anything out.' She enjoyed the rest of the meal.

After lunch they retired to the sitting room, sipping coffee and nibbling After Eights while the children played outside. Tilly could see Peter's eyelids drooping slightly and said with an impressive semblance of regret, 'Robin, we should be getting back. Anne, thank you so much. We've had a wonderful time.'

'I hope this will become a regular event. You will come next Sunday, won't you?'

Tilly caught sight of the framed photos in the corner and shook her head sadly. 'I'm afraid we can't. I promised my mother we'd go to them.'

Robin looked up sharply. 'You didn't tell me.'

Tilly smiled at her husband. 'Didn't I?' she said. 'Silly me!'

'Never mind,' said Anne. 'You must come to us the following week. We mustn't monopolize you! And I'll have finished the sitting-room curtains by then. What do you think, Tilly?'

Tilly fingered the material draped over the small chair beneath the photos. The fabric, pale green and yellow leaves etched on an ivory background, was exquisite and she said so.

'They'd look good in your bedroom,' Anne mused. 'I could make some for you when I've finished mine, if you like. They could be an early Christmas present.'

'Oh, Anne!' Tilly said. 'That *is* kind. We'd be very grateful!'

'I am,' Tilly confessed to Amy the next morning, 'so fed up with being grateful!'

'I don't see why you need to feel grateful,' Amy said. 'If they want to walk the dog and make you curtains, let them! I'd accept with the greatest of pleasure!'

'You don't understand. It's all so . . . so insidious! As we were leaving, Anne insisted we look round the garage and see if we'd like any of their cast-offs. Would we like to replace our sofa with one of theirs? Wouldn't their coffee table look better in our sitting room than our old tea chest? I mean, I *like* our old tea chest! Anne won't rest until our house is a carbon copy of her own. And now they're trying to take over our Sundays.

Because of them I have to tell Mum she's invited us to lunch next week and Dad will make me angry and I don't think Robin believes me anyway . . .'

'Tilly, you do make things difficult for yourself. I'd have murmured something about checking my diary and then later I would have laid down some very firm guidelines to Robin!'

'It's never been easy to talk to Robin about his parents; he has a blind spot where they're concerned. And anyway I was in a state of shock! I'd just seen the Louise photo promoted to the sitting room, side by side with all the other great moments in Robin's life: his christening, his graduation, his perfect woman. I ask you—' Tilly stopped talking abruptly.

The Adonis and his family had strolled into the school playground. This time they had someone else with them: another stick insect. This one was male, dressed all in black, with the same pale face framed by curly dark hair. He had to be a brother. Tilly watched him murmur something to the woman, who laughed. It was a surprisingly loud laugh. Tilly would never have thought she could look so animated.

With a shock she realized Adonis was looking at her looking at them. He was staring at her with insolent deliberation and she reddened and turned to Amy. 'That man,' she hissed fiercely, 'was so foul to me yesterday. I was out looking for Horace and I asked him if he'd seen my dog. He told me I was a hopeless dog-owner and shouldn't be allowed near animals!'

'He didn't!'

'Well, more or less. I couldn't believe it!'

'He's probably a tortured soul. Perhaps he'd just discovered his wife in bed with her lover.'

'If I discovered Robin in bed with someone I'd still be polite to innocent strangers! There is no excuse for gratuitous rudeness. It's so . . . so contaminating. I mean, if someone is horrid to you, especially if it's someone you don't know, it affects you for hours, it makes you scratchy with other people and then they get upset and so they're horrible, and in the end everyone's horrid to everyone. Don't you find that?'

'No,' Amy said. 'If anyone is nasty to me, I just think there's one less idiot I have to smile at. And I'm very busy at the moment, practising my winning smiles for the interview tomorrow. What do you think of this one?'

'You look like you're auditioning for a toothpaste advert. It's frightening. Stop it! All you need to do is spin them the usual Amy charm and you'll be fine.'

Amy *was* fine. Amy was more than fine, she was ecstatic. They were all watching television, with Lucy and Edward squabbling gently over the choice of programme, when the doorbell rang five times in quick succession. When Tilly opened the door Amy almost fell in.

'I've done it! I've done it! I start work next week! You see before you Superwoman Incarnate! Edward! Luke! Come and praise your clever mother! Next month you will both get the new trainers you wanted! Am I brilliant or not?'

'Mum?' Lucy glanced hopefully at Tilly. 'Can I have new trainers too?'

Over supper Tilly told Robin about Amy and his reaction turned out to be remarkably similar to Lucy's. 'Lucky Amy! So she'll be working full-time.' He went over to the stove and helped himself to more quiche. 'I don't suppose there's any chance that you could get more hours at Hurstfield? I've got a mountain of bills at work. If you could get a full-time job, that would really take the pressure off.'

'I don't know,' Tilly said. 'I don't think I could do that yet. What would I do about Sam?'

'Wouldn't Margot be happy to help out?'

'She already does. She has a life of her own. I can't dump Sam on her all the time. Anyway, Arthur wouldn't give me more hours at the moment, he has the entire timetable covered. I could ask him to let me know when any vacancies come up.'

'Would you? At the moment we need every penny we can get . . .' Robin paused and smiled at the sight of his pyjama-clad daughter in the doorway. 'Hello, sweetheart, can't you get to sleep?'

Lucy came in and climbed onto her father's lap. 'We're not allowed to have crisps at school any more,' she said.

'That's all very well,' said Tilly, 'but that doesn't explain why you're out of bed.'

'It's Sam,' Lucy said carelessly. 'He's very ill.' She turned back to her father. 'They won't let us have chocolate now either.'

Upstairs, Sam was sitting on his bed, his eyes full of tears, his duvet caked in vomit.

'Me tummy's fallen out,' he said piteously. 'Me have nothing left!'

'Poor Sam!' Tilly pulled back the duvet and picked up her son. 'You'll feel better *very* soon!'

But Sam didn't. At three in the morning he woke up in tears and a few minutes after Tilly had finally settled him she heard Lucy, who had heroically made it to the bathroom, discharging the contents of her stomach. A couple of hours later Tilly had to make her own emergency dash.

When Robin went to work, he left his family huddled in

bed together, listening to the *Harry Potter* tapes. When he came back from work that evening with flowers for Tilly and puzzle books for the children, they were *still* listening to the *Harry Potter* tapes.

By Thursday, both the children were back to normal and Tilly felt well enough to make a beef casserole though not, as she discovered at dinner, well enough to eat it. Robin insisted on making her an omelette and she sat and pecked at it, grateful for his concern.

The phone rang and Robin leant back on his chair to pick up the receiver. 'Dad, how are you?'

How good-looking Robin was with those rich dark eyes and extravagantly long eyelashes. Most of the time she took his appearance for granted, but there were moments when she saw the way a woman talked to him or when he smiled in a particular way – at such moments she found herself utterly subjugated to him.

He was laughing, scratching his head so that his hair stood up in tufts, making him look absurdly boyish. 'Well, if you're going to be chief dog-walker, I shall have to get you your own key! No, it will be easy. I'll see to it.'

Tilly stood up abruptly and began clearing away the plates. When Robin finished his phone conversation, she came back to the table and sat down opposite her husband.

'That's nice,' Robin said. 'Dad's coming round tomorrow to walk Horace.'

'I heard. Did I also hear you say you'd get a key for him?'

'Yes. Why not? Why are you looking like that? What's the problem?'

'Robin, this is our home. I don't want you handing out keys so your parents can drop in any time they feel like it.'

'Why not? They're my parents!'

'So are mine!'

'What?'

'I have parents too. My mother came round every day after I had Sam and I never once suggested she had a key.'

'So what? You could have done. I wouldn't have minded.'

'But I would. This is our home. It doesn't belong to anyone else. It's as if you've lowered the drawbridge . . . they can pop round any time they like, whether I want them to or not.'

'Tilly,' Robin rubbed his forehead with his hand, 'aren't you getting this out of proportion? My parents have no intention of popping round every day. They want to help, that's all. There is no hidden agenda here: they are a couple of elderly people who wish to help their son and his family. The issue of the key is unimportant.'

'Not to me! It matters to me! I admire your parents and I appreciate how kind they are but I don't want them to have a key! You should have talked to me first.'

'You're right.'

'What?'

'You're right. I'm sorry. I didn't think. Would you like me to ring them back?'

'And say what? That Tilly says they can't have one?'

Robin leant forward and took her hands. 'Tilly, I'm sorry. Truly, I am. I'm an insensitive oaf. I've been so busy trying to make Mum and Dad feel welcome, I haven't even thought about how you might be feeling. I know you don't find them easy . . .'

'It's not that. I don't want you to think I don't like them. It's just that . . . It's difficult to explain.'

'Try me. I want to understand.'

83

'It sounds so pathetic. They're both so glamorous and successful and charming. Your mother dresses beautifully, is a brilliant cook, has a vast circle of friends. She's had a brilliant career and now she'll have a brilliant retirement. She makes me feel so inadequate.'

'Inadequate? Tilly, that's crazy! Why should you feel inadequate? Because you're different from my mother? Do you know something? The first time I knew I loved you was a few weeks after we'd started seeing each other. You'd been to that doctor, remember?'

'Of course I remember. And I have to tell you that if you're trying to make me feel better about myself, reminding me of the doctor episode doesn't help. That would *never* have happened to your mother.'

'No, it wouldn't. But it was very funny. You made me laugh. You often make me laugh. You make life fun. So you don't throw glamorous dinner parties. Thank God for that. I *hate* glamorous dinner parties. I love you.' He touched her cheek with the palm of his hand. 'You are a wonderful mother and a perfect wife and I love you very much.'

He always did this. Every time. A sudden capitulation, a rueful grin, warm words and a loving caress, and somehow she discovered he'd won. As always she let him kiss her and lead her up to bed. Later, while she slept, she dreamt of giants knocking her house down.

CHAPTER SIX

'There is no greater risk, perhaps, than matrimony, but there is nothing happier than a happy marriage.'

DISRAELI

There was something different about Rhona, nothing tangible, no new hairdo or clothes, but when she called out 'Good morning!' Tilly could sense a new dynamism and confidence. Had Tilly been less anxious to offload her request onto Arthur she would have lingered in the staffroom. As it was, she sped along the corridor rehearsing her carefully crafted question.

The carefully crafted question flew out of the window when she arrived at Arthur's door and saw the poster with the words THE EXTRA AID DEPARTMENT emblazoned on it in green and white stripes. 'Arthur!' she said. 'You *have* changed the name!'

Arthur looked up from his desk and gave Tilly a sheepish grin. 'Tilly! Good to see you back. I trust you're fully recovered. Good! Yes, I thought we'd go with my suggestion for a few weeks since none of you came up with anything else. Is that what you wanted to see me about? Have you a better idea?'

'Oh, no.' Tilly flashed him an ingratiating smile. 'I think that's fine.' She sat down and took a deep breath. 'I . . .

85

Arthur, I don't suppose you'd be able to give me more hours? I mean, I just thought I'd let you know I'm available if you need more help . . . I'm sure you don't but if you do . . .'

Arthur blew out his cheeks and shook his head sadly. 'I'm sorry, Tilly, I can't give you more than your three mornings at present. But if anyone leaves or if we're given more funding, which we won't be, saving a miracle, I'll come to you first.' He leant forward. 'Is everything all right? No problems at home, I hope?'

'Oh, goodness no, I'm fine. A little more money would be helpful, that's all. Well.' Tilly stood up. 'I won't keep you.'

'Right. And Tilly –' he paused to give her a sympathetic smile – 'if you ever want to talk, I'm always here for you.'

'Thanks, Arthur.' Arthur would indeed be a marvellous confidant: kind, helpful, concerned. He'd obviously been wonderful when Pam had had her problems last year, and hopefully Pam would never find out that Arthur had told them all in confidence the reason for her protracted sick leave.

At least Tilly could now, in good faith, tell Robin she had tried to get more work. She went off to her maths lesson with a lighter heart, which remained undaunted throughout a series of devilish worksheets.

When the break bell went, Tilly ran down the stairs determined to talk to Rhona. In the corridor, however, she came to a grinding halt at the sight of Gemma in tears. It was not a pretty sight. Poor Gemma was the sort of child who makes one question the arbitrary way in which natural advantages are handed out at birth. Fat and pasty-faced, with lank, greasy hair, asthmatic and with limited intelligence, she made Tilly want to rage at the unfairness of it all.

Gemma was accompanied by Kayleigh, an anaemic blonde, thin as a piece of string, who informed Tilly, somewhat unnecessarily, that Gemma was upset.

'What's happened, Gemma?' Tilly asked gently. 'Has someone been horrid to you?'

Gemma's small eyes were red and puffy. 'My dad's left home, miss. I got back from school yesterday and he was packing his suitcase and now he's gone and Mum says he won't come back.' Her broad shoulders heaved and she sniffed hugely.

'Oh, Gemma, I'm so sorry.' Tilly put an arm round her. 'Perhaps they've just had a row. Perhaps your dad will come back when he's calmed down. We all do things when we're angry that we feel bad about later. . .'

'Not this time, miss. He's never taken his videos before.'

'This time?' queried Tilly. 'Has he left home before?'

'Lots of times, miss!' Kayleigh broke in, eager to provide information. 'He's always going off and coming back and going off and coming back. When he quarrels with Gemma's mum he goes to his other woman and when he quarrels with her he comes back to Gemma's mum.'

'He won't this time,' Gemma insisted stubbornly. 'He's taken the videos! He's never taken the videos before!'

'*I* couldn't get to sleep last night, miss,' Kayleigh said. 'My mum and stepdad were shouting at each other.'

'Oh, dear,' said Tilly weakly. 'I'm sorry to hear that. But Mums and Dads do argue sometimes, you know.' She was beginning to feel like Joyce Grenfell.

'My stepdad's upset,' Kayleigh continued remorselessly, 'because my mum wants to leave him.'

'Oh, dear,' Tilly repeated. 'I'm so sorry.'

Kayleigh shook her head. 'No, it's good, miss, because she wants to go back to my real dad.'

'Really?' said Tilly. 'Well, I suppose that's good . . .'

'Yes, but my stepdad's upset because he'll miss me and I'm not sure who I should go with.'

'Well, I tell you what,' Tilly said breezily, with a brazen display of counterfeit confidence, 'if you're not sure then I should leave the decision to your parents. I'm sure they know best. Now I must dash, but do let me know how things go.' And Tilly scuttled off, inwardly seething at the useless adults who dared to call themselves parents and at herself for yielding to the need for coffee when she should have been trying to help.

Rhona had saved her a seat and with eight short words dispatched the problems of poor Gemma and Kayleigh into the ether. 'Oh, Tilly!' she said. 'You'll never guess! I'm in love!'

'What? Since when? With whom? Tell me quick!'

'It's so romantic, you won't believe it. I'm not sure *I* believe it! I keep thinking I'll wake up and find it was all a dream.'

'Rhona, control yourself. We have about ten minutes for you to tell me everything. Where? When? How?'

'You know I always run the handicrafts stall at the Agricultural Show? Well, last week I was talking to a customer when I noticed this man watching me.'

'What did he look like?'

'Well.' Rhona put her head to one side. 'He was a sort of combination of Harrison Ford and Tom Cruise with a little bit of Noel Gallagher. Does that make sense?'

'Absolutely. I can visualize him perfectly!'

'Don't mock, Tilly, he was gorgeous! He kept going away and then he'd come back and he didn't say anything. He just watched me. After that, whenever I looked up, there he was, watching me.'

Tilly grimaced. 'Spooky!'

'No, but it wasn't. He wasn't watching me in a weird or obsessional or guilty way. He was just . . . there, and . . . interested. And then when I was packing up he came over. He asked if he could speak to me and I said yes, and he looked so pleased. I knew if I'd said no he'd have disappeared at once. Tilly, he was so nice! He said he'd seen me at last year's show but hadn't dared approach me. He said he'd thought about me all year. Can you believe it? He asked me if I'd go for a drink and I said I had to give my daughter some tea but if he wanted I could meet him later. Do you know what he said?'

'Tell me!'

'He said, "I do want," just that, and then he smiled!'

'That is romantic,' Tilly said approvingly, 'and stylish. Brief, to the point, manly.'

'It gets better. We went to the Fox and Hounds and he bought us champagne. Oh, Tilly, the things he said! I felt I was the most beautiful woman in the world! We talked and talked and in the end I invited him back for coffee . . .'

'Rhona!' Tilly exclaimed. 'On your first date! You reckless woman!'

'I know! I've always been so careful, but none of this is like me. I've never felt like this before. He is . . . wonderful!'

'Oh, Rhona!' Tilly looked at her friend with genuine delight and a new respect. How wonderful to be able to inspire such instant adulation! 'When can I see him? I'm dying of curiosity! Robin and I could meet you for a pub supper. What do you think?'

'I think I need to make sure I'm not dreaming first!' Rhona

laughed. 'No, it sounds great. I'll suggest it to Nigel once I know he's real.'

'Good. What does Chloe think about it all?'

'She thinks I'm mad! You know something? The day before I met Nigel I realized I was jealous of Chloe. How low is that? To be jealous of your thirteen-year-old daughter! Nigel's rescued me from that. Oh, Tilly, isn't love wonderful?'

'I can't remember!' Tilly grinned. Later, at about half past nine, she would remember that remark and wonder why she'd found it funny.

This was obviously a day for surprises. When Tilly arrived home with Sam, she found there was something different about her house. Horace's unusually languid greeting should have alerted her but since her head was full of Rhona and love, it didn't. She stood in the kitchen with furrowed brow and sniffed the air. Sam did the same. 'It smells clean!' he said.

He was right. The floor had been washed. Tilly knew how the seven dwarves felt when they came home and found Snow White had been interfering with their house. Grimly she walked into the sitting room and then up the stairs, half-expecting to find her mother-in-law asleep in her bed.

She wasn't. Worse, Anne had made the bed. The coverlet lay, as it had never lain before, neatly tucked around the pillows, and when Tilly lifted a corner of it she found her nightshirt meekly folded on her pillow. If ever a garment could look subdued it was her nightshirt.

Downstairs in the kitchen a small green casserole dish stood on the stove. On the table was a letter. '*Dearest Tilly, Thought you might like some of our Hungarian Goulash for supper. I did a little tidying while Peter walked Horace. Don't thank me, I enjoyed it! Love, Anne.*'

Tilly ground her teeth. She knew Anne would be waiting by the telephone, ready to receive Tilly's rapturous gratitude. The telephone rang and Tilly jumped. It was Robin. 'Hi, Tilly. Look, I'm going to be late so don't cook me anything. I'll tell you about it later. Expect me when you see me.'

'Robin,' Tilly said, 'I want to talk to you.'

'Me too. Got lots to tell you! Take care! Must go!'

Tilly put the casserole in the fridge, childishly pleased that Robin would not be eating it this evening. Then, false smile in place, she rang her mother-in-law to say thank you.

Robin arrived back at nine, bathed in benevolence. 'Tilly,' he said, 'you look beautiful.'

Tilly had spent the last half-hour cleaning out the cooker and neither felt nor looked beautiful. Either Robin needed an optician or he was in a very good mood. She was not. She hated cleaning the cooker and had only done so to prove to herself that there was at least one area of the house over which she had control. 'Tell me,' she said. 'What's happened?'

Robin took out a beer from the fridge. 'Something wonderful has happened, something very wonderful. The last few months, it's been like Custer's Last Stand at work. And now, just possibly, the cavalry has arrived.'

'General Custer got killed. The cavalry never *did* arrive. That's why it's called Custer's Last Stand.'

'Well, in that case I'm a lot luckier than poor Custer.' Robin rummaged around in the cutlery drawer and pulled out the bottle opener. 'Have you ever heard of Peter van Duren?'

'The multimillionaire who's bought the Grange?'

'The very same! Guess who he's asked to design a garden tree house for his teenage boys?'

'Robin! That's brilliant!'

91

'I know!' Robin opened his beer. 'I can't believe it! It's all down to Josie. She sent him our brochure as soon as she heard he'd bought the place. He says he wants the ultimate den, money no object. You realize we could be talking *Homes and Gardens*, *Country Living* . . . it's a dream come true. The perfect client! It's just what we need! This could really put us on the map! I rang Dad this afternoon. He knows the man who designed van Duren's London penthouse. Apparently, he's been inundated with work ever since.' He took a swig of his beer. 'Dad said they'd been over here today.'

'They were,' Tilly said grimly. 'Anne made our bed while I was at work.'

'Really?' Robin yawned. 'That was nice of her.'

'Robin, it was not nice. I didn't want her to make our bed. She also cleaned my kitchen floor and left a Hungarian Goulash, which you can eat tomorrow.'

'So? That's great, isn't it? Why do you make it sound as if she's murdered Horace?'

'How would you feel if someone came into your office while you were out, looked through your papers, tidied them up in neat piles and made a few changes to your latest designs?'

Robin grinned. 'It's not quite the same, is it? Since when did you get so proprietorial about making the bed and cleaning the floor? You hate cleaning the floor! You must see how funny you sound!'

'I don't see anything of the sort! And don't be so patronizing! This isn't about making beds. It's about your parents invading my space, my castle, my nest. I knew this would happen, I knew it. In a few months I won't recognize this place. It will be the Anne Taylor Residence Mark Two!'

Robin crossed his arms. He was no longer smiling. 'I don't understand any of this. If you were a woman whose sole aim in life was to keep a perfect home, it would at least make some sort of sense . . . But you loathe housework. If you had a full-time job you'd jump at the chance of paying for a cleaner. But you don't have a full-time job and you're not that interested in cleaning the house. I can't believe I'm hearing this. Shock horror: my mother has made a nice dinner for us and cleaned up our house! Most people would be very grateful. You know what really gets me? I come back with potentially the most prestigious order of my career and all you can do is complain about Mum making the bed! If you don't want her help, then tell her yourself. I'm not going to. It's late, I've had a long day and I'm seri-ously in need of some mindless television.' He stood up and whistled to Horace, who followed him through to the sit-ting room.

Tilly stood alone in the kitchen and raised her hands to her flaming cheeks. She hated arguing with Robin. They hardly ever argued. Before his parents had arrived, there had been no need. She hated the fact that he made her feel childish and petty and preoccupied with trivia. She hated the fact that Robin, who had always understood her so well, had just refused to understand her feelings about his parents and espe-cially his mother. Most of all, she hated the fact that everything was horribly, dangerously different.

Tilly's father was impressed. 'I've got to hand it to you, Robin,' he said, leaning back in his chair. 'When you and John first decided to set up on your own I was worried. I thought you were too young. I was wrong and I freely admit it. To land van Duren like that, well, you're moving into the big league. You must be proud of him, Tilly!'

'Of course I am,' Tilly said and continued to lay the table.

'Poor old Tilly,' Robin said. 'It's not going to be easy for her for the next few months. I'm going to be working flat out. I can't afford to get this job wrong.'

'Women!' Harry Treadwell chuckled. 'They love to see the money come in; they don't understand we have to work for it!'

Tilly, horribly afraid she would be disappointed by her husband's reaction to her father's observation, walked through to the sitting room before she could find out.

Lucy and Sam were sprawled on the floor, surrounded by a sea of Lego. 'It's lunch, kids,' Tilly told them.

'We making a house,' Sam said.

'It's not a house,' Lucy said impatiently. 'It's a museum.' She added another piece to her tower and stood up. 'I'll show it to Granddad after lunch. He'll think it's brilliant.'

Tilly had read somewhere that children were more likely to take after their uncles and aunts than their parents. Certainly, Lucy's character seemed to vindicate such a theory. She was far more like Charlotte than Tilly. Tilly admired Lucy's confidence and hoped passionately she would never lose it. If a good fairy were to offer her just one gift for her children she would dismiss beauty, wisdom, wealth, whatever and go straight for self-confidence. As Tilly had once said to Lucy, 'If you believe in yourself, you can do anything!' ('Oh,' Lucy had said dismissively, 'I know that.')

In the dining room Margot was setting out the vegetables while Harry carved the chicken. Lucy and Sam sat down on either side of him. 'Breast or bone, children?'

'Breast,' said Lucy.

'Bone,' said Sam.

'Breast for both,' said Tilly firmly.

'There's enough meat here to feed an army,' Harry said. 'I hope you're all hungry.' He passed Sam's plate to Tilly. 'You're looking a bit pale, Tilly. You're not dieting again, are you? You have no need to, you know.'

'I'm not. I don't think I'm completely over that sick bug yet. I haven't been sleeping very well.'

Harry handed Tilly a plate for Lucy. 'Ah, that explains it.' He smiled at Robin. 'Tilly's always needed a lot of sleep. When the girls were young she'd fall asleep as soon as her head hit the pillow. Now, Charlotte was quite different. She'd stay awake half the night, and I'd go up and tell her to sleep and she'd look at me and say, "I can't, Daddy. I'm thinking too much!" I always knew she'd amount to something!'

'Really? And what,' asked Tilly, 'did you think I'd amount to?'

Harry passed Tilly another plate and beamed at her. 'You, my love, are just like your mother!'

'What does that mean?'

'You look after your menfolk.'

'Oh,' Robin caught Tilly's eye and laughed, 'is that what Tilly does?'

'One potato or two?' Margot asked Lucy.

'Two, please.'

'I don't think,' Margot protested mildly, 'that Tilly and I were put on earth simply to look after you and Robin. One day we'll surprise you all.'

'You already have, my love!' Harry winked at Robin. 'Margot is doing a computer course!'

There must have been a time, Tilly thought, when her father did *not* adopt a patronizing tone whenever he spoke to or about his wife. For as long as she could remember, it had set Tilly's teeth on edge and she couldn't understand why Margot remained so placid in the face of such constant provocation. Whenever Tilly tried to remonstrate, her father responded by patronizing *her* as well. In the circumstances, Sunday lunch with the Taylors was almost preferable. Except, of course, Anne was just as condescending as her father. She ought to get the two of them together. Or not.

Hours later, her father's behaviour was still giving her a bad case of emotional indigestion. She heard the telephone ring while she was tucking Lucy up and fervently hoped it wasn't for her. When she finally went downstairs she felt at once the air of suppressed excitement in the kitchen. Robin said carelessly, 'I'll go and say goodnight to Lucy. Is Sam awake?'

'Flat out,' Tilly said. She took a tin of dog food from the cupboard and wondered what she'd done with the opener. 'Who was on the phone?'

'Only Mum. She had some rather intriguing news. Louise Honeytree is coming to stay with them in a few weeks' time.'

'Louise Honeytree? That's a blast from the past! How extraordinary!'

'I know. It's funny, I had no idea they kept in touch all these years. Mum's very keen that we meet up. She says Louise has loads of media contacts and might be able to help with the business. I wonder if she's changed.'

'I wonder,' said Tilly.

'Well,' Robin said happily, 'we'll soon find out.' He smiled. 'I'll go and see Lucy and then I'll get us a glass of wine.'

She could hear him whistling as he ran up the stairs. Tilly

couldn't remember the last time he'd looked so vital and alive. Even the van Duren contract hadn't wrought this transformation. His eyes were shining as brightly as Rhona's had done on Friday morning.

Tilly found the tin opener and told herself it was silly to be upset. Even sillier to wish that *she* could still have that effect on him. You fall in love, you want to spend every minute with your lover, you want to find out everything you can about each other. So you get married and you do indeed find out everything, and possibly more than you want to know. The trouble with marriage was that after that first wonderful moment of public affirmation of mutual love, there was no way to go but down. She knew Robin suffered from occasional heartburn, was hopeless at buying Christmas and birthday presents, cared too much about his parents' good opinion and fell asleep in front of the television. *He* knew she was always depressed before her period, was scatty and disorganized, had a tendency to get people's names wrong and had never recovered her waistline after the birth of Lucy. How could romance possibly survive in the face of such unremitting intimacy?

If you were lucky – and Tilly knew she was very lucky – you exchanged romance for a relaxed comradeship in which sex provided the necessary spice. The heart-churning headiness of young love might have gone but so had the desperation and the uncertainty.

Beside her, Horace made a polite little bark and she realized she was still chopping up his dinner. 'Sorry,' she said and set the bowl down in front of him.

What was important was that Robin knew she loved him and she knew he loved her. True, he'd been impatient and irritable with her lately but any marriage had its down patches. She had no need to worry even if Louise Honeytree was the most glamorous ex-girlfriend in the world . . . and Louise surely was the most glamorous ex-girlfriend in the world. It was even possible that she'd got fat or developed a skin condition or become a deeply boring person. She might even be fat, spotty *and* boring. In which case, Tilly thought, she'd be *very* pleased to see her again.

CHAPTER SEVEN

'Jealousy is the jaundice of the soul.'
JOHN DRYDEN

Relations with Robin did not improve. It seemed to Tilly that every time they edged towards an understanding, Fate stood chuckling on the sidelines, ready to hurl another missile at them. Mr van Duren was proving to be the client from hell. He disliked Robin's initial designs and when Robin, after working flat out for a fortnight, produced alternative suggestions, he accepted them grudgingly, adding casually that his elder son wanted a tower and could Robin please incorporate one into the new design?

On the home front, Peter took to walking Horace twice a week, invariably bringing with him a sample of Anne's culinary expertise. Anne obviously felt her son was suffering from a lack of good food. Robin, preoccupied with work, failed to notice his wife's lack of enthusiasm for his mother's offerings.

The situation wasn't helped by the fact that his parents' contributions only seemed to exacerbate Robin's irritation with Tilly's domestic shortcomings. 'Just once,' he said after arriving home late one evening and nearly falling over Sam's Duplo train set, 'just once in a while, it would be nice to come back to a civilized home. Now that Mum and Dad do so much, it shouldn't be too much to ask.'

'Your parents,' Tilly responded shortly, 'are very kind and do all sorts of things for me that I never did in the first place and never asked them to do now!'

'Come off it, Tilly, are you saying you didn't like the apple pie we had last night?'

'No, the apple pie was lovely but I never make puddings myself. However many apple pies your mother makes, I still have housework and children and job.'

'*Job?*'

'What do you mean, "*job*"?'

'I don't mean anything. I'm sorry. I've had van Duren treating me like a piece of dirt all day and I'm tired and bad-tempered. As you can see. Is there anything to eat?'

'Yes, of course there is. I'll put the spaghetti on right away.'

'Fine.'

No resolution, no reconciliation, just layer on layer of irritation that left a permanent residue of bitterness, like sediment in a glass. Tilly continued to sleep badly at night which made her fractious and exhausted by day. She had lost her appetite and was losing weight. Rhona said her body was mounting a demonstration against Anne's invasion of her kitchen. This theory pleased Tilly: at least one part of her was striking a spirited opposition.

Amy and Rhona were enjoying their lives, which should have pleased Tilly, and the fact that their happiness only fuelled her rampaging self-pity merely added self-loathing to the menu. Amy was absorbed in her new job, full of stories of eccentric artists and future plans. She presided over her empire like a gaudy bird of paradise against the bleached colours and church-like calm of the gallery. She did try to listen sympathetically to Tilly's complaints about her in-laws, but even to Tilly's ears her moans sounded lame and churlish: feeble gripes from an insecure woman with no real problems.

Rhona was unfurling like a flower that has had its first dose of sunlight in years. Nigel was her soulmate, her better half, her true companion who had for ever banished loneliness, jealousy and misery from her life. 'I really want you to meet him,' she told Tilly. 'I know you'll like each other. What about Saturday night? We could go for an Indian meal.'

'Sounds great. Robin and I haven't been out for a meal in ages.'

'Good. Let's go to the one on the bridge. Nigel likes that one. About eight?'

'Fine. I'll get a babysitter.'

'I know you'll like him! He's so perceptive about me and Chloe. He thinks we've been too close to each other for too long, that I'm scared of losing her. Chloe's started staying with her father at weekends and we get on so much better . . . it gives us the breathing space we need. And I think Chloe really likes Nigel. She knows it takes the heat off her and Martin, I suppose.'

'What about her and Martin? Any more luck with the condom question?'

'Chloe assures me they're not sleeping together. She's not a liar. Isn't it odd how, if you're happy, everything falls into place?'

'I wouldn't know,' Tilly said sourly.

'Tilly, you sound like Eeyore. So you've had a few rows about your mother-in-law. You and half the population! If you love someone – and you do love Robin – then everything will work out.'

Great, Tilly thought. She had one friend who was a walking Mills and Boon and another who'd turned into Superwoman. Even her mother, hitherto a stalwart supporter, seemed to be curiously remote and unsympathetic, briskly handing Sam back to Tilly on school mornings, too busy, apparently, to offer lunch.

Tilly was sufficiently unsettled by her mother's aberrant behaviour to ring Charlotte.

'Quite frankly,' Charlotte said, and Tilly immediately regretted her impulse because whenever Charlotte said those words they heralded the arrival of unpalatable opinions, 'I'm surprised at you. At long last, Mum has emerged from Dad's shadow and is acquiring some professional skills. You should be happy for her. She's nursed you through both your pregnancies, she looks after Sam for you; surely you don't begrudge her a little independence now, do you?'

'Of course I don't! That's not what I'm saying! I'm glad she's enjoying her computer course, I really am. I'm merely commenting on the fact that she's changed quite a lot, that's all. She seems to be . . . I don't know . . . dissatisfied with her life.'

'Then it's about time,' said Charlotte briskly. 'Perhaps she realizes she deserves a life of her own at last. By the way, I've invited Mum and Dad to spend Christmas with us this year. I expect we could squeeze you lot in if you'd like to come . . .'

'Thanks, I haven't really thought . . . I'll talk to Robin.' There was no way she was spending Christmas with her sister. One telephone call was quite enough.

Robin came home with a face as black as thunder. 'I sometimes wonder if this job is worth all the pain. I'm so fed up with having to be charming and polite to ill-mannered idiots who have no idea how long it takes to make something that's any good. In my present mood I could pack the whole thing in, dig out my rucksack and go off to India.'

'Can I come too?' asked Tilly.

'Yes.'

'And Sam and Lucy?'

'If they carry their own rucksacks.'

'And we'd have to take Horace.'

'Perhaps India's a little ambitious.'

'How about Weymouth?'

Robin smiled. 'Weymouth and rucksacks: sounds unmissable! Do you want a drink?'

'Yes, please. I'll just get the washing in.'

When Tilly came back in, bearing her load of sheets, she found a changed Robin. His eyes were shining and he looked as if he'd been injected with a shot of adrenalin. 'I've been talking to Mum,' he said, 'and it's definite. Louise is arriving on Saturday and we're all going to lunch there on Sunday!'

'Oh, good,' said Tilly and she began to fold the sheets.

At least the news roused her from her lethargy. On Thursday she went to the chemist to get some vitamin pills and on Friday afternoon she and Sam visited the Oxfam shop where she found a pair of dark green corduroy trousers and a pale yellow jersey, all for seven pounds. She returned home in high good humour, determined to emulate Pollyanna henceforth. If Robin was cheerful because of Louise she would give silent thanks to Louise. If Anne wanted to suffocate her with perfect casseroles she would be grateful. Perception, Tilly decided, was all. She would perceive everything in the best possible light. Even her mother-in-law.

In the midst of all these strenuously good intentions it was a relief to look forward to a social gathering with genuine pleasure. Rhona and Nigel were already eating poppadoms when they arrived at the restaurant. 'I'm sorry we're so late,' Tilly said breathlessly. 'Our babysitter was late because she'd dropped in on her boyfriend and they'd had a row, so she'll probably be on the phone all night, trying to carry on with the argument!'

'Have some wine,' Rhona soothed. 'Robin, Tilly, this is Nigel!'

The man beside her smiled. He was very handsome. He had a long, narrow face and a close-cropped haircut that on many men would have been too severe. In his case, it only served to emphasize his intense grey eyes. He wasn't Tilly's type and he certainly didn't look like Harrison Ford or Tom Cruise or even Noel Gallagher, but she could fully appreciate why Rhona was so mad about him. He took Tilly's hand in his. He had beautiful hands with long slender fingers, artists' fingers. 'It's good to meet you,' he said. 'I know how important you both are to Rhona.' He smiled and nodded to Robin. 'I've heard all about your heroic behaviour at the Glastonbury Festival!'

Tilly grinned. 'Robin, heroic? I just remember him laughing when I fell in the mud!'

'Oh, but Tilly, he was!' Rhona exclaimed. 'Do you remember when the White Stripes were on? I was so excited and then I couldn't see anything because those two giants were in front of us, and Robin knew how much I adored the White Stripes and he simply set me up on his shoulders for the entire set. If that isn't heroic I don't know what is!'

'Rhona,' Robin said gravely, 'it was a pleasure. Nigel, I hope for the sake of your future with Rhona, that you like the White Stripes?'

'I don't think I've heard of them,' Nigel said. 'I'm not very good on pop music. I used to like Oasis.'

'You like Oasis,' Robin said. 'That could be a problem.'

'Don't listen to him,' Tilly laughed. 'You're obviously made for each other!'

Nigel took Rhona's hand. 'We are,' he said simply.

'Oh!' Tilly breathed. 'That's lovely! Robin, don't you think that's lovely?'

'I think,' Robin said, 'it's time we ordered some food.'

It was a very pleasant evening. The transparent happiness of Nigel and Rhona spread like sunshine, enveloping Tilly and Robin in its warmth. On the way home Tilly said, 'Did you notice how they kept touching each other? Even when I was talking to Nigel he couldn't stop looking at Rhona. He's completely smitten.'

'So's Rhona,' Robin said. 'I hope it works out. She deserves to be happy. What did you think of Nigel?'

'Well,' Tilly said cautiously, 'I thought he was very nice. What about you?'

'Very nice,' said Robin. 'Rather serious, though, wasn't he?'

'Very serious.'

'He didn't understand my joke about the elephant and the tarantula.'

'Robin, no one understands your joke about the elephant and the tarantula.'

'Yes, but at least you and Rhona laughed.'

'She looks so pretty these days!' Tilly sighed happily. 'Isn't love marvellous?'

'You are such a romantic!' Robin laughed but he reached out and took her hand in the darkness.

The next morning both Robin and Tilly dressed with

elaborate care while pretending to do nothing of the sort. Tilly washed her hair and made up her face. She even used the lipstick Charlotte had given her for her birthday.

'You look nice,' Robin said. 'Is that a new jersey?'

'Oh,' said Tilly carelessly, 'it's just some old thing I found in the Oxfam shop. You look good too. You haven't worn that blue shirt in ages.'

'Haven't I?' said Robin, glancing at his shirt as if he was hardly aware of what he was wearing.

Honour thus maintained, they set off with the children in a pleasant state of harmony.

'Louise is in the kitchen!' Anne said, as if Louise were some rare and beautiful painting she couldn't wait to show off. Louise was indeed in the kitchen and unfortunately Louise looked better than ever. Her blonde hair was shoulder length and shining, her complexion flawless and her grey moleskin trousers encased a bottom a fitness class would die for.

'Robin!' Louise exclaimed and held out her arms. Like a homing pigeon, Robin made straight for her. Tilly would have felt happier if he'd told her how gorgeous she looked. Instead, he embraced her, took her hands and simply smiled at her.

Lucy, with her unerring instinct for knowing where the spotlight was, marched straight up to Louise. 'Hello, I'm Lucy.'

'Lucy.' Louise shook her hand. 'I've heard so much about you. Aren't you beautiful? You have your father's mouth.' The matching mouths smiled smugly. 'And this must be Sam!' Louise turned towards Tilly. 'You must be so proud! And look at you, you've hardly changed at all!'

There was a sudden pop as Peter opened a bottle of champagne. 'A present from Louise!' he said.

Robin glanced at Tilly. 'It is your turn to drive back, isn't it?'

'Yes,' Tilly said. She wished it wasn't. She would very much have liked to drink far too much.

'Great!' Robin held out his glass. 'Fill it up, Dad!'

'Louise,' Lucy said, 'would you like me to show you Granny's house in the garden?'

Louise smiled. 'I would like that very much.'

'Can I come too?' asked Robin.

'Yes,' said Sam. 'You come with me.'

Tilly watched the two adults being led outside and restrained an impulse to tag along behind them. 'Louise is wonderful with the children,' she said brightly. 'They love her already! So tell me, what brings her down here?'

'You know she used to work on *Country Living*?' Anne said. 'Last year she opened a small wallpaper business in London with a friend but she hasn't stopped doing freelance work for the glossies. I always knew she'd be successful.'

'So did I. And is she down here just to see you?'

'She's doing an article on old churches that have been turned into homes. Apparently, there are lots of them round here. She visited three of them yesterday. It's such fun to see her again. Horace, do get out of the way, dear.'

'Horace!' Peter said. 'Come!'

Horace took one last, lingering sniff round the Aga and plodded back to Peter.

'Lie down!' said Peter.

Horace lay down. 'Peter!' Tilly gasped. 'You're brilliant!'

'I'm trying to teach him to heel at the moment but I think

107

that might take a little longer. You just have to show him who's boss. Dogs like to know where they are.'

They're not the only ones, thought Tilly, wondering when Robin and Louise would come back.

Lunch was very jolly. Louise, though Tilly hated to admit it, was extremely likeable. She showed genuine interest in Tilly's job, initiating a discussion about the growth of special needs in education in which Tilly surprised herself by participating with confidence. She teased Anne gently about her love of cleanliness, encouraged Lucy to recite a poem she'd learnt at school and was anxious to hear all about Robin's business.

'How did it start?' she asked. 'Tell me everything!'

'Do you remember Josie?' Robin asked. 'We went to her party one New Year's Eve.'

'Of course I do. She's one of your oldest friends. You met her at a party when you were fifteen and you pushed her out of the way just as her boyfriend was about to throw up over her.'

'That's the one! She always had appalling choice in men. When Tilly was pregnant with Lucy she wanted to come down to Exeter with her latest boyfriend . . .'

'We weren't terribly excited,' Tilly said, 'because the previous one had smelt like a pig farm and the one before that came down in the night and ate the entire contents of our fridge.'

'However,' Robin continued, 'for once in her life she'd struck gold. John was great. Josie, being Josie, had had no idea how to cope with a man who was kind and considerate. She had been about to dump him when she found he was dead.'

'Only he wasn't.' Tilly explained, 'He'd gone to a rock concert in Denmark – Pearl Jam were playing – and people at the back pushed forward to get a better view. Some of the spectators were crushed to death. Josie heard it on the news and tried to get John on his mobile. By the time he rang her three days later, she was ready to fall in love at once.'

'So they came to see us,' Robin said, 'and John told us he made garden houses for his uncle near Frome and Tilly told him her parents lived in Frome and he told us his uncle wanted to retire in a couple of years—'

'And by the end of the evening,' Tilly said, 'we'd decided to move up to Somerset. Within a year, Robin and John had set up Garden Magic. When Josie married John, she joined the company. Now they make tree houses, pool houses, garden furniture . . . You ought to see the things they make, some of their tree houses are incredible.'

'I'd love to see them,' Louise said, 'I might even be able to help. Garden Magic could be a rather good subject for an article. It's the sort of thing *Country Living* would love. Have you any interesting photos? Are there any orders you're particularly proud of?'

Robin nodded. 'My favourite is an order we did for a family in Cornwall last year. They wanted a retreat for their teenagers. It has a wood-burning stove, it's wired for electricity. It worked really well.'

'What materials did you use?'

'Oak and red cedar with chestnut roof slates and weatherboards. All the wood is handcut and then it's jointed using clefts and pegs. No two pieces of wood are identical. We wanted the building to look irregular, almost organic.' He smiled. 'Am I boring you?'

'Of course you're not, it's fascinating.' Louise leant forward. 'What are your starting prices?'

'Fifteen thousand. But most of them cost a lot more.'

'Good.' Louise smiled at everyone. 'I can definitely make something out of this. And I could talk about your pool houses and greenhouses too. Let me speak to a couple of people and I'll get back to you.'

'Well!' Anne said. 'I think this calls for another bottle!'

'There's a rather good red in the box I brought down,' Louise said.

'Louise has been far too generous,' said Anne. 'We've been drinking our way through her bottles the entire weekend!'

Louise laughed. 'Nonsense! I've been drinking most of it. Besides, I can afford to be generous. I have no children, as my mother is always complaining!'

'Very sensible.' Robin grinned. 'They cost you a fortune!'

Lucy bridled. 'No, we don't!'

'Ah,' Louise said, 'if I knew they'd be like you and Sam, I'd be tempted to find a husband at once!'

'Perhaps,' Lucy suggested, 'you could find a husband like Daddy and then you could have a daughter like me.'

'That's good advice,' Louise said. 'I have tried to find a husband like your father. So far I haven't met one.'

Lucy sighed. 'It's a pity Daddy hasn't got a brother. Then, you could marry *him*.'

'That would have been very nice,' Anne agreed. 'I'd love to have Louise as a daughter-in-law.'

'What about you, Robin?' Louise said. 'Would you like me as a sister-in-law?'

'I think . . .' Robin began and then he paused. 'No comment,' he said.

'I'm not going to get married,' said Lucy.

Anne laughed, rather immoderately, Tilly thought. 'Why not, darling?'

'Because I don't want to spend all my time washing up!'

'Oh, Lucy!' Tilly exclaimed. 'What a terrible role model I am!' and she waited in vain for someone to contradict her.

Sam, who had either not understood the conversation or else divined the essential truth of it better than any of the adults round the table, rested his head on his mother's arm. 'Never mind, Mummy,' he said, '*me* mawwy you!'

'Thank you, Sam,' Tilly said and felt absurdly comforted.

By the time they climbed into the car it was after six. Almost immediately, Robin fell asleep. Tilly, anxious to prevent the children doing the same, encouraged them to join her in singing nursery rhymes.

Once home, Robin staggered into the sitting room and fell onto the sofa where he remained comatose for the rest of the evening. In contrast, Tilly was a veritable tornado of energy. She fed the children, bathed them, washed their hair, put them to bed, fed Horace and prepared Lucy's sandwiches for the next day.

By the time she'd finished, Robin was no longer horizontal. 'Hello,' he blinked, 'have I been asleep long?'

'Hours. I'm just taking Horace out for a quick walk. I won't be long.' She put Horace's lead on and walked out into the cool night air. She heard a distant screech and wondered if it were a badger or a fox. Did foxes screech? It must be good to be a fox. Foxes led such simple lives. All they had to worry about was the possibility of being torn apart by any hounds who didn't realize the government had banned them. She

111

shivered and began to walk briskly, pulling at Horace's lead whenever he stopped to smell something interesting.

Later, when she and Robin were in bed, she whispered, 'Are you asleep?'

'Yes.'

'Robin. All those years ago, was it Louise who broke it off with you or did you break up with Louise?'

'Louise left me,' he murmured. He gave a sleepy chuckle. 'I'm sure she's regretted it ever since!'

Tilly thought grimly that that was very probably true. 'It's funny,' she said hesitantly, 'I always assumed it was the other way round. I mean . . . I don't mind, it's interesting, that's all . . . Robin?'

But Robin was asleep.

Tilly lay still beside him. She felt horribly awake. Trying to be Pollyanna was more difficult than she had thought.

CHAPTER EIGHT: Past

'Pains of love be sweeter far
Than all other pleasures are.'
JOHN DRYDEN

In Robin's last year at university he took on a Saturday job with a wheelwright and woodworker near Dawlish. When he was offered a permanent position there after his finals, he decided to accept, partly because he wanted to be near Tilly and partly because he enjoyed the work.

Life with Robin began to acquire a delicious permanence for Tilly. She started doing bar work at the Black Horse on Thursday and Friday evenings. Often at weekends she and Robin would take off with a tent and sleeping bags and explore Dartmoor, occasionally venturing into Cornwall. Life was good.

Then, in March, Robin received a belated twenty-first birthday present from his godfather: a cheque for five hundred pounds. 'This is to be spent on travelling,' his godfather wrote, 'before you're too old to sleep under the stars.' Four weeks later Robin's cousin, Tony, came down for a weekend and told Robin he was going to India in September.

'Do you know where you want to go when you get there?' Robin asked.

'I'll start off in Goa,' Tony said, 'and see what happens. I'll come back when the money runs out. Why don't you come with me?'

'I don't think so,' Robin said. 'I've got my job and there's Tilly and . . .' He hesitated. 'When did you say you were going?'

He told Tilly he'd be back by Christmas. He told Tilly he'd send her hundreds of postcards. He sent her three. Christmas came and went without a word and Tilly was too proud to ring his parents for information. In a funny sort of way his silence was a relief. She had always assumed Robin would tire of her and now that the worst had happened she could at least get on with her life.

But oh, the loneliness and the aching misery that his absence inflicted on her! Tilly lay in bed at night, tossing and turning, desperate for Robin's body to be next to her own. Was it perhaps possible that her body had become physically addicted to his and that she was now suffering from severe withdrawal symptoms? It was a fascinating theory and Tilly would have liked to consult her doctor for confirmation, but she suspected he would simply prescribe more stomach-jumping.

She pestered her friends for their views on the state of the Indian postal service and the possible dangers Robin might encounter in the form of deadly tigers or scorpions. At last even Kathy told her to get a life. 'This is your last year at university,' she said, 'you should be having fun.' Tilly started working on Saturday evenings at the Black Horse.

One Saturday evening in February, Tim Shaw, one of her first-year tutors, came into the pub and hailed Tilly. 'I didn't know you worked here,' he said. 'I'd have come more often if I'd known!'

Tilly raised an eyebrow. 'You obviously haven't been here for a long time.'

'Two years, to be precise!' he said and looked so sad that Tilly was intrigued.

'So why are you here now?' she asked.

'My wife has left me. I'm lonely.'

Tilly grimaced. 'Tell me about it.'

'I'm sorry?'

Tilly bit her lip. 'Don't pay any attention to me. I've become so self-absorbed. I didn't mean to be flippant. How terrible for you. I am so sorry . . . it's just that I know about loneliness.'

'Do you? How surprising. Can I buy you a drink?'

Tilly cast a sidelong glance at her employer. 'Albert doesn't really approve of customers buying us drinks. He likes his employees to remain sober.'

'I tell you what. Give me two white wines and you can sip one of them when Albert's not looking.'

Tilly laughed. 'You're on!' She poured out the wine and collected his money. 'Perhaps your wife will come back,' she said.

'I doubt it.' Tim laughed shortly. 'Isn't it funny the way you start off by worshipping someone and then four years later you're arguing about dirty baths!'

'Well,' mused Tilly, 'I do sympathize with your wife there. Perhaps if you learnt how to clean—'

'I always clean the bath after me,' Tim said. 'My wife, on the other hand, is perfectly happy to wallow in brown-rimmed squalor!' He took a deep breath and shook his head like a dog trying to throw off fleas. 'Never mind. Tell me about you. If I talk about me it just raises my blood pressure. Why are you lonely? Someone as pretty as you shouldn't be lonely.'

'I'm fine, really. I was being silly.'

'No, you weren't. Tell me about it.'

So Tilly, in between serving other customers and drinking Tim's wine, did.

'Do you want me to be kind or brutal?' Tim asked.

'Kind,' said Tilly, swigging another gulp of wine. 'No. Be brutal!'

'India,' he said, 'is an extraordinary country. It attracts free spirits. I'm sure Robin was crazy about you but the country changes people. I think you should accept that you probably won't see him again.'

'Right,' said Tilly, nodding furiously and blinking hard.

'I think,' Tim said, 'that we both have to wipe our slates clean.'

'Right,' said Tilly again, 'along with our baths.'

At the end of the evening Tim walked her home. Outside her front door, he took her face in his hands and told her she was beautiful. He kissed her lightly on the mouth and said he'd had the best evening he could remember in a long time.

'Thank you,' Tilly said. 'Thank you for the drinks and for listening.'

'I like listening to you. I like being with you. I'd like to listen some more.'

Such concern, such kindness! Tilly smiled. 'Would you like some coffee?'

In the room he admired her posters and picked up her book of poems by Thomas Hardy. 'No wonder you're depressed,' he said and Tilly laughed. She went through to the tiny kitchen and spooned Nescafe into two mugs. She tried not to think of Robin communing with free spirits in India.

When she brought the coffee into her room, she found Tim

had been busy. He'd lit the gas fire. He'd switched on her bedside lamp and switched off the main light. He'd taken off his jacket, which lay neatly folded on the small table in the corner. His T-shirt was no longer tucked into his trousers and he was sitting on her bed.

'Come here, Tilly,' he said and held out his hand.

Tilly stared blankly at him. 'Don't you want your coffee?' she asked.

'No, I don't,' Tim said. 'I want you.'

'Tim,' Tilly said, 'I like you but . . .'

'My wife's left me, Robin's left you. Let's forget them tonight.'

He's right, Tilly thought, he's absolutely right. She set the mugs on the mantelpiece, moved towards the bed and allowed Tim to pull her down beside him. He buried his face in her neck and she saw a condom, neatly propped up against the base of her lamp.

'Tim,' she marvelled, 'you're so well-organized, it's frightening!' She felt his hand creep up round one of her breasts and she murmured, 'Actually, Tim, I'm not sure about this.'

'Yes, you are,' whispered Tim. His hand left her breast and tiptoed round to her back where his fingers fumbled for and found the hook on the back of her bra.

'You know, Tim—' Tilly began.

'Be quiet, Tilly,' said Tim, and he fixed his mouth onto hers.

Later, Tilly wondered what would have happened if the doorbell hadn't rung at that moment. But ring it did, long and unremittingly, and Tim released her instantly.

'Tim,' Tilly hissed, 'will you do up my bra?'

'Right,' said Tim, 'right. Shouldn't you answer the door?'

'*Will* you do up my bra?'

Tim did up her bra and Tilly pulled down her top. 'All right, all right!' she shouted. She ran out of the room, into the hall and opened the door. 'Do you *want* to wake everyone in the street?' she demanded and then froze. She felt as if she'd been punched in the stomach. She managed to utter hoarsely, 'Robin?'

Robin stood in the doorway, dressed in the same old mac he'd bought in the Oxfam shop six months earlier. 'Hello, Tilly,' he said.

She looked at him stupidly. She had envisaged his return so many times. As the weeks had gone by, the scene had shifted from a passionate reunion to a vision of a haggard Robin desperate to see her to explain he'd been in a coma since the day he'd sent her her third postcard. She had never expected him to turn up on her doorstep so casually, so carelessly, with no hint of apology or explanation for his silence. She wanted to slap him very hard. She asked coldly, 'Do you know what time it is?'

'I know it's late. Were you getting ready for bed?'

'Sort of. What do you want?'

'I thought you might like to hear about India.'

'Now? Robin, it's after midnight.'

'I won't stay long. I could die for a cup of coffee.'

'You've lost weight,' she said.

'I have.' He glanced up at the naked light bulb in the hall. 'Nice corridor,' he said.

Tilly bit her lip. 'I suppose you want to come in?'

'If you insist,' Robin said.

Tim was standing in front of the gas fire. He'd put on his jacket and he'd tucked his T-shirt into his trousers. 'Hello there,' he said breezily.

'I'm Robin,' said Robin. 'Nice to meet you.'

'Yes, indeed. I'm Tim.'

Tilly stared fixedly at Tim. 'Robin's an old friend of mine. He's been travelling in India.'

'Oh,' said Tim, 'what a country!'

Robin took off his mac and sat down in the only chair. 'You've been there?' he asked.

'Unfortunately not,' said Tim. He looked down at his feet and then, spotting his shoes at the foot of the bed, made a sudden lunge for them. 'Well,' he said, 'goodness, it's late! Just look at the time! I think I should be going!'

'I'll see you out,' said Tilly.

In the hall, Tim clutched Tilly's arm. 'That's *him*?'

'Yes. I had no idea he was back. I'm sorry . . .'

'No, no, that's fine. A little frustrating, perhaps, but . . . fine.' He leant forward to kiss Tilly and froze.

'Excuse me,' said Robin politely, holding out the condom, 'but I thought this might belong to you.'

Tim's face turned the colour of ketchup. He took the condom, muttered an anguished sound that could have been 'Goodbye', wrenched open the door and fled.

Tilly shut the door behind him and turned back to Robin. Robin was smiling.

'You are truly vile,' Tilly said.

'Sorry,' Robin said. He walked back into her bedroom. Something about the smug, careless air with which he reclaimed the chair and threw his keys on the floor filled her with such venom she could hardly speak. She managed it. 'I think you should go,' she said.

'I've only just arrived.'

'I know. At midnight. You've got a bloody nerve, Robin,

you really have. I'll send you hundreds of postcards, Tilly. I'll be back by Christmas, Tilly. Just hang around long enough, Tilly, and I'll fit you in at midnight, Tilly. Well, amazingly enough, Robin, I've survived very well without you and all your free spirits.'

'My what?'

'You know very well what I mean. You happen to have interrupted an extremely interesting evening and I think you should go before I get really cross.'

'I'm so sorry, I had no idea,' Robin said mildly. He stood up and took his mac from her outstretched hand. 'By the way, are you actually sleeping with Condom Man?'

'None of your business. It doesn't concern you at all.'

'No, of course it doesn't. Well, I do apologize for ruining your evening.'

Tilly went out into the hall and opened the front door.

'Goodbye,' Robin said. He walked down the steps and turned back to look at Tilly. The street light lit up his face and she could see he was smiling. 'I take it you *are* sleeping with him?' he asked.

'What? What sort of question is that?'

'I just wondered.' He waited a moment, shrugged lightly and began to walk away.

'Not yet!' shouted Tilly. 'But I will be. I really, really, will be!'

She walked back into the house, slammed the door and burst into tears. When she couldn't cry any more she washed her face, changed into her nightshirt and cleaned her teeth so hard her gums began to bleed. I hate him, she thought, I really do hate him. I'm so glad he came round because I shall never miss him again. Ever. She splashed cold water over her face in an effort to stop any further tears. Now her nightshirt was wet, and that was saddest of all.

The doorbell went again. Tilly scraped her towel across her face and went out into the hall. She slumped against the door and said, 'What do you want?'

Robin's voice sounded apologetic. 'I've left my keys in your room.'

Tilly shut her eyes for a moment and said, 'I'll get them for you.' She went back to her room, found the keys and padded back to the door. She opened it slightly. Outside the street lamp blinked and went out.

'There you are,' she said and thrust out his keys.

'Can I come in for a moment?'

Tilly hesitated. 'What's the point?' She shivered. The draught of cold air was circling round her body and threading its way into her home.

'Look,' Robin began and then stopped. He stared at his feet for a few seconds and then met her eyes again. 'I'm hopeless at situations like this. I know I should just be honest and straightforward and say what I think, and instead I hear myself being a stupid prat who's doing his level best to make you mad. I don't know why I do it. I mean, I know you have every right to throw me out but I would like the chance to explain. I won't stay long. Please?'

Tilly shivered again and with an impatient wave of her hand said, 'Oh, come in, then, but only for a minute. And shut that door, it's freezing.'

She went back into her room and sat on the end of her bed.

'Tilly,' Robin said. 'You've been crying.'

'I have an eye infection,' she said. 'And it's very infectious.'

'Tilly,' Robin said, 'please don't cry!'

'I'm NOT CRYING!'

'Tilly, I'm sorry. I was jealous, that's all.'

'You were *laughing*!'

'I was hurt. I wanted to hurt you back.'

'You left me. You had no right to be hurt.'

'I know. I should have written. I'm sorry. I never meant to leave it so long. I wasn't well for a while but, you're right, I should have written. I came round earlier and since you weren't here I thought I'd try the pub. I saw that man chatting to you and I wanted to go up to you, but I got cold feet. I didn't know if I was interrupting something and I wouldn't blame you if you'd met someone else. I followed you both back. I thought, I'll see what happens; if he goes in with you then I'll know it's over and I'll slip out of your life in dignified silence.' He gave a lopsided smile. 'I'm not very good at dignified silence.'

'That's the understatement of the year.'

'I know, I know. But when I saw him kiss you I wanted to kill him.'

'Really?' Tilly gave what she hoped was a sceptical glare, but inside her heart was singing. Robin felt murderous because of *her*! Robin was jealous about *her*!

'It was terrible. I've never felt like that before. I couldn't bear it, Tilly. When he went inside with you, I meant to leave. I thought I'd lost you. But I couldn't bear to think of him in here with you and once I rang the bell I couldn't stop. When I saw him I felt so angry, I . . . well, that's why I was the way I was. Tilly, do you really like him?'

'Do you really care?'

'No, I spend my life skulking in doorways wondering whether to murder overweight men in silly trousers.'

122

'He isn't overweight.'

'He is. And his trousers are silly.'

'Robin,' Tilly said, 'I really hate you.'

'I don't blame you.'

'It would serve you right if I went off to Argentina.'

Robin looked startled. 'Are you planning to?'

'No. But it would serve you right.'

'I know it would.'

'I've missed you so much.'

'I missed you too. I didn't want to. I tried not to. But I missed you like hell.'

'Good. Because if you ever go away again—'

'Tilly,' Robin said, 'I shall never go away from you again.'

Two minutes later, he asked her to marry him.

CHAPTER NINE: Present

'If you're afraid of loneliness, don't marry.'
ANTON CHEKHOV

There was no way that a mature, happily married mother of two would waste her time worrying about the fact that many years ago her husband's former girlfriend had been the one to terminate the relationship. Since this fact was flashing in Tilly's brain like the irritating security device that Anne had recently had installed on the front of her cottage, this suggested a range of possible explanations:

1: Tilly was not mature.

2: Tilly was not happily married.

Tilly dismissed Point One without a qualm. In her experience, there were very few adults who *were* mature, they were merely better at disguising their quivering egos than children and adolescents. Point Two was more of a problem. Point Two squatted in her mind like the huge mound of dung currently residing on her neighbour's side of the fence. That Tilly's marriage was happy had always been axiomatic. Now, for the first time, doubt was creeping in, twining itself round her cherished beliefs, strangling confidence and certainty and peace of mind.

None of this would be happening if Louise had remained

safely immured in her London wallpaper shop. None of this would be happening if Louise was a lactating mother of six or cosily ensconced in a loving relationship. Which raised an interesting question: why *wasn't* Louise cosily ensconced in a loving relationship? What was she doing coming down to Somerset and making it crystal clear that she wished she never *had* terminated her relationship with Robin?

In those first heady months that Tilly had spent with Robin they had delighted in shining spotlights on every dusty corner of their lives in the confident knowledge that the other would find it fascinating. Yet Robin had never talked about the end of his relationship with Louise. Tilly had once asked with scantily understood caution whether he still cared for his ex-girlfriend. He had said, 'I love you because you are so different from Louise.'

At the time she had been pleased and flattered by his response. Now she saw that his answer had been horribly revealing. He had fallen in love with her because and only because she had helped to soften the hurt that Louise had caused. Where Louise was challenging, demanding, competitive, charismatic and exciting, Tilly had been simply and unquestioningly adoring, ready to follow him wherever he went, deeply conscious of his superior abilities. No doubt she had provided a delicious balm to his troubled soul, the perfect medicine for his dented confidence.

Unfortunately, Tilly thought, medicine cabinets were only valued when people were ill. Tilly had watched Robin and Louise at the Taylors'. She had heard Louise suggest five different strategies for coping with the spoilt but insecure multimillionaire that was Mr van Duren. Tilly had seen Anne Taylor regard Louise with a contemplative eye and knew she must be wondering what Robin's future might have been with such a golden girl by his side.

Tilly was aware she was skirting perilously close to the great chasm of self-pity; it seemed to be a permanent feature of her personal horizon these days. It didn't help that she felt constantly unwell at the moment. As she walked into the health centre with Sam, she made a clutch of instant resolutions. She would get herself physically sorted out with a course of iron tablets or whatever doctors gave these days; she would begin to take a detailed interest in Robin's work; she would start to study the serious job pages; she would even follow her mother's example and do a computer course. She would out-Louise Louise.

Twenty minutes later her plans lay trampled on the purple carpet of her doctor's consulting room.

'I know it's a shock,' Dr Sheldon said easily, 'but believe me, another baby isn't the end of the world. I should know. I have four of my own, you know!'

Yes, Tilly thought, along with a big house, a rich wife and an au pair. 'It's impossible,' she said. 'I don't understand. I never ever forget to take my pill. I keep the packet right next to my toothbrush mug. How on earth could I get pregnant?'

Dr Sheldon shrugged. 'Even the pill isn't totally infallible. I don't suppose you've had any infections in the last few weeks?'

Tilly nodded. 'The children and I had a tummy bug a few weeks ago. We were throwing up all over the place.'

Dr Sheldon gave a triumphant smile. 'There you are, then! I'm willing to bet that you didn't use any other contraceptive around that time?'

Tilly frowned. 'Well, no, I didn't . . .'

'Ah,' said Dr Sheldon, shaking his head with a sorrowful expression that Tilly found extremely irritating, 'if you had read the instructions inside your packet of pills, you would know that your pill cannot be guaranteed to work while you are sick. You should have read your instructions.'

'Well, funnily enough,' Tilly said, with little attempt to conceal her fury, 'when your children are vomiting in stereo and you're doing your level best not to vomit yourself, you don't have much time to read the small print in your box of pills.'

'Of course not,' soothed Dr Sheldon. 'Although,' he paused and gave a grave sigh, 'it is something that most people know about.'

'Well, I didn't.'

'Evidently,' said Dr Sheldon, glancing at his watch. 'Anyway, I know everything will be fine. Just don't overdo it. You'll soon adjust to the idea. And you have family around, don't you?'

Tilly nodded.

'Well, then! Use them! I'm sure they'll be anxious to help in any way they can.' He glanced at his watch again, with ill-concealed impatience. 'You'll be delighted once you get used to the idea!'

Tilly, aware she was on the brink of tears, stood up abruptly, thanked Dr Sheldon, and walked out with Sam through the reception area and into the sunshine. She felt sick: sick, depressed and devastated. She glanced down at her tummy in fear and loathing. She felt she was carrying a time-bomb.

It had taken months of campaigning on her part to persuade Robin to agree to a second baby. As an only child, Robin had little understanding of any advantages a sibling might bring. Admittedly, her campaign had not been helped by the fact that at its height she and Charlotte had had a spectacular falling-out after which she had told Robin that her sister was a total waste of space. Ever since he had taken on the wretched new premises at Radstock, Robin had spoken forcefully of the need for Tilly to work full-time once Sam started school. And now – oh, God – and now, what on earth would he say?

Sam tugged at her hand. 'Playgwound, Mummy!' he commanded.

'All right,' Tilly said. She strapped him into his buggy and wheeled him across the road to the park. For the next half an hour, as the two of them went round and round on the creaky old merry-go-round, a small insistent voice within her kept asking the same question: how was she going to tell Robin?

That afternoon, she stood in the school playground watching Sam playing his own unique brand of hopscotch while they waited for the doors to open. She saw Amy approach and could barely muster a smile.

Amy raised an eyebrow. 'You look like you've just eaten one too many of your mother-in-law's meals! Tilly . . . Tilly, what's wrong?'

Tilly blinked hard and looked straight into the eyes of Adonis, who stood a few feet away watching her with a curiosity that was all the more insulting because it was so patently uninterested. She raised her chin and stared back at him defiantly before turning to Amy and saying flatly, 'I'm pregnant.' She bit her lip. 'I don't know how to tell Robin. He'll go mad.'

'Oh, Tilly!' Unusually, Amy was at an obvious loss as to what she should say.

'We had lunch with his parents yesterday. Did I tell you Louise was going to be there?'

Amy stared blankly. 'Louise?'

'Louise! Robin's old girlfriend! You know, the one in the photo! He's still in love with her, Amy. I think he's always been in love with her.'

'Rubbish!' Amy said briskly. 'That's just your hormones speaking!'

'What do you mean?'

'Your body knows it's about to start resembling a potato. Throughout both my pregnancies I was convinced that Derek was lusting after every woman I know. Mind you,' Amy paused, 'he probably was. Tilly, you and Robin are one of the sanest couples I know, and in all the time we've been friends Robin has never given me the slightest impression his heart is pining for some distant love.'

'Really?'

'Cross my heart. If I were you I'd wait until Robin's in a very good mood and then I'd break it to him gently. Once he gets used to the idea he'll probably be thrilled. He adores Lucy and Sam. Come on, Tilly, it's not the end of the world.'

'That's what Dr Sheldon said.'

'Oh, well, if Dr Sheldon said it, it must be true! His wife came into the gallery on Friday and managed to buy the only dud painting in the entire exhibition. I can't tell you what pleasure it gave me to sell it to her. Oh, look, here come our little angels! Now just remember, pick your moment carefully and it'll be fine!'

Perhaps Amy was right. She usually was. When Robin came home late from work the omens were good. He had a smile on his face and a spring in his step.

'It was brilliant!' he said. 'I saw van Duren today and I suddenly snapped. I knew I couldn't take any more of his rants about costs. So I waited for him to finish shouting and I gave him the addresses of two other firms. "Look," I said, "these people will provide you with a cheaper product. Inferior certainly, but definitely cheaper. I never compromise my standards so if you reimburse me for the work I've done, that's fine and we'll call it a day." You should have seen his face!'

'What did he say?'

'He caved in completely! Louise was right. Do you remember her saying that the only way to deal with bullies was to stand up to them? He's given me carte blanche. Oh, it felt good! After all these weeks of misery and humiliation, it felt good! The trouble is, rich people always make the rest of us feel inferior. I mean, why should they? I have a talent for making beautiful garden houses and furniture. Why is that less of a talent than van Duren's one for making money? Why does everyone think making money is the best talent in the world? It's crazy. You'd think by now we'd have learnt our lesson but no, Greed is still Good. And I'm as bad as everyone else. You should have seen his face, though! He looked like a great red punctured balloon. Are the kids asleep?'

'Sam is. Lucy's waiting to show you she can read the whole of *The Three Billy Goats Gruff*.'

'I'll go up now. What's for supper?'

'Chicken pie and I've made a pudding! Rhubarb crumble.'

'Perfect!' Robin kissed Tilly. 'I won't be long.'

He was whistling as he went up the stairs. It would be all right. It wasn't the end of the world. Tilly even offered up a silent prayer of thanks to Louise.

Tilly encouraged Robin to relive the day's successes over dinner. 'You know,' he mused, 'ever since we set up the company I've been living in fear, wondering if we weren't just fooling ourselves. It's like we've been pushing against a huge door. And now, for the first time, I really think the door might be opening. Any more pie?'

'I'll get you some.' Tilly stood up and took his plate. 'Robin, I'm so glad.'

'Of course it's still early days but if Louise gets the glossies interested in us . . . *Down in the depths of Somerset, two young craftsmen are making the sort of hideaways we'd die for . . .* and then there'd be a photo of John and me . . .'

'. . . exposing your manly chests as you clear a couple of trees!' Tilly laughed and handed Robin his plate. 'Sex always sells!'

Robin grinned. 'Josie's already planning our wardrobes for any possible photo shoots. *And* she's putting John on a diet. By the way, I've invited them to dinner, not this Saturday but the next. We're not doing anything then, are we?'

'I don't think so.'

'We got another client today. He wants a garden house in the shape of a beach hut. He was brought up in Frinton-on-Sea and his parents had a blue-and-white-striped beach hut. If things carry on like this, we might even be able to treat ourselves to a proper holiday next summer. We haven't been abroad in years. We could go camping in France.'

Tilly helped herself to a glass of water. 'That would be nice,' she said.

'There've been so many times when I thought the business was about to crash. I know I've been a pain to live with but, touch wood, I think, I really think at last, that things might work out. And once both the children are at school, you'll be able to bring in more money and—'

'Robin!' Tilly couldn't bear it any longer. She had to tell him or she'd explode. 'Sam and I went to the health centre today.'

'Why? What's wrong?'

'Nothing. Well, sort of nothing. Nothing serious. I mean, it is serious but I'm not ill. The thing is, Robin, I'm pregnant.'

She watched the colour, along with the good humour, drain from his face. He pushed his plate away. He didn't say anything, he simply looked at her as if she'd put a dagger through his heart.

'Robin, I'm so sorry. It was as much a shock to me as it is to you. I had no idea.'

'You are definitely pregnant?'

'Yes, and I know it's a disaster and I'm so sorry . . . Robin?' She wished he'd say something. 'I've been feeling off-colour for weeks but I never thought . . . I know this is a bad time . . . I'm so sorry.'

Robin stared blankly ahead of him and then slowly, as if it were a great effort, turned his attention back to Tilly. 'No, you're not.'

'Well, of course I am.'

'At least do me the courtesy of not pretending. You always wanted another child. You have exactly what you wanted.'

'Of course I haven't! What are you saying?'

He didn't reply. He put his face in his hands and said nothing.

'Robin,' Tilly said, 'talk to me. Please.' She waited for a few seconds and tried again. 'If you're implying that I deliberately engineered this pregnancy, you're wrong! I would never do that! I know how worried you've been about work—'

'No, you don't.' He spoke the words flatly as if he were drugged or hypnotized. 'You have no idea at all.'

'How can you say that? Of course I have.'

He stared at her now. 'We've been on a tightrope for months. You have no idea what it's like. I have a drawer full of bills at work and I spend an hour every day working out which ones I can afford to pay. And now you tell me you're pregnant.'

'I'm sorry. I'm really sorry, but—'

'I don't know what we're going to do.'

'Listen,' Tilly said, 'remember how worried you were about us having another child after Lucy? And then we had Sam and we were fine! The world didn't crash, the planet kept turning. All right, it's going to be difficult, but we will cope. I know we will. I have no worries about that.'

'I know you don't. It's very easy not to worry if you don't have anything to do with the finances.'

'That's not fair. I'm just saying . . .' Her voice faded away as she saw him push his chair back and stand up. 'What are you doing?'

'I can't talk to you at the moment,' Robin said. 'I'm angry and I'm upset and I don't want to say anything I might regret later. I'm going for a walk.'

She sat motionless. She heard the front door slam behind him. She thought of the uneaten rhubarb crumble. She should have waited until he'd eaten his rhubarb crumble.

Later, much later, she lay sleepless and alone in their bed. She heard him come up the stairs and shut her eyes. She heard him move about the bedroom and then he was off to the bathroom. Tilly wondered if she should say anything when he came back. In the event, she didn't have to. Robin took himself off to the spare room. In ten years of marriage it was their first night apart.

CHAPTER TEN

'. . . Love is not love that alters when it alteration finds.'
SHAKESPEARE

Tilly hoped, indeed she realized later she'd assumed, that there would be some speedy reconciliation or at the very least discussion. Robin thwarted her wish by removing himself from the house before she'd finished dressing Sam.

She said goodbye to Lucy at the school gates and spotted Adonis with his son. The stick insects rarely appeared these days. Perhaps they were fed up with Adonis. The idea cheered her.

She had a phone call in the afternoon from Josie. 'Tilly! Hi!' Was it her imagination or was Josie's enthusiasm rather too forced?

'Hi!' Tilly responded brightly. 'I gather you and John are coming to supper next week.'

'Yes. We're looking forward to it!'

She knows, Tilly thought; damn Robin, she knows!

'Tilly, I've got to rush but Robin asked me to ring you. He got to work this morning and discovered this week's his last chance for ages to visit some prospective clients: two in Cornwall, one in Devon and another near Yeovil. Great panic all round! So he's dashed off today and asked me to tell you

135

he'll be back on Thursday. I know it's a pain but you have to jump when the punters get restless, don't you?'

Tilly laughed. 'Don't I know it! That's fine, Josie. See you soon!'

Tilly put down the receiver and went upstairs. His toothbrush was not in the bathroom and the airing cupboard revealed signs of intrusion. So, he had known before he left home that he would be staying somewhere else tonight. Furthermore, he could have easily rung Tilly from his car on his mobile. She hated the fact that Josie had been co-opted into the whole horrible mess. What was clear was that Robin wanted to get away from Tilly. Fine. If that was what he wanted, Tilly would make no effort to contact him.

Work provided a welcome diversion and on Wednesday morning, after Arthur's meeting, Rhona clutched Tilly's arm and whispered, 'I'm going to marry Nigel!'

Tilly's eyes widened. 'You're going to *marry* him? You've only known him a month!'

'I know!' Rhona laughed. 'And in another month he'll be my husband!'

It was true what they said: love did transform people. Rhona's face glowed with happiness, her hair shone. Confidence had made her beautiful. Tilly had time only to give her a quick embrace before rushing off to Matthew's maths lesson. She then remembered that Arthur had asked her to transfer to Joseph and French. She stopped for a moment and waited for the feeling of nausea to subside. Then she turned and proceeded to Room Eight.

Joseph was a charming twelve-year-old, friendly and good-humoured. The son of a tenant farmer, he possessed a serene belief in his inability to learn anything that wasn't directly related to his longed-for future on the tractor. Unfortunately for Joseph, and despite sympathetic pleas from his parents, he was not allowed to give up French. Joseph, who found English lessons quite difficult enough, allowed the strange sounds uttered by his French teacher to float over his head like exotic birds in the sky. He sat at his desk, placid and uncomplaining and taking in nothing. Tilly had been called in to help because they were doing a lot of oral work at the moment and the French teacher had noticed that Joseph's mouth remained politely but resolutely shut.

'Bonjour, Joseph!' Tilly said.

'Sorry, miss?'

'Bonjour, Joseph.'

'Bonjour, miss.'

'Good! What does that mean?'

'Haven't a clue, miss!'

'It means "hello". You've just said "hello" in French! Well done! Say it again!'

'Bon . . . what was it, miss?'

'Bonjour!'

'Bonjour, miss!' He grinned sympathetically. 'It's no use, miss, it's stupid me doing this. I can't do any of it. I'm thick, miss!'

'Joseph,' Tilly said gravely, 'that is such a cop-out. You are not thick! You'll never get anywhere if you think you're thick. Now say it again: bonjour, Madame Taylor!'

'Bonjour, Madame Taylor.'

'Good. And what does it mean?'

'Can't remember, miss.'

'Joseph!' Tilly said. 'You can do anything you want to do!'

Joseph gave a supremely Gallic shrug. 'Some of us can, miss, some of us can't.'

'Some of us,' Tilly corrected him sternly, 'are prepared to make an effort, some of us aren't.'

Joseph sighed. 'The thing is,' he said, 'I know I can't do French.'

'But how do you know if you don't try?'

'Are you good at maths, miss?'

'Not particularly.'

'You see?' Joseph regarded her with triumph.

Tilly's eyes narrowed suspiciously. 'How did you know I wasn't good at maths?'

Joseph gave a nonchalant smile. 'I could just tell. Like I know I'm no good at French.'

Tilly was pleased when the bell went for break.

Rhona was waiting for her in the staffroom and Tilly gave her a hug. 'I haven't been to a wedding for ages! I might even wear a hat!'

'Well, actually,' Rhona said, 'it's going to be very small . . . just Chloe and Nigel's brother . . .'

'Oh, right, I quite understand,' said Tilly, who didn't.

Rhona had gone a little pink. 'It's stupid, really. It's Nigel. He wants to keep the wedding very small and he doesn't want anyone from school to come along. He's got it into his head that Arthur's interested in me . . .'

'*Arthur*!'

'Yes, I know it's silly but you don't know Nigel. He seems to think that a man only has to look at me to fall in love. It's rather sweet in a way. Arthur called round a few weeks ago with some worksheets he wanted me to try out on the group in 7F and Nigel appeared and acted like Arthur was trying to seduce me.'

'Arthur!' Tilly said again and grinned.

'Yes, I know, but Nigel was very upset. So now he says he doesn't think the wedding has anything to do with anyone but us. I told him that's daft but . . . Well. It's not worth making a fuss about. I think Nigel's been badly hurt in the past. He doesn't like talking about himself but I do know his mother left him and his father when he was only six and he's never seen her since. Nigel says his father never got over it and I don't think Nigel has either. He's always saying he can't believe I love him.'

'He doesn't know how lucky he is,' said Tilly stoutly. She stood up abruptly. 'I'll be back in a minute.'

'Tilly? You're not offended? You do understand?'

'Of course I do, stupid, I just need to go to the loo.'

'Are you all right? You look terrible.'

'Tummy upset,' Tilly lied. She dashed to the ladies' cloak-room where she discovered that it was well-nigh impossible to be sick without making a noise.

When Tilly collected Sam from her mother's house at lunchtime, Margot was sufficiently concerned about Tilly's pallor to invite her in for lunch. Since the thought of food made Tilly feel even worse she refused, using the improbable excuse that she had cupboards to clean.

At night she lay in bed and wondered why she could not face telling either Rhona or her mother about her condition. Of course she knew the answer. She was hoping that if she said nothing the new life inside her would somehow realize its error and meekly withdraw, die, miscarry. She hated herself for thinking such thoughts.

On Thursday she had another message from Josie. Robin had been delayed in Taunton for another day. He'd be back late on Friday evening. Tilly wasn't to wait up for him.

'Where's Daddy? Has he come back?' Lucy and Sam stood like prosecution lawyers at the end of the bed.

Tilly pushed her hair back wearily and wondered how it was possible to wake up after a night's sleep and feel so exhausted. 'He got back very late last night. I expect he didn't want to disturb me. He's in the spare room.'

'Can we wake him?'

'No! Let him rest.'

Later, she went upstairs bearing a cup of tea. She had intended to shame him by first knocking on the door and then placing his drink next to him with silent dignity. Sam, however, ran ahead of her, shouting, 'Wake up, Daddy!' and jumping on the bed.

'Monster!' Robin groaned. Sam shrieked in delight and sat astride his father.

Tilly opened the curtains and told Sam curtly that if he knocked over Robin's tea he'd be in trouble.

'I'm going into town,' she said coldly. 'Do you want me to take the children?'

'No. I feel as though I haven't seen them for a month.' He put his hands on either side of his son's chest, swung him into the air and grinned as Sam squealed with delight.

Tilly left the room and went downstairs. She scooped up her bag and car keys and walked out into the garden. Lucy was attempting to play ball with Horace.

'He's stupid, Mum! Whenever I throw him the ball he won't give it up, even though I know he wants me to throw it to him again. Are you going shopping? Can I come?'

'No. Your dad's awake. He wants to see you. Take Horace in so I can open the gate.'

Tilly drove out onto the lane, got out of the car and went back to close the gate. She waved at Mrs Harris across the road and swallowed. When she got back into the car she took a few deep breaths but by the time she reached the roundabout the nausea was back. The shopping could wait. Tilly veered sharply to the left and made for her parents' house.

Her father was painting the front door. 'Watch the paint, Tilly. Tell Margot to put the kettle on, I've almost finished.'

Margot, caught in the act of dipping a finger in the bowl of chocolate icing, said, 'I'm baking! I'm in charge of the cake stall at the Save the Children Fete. What do you think of my Viennese tarts?'

'Shouldn't they have bits of jam on top?'

'They should! You don't fancy doing that for me while I ice my chocolate cake, do you? Or is this a flying visit?'

'I'm supposed to be doing the shopping,' Tilly said, sinking onto a chair, 'but I'd much rather help you.'

'Good. There's the jam and when you've done that the cakes need to be dusted with icing sugar. And while you're doing that you can tell me what's wrong.'

'Nothing's wrong. I'm fine.'

'So why are you here? And why are your eyes so red?'

With great deliberation, Tilly deposited a small dab of jam onto the first cake. 'I've had a silly row with Robin, that's all.'

'You told him you're pregnant?'

'How did you know I was pregnant?'

Margot smiled. 'You've stopped drinking coffee and you

look like a ghost when you bring Sam over . . . Go easy on that jam! Oh, Tilly, it's so exciting! Another grandchild!'

'It isn't exciting. It isn't exciting at all, it's a disaster.' Tilly bit her lip. 'I don't want this baby. I feel so guilty. It's growing every day and . . . I don't want it. Robin is furious. He thinks it's all my fault.'

'Did he say so?'

'In so many words. He can hardly bear to look at me. He says it's a disaster.'

Margot slapped the cake viciously with a huge dollop of icing. 'He's not thinking rationally at the moment. He's been like a bear with toothache ever since he bought those new premises. He should never have taken them. He should have listened to you. You're a lot wiser than he is.'

Tilly smiled. 'You're hardly impartial!'

'I know what I know. Oh, Tilly darling, don't cry!'

Tilly blew her nose. 'Don't worry, I cry over anything at the moment.'

'Oh, Tilly!' Margot said again and came over and gave her daughter a hug.

'Any chance of a coffee?' Her father stood in the doorway. 'What's going on?'

'We're both feeling rather emotional,' Margot said. 'Tilly's pregnant.'

'Good heavens, not again? Poor Robin!'

'Excuse me,' Tilly said, 'I have to go to the bathroom.'

When she came back her mother was finishing the tarts. Her father shifted his bulk uneasily in his chair and set down his mug. 'Tilly, I'm sorry. I hadn't realized that . . . well, never mind. It's not the end of the world.'

'I wish people would stop saying that.'

'Well, it's true.' Harry attempted a chuckle. 'I don't know, the messes you women get yourselves into! You should see your mother with the computer!'

Margot handed Tilly a cup of tea. 'My computer and I are beginning to understand each other very well.'

'Margot, my love, you have many qualities but understanding computers is not one of them! Where are you off to, Tilly?'

Tilly picked up her bag. 'I need to go to the supermarket. I must go. Have a good fete, Mum.'

Tilly got home at midday to find only Horace waiting for her. A note on the table informed her that Robin had taken the children to lunch with John and Josie.

She wondered how long Robin was going to avoid her company. Fine. She was fed up with being made to feel like a criminal. He was being quite impossible and if he was waiting for her to grovel in front of him he would have to wait for a very long time.

Horace watched her intently, his head cocked to one side. 'Hey, Horace,' she said, 'I'll put away the groceries and then we'll have a walk.'

Horace understood only the last word and he barked joyfully, dashing to the door, then back to Tilly and then around the supermarket bags. It was a pity, really, that humans couldn't learn from Horace. He was wired for happiness. One only had to say, 'Dinner!' or 'Walk!' or scratch his tummy and he'd be in seventh heaven. What a pity people couldn't be like that. Wouldn't it be great if she could yell, 'Sex!' or 'Steak!' or 'Hot bath!' and watch Robin bound up to her and run round happily in circles.

It was mid-afternoon when the family returned. Tilly was

in the garden pruning the roses. The children shot out of the car and ran over to her. 'We had chow mein for lunch,' Lucy told her.

'Me cooked it!' Sam said proudly.

'No, you didn't,' Lucy said. 'Josie let you stir it, that's all. And after lunch we watched *Fantasia* and it was very boring so Daddy brought us home.'

'Well, if you've been in front of the television all afternoon,' Tilly said, 'you'd better get some fresh air. Go and get your boots on. You can help me in the garden.'

She was about to follow them into the house but she was stopped by Robin. 'Tilly, I'm sorry I rushed off like that. I needed to talk to John and Josie.'

'And I'm sure they were very sympathetic,' Tilly responded coolly. She had no intention of alleviating his guilt. She welcomed the cold anger she felt. At the moment it seemed the only effective antidote to tears.

'They send their love,' Robin said, still trying. 'They say they're looking forward to seeing you next week.'

'That's nice.' Really, it was far better not to talk to Robin at all.

It was a perfect late-autumn afternoon. The sun was warm and inviting. The occasional plane traced patterns across the sky. Any pilot might have looked down on them and thought he was watching a charming family scene: Robin mowing the lawn, Tilly clearing the worst of the weeds, the children looking for worms. Only a close observer would have noticed that in two hours never a word passed between husband and wife.

Tilly maintained her icy reserve until half past seven. She had opened a tin of dog food and its pungent aroma revitalized her ever-present feelings of nausea. She ran upstairs and re-emerged from the bathroom a few minutes later.

Robin was hovering at the bottom of the stairs. 'Are you all right?'

'Yes, thank you.' Tilly returned to the kitchen, saw Horace regarding her with anticipation and swallowed hard. 'Robin, would you mind giving Horace his food?'

'Of course.' Robin eyed her apprehensively. 'Do you want to lie down?'

'No.'

Robin set down Horace's food in front of him. 'Tilly, look, I can't pretend I'm happy about the baby, but I'm sorry I . . . well, I'm sorry, that's all. It was all rather a shock. Just as we're getting to the stage when you can earn some more money, you go and . . . anyway, it's done now. You've got to give me a while to get used to it.'

Tilly stared directly at him. 'Do you want to go on staying in the spare room?'

'No, of course I don't. I was being silly.'

In bed that night it occurred to Tilly that Robin had still not conceded that her pregnancy was a mistake. She lay, open-eyed and sleepless, and reflected that there were few lonelier situations than sharing a bed with someone who's become a stranger.

CHAPTER ELEVEN

'The more I see of men, the more I admire dogs.'
MME DE SEVIGNE

Sunday lunch with the Taylors did not improve Tilly's state of mind. She knew Robin had told them about the baby and hoped they would not display an enthusiasm in which she could not share. Even so she was dismayed by their reaction. From the moment she was ushered through the door, she felt she'd been diagnosed with a terminal illness.

Anne maintained a bravura display of inconsequential chatter throughout the meal which depressed everyone. Even Lucy and Sam were subdued. Then, as they were leaving, Anne took Tilly aside and whispered, 'Don't worry, darling, everything will be all right. We'll see this through together,' and for the life of her, Tilly couldn't think of an appropriate response. Peter pressed her hand and murmured, 'Take care of yourself now,' which was even worse because it made her want to cry.

Tilly finally told Rhona her news on Tuesday, dreading the expected sympathy and aggrieved when she did not receive it. 'Tilly, you are so lucky, that's wonderful! I am *so* jealous! I'd love to have another baby. I remember the way Chloe used to press her face tight against mine as if she couldn't get close enough. There's nothing like it, is there? The love between a

146

mother and her baby . . . I mean, it's the purest sort of love there is: unconditional, unquestioning . . . marvellous!'

Tilly took a few moments to answer. She was beginning to wonder if she and Rhona inhabited the same universe. 'The thing is,' she said, 'even the purest sort of love can be . . . derailed . . . by certain factors.'

'What sort of factors?'

'Oh, you know, a father who doesn't *want* to be a father, a rapidly diminishing bank account. . .things like that.'

'None of that matters,' Rhona said confidently. 'When a baby is born and smiles at his parents, nothing else matters.'

Tilly was tempted to remind Rhona that newborn babies couldn't smile for at least six weeks, by which time Robin would probably have left her. She decided that, on balance, it was safer to change the subject. 'Tell me about Chloe. How is she?'

'She's decided to go and live with her father . . . permanently.'

'Oh, Rhona, I'm sorry.'

'You needn't be. It's all quite amicable. We didn't have any great rows about it. It was just the *way* she told me that hurt: very calm, very reasonable and so grown-up, it was horrible somehow. She said she'd talked to her father, she said Nigel and I needed our own space . . . honestly, I felt as if we were in some American soap opera. She said she wanted to spend more time with her father, it was only fair, it was his turn. And she's moving out properly after Christmas. I couldn't even discuss it with her.'

'It all seems so sudden. Do you think she really means it? Perhaps she thinks you want to be alone with Nigel? Perhaps she hopes you'll beg her to stay?'

Rhona shook her head. 'She's already chosen the paint she

wants for her room in Mark's place. Nigel says I'm being silly to mind. He thinks I'll get on far better with Chloe once we stop living together. I'm sure he's right. And I suppose it will make life easier. Nigel's never had children, he isn't used to them and living with adolescents is difficult at the best of times. So it's probably all for the best.'

'Does Nigel want children of his own?'

'He won't even consider it. Why do you think I'm so envious of you? He says he's too old to start changing nappies. I think living with Chloe's probably destroyed any paternal feelings he might have had! You may not think so now, Tilly, but you are very lucky. So cheer up!'

Josie was equally upbeat when she and John came to supper on Saturday. When the men went through to the sitting room, she lingered in the kitchen while Tilly put the finishing touches to the lasagne and the salad. 'I know Robin's upset about the baby . . .' she said.

'That,' Tilly said, slicing a cucumber with frightening speed, 'is the understatement of the year.'

'All I want to say is that you need to see *why*. It's just lousy timing.'

'Josie,' Tilly said, 'contrary to what Robin has probably told you, I did not *intend* to have this baby.'

'He hasn't told me you did and I'm sure you didn't. The thing is, we're all very jittery at the moment. The last few months have been scary. Did he tell you that a few weeks ago we were seriously considering bankruptcy?'

'No,' Tilly said, 'he didn't.' She put down her knife and tipped the cucumber into the salad bowl. 'You see, on the one hand, Robin implies I take no interest in his work, and on the other, he fails to tell me anything about it. I can't win.'

'He probably didn't tell you how bad things were because he knows you were the only one with enough sense to see the dangers of trying to walk before we could crawl. I happen to believe we'll come through it now. Just give Robin time.' She leant forward and helped herself to a slice of cucumber. 'John and I are talking about children.'

'Seriously?'

'We think we might have a baby in a couple of years. Or a kitten. We can't decide which.'

Tilly grinned. 'I'd buy a kitten. Cat litters are a lot cheaper than nappies.'

Robin and Tilly were both subdued over dinner but fortunately John and Josie talked enough for all of them. John, a committed Liberal Democrat, was particularly exercised by Josie's announcement that she didn't see any point in voting in the next general election. John said that of all emotional states, pessimism had to be the most pointless. Josie retorted that optimism was an essential requirement for a Liberal Democrat. John said that without optimism they would all have given up on Garden Magic months ago. Josie graciously conceded that this was true.

By the time Tilly had made coffee, the other three were happily tearing apart Mr van Duren. 'The man's a monster,' John said. 'I've never met anyone like him. He'd try to teach physics to Stephen Hawking.'

'When he came in the other day,' Josie said, 'he told me he wasn't feeling very well. I asked him why and he said he hadn't had sex the night before. He said he could never concentrate well unless he'd had sex the night before. Then he asked me if I were the same.'

'Yuck.' Tilly grimaced. 'What did you say?'

'I told him I preferred coffee.'

Tilly laughed. 'Is he physically attractive?'

'Very,' said Josie, 'if you fancy ET.'

'The man's a moron,' John insisted, 'but he's also a rich moron. Let's hope we can get some newer and nicer clients soon.' He glanced at Robin. 'How did you get on with Louise on Thursday? Did you take her somewhere nice for lunch? Josie said you were out for hours.'

For a moment, Robin's eyes met Tilly's and then they slid away. Briefly, he reminded her of someone she knew but she couldn't remember who.

'She deserved a good meal,' Robin said. 'She gave up most of the day for us and she's won a definite go-ahead from *Homes and Gardens* and a possible commission from one of the Sunday papers.'

'What about photographs?' Josie asked.

'I've given her a few of the Cornwall place and all the usual brochures. She said she'd ring you on Monday about a date for her photographer to come.'

Tilly remembered now who Robin reminded her of: Horace, last week, when she'd caught him digging up her parsley plant. She handed him his coffee. 'You didn't tell me you saw Louise on Thursday.'

Robin gave a careless shrug. 'I don't tell you everything.'

'These days,' Tilly said, 'you don't tell me anything.'

There was a brief, uncomfortable silence and then Robin said lightly, 'We shouldn't argue in front of our friends. It is unforgivably boring.'

'Don't worry,' Josie said breezily. 'It's always reassuring to see other couples getting cross with each other!'

'Very healthy,' John agreed. 'Did I ever tell you my great-aunt's favourite story? She once spent three years looking after a glamorous couple in Cheltenham. They were the life and soul of every occasion and their parties were legendary. Everyone adored them. They were incredibly sociable and, even when they stayed in, they always dressed for dinner. But what people didn't know was that they only spoke to each other in public. In private they communicated by notes or occasionally through my great-aunt. Now that *is* sad!'

Tilly had heard the story before, which meant that John's wife must have heard it at least ten times. Josie's response of delighted mirth was a noble attempt to lighten the atmosphere. 'People are so weird,' she smiled. 'My uncle has been married four times and you can always tell when he's about to jump ship because he starts canoodling in public with the latest casualty. And at his age PDA is pretty disgusting, I can tell you.'

'Don't get Josie started on PDA,' John said, despite the fact that Tilly and Robin were saying nothing at all. 'Public Displays of Affection. It's her pet hate!'

Tilly appreciated the efforts her guests were making to salvage the evening even though she wished they'd chosen a subject other than bad marriages in which to do so. She tried, belatedly, to make amends. 'Anyone for more coffee?' she asked, with a hopefully cheery smile.

'Actually,' Josie said, staring meaningfully at her husband, 'we must be going. We're taking part in a charity run tomorrow: fifteen miles, would you believe! Don't get up, either of you. Thank you, Tilly, for a lovely meal. Stay there! We'll just slip out.'

John was already out of his chair. 'Thanks, Tilly. See you Monday, Robin.'

Robin and Tilly continued to sit in silence at either end of the table, just like John's aunt's employers. Tilly heard the car drive away and said flatly, 'They couldn't get away quickly enough.'

'Do you blame them?' Robin said.

'Not at all. Robin, just how long are you going to go on like this?'

'What do you mean?'

'Oh, please! If you think, if you really think, I planned all this, that I set out deliberately to have children you don't want, then we might as well end it now.'

'I don't think that,' Robin said wearily. 'I don't think you consciously meant to get pregnant.'

'What does that mean? You think I unconsciously meant to? Robin, I didn't plan anything.'

'No,' Robin said. 'You never do.'

'What does *that* mean?'

'Nothing. It's a simple observation. Let's leave it.'

So they did and with every passing day Tilly felt the wall between them grow bigger than Jack's magic beanstalk. Her parents-in-law were more assiduous than ever in their efforts to help, Robin remained clipped and distracted, and neither of them talked about the baby. Tilly felt as if her identity were swilling around in some gruesome mixing bowl, being pushed and pummelled into some shapeless, alien form. Before the arrival of the Taylors she'd believed she presided over a happy family life. But now, every time Anne cooked a meal for her or did some sewing or even, once, some gardening, Tilly felt her increasingly tenuous hold over her domestic domain slip further away. Anne, Peter and even, in fact especially, Robin, seemed to think of her as a helpless scatterbrain, a twenty-first century equivalent to Charles Dickens's Dora, only without the fetching curls. The really scary fact was that she was beginning to share their opinion.

Her visit to the antenatal clinic didn't help. Everyone else seemed to be at least ten years younger than her and the waiting room buzzed with excitement and pride and anticipation. Tilly felt old and sour, like a withered apple in a bowl of fresh strawberries.

The weather was appalling too. Day after day the skies tipped oceans of water on the fragile communities below. Tilly began to wonder if they'd ever see the sun again.

Rhona's wedding in early December increased still further Tilly's general feeling of isolation. Only after it had happened did Tilly realize that she had assumed Rhona would invite her in the end. The fact that she didn't seemed to prove that Rhona no longer valued their friendship.

On the last day of term Tilly heaved Sam's buggy awkwardly down the playground steps. The stick insects were there. Adonis stood a little apart. The child was talking to him but received little response and as soon as he left to join the queue of children Adonis turned on his heel and left with barely a glance at the stick insects. Tilly felt almost sorry for him. She knew how he was feeling.

As Christmas approached, the atmosphere at home was like the air before a thunderstorm: thick, claustrophobic, unnaturally silent. Tilly, too weak to force a confrontation, threw herself into the Christmas festivities.

She and the children made tree decorations out of modelling clay and stuck together paper chains which spent the rest of the holiday hanging disconsolately from various points on the ceiling. After reading an article on the joys of home-made Christmases, Tilly spent a morning making heart-shaped shortbread biscuits to hang from the tree. This proved not to be such a good idea since Horace assumed they were a special treat for him and nearly caused a disaster when he tried to pull them down. Even Robin found that funny and the incident provided an aching reminder of how things used to be.

Christmas Day was fine, despite the fact that it was spent with the Taylors. Anne produced a superb dinner and the children loved their presents. Tilly thanked Robin politely for the jersey he'd given her and which she knew by its understated elegance had been chosen by Anne.

The storm, when it broke, was brutal. A week after the new term began, Tilly came back from the supermarket to find that Horace was missing. She and Sam set about trying to find how he'd escaped. It didn't take long. In the corner of the garden, behind the compost heap, three slats had fallen down.

Fastening Sam into his buggy, Tilly set off down the road, asking neighbours if they'd seen him and stopping periodically to call his name.

At half past seven the doorbell rang. It was Richard Stevens, a farmer from half a mile away. 'Tilly,' he said gently, 'I've got Horace in the trailer. We found him by the side of the road. Would you like me to bury him for you?'

Tilly stared at him, her eyes wide with horror. Thank heaven the children were asleep. 'That's very kind. Can I see him?'

'Of course. Maggie said you were looking for him. I'm so sorry.' He led Tilly out to his tractor. Tilly looked at the limp pile of fur that had been Horace and stroked him.

'It would have been very quick,' Richard said.

'I hope so,' Tilly said. 'Do you know he was only five?'

'Best leave him now,' Richard said gently.

Tilly watched him drive away and walked back slowly into the kitchen. She sat down and wept for her big, beautiful dog. This is my fault, she thought. I'm responsible.

Robin came home half an hour later and agreed with her. 'What on earth possessed you to leave him in the garden while you were out? You know he's escaped before. He'd have been quite happy indoors.'

'He didn't want to come in and the sun was shining for once. We were only away for about fifteen minutes. I thought the fence was secure.'

'You thought that the last time he went missing. You know what Horace is like.' Robin's face hardened. 'You know what Horace *was* like.'

Tilly burst into tears. Robin reached silently for the box of tissues and handed it to her. She blew her nose loudly. 'I know it's my fault and I don't need you to tell me so but if you were so concerned about the fence you should have had a look at it yourself.'

'I haven't the time. I am working flat out to provide enough money for your latest baby.'

'It's our baby, Robin, not mine.' Tilly walked over to the bin and threw in her tissue. 'I'm fed up with being made to feel guilty about everything that's wrong in your life, I'm fed up with having to tiptoe round the house waiting to see what's going to irritate you next, and I'm fed up with getting

155

no support from you. If living with me is so bad then perhaps you should go and live with your precious parents!'

Robin sat down at the table and threw his head back. At last he sighed very heavily and looked at Tilly. 'Actually,' he said slowly, 'I think perhaps you're right.'

CHAPTER TWELVE

'Despair of peace as long as your mother-in-law is alive.'
JUVENAL

For sheer versatility no computer will ever match the human brain. Tilly's brain was surpassing itself. While on the one hand it was instructing her heart and stomach to perform internal gymnastics of Olympian dimensions, it was also directing her limbs and lips with such precision that she was able to take a seat opposite Robin and say with apparent composure, 'If that's what you want.'

'I honestly think it's for the best,' Robin said. He pushed both his hands through his hair and started kneading the back of his neck. He looked utterly exhausted. 'If we carry on like this, we'll end up hating each other.'

'I won't hate you.'

'Yes, you will. It's no good for the children to live with parents who are barely talking to each other. It's far more honest to admit that things aren't working out. Don't you agree?'

'I don't know,' Tilly said. 'I'm not sure I do.' Why was she saying this? She knew very well she didn't, of course she didn't. She was utterly bewildered. Was he being serious or simply lashing out at her? How had they got to this? How had this happened? She wanted to ask him a thousand questions: was this to be a permanent separation? Was it because she'd let Horace die or had he been thinking about this for some time? Did he no longer love her at all? Did Louise figure in any of this? She wanted to tell him he was in shock over Horace, they were both in shock, he was being ridiculous, they could work it out, this was silly, this was utterly stupid. But she sat and said nothing and waited for him to explain himself.

'When I talk to you these days . . .' Robin leant forward and blinked before throwing up his hands in the air. 'I don't know, I can *hear* how unpleasant I am. I nag you about silly things, I'm cross, I'm bad-tempered. You *make* me like this.'

'So it's my fault?'

'No, no, it isn't. It's just . . . I'm not a nice person when I'm with you any more. It's not working.'

'So you want to leave it behind?'

'I want to see what happens when we separate. We both need a breathing place. I don't want . . . I don't want to live like this any more.'

'I see.'

'Do you?'

'Not really.'

'Something's going wrong and I don't know how to fix it.' He shook his head. 'I can't live with you at the moment.'

'That's honest, at least.'

Robin rested his elbows on the table and sighed. He began to rub the back of his neck with his left hand. 'I just think,' he said slowly, 'that if we have some time away from each other, we can work things out. At the moment, I come home at night and I feel so angry with you and I know it's unfair, I know it's not right, but I just can't deal with it any more. I need to get away, to get some sort of perspective on everything. I'm not talking about anything permanent but . . .' He paused and shook his head again, helplessly. 'At the moment, I really don't think I can stay here with you.' He sighed. 'I know you're unhappy. So am I. It's like we're both standing in front of a huge wall and we don't know how to get round it. If we spend a few weeks apart from each other we might find the answer.'

'I see.' Tilly bit her lip. 'And what do we . . . what do *you* . . . tell the children?'

'We admit we've had a few arguments and I'm moving out for a little while until we can resolve them.'

'So that will be all right, then.'

'Tilly, please . . .' He stared at her for a moment and then his face hardened. 'I'll go at the weekend.'

'No,' Tilly said.

'It's only for a little while, I'm sure that—'

'No. I mean, don't leave it until the weekend. Pack some things and go now.'

Robin stared at her. He had the same expression on his face that he'd had at breakfast when he'd discovered that his cornflakes were stale. 'Tilly, that's stupid. What will the children think? We have to put them first.'

'I am putting them first and I don't want them to see their parents unable to talk to each other. If you want to leave me, that's fine, but it's much better if you don't hang around. Just go.'

'I thought you wanted me to tell them.'

'You can. You can see them on Saturday and explain everything, because for the life of me I can't.'

'This is stupid. We need to talk sensibly and coolly.'

159

'Fine. Can you tell me, sensibly and with great coolness, why you want to leave this marriage?'

'Now you're being melodramatic. I'm simply saying we need to have some time away from each other. We're not any good with each other right now. I think we need to sort out where we go from here.'

'Robin, do me a favour and stop talking about "we". *You* need to sort out how *you* feel, *you* need to be away from me. Fine. Go, then. I think it's a good idea. So far you've accused me of deliberately plotting a secret pregnancy, of killing Horace and of being a completely useless wife and mother. I can quite understand why you don't want to live with a woman like that. I wouldn't want to live with her either. So get your things and go!'

'If you're going to be like this then I might as well—'

'Good. Yes! I quite agree! Hurry up!'

'There's no need to get hysterical.'

'I am NOT getting bloody hysterical.'

'All right.' Robin stood up. 'I'll go and pack a few things.'

She couldn't believe it. He was really going. 'Fine,' she said.

'Do you want to know where I am?'

'Not particularly.'

'I'll go to John's tonight. After that I'll go to Mum and Dad.'

'Great.'

'Right. I'll go and pack, then.'

'Wonderful.' Tilly sniffed. 'By the way, is it all right for me to go on using the joint bank account? I'm not sure I can manage on just my salary.'

'Of course it's all right. Look, Tilly, I just need a bit of time—'

'Fine, that's fine. Now go and pack.'

Robin cleared his throat, murmured, 'Right,' again and disappeared upstairs.

Tilly stood and set about gathering up all signs of Horace's existence: his blanket, his bowl, his lead and his well-chewed yellow ball. She put them all into a dustbin bag and took them out to the shed. It was quite something to lose a dog and a husband in the space of one evening. Of the two she would miss Horace the most, no question.

Half an hour later Robin came down with a bulging suitcase. Tilly leant against the sink and folded her arms. 'I see you're travelling light,' she said.

Robin almost smiled. 'I was always hopeless at packing. Look, are you sure you want me to go tonight?'

'I am absolutely sure. Goodbye, Robin.'

'You know where I am. If you want anything.'

'I don't. Go away.'

'I'll ring.' He left then. She heard him go outside, she heard the car drive off and she realized that right up to that moment she hadn't really believed he'd go, that right up to that moment they'd been playing some game of bluff and now he'd won.

She switched out the lights and went upstairs. She heard Lucy calling her and found her sitting up in bed. 'Lucy!' she admonished. 'You'll wake Sam.'

'Has Horace come back yet? Can you get Daddy to come and say goodnight?'

'Shall I make you some hot milk?' Tilly suggested. 'It'll help you get back to sleep.'

Telling Lucy about Horace proved easier than prevaricating about Robin. After an initial bout of tears Lucy was cheered by the thought of Horace chasing rabbits in heaven. She was not impressed by Robin's absence. 'He said he'd help me with my tables. He didn't even say goodnight!'

'He wanted to but he had to dash off. He's very busy at the moment. He'll see you on Saturday. Now go to sleep.'

Tilly went back downstairs and stood in front of Horace's basket. She couldn't bear to take it out to the cold, dark shed outside. She knelt down beside it and breathed in Horace's smell. Any moment now he would nudge his face gently underneath her arm and press his cold nose against her skin. Except, of course, he wouldn't. He never would again.

In bed, she kept rewinding the confrontation with Robin. It had all happened so quickly, she felt as if she'd been pushed onto an escalator that wouldn't let her off. But that was stupid. She could have stopped it, they could have talked it through. He'd wanted to talk and she'd said no. Why had she said no? Was it pride or fear of what he might say? Either way, she'd been criminally irresponsible.

The next morning Sam was remarkably phlegmatic about the absence of Horace, although he did display a lurid interest in the circumstances of his death. When Tilly came to pick him up from playgroup, he presented her with a graphic painting of a car under which red paint had been heavily applied. 'That's Howace's blood,' he said.

'Lovely,' Tilly said faintly. As long as she didn't have to talk or think about Robin, she could almost convince herself nothing had happened. Except, of course, she had to tell the children about their father.

She sat down with them while they ate their tea and said brightly, 'I have to tell you something about Daddy.'

'Does Daddy know a car squashed Howace?' Sam asked, his mouth full of banana.

'Horace wasn't squashed and, yes, Daddy does know.'

'I've brought my Tables Book home to show him,' Lucy said.

'I'll help you with your tables.' Tilly picked up the banana skin by Sam's plate and squeezed it hard. 'Daddy isn't coming home tonight.'

'Why?' asked Lucy.

'Well,' Tilly began, 'you see, Daddy and I have been having some silly quarrels lately.'

'Why?' asked Lucy.

'Oh,' Tilly swallowed. 'All sorts of silly things. But because we've been getting cross with each other, Daddy's decided he should go and stay with Granny and Grandpa Taylor for a while.'

'Why?' asked Lucy.

'Because,' Tilly said, pinching and pummelling the banana skin, 'we can't seem to be nice to each other at the moment.'

'Why?' asked Lucy.

'I don't know, we just can't. But you'll see him on Saturday; he wants to see you very much and you'll have a lovely time with him.' She stopped, aware of two sets of eyes, one puzzled, one accusing, staring at her intently.

'You always say,' Lucy declared, 'that it's wrong to quarrel. You always say Sam and I shouldn't quarrel, you always say we should make up and be friends, you always say—'

'I know I do,' Tilly countered, 'and that's absolutely right and that's what Daddy and I are trying to do. But sometimes adult arguments are rather difficult to work out, I don't know why, they just are.'

'Where's Daddy?' Sam asked.

'He's with Granny Taylor. You'll see him lots.'

'Doesn't he want to live with us any more?' Lucy's bottom lip was quivering.

'Yes, of course he does,' said Tilly, hating Robin. 'And I'm sure we'll sort this all out. Daddy loves you very much.'

'Then why doesn't he stay?'

'I'm sure he'll come home soon. Very soon.'

Lucy burst into tears. 'I hate you!' she shouted. 'You're horrible!' She ran out of the room.

Sam's lip was trembling now. 'Me want Daddy,' he said.

'I know,' Tilly said. 'I know.'

Robin rang a few hours later. 'Have you told them?' he asked. 'What did they say?'

'They wanted to know why you didn't want to live with them.'

'So you explained? You told them I—'

'I said we weren't getting on. I said you'd see them on Saturday. Be here at ten. They're very unhappy. Have a good meal.' She slammed down the receiver and hoped he'd choke on his mother's dinner. He wouldn't, of course. His mother's dinner would be delicious. He'd probably have second helpings. And at breakfast, he wouldn't be eating stale cornflakes either.

The next morning, Tilly kept out of the staffroom at breaktime. If she saw Rhona she'd be tempted to tell her about Robin, and if she started talking about Robin she would be in no state to help children with maths or French or anything at all. At lunch, she went to collect Sam from her mother, ready to zoom in and zoom out. 'Sam's asleep,' Margot said, 'and I want you to tell me why he says his daddy's gone away. So come in and don't pretend you're in a hurry. I've made some soup, it's nearly ready.'

Tilly, accepting defeat, followed her mother into the kitchen and collapsed onto a chair. 'Robin's going to stay with his parents for a while. He's gone.'

'*Gone?* Why? It's crazy. You're expecting a baby, for heaven's sake! I don't understand.'

Tilly shrugged. 'Join the club.'

'But it's all so sudden. What did he say? Did you try to stop him?'

'No. The last few months have been horrible. What's the point in him staying if he doesn't want to?'

'I can think of two, soon to be three, very good reasons. One of them is asleep upstairs. I can't believe you're being so selfish!'

'Me! Mum, I'm not the one who decided to walk out!'

'No, but you're not doing anything to stop him. Tilly, this is serious. It's not just about you and Robin. You can't afford to be all proud and noble, you should have made him stay. Have you any idea what this will do to the children?'

'Of course I do, but if Robin wants to go I can't stop him. Ever since his parents moved down here, I've seen him look at me, comparing me to his perfect mother. I irritate him. Everything I do irritates him. It's not very nice to watch that happening.'

Margot poured out two glasses of water and sat down opposite Tilly. 'We played bridge with them last week,' she said.

Tilly stared incredulously at her mother. 'You can't play bridge!'

'I know,' Margot said. 'It was awful.' She smiled suddenly.

'Actually, it was quite funny. Harry got crosser and crosser with me and the Taylors kept trying to explain the rules to me very slowly, and of course I got more and more confused and I could feel my brain shut down!'

Tilly smiled. 'I wish I'd been there!'

'You don't. You'd have been cringing with embarrassment. Harry lectured me all the way home!' Margot laughed, a little longer than was natural. 'I'll serve out the soup, then, shall I?'

For a few minutes they ate their food in silence. Then Tilly said, 'I'm not completely spineless, Mum. If I make Robin stay, it won't change anything. You know what Anne's like: she'll be all over him at first and then after a week or two she'll slip back and start bossing him about, just like she does Peter. She'll have him washing up and cleaning the car, and he might just begin to remember that living with me wasn't so bad. Perhaps it's all he needs, you know? After a week or two I'll try, I really will try to get him back.'

Margot frowned. 'A fortnight, then. No longer.'

Tilly nodded. 'Agreed. A fortnight's not so long.'

Tilly was wrong. It was an eternity. She went to work, she cooked, she cleaned, she tried to persuade herself that it was wonderful to live without Robin's glowering disapproval. The children were unhappy, querulous and confused. As Tilly's tummy swelled, the shadows under her eyes deepened.

She wasn't the only one who was suffering. At school the big, blond Adonis no longer accompanied his son. The little boy stood silent, small and vulnerable between the stick insects. Tilly wanted to wrap him in her arms and hug the misery out of him. He reflected all too clearly the gloomy half-life which she and her children were living.

After a week, she'd had enough. She rang the Taylors for the first time since Robin had left and asked to speak to him. 'Tilly, how are you, darling?' Anne used the hushed tones of the hospital visitor. 'I've so wanted to ring you but Peter and I felt you both needed space to sort things out. I can't believe any of this. It's just too dreadful. There's nothing sadder than the end of a marriage.'

The end of a marriage? Was this what Robin had said? Was this what he intended? Tilly's mouth felt horribly dry and she moistened her lips and strove to keep her voice level. 'Would it be possible to speak to Robin?'

'Ah.' There was a pause. 'Has Robin not told you?'

'Told me what?'

'Well,' Anne said carefully, far too carefully, 'he's decided it's easier if he stays near Radstock during the week.'

'Where is he? With John and Josie?'

'No. He's staying at a friend's house.'

'Who is this friend, Anne?' But of course Tilly knew. She knew by the barely suppressed excitement in her mother-in-law's voice.

'Louise,' Anne said, 'Louise Honeytree.'

CHAPTER THIRTEEN

'Marriage is like life in this – that it is a field of battle and not a bed of roses.'

ROBERT LOUIS STEVENSON

Charlotte's invitation was suspiciously spontaneous. 'Tilly, I've suddenly had a great idea! Why don't you come up to Crouch End? On Saturday. Do you realize Michael and I moved here eighteen months ago and you've never seen the place? You might as well enjoy your free weekends while you can. When does Robin bring the children back?'

'Sunday afternoon . . . usually about five.'

'Fine. You can stay for an early Sunday lunch. Tell him you'll be a little late. It will do you good to get out. And we can have a good talk.'

Tilly didn't want to have a good talk with Charlotte. She knew what Charlotte's good talk would involve: Take charge of your life, Pull yourself together, Organize, Make lists, Shape events, don't let events shape you . . . Just thinking of Charlotte's good talk made her feel tired.

Nevertheless, Tilly accepted Charlotte's invitation because anything, even Charlotte's homilies, would be better than remaining at home on her own. She felt like an uprooted weed, exposed and homeless, suspended in the hand of a

168

whimsical, malevolent gardener whose face bore a remarkable similarity to that of Robin.

She bought a magazine at the station, lured by its promise to show her How To Bring the Sparkle Back into Your Marriage. Don't take your man for granted, said the writer. Had Tilly taken Robin for granted? She didn't think she had. Indeed, she'd never stopped feeling lucky that he'd married her. Listen to his problems, the writer said, and don't go on about your own. Which seemed a little unfair. Be seductive, said the writer, buy a set of sexy underwear. It could be the best investment you've ever made. Tilly leant her head against the window of the train and tried to imagine herself seducing Robin.

Perhaps in a few months, when she'd had the baby and the novelty of Louise had begun to fade, Tilly could call in on Robin's love-nest. Louise would be in the kitchen, wearily stirring a coq au vin, her hair tied back in a greasy ponytail.

– Tilly knocks lightly on the door. Robin opens it and the colour drains from his face. 'Tilly,' he begins, 'what are you—'

Tilly interrupts softly. 'Hello, Robin.' She is wearing a long, black velvet dress that clings to her body. Silently, she leads him to the bedroom and slowly and deliberately unzips her dress. Robin stares at her hungrily, feasting on the skimpy black knickers and the lacy maternity bra.

'Unhook me, please,' Tilly whispers, and as Robin, with trembling hands, does so, her breast pads fall soundlessly to the floor.

'My God, Tilly, you're beautiful,' Robin murmurs and finds his fingers drawn to the tantalizing, teasing stretch marks etched on Tilly's opulent tummy. Robin grabs her fiercely and mutters hoarsely, 'Oh, Tilly, I've made the most terrible mistake. I've missed you so much.'

169

Tilly pushes back her long blonde hair (which has grown incredibly in the last few months and has been bleached and styled by Frederick). 'But Robin,' she points out, 'you have Louise.'

'Louise!' Robin gives a mirthless laugh. 'I'd forgotten how boring she is. And selfish. And she has smelly feet and she's hopeless in bed. And she snores. Oh, Tilly, please forgive me. Say you'll take me back!'

Suddenly, the door opens and Louise appears in the doorway. She is wearing an oil-splattered apron around her waist. 'Robin!' she cries. 'How could you? I can't fight any longer. It's Tilly, isn't it? It's always been Tilly, I know that now. Do you want to know what really hurts?' –

Tilly's eyelids drooped. She slept like a baby all the way to Paddington.

Charlotte had told Tilly to take a taxi to Crouch End, which betrayed a touching if misguided optimism about the state of Tilly's finances. Tilly took the tube and after a protracted journey, which somehow involved going to Harrow and back again, she arrived at Highgate. Armed with her A to Z she successfully navigated the long and weary way to Charlotte's house.

Charlotte flung open the door and gave Tilly a brisk embrace. 'Hello,' she said. 'I was about to call out a search party. Did you get lost?'

'Of course not.' Tilly laughed at such an outrageous suggestion. 'Charlotte, I love that rug . . . and the mirror . . . this is lovely!'

'Thank you. I'll give you a guided tour after tea! You would like some tea?'

'Yes, please, I'm dying of thirst. And you've bought some gingerbread! Delicious!'

'It's a weakness of mine.' Charlotte tossed tea bags into two green mugs and turned to Tilly. 'So, what's the state of play at the moment?'

Tilly sighed. 'Robin's staying with his parents when he's not living in some love-nest with his girlfriend.'

'What? Are you sure? Perhaps she's just a friend.'

'Louise was never just a friend. He used to go out with her before he met me. She used to be the love of his life. I suspect she's always been the love of his life. And he's obviously been her's. Why else would she rush to take a flat near his work-shop the moment he's on the loose? Robin says it doesn't belong to Louise. I did think about giving him my opinion on the semantics of letting and buying, but I couldn't be both-ered. It's so pathetic he feels he has to lie. I don't feel I know him at all any more.'

'Are you sure he's lying to you?'

'Oh, yes. His mother told me everything. Of course she pre-tended she hadn't meant to say anything, she said Robin would be furious if he knew, but I could tell she was loving every minute of it. She never thought I was good enough for her son.'

Charlotte shook her head. 'I can believe your mother-in-law is a bitch. I still can't believe Robin could really want to leave you and the children. What a bastard!'

'He isn't,' Tilly said, 'not really.' She wasn't sure why she wanted to defend him to Charlotte, heaven knew she hadn't been defending him to herself.

'Excuse me, Tilly, the man leaves his pregnant wife and two small children. That is not something a good man does.'

'It's not as simple as that,' Tilly said, which was a stupid way of trying to bring an irritating conversation to an end because of course Charlotte immediately asked, 'Why not?'

Tilly sighed. 'I bullied him into having Lucy, I bullied him into having Sam and now I'm pregnant again. He's working very hard, he's worried about money, he just can't cope.'

Charlotte snorted. 'Trust Robin to have his mid-life crisis ten years before anyone else. I'm sorry, but I think he's pathetic. So, what are you going to do?'

Tilly stifled a yawn. It had been a long journey and getting lost always exhausted her. She wished she could go to bed and fall asleep for the rest of the weekend. 'What do you mean?'

Charlotte set the tea tray on the table and sat down. 'Robin has left you. Are you going to stay in the house or sell it? What are you going to do about money? I mean, you can't simply put your head in the sand and hope it will go away. What are you going to do?'

'I don't know.' Tilly glanced at the front door. She felt overcome by exhaustion. She hoped Michael would get back soon. Very soon. 'I suppose I'll wait and see.'

Charlotte took a sip of her tea, set the mug on its coaster and placed her hands together on the table. 'What exactly has Robin said? Does he want a divorce?'

'No. At least, I don't know.'

'Well, ask him, Tilly. You're always waiting for other people to tell you what to do. He has to tell you what his plans are. You need to know!'

Tilly exploded. 'I don't need to know! Please, Charlotte, don't lecture me. I won't bring up divorce unless he does. I don't want a divorce, I want Robin back!'

The front door opened and Michael came in. 'Tilly!' he beamed. 'How *are* you?'

'I'm fine,' said Tilly and burst into tears.

An hour later she lay in the bath and wondered what on earth she was doing here. She might have known Charlotte would reduce her to a gibbering wreck and Michael must think her a spineless hysteric. And to cap it all, they were having a dinner party! A dinner party! And they thought she'd be pleased!

'Just a few friends,' Charlotte had assured her. 'Fred and Andrea Spencer and Colin Drew. Fred's an antique dealer, Andrea's in television and Colin's a doctor. You'll like him.'

Tilly lay back in the perfumed water and shut her eyes. It was obvious. Robin was already dispatched, out of bounds, discarded, forgotten. Colin Drew, poor man, was the chosen replacement. Never mind that Tilly was pregnant and had brought nothing to wear and felt like death. Typical. She heard a knock on the door and raised her head. 'Hello?'

'Tilly, I've put a couple of things on your bed. Try them on. And take your time. Wear some make-up. Have fun!'

Surprisingly, Tilly did. Charlotte might be irritating but she had a wardrobe to die for. Tilly chose a long, pale blue dress which concealed her lump and did wonders for her morale. She was even able to greet Charlotte's terrifying friends with relative equanimity.

Even more surprisingly, they proved not to be terrifying at all. Fred had short, closely shaven hair like Bruce Willis. Tilly thought Bruce Willis ought to receive a medal for showing balding men how they could still be attractive. Fred endeared himself to Tilly by saying, 'You're Charlotte's little sister? Poor you! Does she tell you what to do all the time? Of course she does!'

Andrea was small and plump and cosy, with earrings that kept falling off. She was quite unlike Tilly's idea of Someone Who Worked in Television.

Colin Drew arrived late. He was thin and wiry with a shock of black curly hair and a manner of talking very fast, as if he were afraid he would be interrupted at any moment. Tilly liked him at once.

'I'm sorry I'm late,' he said. 'My sister rang up and refused to believe I was on my way out. I had to hear about the rising damp in her sitting room followed by a lurid account of her attempt to get her poor poodle impregnated. And then she told me she's decided to train to become a counsellor. Every woman she knows has become a counsellor, they'll all end up counselling each other and why do they think people want to be counselled anyway? If I'd just survived a plane crash the last person I'd want to see would be some woman I don't know telling me to tell her all about it and to feel free to cry on her shoulder.' He glanced suddenly at Tilly. 'You're not a counsellor, are you?'

Tilly laughed. 'No. I take it you don't have a very high opinion of them?'

'I have an extremely low opinion of them. They encourage people to blame their parents for everything they're doing wrong in their lives. I mean, do *you* think it's healthy to get someone to talk about nothing but themselves for over an hour and pretend that they're being interesting while they're doing so? I don't think so!'

'Colin, you are talking utter drivel,' Charlotte said, 'and you don't know what you're talking about, or rather you do know what you're talking about so you have no excuse at all. Now come and sit down. Michael, will you pour the wine?'

Tilly took her place with the delightful knowledge that she was going to enjoy herself. She was surrounded by people who were easy to listen and talk to. The conversation ebbed and flowed like the sea. By the end of the main course the party had considered the state of: education (possibly depressing) the NHS (possibly promising), the long absence from the screen of *Buffy the Vampire Slayer* repeats (tragic), and even the meaning of life (there was none).

Andrea said suddenly, 'How terrible! Do you realize we've drunk three bottles of wine and Tilly and Charlotte are on water! Three bottles between four of us!'

Tilly glanced at her sister. 'What's this, Charlotte? Have you gone teetotal?'

Fred laughed. 'You know Charlotte. Her little embryo has got to be the healthiest baby in London!' He looked from one sister to the other. 'Didn't you know? Oh, lord, have I put my foot in it?'

'No, I didn't know,' said Tilly slowly. 'Charlotte, that's wonderful. I just thought you'd put on weight! Why didn't you tell me?'

Charlotte looked embarrassed. Tilly had never seen Charlotte look embarrassed before. 'I thought . . . you've been so depressed about your own pregnancy . . . I didn't want to . . .'

'You thought I wouldn't be happy for *you*? I'm not quite as selfish as that!'

Charlotte's eyes flickered away towards her husband and then back to Tilly. 'Of course you're not.'

Colin rested his elbows on the table and leant towards Tilly. 'It's not just you,' he assured Tilly kindly. 'She'd never have told me either if Michael hadn't let it out. My wife's pregnant, you see.'

Tilly frowned. 'I don't understand.'

'I'm not the father.'

'Oh,' said Tilly, 'I'm so sorry.'

'So am I,' said Colin without any noticeable rancour. 'It's all a big con trick really.'

'What is?'

'Love. Of course it's all about chemicals.'

Michael stood up and began to clear the plates. 'Don't encourage him, Tilly. We've heard it all before.'

'But it's interesting,' said Tilly. 'What has love to do with chemicals?'

Michael gave an exaggerated groan. Colin ignored him and turned to Tilly. 'You know how when you're in love you feel giddy, elated, ecstatic. Right? Right! Well, believe it or not, that's all down to two little neurotransmitters called nor-adrenaline and dopamine. Meanwhile, the good old pituitary gland gets busy producing oxytocin and vasopressin during arousal and orgasm. Now the interesting thing is, we know these hormones produce bonding and monogamy in American prairie voles.'

'Do we?' asked Tilly. 'How do we know? And anyway why should we assume that they do the same in us? Isn't that jumping to conclusions?'

Colin shrugged. 'It's the obvious deduction. I'll tell you something else: all these hormonal actions are *most marked* in the first year or two of a relationship. You see, Nature is so clever. It keeps the hormones beavering away just long enough for a couple to bond, conceive and nurture a newborn child. Evolution needs reproduction, and love is just a means of achieving it.'

Andrea pulled off her earrings and leant forward. 'What

you are saying is that we are simply the product of our chemicals. If that's true there's no point to anything, and I refuse to accept it. You can't reduce love to a load of old hormones!'

Colin tapped a triumphant finger on the table. 'Italian researchers have found that couples in love have lower than normal levels of the neurotransmitter serotonin. Similar falls are seen in patients with obsessive compulsive disorders. Why else do we talk about people being *madly* in love?'

'But in that case,' said Tilly, 'why are there so many happy marriages that endure long after the oxy thingies have gone back to sleep? Going by your theory, every marriage must have a limited shelf life.'

'Exactly!' Colin paused only to finish his wine. 'All the pressures that kept people together in the past – family, religion, social expectations – they're all falling apart. People don't have to stay together any longer and an awful lot of them are choosing not to. The trouble with marriage is all the baggage that comes with it, all the huge expectations provided by those poisonous chemicals. When they wear off, what's left? Two people who don't even want to hold hands any longer! The only thing keeping most couples together is apathy!'

'Rubbish!' said Andrea. She leant forward again and wagged a finger at Colin. 'I know far more people who choose to stay married than people who don't! If you take your argument to its logical conclusion, then it follows that once the romance has left a marriage, couples will just pack their bags and move on. Which is fine if you don't mind spending large chunks of your life clearing up the messes you leave behind. I don't want to spend weeks, months, years working out complicated visiting rights with innumerable ex-partners. I'd rather spend my time making a good relationship work and keeping my children happy. That's not apathy, it's common sense!'

'Fine,' Colin said, 'if that's what you want. But just tell me this. How many long-term couples do you know who really are happy? How many people do you know, do you *really* know, who are truly, genuinely happy?'

'I am!' said Andrea stoutly.

Charlotte smiled. 'So what's your secret? What do you do when romance begins to fade?'

Andrea screwed up her face in thought. 'Negotiate,' she said at last, 'and compromise. And empathize. My mother always says instead of asking how I feel I should try asking Fred how he feels.'

'In that case,' said Fred, 'since you understand my love of sport, will you please let me get a satellite dish?'

'Rule Number Two,' said Andrea sweetly: 'never negotiate in public.'

Later, when the guests had gone, Michael said, 'You two go to bed. Since I'm the only person who's not pregnant round here, I'll wash up.'

Tilly yawned. 'Are you sure?'

'Come on,' Charlotte said, 'before he changes his mind!'

Tilly saw her gently stroke her husband's back and felt a pang of jealousy. She stood up, said goodnight to Michael and followed Charlotte upstairs. On the landing she said, 'Charlotte, I'm really pleased that you're pregnant. You should have told me.'

'I know. I'm sorry.' Charlotte gave a small laugh. 'It's silly, you know; I was very cross when I heard you were pregnant.

Purely selfish. I thought: now Mum won't be able to come and look after me!'

'Well, of course she will!'

'No, she won't. You need her more. Goodnight, Tilly.'

'Hang on a moment. This is your first baby and, if our dates clash, Mum will want to come up and be with you. And I will want her to come up and be with you. Just so you know. All right?'

'All right. Thank you.'

'You have nothing to thank me for. And, Charlotte . . .'

'Yes?'

'You've been with Michael for six years. How have you stayed happy?'

Charlotte smiled. 'I'm not sure. I suppose . . . I've never expected him to be my meaning to life. Goodnight.'

'Goodnight, Charlotte.' Tilly went to her room and kicked off her shoes. She wondered if she had just been rebuked.

CHAPTER FOURTEEN

'Love is a temporary insanity, curable by marriage.'
AMBROSE BIERCE

Tilly decided to think on the way home. She found train journeys, or rather train journeys without children, extremely conducive to disciplined thinking. Whether it was the regular, pulsating rhythm or the hypnotically mutating landscape passing seamlessly from urban sprawl to towns to countryside, Tilly wasn't sure; she always found that on trains her brain could travel from A to B without succumbing to its usual temptation to take in H and P and Z on the way.

She was lucky too in that her carriage seemed to be exempt from the mobile phone virus. The only other occupants were an elderly lady who was knitting and a sleeping vicar. Tilly took out her notebook and pencil from her bag and wrote down her chosen subjects for contemplation:

> Empathy
> Charlotte
> Meaning of life
> Decisions

Initially, Tilly decided to try to be empathetic towards Robin but after a few minutes of being in Robin's shoes she felt so miserable that she decided to go on to Charlotte. The visit to her sister had been a revelation. Charlotte might be opinionated and patronizing and tactless but she could also be charming, kind and considerate, and her friends clearly held her in great affection.

Equally clearly, Charlotte found her sister irritating and exasperating and incapable of looking after herself. In Charlotte's eyes, she had monopolized their mother's attention, she was needy and pathetic, incapable of making a decision and congenitally unable to make any direct intervention in the way that her life proceeded.

Was Charlotte right? Was she needy? Had Robin found her so? He'd once told her he'd fallen in love with her because she *did* need him. On the other hand, the qualities that make a young man fall in love are not necessarily going to inspire the same enthusiasm ten years on. Had she depended on Robin too much? Was that what Charlotte had meant by her cryptic comment of the night before?

Tilly sucked the end of her pencil and decided to tackle the meaning of life. She presumed that Charlotte was trying to say it was unfair to expect a man to provide a woman with the meaning to her life. Charlotte had a point. Grandma Treadwell had once told Tilly that nothing mattered in the world except love and look what happened to her: Grandpa Treadwell dies and she falls apart.

Tilly blew out her cheeks and was momentarily diverted by the resultant fine mist that obscured the window. She wrote CONCENTRATE on the glass and studied her list again. Under Decisions she drew a line and added:

No more self-pity

Be strong not needy
Take control

She would make Robin see what his departure had done to the children, she would impress him with her calm determination and her new maturity, she would win him back. It all seemed quite easy.

An abrasive approximation of the first chords of Beethoven's Ninth abruptly filled the carriage. Tilly looked up and saw the elderly lady put down her knitting and extract a brilliant-yellow mobile phone from her bag. Tilly closed her notebook and decided she'd done enough thinking for one day.

It was odd to arrive home and find Robin sitting in the kitchen with Sam on his lap and Lucy beside him. For a moment Tilly could almost believe the whole horrible break-up had never happened. Then she saw Robin's stilted smile of forced welcome.

'We're playing dominoes,' Lucy said, 'and I'm winning!'

Sam held out his arms and Tilly gathered him up. 'Hello, monkey!' she said. 'I've missed you. Have you had a good weekend?'

Sam laid his face on Tilly's shoulder. 'Gwanny was cwoss,' he said.

Tilly raised an eyebrow at Robin. 'Really? Why?'

'Not for very long,' Robin said quickly. 'Sam brought some mud into the sitting room. We cleared it up for her, didn't we, Sam?' Sam responded by burying his face in Tilly's neck. Robin asked Tilly politely, 'How was Charlotte?'

'Very well. I had a lovely time.'

'Good. Fine.' Robin clapped his hands together. 'Well!' he said. 'I suppose I'd better be going.'

Lucy looked at him with horror. 'You can't go yet! We haven't finished our game! Tell him he can't go yet, Mummy!'

Robin hesitated. 'I think it's probably your bath time.'

'That's all right,' Tilly said sweetly. 'You finish the game while I bath Sam. Say goodnight, Sam.' Sam raised a weary hand.

'They're very tired,' Robin said, 'I took them for a long walk this afternoon.'

'Was that before or after the incident with the mud?'

'After,' Robin admitted with the ghost of a smile.

Tilly laughed and took Sam upstairs. She was in control. She was doing well. When she came back to the kitchen Robin and Lucy were clearing away the dominoes. 'Right, Lucy,' Tilly said, 'say goodnight to Daddy. You have school tomorrow.'

Lucy stuck out a quivering lower lip. 'I want Daddy to put me to bed.'

'Daddy has to go.'

'No, he doesn't! Daddy, *you* put me to bed, I want *you*!' She began to cry. 'I don't want you to go! I want you to stay here and put me to bed!'

Robin glanced helplessly at Tilly. She stared back blankly at him. 'Now look here, sweetheart,' he murmured.

'I don't . . . want . . . you . . . to go! It's not fair!'

'All right, all right,' Robin said, 'I'll take you to bed. Come on, Luce, let's go.'

'And you'll read me a story?'

'If you're very good.'

As soon as Robin had gone upstairs, Tilly went out and brought in some logs from the garage. She laid and lit the fire and tidied the cushions on the sofa. She switched off the main light and switched on the reading lamp in the corner. She closed the curtains and tidied the pile of Lucy's books on the small coffee table. When Robin came down he found her curled on the sofa apparently absorbed in her novel.

'I said you'd go up in a minute,' he said. 'I think she's worn herself out.'

'She's upset,' said Tilly. 'She doesn't understand what's going on.'

'Well . . .' Robin said. He stood, jiggling the change in his pockets, fixing his gaze on the fire. 'Well, of course . . . this isn't easy for any of us.'

'No,' Tilly said, 'it isn't. Especially for the children.'

Robin stared at the fire. 'Look,' he said at last, 'I know it's difficult for them to understand—'

'It's difficult for *me* to understand. Lucy keeps asking when you're coming home and I have no answer. Charlotte asks me if we're getting divorced and I have no answer. You've put me in this limbo and I'm just waiting, day after day. It's not fair; Robin, you need to tell me what's going on.'

'I know,' Robin said. He perched awkwardly on the edge of the armchair, his eyes still fixed on the fire. 'The thing is,' he said slowly, 'things are complicated.'

Tilly bit her lip. 'Why? Because you're in love with Louise?'

'For God's sake!' Robin stood up again and thrust a hand through his hair. 'Don't do this, please.'

'Why not? I think I've a right to know. Are you sleeping with her?'

'What?'

'Are you having sexual intercourse with Louise Honeytree?'

'I don't believe this!' He was blustering, playing for time

184

and the realization made her want to vomit. 'What sort of question is that?'

Tilly studied him coldly. 'A yes or no question.'

'Tilly, this is ridiculous. I don't want to get into a shouting match with you, I can't deal with hysterics.'

'I'm not being hysterical. I'm disgusted and disillusioned but I'm not hysterical. If you could see yourself! You can't even look at me. I can't believe I've lived with you for so long and got you so wrong. Are you staying with her tonight?'

'No! Why should I? I'm going back to Mum and Dad this evening.'

'Do send them my regards.'

'Look, Tilly, I'm sorry, I don't want—'

Tilly uncurled her legs and stood up. 'Please don't be sorry. I've found this all very enlightening. And don't worry, I won't ask you to come home again. It would stick in my throat. All we have to do now is decide what to tell the children.'

Robin looked startled. 'Do we have to tell them anything?'

Tilly regarded him with scorn. 'If you can't see how badly they're being affected by this then you're even more stupid than I thought. And don't tell me they're just tired, because in that case they're just tired day in and day out. You know what I find really despicable? You make me feel guilty about being pregnant – and for the record I did not set out to get pregnant and I did not want to get pregnant – and all the time the only reason you left is because you had the hots for Louise. You have no idea how much I despise you.'

'I think it's better,' Robin said, making for the door, 'that I go now.'

'I think you better had. I'm sure you'll understand if I don't see you out.'

Tilly picked up her book. She did not move until she heard the front door close. She felt like a Christian who's lost all faith. Robin had been her hero, her life, her one true love and now he was merely another cowardly philanderer who couldn't even admit what he'd done. What had happened to the glorious, confident boy who always spoke his mind and who was always in control? That friend of Charlotte's was right: love was a con trick.

She went upstairs to say goodnight to Lucy.

Lucy smiled sleepily. 'We had pink ice cream for lunch.'

Tilly tucked the duvet round Lucy's shoulders. 'Granny always gives you lovely things to eat,' she said.

'Yes,' said Lucy, 'but she's very bossy. She made Daddy clear up every tiny bit of mud, and when he said he'd finished she made him do it some more.'

Tilly smiled. 'I bet he loved that!'

'No, he didn't. I could tell!' Lucy's eyelids drooped and closed. Tilly kissed her forehead lightly and tiptoed out of the room.

She went back down to the sitting room. The fire gave it a warm, enticing glow. What a waste of time that had been, she thought, and then remembered her list. No more self-pity. She would enjoy the fire on her own, she might as well get used to enjoying things on her own. In fact she hoped Robin and Louise would be very happy. That was rubbish, of course. Tilly hoped they'd be achingly, gruesomely, destructively miserable. She hoped Robin would come back to her on his hands and knees and beg her to take him back so she could tell him she'd rather marry Keith Chegwin or Attila the Hun.

She felt as if she'd received some seismic revelation. Robin was a rat. And if Robin was a rat, it was time to stop blaming herself for everything that had gone wrong. She might be all those things she thought Charlotte thought she was, but the fact remained that Robin was a rat. Everything was different. Her life had exploded and only the children, the three children, remained. Their security, their happiness was paramount. No more self-pity and actually, Tilly thought, precious little empathy for the time being.

'The point is,' she told Rhona on Tuesday, 'you managed brilliantly after Mark left you. I can cope, I know it.'

'I only had Chloe,' Rhona said doubtfully. 'You'll have three children under ten. Will you give up work?'

'I can't. I thought I'd start looking at things I can do at home as well – you know, like filling envelopes or something. I don't want to depend on Mum for child-minding.'

Rhona began collecting up her files for the next lesson. 'I might be able to help you there,' she said. 'I'm thinking of leaving Hurstfield and setting up at home as a childminder.'

'You're thinking of what? Excuse me?' Tilly stared incredulously at her friend. She wondered if there was something funny in the water: first Robin, then her mother, now Rhona. All of them had gone mad. 'I've never heard anything so crazy. You're a qualified special needs teacher. You're a very good special needs teacher! Why on earth would you give up a job you love in order to stay at home all day, changing nappies of other peoples' babies? You'd go mad!'

'Well, don't say anything to Arthur about it,' Rhona said. 'I haven't finally decided yet. I must go.' She reached for her pencil case and Tilly noticed a large purple bruise on her wrist.

'Ouch!' Tilly said. 'How did you do that?'

Rhona laughed. 'My darling daughter! She came round at

the weekend to pick up some books and managed to slam the door on my arm. I don't *think* she meant to do it!'

'Does she come round a lot?'

'Only when she wants something! It never fails to amaze me how self-absorbed teenagers are . . . I was talking away to Chloe the other day and she was looking at her reflection in the mirror the whole time.'

'So would I,' Tilly said, 'if I looked like her.'

The end-of-break bell rang and Tilly stood up. 'Would you and Nigel and the gorgeous Chloe like to come to lunch with me on Sunday? I could do with the company.'

Rhona hesitated. 'No!' she said. 'I have a better idea! You come to us. We'll have a party!'

On Sunday morning Rhona rang to say she had a migraine. She apologized profusely and Tilly said it didn't matter at all, she had lots of cleaning to do. Tilly put down the phone and thought about the long, empty day that stretched ahead of her. She hated being without the children. She had done copious amounts of cleaning yesterday. The house looked shiny and polished and empty.

No self-pity. Tilly squared her shoulders, put on her coat and her scarf and went out to the car. The last time she had been to White Sheet Hill, it had been a hot summer's day and the children had spent their time chasing after the gaily coloured kites littering the sky, while Horace had chased joyfully and fruitlessly after rabbits.

Today, Tilly was pleased to find she had the place to herself. She parked the car and walked up the stony, chalk track. Two hundred years ago, this had been a major route to Salisbury. Hundreds of years before that there had been

Bronze Age settlements, and hundreds and hundreds of years before that Stone Age people had set up residence in this very spot. And now here was Tilly wondering if Stone Age house-wives had to deal with adultery and betrayal.

The view at the top was worth the walk. On the one side were the rolling flanks of the Wiltshire Downs and on the other, the lush woods and farmland of Somerset. Tilly breathed in the air and raised her face to the morning sun. She ought to do this more often.

She began to walk towards the shallow crater which had probably once been the site of an Iron Age fort. It was only when she reached the rim that she saw the body.

Tilly shut her eyes and opened them again. She had not imagined it. The body lay spreadeagled on its front as if some-one had dropped it from a great height. It was dressed in blue jeans and a black leather jacket.

Tilly suppressed an impulse to run back to the car. She walked slowly, soundlessly, towards the corpse and stretched out a shaking hand. The corpse moved. Its head and shoulder turned and Tilly found herself staring into the unblinking blue eyes of Adonis.

'Don't tell me,' he said. 'You've lost your bloody dog again.'

CHAPTER FIFTEEN

'Accident counts for much in companionship as in marriage.'
HENRY ADAMS

Tilly was too surprised to do anything other than answer his question. 'Horace is dead.'

Adonis turned himself languidly onto his back and propped himself up on his elbows. 'Now why doesn't that surprise me?'

Tilly stared at him outraged. 'What is it with you?' she demanded. 'Do you enjoy being so unpleasant? There is no excuse for anyone to be as rude as you are.'

'Yes, there is. I left my wife three hours ago.'

'That's no excuse at all, and anyway you were rude long before that.' Tilly struggled to her feet with some difficulty. 'My husband left *me* weeks and weeks ago and I don't go round being rude to complete strangers.'

'Yes, you do. You barge in on me when I clearly want to be alone.'

'I thought you were dead!'

'Why would I be dead?' Adonis began to brush strands of grass from his sweater.

'You *looked* dead! Funnily enough, most people don't choose to lie motionless on wet grass in remote places.'

Adonis sniffed loudly. 'You're here so it isn't remote and the ground isn't wet. I was trying to commune with the spirits of my ancestors. Not easy to do when some overweight housewife starts—'

'I am not overweight, I am *pregnant*! No wonder your wife threw you out, and don't tell me you wanted to leave because I don't believe it. The woman must have been crazy to put up with you for as long as she did. And I came here to get some peace and harmony so you'll understand if I walk away from you as far and as fast as I can!'

Tilly turned on her heel. She was rather pleased with that last little speech. It was an exhilarating novelty for someone so indelibly polite to shout at a stranger, particularly since he deserved every insult she could throw at him.

She heard him running towards her and turned sharply. 'What do you think you're doing? Go away!'

He fell in by her side. 'Where are you going?'

'For a *quiet* walk.'

'I'll join you,' he said. 'Why did your husband leave you?'

Tilly decided the best policy was to ignore him. She raised her head in the air and promptly tripped over a rabbit hole. Adonis caught her arm and she thanked him stiffly.

'Why did he leave you?' Adonis repeated mildly.

'Not that it's any of your business,' Tilly said loftily. 'He was angry when I told him I was pregnant.'

'Why? Who's the father?'

Tilly turned on him indignantly. 'Well, for goodness sake! He is the father! He thought I got pregnant deliberately and I didn't. But anyway that wasn't the real reason. He's fallen for someone else, only he was too pathetic to tell me.'

'So . . . basically, he grew bored of you.'

Tilly narrowed her eyes. 'Not half as bored as your wife got with you.'

'My wife didn't get bored,' Adonis said. 'She simply began to see me through the eyes of a loathsome apology of a man. We were fine before her brother came along.'

'And *we* were fine before his parents moved down here.'

'That,' Adonis opined, 'sounds like an excuse.'

'In that case,' Tilly said crossly, 'so is your brother-in-law.'

Adonis shook his head. 'That's different.'

'Oh, for heaven's sake!' Tilly stopped walking and put her hands on her hips. 'Why don't you just go back and carry on communing with your ancestors, except they're probably not your ancestors because you look as if you're descended from Viking hooligans and they never had any manners either.' She wound her scarf tightly round her neck and began to walk towards her car.

Adonis took her arm. 'How did you annoy your husband?'

'Who says I annoyed him?' demanded Tilly, shaking off his hand.

'It stands to reason. If everything had been fine before your in-laws came along it wouldn't have gone wrong when they *did* come along.'

'We were fine! I mean, you can't live with someone for any period of time without annoying each other occasionally, but most of the time we were fine.'

Adonis frowned. 'What is fine? Is it fine in that we don't hate each other, or fine in that we occasionally have a good laugh, or fine in that we have wonderful, orgasmic sex every night of the week?'

Tilly rolled her eyes. 'If you're going to tell me you have wonderful, orgasmic sex every night then, I'm sorry, I don't believe you. No one has seven-nights-a-week sex once a child comes along . . . and don't smile that smug smile because it's incredibly irritating. There is . . . there *was* nothing wrong with my sex life! Why am I telling you this?'

'So why did you annoy your husband?'

Tilly flung out her arms in exasperation. 'I don't know! He didn't like the dust on the mantelpiece and he wished the kitchen surfaces were free of clutter, but that was his fault because I bought some shelves for the kitchen and he never got round to putting them up. He wished I could earn more money. He wished I could cook better too, I expect. He probably found me boring and dull and sexless and fat and, worst of all, I let Horace die!' Tilly burst into tears and reached into her coat pocket for a tissue.

Adonis watched impassively while she blew her nose. 'How did you let Horace die?'

'I failed to notice a hole in the fence behind the compost heap. Horace got out and then he got run over.'

'Poor old Horace. Would you like me to put up your shelves for you?'

'What?'

'Where do you live?'

'Just outside Frome.'

'Good. I could do with a lift. I hitched a ride here. You take me home with you and give me lunch and I'll put up your shelves for you.'

Tilly regarded him doubtfully. 'Do you *know* how to put up shelves?'

'It's what I do best.'

Tilly gave a watery smile. 'You sound like Tigger!'

'Tigger?'

'In *Winnie-the-Pooh*. Don't tell me you've never read *Winnie-the-Pooh*. No, of course you haven't. What's your name?'

'Graham. Why are you smiling?'

They had reached the car now. Tilly said, 'You don't look like a Graham. You're more like a Dan or a Jake or a Luke.'

'What's your name?'

'Tilly.'

'Tilly!' Graham made a sound that could possibly be a laugh. 'Makes you sound like a baby. That's probably your problem. What's it short for?'

'Matilda.'

'Then I'll call you Matilda. Let's go.'

As they climbed into her car, Tilly couldn't decide whether she was at last being decisive in agreeing to give him lunch or indecisive in allowing him to overrule her hesitation. At least his company had to be marginally better than her own. Unless he was mad. Which, judging by the course their conversation had taken, was a distinct possibility.

Neither of them said anything on the way home but Tilly found his silence unembarrassing. It was only as she drew up outside her house that she asked him with genuine interest, 'Why were you so rude to me when I was looking for Horace?'

'I didn't like you.'

'Oh,' Tilly said, and climbing out of the car she shut the door with unnecessary force.

Graham got out of his side and stared at her as if she were stupid. 'I like you *now*,' he said.

Mollified, Tilly found her house key and opened the door. Graham followed her through to the kitchen, looking around him like a dog sniffing the air. 'Who chose the paint?' he asked.

'It was here when we came,' Tilly said. 'Why, what's wrong with it?'

Graham shrugged. 'Where do you want the shelves to go?'

Tilly showed him. Graham tapped the wall a few times and nodded. 'Right. Let's have lunch first. What are we eating?'

'Will mushroom omelettes be all right?'

'Yes. I'm hungry.'

'Well, give me ten minutes and I'll . . .' But Graham had already unlocked the back door and gone out into the garden.

Tilly assembled the ingredients and began to wipe the mushrooms. Glancing out of the window she saw Graham performing what she could only suppose was shadow-boxing or kung-fu or karate. She hoped she hadn't been mistaken in taking him home with her.

Over lunch, which Graham ate in the manner of a man who's been shipwrecked for a month, Tilly asked politely, 'Where do you live? I mean, where are you going to live?'

Graham paused with his fork in the air. 'Why? Are you inviting me to stay here?'

'That,' Tilly said coldly, 'is not funny.'

'I don't know.' Graham swept his plate with his last lettuce leaf. 'If it's any consolation, there are some men who would be very excited by your invitation. There are some men who find pregnant women very attractive.' The lettuce leaf disappeared into his mouth. 'I'm not one of them.'

Tilly sat back in her chair and folded her arms. 'Well, I'm sure I'm disappointed to hear that. And for the record, that wasn't an invitation.'

'It's nothing personal,' Graham assured her. 'Now, where's your tool box?'

'I'll get it,' said Tilly. She went out to the shed and after an exhaustive search found it under an unopened bag of potting compost. She caught sight of Horace's basket, lurching drunkenly against the logs, and she felt a yearning for his sweet nature and his soft fur. The sound of the telephone made her jump and she struggled back to the kitchen with the tool box.

Graham was sitting with his feet on the table and the phone jammed to his ear. '. . . I'm a friend of Matilda . . . There's no reason why you should. Can I give her a message? Wait a moment . . .' Without moving the receiver from his mouth he yelled at Tilly, who now stood beside him, 'Matilda? Do you *want* to speak to your husband?'

Tilly scowled at Graham and snatched the phone. 'Hello, Robin. Are the children all right?'

Robin sounded put out. 'Tilly, who *is* that man?'

Tilly said coldly, 'A friend.'

'He's very odd. Where the hell did you meet him?'

'That doesn't really concern you, does it? What do you want?'

There was a moment's silence and then, 'Just to say I'll bring the kids back about five. I take it you'll be there?'

'Of course I will.'

'Right. It's just you weren't there this morning when I rang.'

'I wasn't expecting the children back this morning.'

'No. Well, I'll see you later, then.'

'Goodbye, Robin.' Tilly hastily replaced the receiver and turned to Graham.

Graham rolled up his sleeves. 'Shall we get on?'

Robin brought the children back at half past four. Graham and Tilly were having a cup of tea. Lucy let go of her father's hand and raced up to Graham. 'You're Jack's dad!'

'I am!' Graham extended a hand. 'You can call me Graham.'

'He's very clever,' Tilly said warmly. 'Look what he's done!'

Graham had indeed surprised Tilly by the speed and the skill he had shown. They had spent the last half-hour squabbling amicably about what Tilly should put *on* the shelves. Graham had watched her pull out her saucepans from the depth of the corner cupboard and had then told her flatly that they were far too hideous to put out on display. He had extracted her three casserole dishes and two fruit bowls. Annoyingly, he was right. They looked much better.

Robin gave Graham a wary smile. 'That's very kind of you to help Tilly.'

'Oh,' Graham said easily, 'I like to help Matilda.'

'Robin,' Tilly said quickly, 'could you give Graham a lift to Frome?'

Graham stood up. 'I ought to go now.'

Robin, who had just sat down, stood up again. 'Well, then, it looks like I'm off. See you next weekend, kids.'

'Goodbye, Daddy,' Lucy said easily. She pulled at Graham's sleeve. 'You can bring Jack next time.'

'I will,' Graham said. 'I might bring him to tea on Wednesday after school. Would that be all right, Matilda?'

'Yes, of course,' said Tilly, feeling like someone who's been swept up by an implacable typhoon.

'Good.' Graham surprised Tilly further by leaning forward

197

and kissing her on the cheek. 'Take care,' he said with a tenderness that Tilly knew was entirely simulated. He straightened himself and nodded carelessly to Robin. 'Shall we go?'

Robin looked as bewildered as Tilly felt. 'Goodbye, then. I haven't had time to ask you how you are, Tilly. Still feeling sick?'

'No,' Tilly said.

'Tilly,' Robin told Graham, 'is expecting a baby.'

Graham nodded. 'I was saying to Matilda over lunch that I find pregnant women unbelievably erotic.'

'What does erotic mean?' Lucy asked.

'Graham,' Tilly said, fixing him with a fierce eye, 'I thought you said you needed to go immediately? We'll come and see you out.' She marched both men from the house and watched Robin drive off. Graham, sitting in the passenger seat, waved sweetly at her.

After they'd gone she felt unaccountably elated. She had no time to analyse her mood since Sam wished to show her the bruise he'd acquired on his knee and Lucy wanted to describe the trip they had made to the cinema on Saturday, their visit to the playground earlier in the day, the lunch they had eaten and Sam's behaviour during the said lunch.

For the first time in what seemed like months Tilly had an entirely uncontroversial evening with the children: no sulks, no tantrums, no arguments. Tilly couldn't help wondering whether much of their recent bad behaviour had been more a reflection of and a reaction to her own moods rather than theirs. There was no doubt about it: unhappiness was contagious. She must remember to add 'Do not be unhappy' to her list of resolutions. It was time to be positive. On the plus side, she was no longer being sick. On the minus side, her tummy seemed to be swelling far too quickly. With Lucy, she had hardly shown anything in the first five months. She could remember feeling quite aggrieved; she had been so eager to start wearing maternity clothes. Stop it, she told herself, forget about the minuses.

Later, when the children had gone to bed, Tilly made herself some cheese on toast. She switched on the television and watched a drama about a group of twenty-somethings who were all desperate to meet their Mr Right. No one seems to care, Tilly mused, how you live with Mr Right once you've caught him.

She heard the doorbell and wondered if it might be Robin (No, I won't have you back unless you prostrate yourself at my feet) or Graham (No, you can't stay here) or her neighbour (Yes, of course you can borrow some more milk). She opened the door.

'Hello, darling.' Margot held a suitcase in either hand. 'Do you mind if I stay with you for a bit? I've left your father.'

CHAPTER SIXTEEN

'Advice is seldom welcome; and those who want it the most always like it the least.'

LORD CHESTERFIELD

Tilly stood in front of the two-for-the-price-of-one pizzas. On the one hand she had not intended to buy any pizzas and she was trying very hard these days to only purchase items on her shopping list. On the other hand she might well want to buy a pizza in a fortnight and who could tell if they would still be on special offer? She thought for a moment, took out her pencil, added pizza to the list and grabbed two boxes.

She looked up and smiled at the man next to her. 'Nigel!' she said. 'How are you?'

'I'm very well, thank you.' He manoeuvred his trolley away from the centre of the aisle. 'Rhona and I did enjoy that evening we had with you.'

'It seems a long time ago.'

'Yes.' Nigel obviously found small talk difficult. 'Do you often do your shopping at this time?'

'Hardly ever. But I've got my mother staying at the moment and it's too good an opportunity to miss. If I have Sam with me, my trolley becomes full of things like jelly babies and Coco Pops!' She hesitated. 'Actually, I'm glad I've seen you. I . . . well, it sounds silly really, but I'm a little worried about Rhona.'

'Rhona? Why?' The polite tone had disappeared faster than melted butter from a knife. She had his full attention. No question, the man was crazy about the girl. 'Has she said anything? What's wrong?'

Tilly hastened to reassure him. 'No, no, she's very happy, don't get me wrong. She's happier than I've ever known her to be. It's only that she's talking about giving up teaching and it seems so ridiculous. She's a brilliant teacher: the kids all love her and she gets fantastic results. She says she might become a child-minder instead and I can't for the life of me understand why. She's always loved her job. It would be such a waste.'

'I think . . .' Nigel paused, scratched his head and sighed. 'Do you mind if I speak frankly to you?'

'Not at all.' Tilly gave him an encouraging smile and wished he wouldn't look at her so fixedly. She was finding his unremitting concentration mildly oppressive.

'Rhona,' Nigel said slowly, 'is a woman who seems very strong and capable and compassionate. She *is* compassionate, she *does* care. Everyone comes to her for advice. I know, for example, that you do.'

'Well, yes,' Tilly admitted, 'but . . .'

'I'm not saying you shouldn't but I don't think you – or anyone else for that matter – realize how draining it is for her. Rhona cares too much. She gets worried and preoccupied and then she gets headaches. She has one this evening, which is why I'm doing the shopping. In her job she is constantly worrying about the children in her care. She feels responsible and, to be perfectly honest, it's beginning to get her down.'

Tilly frowned. 'I had no idea Rhona felt like this. She always seems so cheerful.'

Nigel raised his eyebrows. 'Of course she does! She'd hate people to think she wasn't! That's what she's like. It's only with me that she lets her mask drop.'

'Oh.' Tilly stood aside to let a plump woman with too much perfume reach out for a bag of fresh fettuccine. She looked at Nigel and said with a forced lightness, 'You make me feel terrible. I had no idea Rhona got so upset about things. I thought . . . well, I suppose I always thought she could confide in me . . . as I do in her.'

Nigel shrugged. 'That's Rhona! She puts on a brave face for the world. And she'd be furious if she knew I'd talked to you like this, so please don't tell her. The truth is that Rhona's far more fragile than everyone seems to think. She needs a rest. I hope you know I wouldn't let her make any decision I didn't feel was absolutely right for her.' He glanced at his watch and cleared his throat. 'I must get on. I told Rhona I'd only be a few minutes. Don't worry about her. She has me to look after her now.'

'Right.' Tilly nodded unhappily.

'By the way,' Nigel said, 'I was so sorry to hear that Robin had left you.'

'Thank you,' said Tilly. She watched him wheel his trolley round the corner. She glanced across at the Chardonnay, reduced from £4.99 to £3.99, and pushed her trolley quickly towards the checkout. Nigel was in the next-door queue. She could think of nothing at all to say to him and so spent the next few minutes pretending to rummage around in her bag for her wallet. By the time she reached the car she felt like a piece of elastic that has lost its bounce.

All the way home she kept replaying his comments. He seemed to be suggesting that too many people, and most especially Tilly Taylor, dumped all their problems onto a wilting Rhona. The Rhona he described seemed utterly unlike the friend Tilly had known for the last three years. Of course it was true that human beings were complicated and often behaved quite differently with different people. Tilly knew, for example, that with Charlotte, she herself could be truculent and defensive, without a shred of humour. In Amy's presence she tended to be the naive younger woman, a perfect foil for Amy's cynicism. With Rhona, she was more assured and decisive, a never-ending fount of sensible advice. Both Amy and Rhona were close friends, partly because they made Tilly feel good about herself. They brought out what she liked to think were her more likeable characteristics. If your best friends couldn't make you feel good about yourself then they shouldn't be best friends.

Tilly loved Rhona because she seemed to find Tilly's life every bit as fascinating as Tilly found Rhona's. Now, Nigel seemed to be saying that Tilly's problems gave Rhona a headache. How had Tilly got Rhona so wrong? It was all unutterably depressing and, as Tilly drove home, the only clear conclusion she came to was that she didn't like Nigel. She didn't like him at all.

At school the next day Rhona was nowhere to be seen. Tilly felt a mixture of disappointment and relief. At least, she thought, as she sat next to Joseph in Period One, she knew where she was with Joseph and Joseph knew where he was with her. Both of them knew his French was as bad as ever.

Ten minutes into the lesson, Arthur popped his head round

the door and nodded significantly at her. Tilly murmured to Joseph, 'I won't be a moment,' and walked over to Arthur.

'Tilly,' Arthur whispered, 'I'd like a little word. Do you mind if I drag you away from Joseph's French for a moment?'

Tilly didn't mind at all. She had spent the last five minutes trying to explain the mystery of verb endings to Joseph and felt as if she had thrown herself against a brick wall too many times for safety. With any luck Arthur's little word might extend to the end of the lesson.

In the corridor Arthur leant against the wall, folded his arms and sighed. 'I'm very worried about Rhona,' he said.

Tilly frowned. 'Has she called in sick? I haven't seen her this morning. I know she had a migraine at the weekend.'

'She says she has flu.'

'Don't you think she has?'

Arthur looked hurt. 'Of course I do. I know Rhona too well. If Rhona says she has flu then of course I accept she has flu. What concerns me rather more is that she's handed in her notice. She says she wishes to leave at the end of the school year. Quite honestly, I'm staggered. Has she said anything to you?'

'Yes,' Tilly said, 'but I didn't take it seriously. I think perhaps I should have done. She was talking about child-minding.'

'Why would she want to do that? It doesn't make sense.' Arthur looked genuinely perplexed. 'I want you to talk to her, find out what's really wrong. I don't have to advertise before next term and I'd hate to see her go. She's good at her job. She loves her job. Go and talk to her, Tilly.'

Tilly nodded. 'I will. I'll go today. When I finish here.' Arthur's reaction to Rhona's news was like a tonic. Why, after all, should Nigel know Rhona better than she did? He'd only met her a few months ago, for heaven's sake.

Arthur patted her arm. 'Good, good. I must let you get back to Joseph. And sometime soon we must discuss your plans for the future, in the light of . . .' He waved a hand in the direction of Tilly's bump, smiled awkwardly and beat a rather hasty retreat down the stairs. His embarrassment was entirely understandable since Tilly had never actually told him she was pregnant. She had thought she was safe for a while yet. Presumably, her dashes to the cloakroom had been noticed, along with her expanding tummy.

She should have said something to him weeks ago. Her inability to do so was all a part of her unwillingness to make any long-term plans. The future seemed to be some cold, impenetrable country for which she had no maps or compass. To be honest she had never thought she'd need them. She had Robin. She *had* had Robin. And now Robin was looking after Louise's maps and compass. Except, of course, Louise would never want or need anyone to look after her maps and compass. Perhaps that was her attraction. Apart from her beauty. And her intelligence. And her sweet personality. And her financial self-sufficiency. Tilly returned abruptly to the classroom. 'Hi, Joseph!' she said. 'Let's have a great time with French verbs!'

Rhona's front garden had been ruthlessly tamed, presumably by Nigel since Rhona's idea of gardening was to prune the weeds every few months. Now they had been eliminated, leaving the borders subdued and empty. The small patch of lawn, now fully revealed, lay clipped and oddly vulnerable. The garden, Tilly felt, liked Nigel as little as she did.

Tilly rang the doorbell, waited for half a minute and rang again. She turned back towards the road, saw Rhona's car and retraced her steps. She could hear the measured tones of a Radio 4 newsreader in the kitchen, and when she glanced at the upstairs window she could swear she saw a curtain twitch.

She bent down and opened the letter-box flap. 'Rhona? Are you in there? Please let me in.' She could almost feel the house hold its breath. 'Rhona! Are you all right? Do you need a doctor? Rhona, please answer me.' Tilly paused and then tried again, fear making her voice unnaturally loud. 'Rhona, don't worry, I'm going to get help. I'll be there in a minute, all right? If you're really ill we'll get you sorted. Don't worry!'

'Wait!' The voice was unmistakably Rhona's and was followed by the sound of footsteps on the stairs. 'Tilly,' Rhona was now on the other side of the door, 'I'm here, I'm fine, don't get anyone. Please go away. I'm fine.'

'Good. That's great. Can I come in for a few minutes?'

There was a short silence. 'I'm really not well. You'd better go.'

'I will. I only came for a quick chat.'

Another pause. 'I have a virus. I'm contagious.'

'Good, you can breathe all over me and I'll make sure Robin gets my germs next week. Come on, Rhona, let me in. I'm feeling pretty silly shouting into a letter box. People,' she added craftily, 'are beginning to stare.'

Rhona was wearing a faded blue dressing gown over green-and-grey-striped pyjamas. Her hair fell limply over her face but failed to disguise a large, discolouring bruise on one side of it. Her left eye was streaked with thin red lines as if someone had thrown paint at it.

Rhona caught Tilly's appalled gaze and said quickly, 'I fell and hit my face on the coffee table. Pretty stupid, I know!'

'Ouch!' Tilly winced in sympathy. 'It looks horrible.'

'Thank you,' Rhona said drily. 'Actually, it's not too bad. I've only myself to blame. I'm getting really clumsy in my old age!' She smiled nervously, an unfamiliar smile in which the lips stretched slightly while the eyes strained anxiously. 'Do you fancy a cup of tea before you go?'

Tilly settled herself at the breakfast bar and listened politely while Rhona continued to rail against her curious lack of coordination. There was a hiatus while Rhona threw tea bags into two mugs, poured boiling water on them, then threw out the tea bags. Rhona handed Tilly one of the mugs and Tilly thought about asking for milk but decided against it.

Rhona sat down on the other side of the bar. 'I'm sorry I had a migraine on Sunday,' she said. 'I meant to give you the perfect Sunday lunch as well, roast chicken *and* bread sauce!'

'So,' Tilly took a sip of her tea and tried not to grimace at the taste, 'did Nigel hit you on Saturday evening or earlier?'

Rhona's face turned brick red. 'Tilly! What *are* you talking about?'

Tilly put her mug to one side and leant forward. 'Look, I know I'm forever blabbing on about my own problems and it's quite understandable that you think I'm too stupid to see that a bruised wrist and a beaten-up face are not the results of bumping into furniture. But what I don't understand is why you're trying to protect the man who did this to you.'

Rhona bit her lip hard. 'You're trying to make a huge melodrama out of nothing at all.'

The kitchen tap had been releasing one teardrop of water every three seconds. Tilly stood up and moved to the sink to turn it off. 'Do you remember the day we found Stuart Miller beating up Andrew Maggs by the games hut? You told Stuart that anyone who hits someone just because he can does not deserve to be called a human being. You told him that the lowest form of human life was the bully. You were brilliant. Well, Nigel is just another Stuart Miller, so what the hell are you doing covering up for him?'

Rhona said nothing. Tilly fished out the discarded tea bags from the sink and threw them into the kitchen bin, which was lined with a proper bin-bag instead of Rhona's usual supermarket ones. Nigel had apparently colonized the house as well as the garden. A strangulated sound made Tilly turn round and Rhona whispered, 'He loves me,' before breaking into ugly rasping sobs.

Tilly couldn't bear it. She knelt down and threw her arms round Rhona without saying anything, because the murderous indignation she felt towards Nigel must, she knew, be sheathed for the time being. At last she rose and found a glass of water. 'You know,' she said carefully, handing Rhona the glass, 'I'm sure Nigel thinks he loves you. But it's a funny sort of love that inflicts pain and humiliation. It's not what I call love.'

Rhona gave a little exhalation of breath. It reminded Tilly of Lucy; she always signalled the termination of a tantrum by the same tired sigh.

'He gets jealous,' Rhona said. She began to trace a crack on the breakfast bar with her finger. 'It's not his fault, he can't help himself. He feels everything so intensely, you know? He told me he left the army because he couldn't bear the misery he saw. He does love me, Tilly, whatever you say, he really does and I've let him down. If you knew what his life's been like you'd understand. His mother ran off with someone else when he was only six and she's never tried to make contact since. His father took all her things and burnt them in front of Nigel and his brother. He brought them up to believe that all women are callous and cruel and never to be trusted. Is it any wonder that Nigel is like he is? He's so damaged he can't believe anyone can love him and yet he can't bear the thought I might not. Every time he loses his temper he feels dreadful afterwards. If you could have seen him after –' Rhona pointed to her face – 'after he did this. He was crying, Tilly, he said he wanted to kill himself.'

'And next time he'll probably kill *you*! Rhona, this is crazy. There is never, ever, any justification for unprovoked aggression. Even if he had the most deprived childhood in the history of man there is still no excuse.'

'I'm not justifying, I'm trying to explain.'

'So was Stuart Miller and I seem to remember you shut him up pretty fiercely.'

'I wish you'd stop going on about Stuart Miller. Nigel is my husband. My first marriage failed and I don't want my second one to. If I can make him see he has no need to worry—'

'He never *did* have any reason to worry. How can you stop his worries when they're totally irrational in the first place? You can give up work at school, you can become a hermit at home and renounce all contact with the outside world and it still won't be enough, it never will be enough. I mean look at Othello! And Nigel doesn't even have an Iago!'

'Tilly,' Rhona said, 'what are you going on about?'

'I'm saying that I can't believe you are actually giving up your career! And for what?'

Rhona gave a crooked smile. 'For love?' she offered.

Tilly snorted rudely. 'I'm beginning to think love is just an excuse for all sorts of rubbish behaviour. Robin loves Louise so it's all right for him to abandon his children and his wife. Dad loves Mum so it's fine for him to tell her she's stupid all the time because, hey, everyone knows he loves her. And you love Nigel so it's fine if you ruin everything else in your life, your job, your home, Chloe . . .'

'That's not true, I wouldn't let anything happen to Chloe!'

'I know you wouldn't,' Tilly said quickly, 'but Chloe obviously felt something was wrong otherwise why would she decide to move in with her father?'

Rhona stood up and tightened the belt of her dressing gown. 'Tilly, I didn't ask you to come here and I didn't ask for your advice about my daughter or my husband. And since your marriage has turned out to be a complete failure, I don't think you're entitled to tell me how to make mine better. Now please just leave me alone.'

'All right,' Tilly said. 'I was only trying to help. This isn't right. You know it isn't right!'

'Tilly!' Rhona glared at her. 'Will you please leave my house?'

'I'm going,' Tilly said. 'I'm sorry I bothered you.' She walked out of the room and through the front door without looking back. She was furious with Nigel, furious with Rhona and furious with herself for handling it all so badly.

Tilly's father rang that evening and Tilly said awkwardly, 'Hello, Dad. How are you?'

'Bearing up, you know, bearing up! I made myself a rather good lamb stew last night. Not at all bad.'

'Sounds great. You'll have to give me the recipe!'

Harry Treadwell chuckled. 'I made it up! I looked in the fridge and threw things in and it turned out to be delicious. Now, is your mum looking after you?'

'Yes,' said Tilly faintly, 'yes she is.'

'Good. I'm glad to hear it. Could I have a word with her? I think she may have forgotten we were going to the pub quiz night on Saturday.'

'Really?' For the life of her, Tilly could not think of a suitable response. She took the coward's way out. 'I'll go and get Mum. Take care!'

'And you. See you soon!'

Tilly called her mother and tactfully withdrew to the sitting room where she began to clear away Sam's Duplo. She could hear the intonation of her mother's voice as it rose and fell, first polite, then irritable. Tilly stood up and shut the door. She had no wish to be a witness to the death throes of her parents' marriage.

When Tilly returned to the kitchen, her mother was sitting at the table mending a hole in Sam's jumper. Tilly had been studying the jobs pages of the local paper when her father had rung and now she sat down and made a great play of resuming her perusal. Her mother's sigh seemed to indicate a wish for conversation so Tilly said, 'Everything all right?'

Margot shook her head crossly. 'It's like talking to a brick wall. He refuses to accept I've left him. He tells me about the pub quiz so I say I'm not coming to it and he says he'll let me know the date of the next one. I tell him I'm not going to any more quizzes with him and he asks me how long you will need my help because it's his office social in three weeks. I explain to him very simply that my leaving him is nothing to do with you and he says he'll give me a ring in a few days. I mean, what can I do to make him understand what I've done?'

Tilly cleared her throat. She had no idea how she was supposed to talk to this strange, angry woman who had replaced her own amiable mother. 'Perhaps,' she suggested tentatively, 'he can't face the fact you don't want to be with him. I mean, from his point of view, why should you suddenly decide to go?'

Margot looked up sharply. 'Are you saying I've no reason?'

'No, Mum, I'm simply saying that you never showed him how fed up you were before, so why should he understand you now?'

'I told him,' Margot said. 'I was quite clear. I said I couldn't remember the last time I thought I loved him; I said I couldn't remember why I loved him in the first place; I said I realized I didn't enjoy living with him so it was logical to leave.'

Tilly blinked. She actually felt sorry for her father. 'What did he say?' she asked.

'He told me not to worry. He said it was my hormones talking and that I should visit the doctor.'

'Oh,' Tilly said. She no longer felt sorry for her father. 'As a matter of interest, why did you fall in love with Dad?'

Margot narrowed her eyes in thought. 'He seemed to know so much,' she said.

'So why did you stop loving him?'

'Because,' Margot sighed, 'he seemed to know too much.'

Tilly looked at her mother and burst out laughing. Margot grinned and said, 'Really, Tilly, you've made me prick my finger.' She cut the wool, shook out Sam's jumper and folded it neatly.

'Look at us,' Tilly said. 'Who would have thought even a year ago that you and I would be living here together without our husbands?'

'It's funny,' Margot said. 'I never thought you and Robin would split up. You seemed so . . .'

'So what?'

Margot closed the lid of the sewing box. 'You always reminded me of Mummy and Daddy.'

'I know. I thought the same,' Tilly said. 'That was my big mistake.'

In bed that night, Tilly thought about love: how it could make someone like her mother believe she could live happily with someone like her father; how it could turn an independent, sensible woman like Rhona into a battered dupe; how it could make her betrayed self continue to miss Robin's presence in bed beside her even though she'd never have him back in a million years. Possibly.

None of it would matter, of course, if it weren't for the children. Nature might have been fiendishly clever in making people fall in love with each other but it should have done something to make the magic last until the children grew up. In fact, Tilly thought bitterly, Nature should take a look at Sam, who was wetting the bed at night, and Lucy, whose tempers and truculence were painfully transparent signs of her shattered security.

Last week Tilly had been sitting in on a Year Five English class. The teacher was reading a story about a fairy who could make one wish come true for a man and his wife. When she'd finished the story, the teacher said, 'Let's ask Mrs Taylor what she'd wish for if the good fairy came to see her!'

Startled, Tilly said lightly, 'A new washing machine?'

The teacher, as unimpressed as the class by Tilly's answer, turned to her pupils, 'What about everyone else? Keira, what about you?'

Keira said, 'I'd like a dog with a big tail!'

'That would be nice! And what about you, Ben? What would you like?'

'I'd like a PlayStation Two!'

The teacher gave a merry laugh. 'My son wants one of those! Anyone else? Simon? What would you like?'

Simon had round glasses that kept falling off the edge of his nose. He looked at his teacher and his mouth quivered and he said, 'I'd like my daddy to come home. And I'd like my mum to stop getting cross with me all the time.' He bit his lip. 'I want my daddy.' Then he started to cry.

Two tables in front of him, Hannah Skinner let out a cry. 'I'd like *my* daddy to come home.'

'So would I!' said Luke Austin.

Then another child started weeping. The teacher looked round her class, like a tourist who's inadvertently started a bush fire. She turned for help to Tilly and hissed desperately, 'Why are *you* crying?'

'I'm sorry,' Tilly whispered, furiously blowing her nose, 'but I'd like my husband to come home.'

CHAPTER SEVENTEEN

'One change leaves the way open for the introduction of others.'
MACHIAVELLI

Clutching a bag of cod fillet in one hand and Sam's wrist in the other, Tilly walked down the street and peered through the large window of the Curved Wheel. She could see Amy sitting straight and intent like a noble queen in her palace. Indeed, she looked so noble and intent that Tilly was about to move on without disturbing her. Then the queen yawned and so Tilly knocked on the window.

Amy turned, smiled broadly and beckoned Tilly in. Tilly opened the door and stood aside to let out the only other occupant, a bald-headed man in a dark suit and a red tie. Amy bent down to give Sam a hug. 'Come in, come in! I am so bored, you wouldn't believe it! Look, Sam, here's a box of toys for you to play with.' She glanced up at Tilly. 'Do you know, there were no toys for children when I came here? I said to them, "Do you think young mothers aren't interested in Art?"'

Tilly raised her eyebrows. 'I'm not sure young mothers *are* interested in Art. In my experience, young mothers are too tired to be interested in Art.'

'Yes, but you're a philistine,' said Amy, 'and anyway you're over thirty so you don't qualify as a young mother.'

'You don't need to remind me. We've just come from the antenatal clinic. The other mums look as if they've just left school. I keep reading that women are having babies later these days. How come I live in the one part of Britain where you're considered a freak if you're over twenty-one and pregnant?' Tilly picked out a shape-sorting toy for Sam. 'Look, Sam, do you know how to get the blocks out? And then you have to put them through the correct holes.'

'Me know,' said Sam, pulling them out. 'Me do it at playgroup.' He sat on the floor, legs splayed out and began forcing a triangular shape into a square-shaped hole.

Tilly looked about her and sat down. 'I love this place,' she said. 'Neutral walls, neutral floor, neutral pots. It's so peaceful.'

'It is peaceful,' Amy agreed. 'It's very peaceful. Very peaceful indeed.' She paused. 'To be perfectly honest, I'm beginning to think peace is rather overrated.'

'Not for me, it isn't.'

'Yes, but that's because you haven't got it. I've had only two people in here this morning. The first was a young man who kept scratching his beard and then his groin. He was wearing a Greenpeace sweatshirt and denim jeans and he had a skull and crossbones key-ring hanging from his pocket. He had terrible skin, greasy hair and a love bite on his neck. I kept wondering what sort of woman would want to give a love bite to a man like that?'

'Plenty!' Tilly said. 'It's only women who have to be good-looking to be sexy. I've always thought that was very unfair.'

'I forgot to tell you,' Amy said darkly. 'He also had BO.'

'Perhaps his girlfriend has sinusitis and can't smell. Perhaps she finds body odour manly.'

'Shall I tell you about my second visitor?'

'I saw him. In a suit and red tie.'

'He's been in three times this week. How does anyone with a job find time to come and look at a collection of pots three times a week?'

'Does he stay long?'

'About twenty minutes. It's always in the morning. I reckon he's either been sacked and is pretending to his wife that he's still working, or he hates his colleagues so much that whenever his anger threatens to overwhelm him he comes here to calm down, or he's hankering after his long-lost love who happened to be a potter. Or perhaps he's in love with me and is too shy to say anything. I hadn't thought of that.'

'Amy,' Tilly said, 'you ought to write a novel.'

Amy sniffed. 'The point is, on mornings like these I'm reduced to making up fantasies about people I don't know and don't even wish to know. I mean, that is very sad, don't you—' She broke off abruptly and her face went into a frozen rictus grin. 'Sam!' she murmured faintly.

Tilly followed Amy's anguished gaze. In the far corner of the gallery Sam had lifted from its plinth a large brown pot and was holding it in front of him. He looked like Pooh Bear about to attack the honey jar. Tilly gulped. 'Sam,' she said levelly. 'Would you mind holding on to that pot very carefully for a few moments?'

'Tilly!' Amy breathed. 'Sam is holding six hundred pounds worth of pot there!'

Sam was aggrieved. 'It not got anything in it!' he said.

Tilly walked over to her son and relieved him of the pot. 'Amy,' she said, 'you don't think it might be worth revising your policy of encouraging young mothers here? Sam, I think it's time we went.'

'Yes,' Sam said, 'it's bowing here.'

'Correction,' Amy retorted. 'It *was* boring here.' She took the pot from Tilly's hands and set it on her desk. 'You don't have to rush off, you know. I haven't had a proper chat with you for ages.'

'I'll tell you something,' Tilly said. 'Do you remember Adonis in the playground? The one who was horrid to me about Horace?'

'Big, blond and good-looking, in a leather jacket? Tiny wife. Yes, of course I do. What's he done now?'

Tilly picked up her fish and took Sam's hand in her own. 'He had lunch with me!'

'What? How? Why? Tilly, you can't leave now, my imagination will go wild!'

'I'll ring you!' Tilly grinned. As she walked back to the car she was still smiling. She rather liked the idea of being a heroine in one of Amy's day dreams. Graham, however, would make a lousy hero, not least because he was totally unreliable. He had not turned up for tea yesterday despite having initiated the invitation on Sunday. The thought of Graham making passionate declarations of love made her laugh out loud and Sam demanded to know what was funny.

'Nothing!' Tilly assured him. 'I'm going mad, that's all.'

'Oh,' said Sam, accepting the explanation without a murmur.

The following Wednesday, at four o'clock, Graham came round with his son.

'Hello,' Tilly said politely. 'How nice to see you.'

'We've come to tea,' Graham said. 'You invited us.'

'I did?' She saw the little boy glance uncertainly at his father, and said quickly, 'Of course I did. Do come in.' She smiled at Graham's son, who stood so stiffly and gravely beside his father. 'You must be . . .'

'This is Jack,' Graham said. 'Say hello to Matilda, Jack.'

'Hello, Matilda,' said Jack.

'Hello, Jack! Well! Lucy and Sam will be pleased to see you! Come on in and we'll find them, shall we?' She led them through to the sitting room where Lucy and Sam were sitting side by side on the sofa, watching a cartoon. 'Look, you two. Isn't this nice? You have a visitor!'

Lucy said hello without taking her eyes from the screen. Sam took his thumb out of his mouth, glanced at Jack, replaced his thumb in his mouth and turned back to the programme. Jack sat down on the edge of the armchair.

'Good!' Tilly said. 'You can all watch this and then we'll have some tea. Good!'

Graham followed his hostess back into the kitchen. Tilly swept Lucy's school bag from the table and glanced anxiously towards the sitting room. 'I hope Jack's all right in there. Lucy isn't usually so unfriendly. She's had a bad day at school. She seems to be having rather a lot of bad days at the moment. Still,' she opened the fridge door to survey the contents, 'you know what children are like. You introduce them to each other and they don't say a word, and when it's time to go they suddenly become bosom pals! Does Jack like cheese on toast?'

'Jack likes anything.' Graham wandered restlessly round the table and added pointedly, 'And so do I.' The room seemed much smaller with him in it. 'You'd forgotten you invited us.'

'I seem to remember,' Tilly said tartly, 'you invited yourself. And anyway that was for last week. I never thought you'd actually come. I assumed you were trying to irritate my husband.'

'I was. What on earth did you see in him?'

'I don't think you bring out his best side.'

'Does he have one?'

Tilly smiled sweetly. 'And how is your dear wife?'

'I don't know,' Graham said, 'and I don't care. I've decided she doesn't deserve someone like me.'

'She'd probably agree with you. So where are you living at the moment?'

'I'm staying with a friend in Station Road. He has a computer.'

'Well, that's all right, then. Do you want a cup of tea?'

'Thank you.' He stopped in front of the new shelves. 'They look good.'

'They do,' Tilly conceded. She added politely, 'It was very kind of you to put them up for me.'

'That's all right. I like you.'

Embarrassed but absurdly pleased, Tilly said, 'Thank you.'

'Even if you do have a rotten taste in husbands.'

Tilly sighed and waved her bread knife at Graham. 'If you want to be friends with me you are going to have to stop being rude about Robin. I am trying very hard to develop a civilized attitude towards him.'

'All right.' Graham pushed back his sleeves. 'Shall I grate the cheese for you?'

'Please. The grater's in the cupboard in front of you.'

'Got it. Matilda?'

'What?'

'I do want to be friends with you.'

'Really?' Tilly grinned suddenly. 'Even though you find me physically repulsive?'

'I never said that!'

'Not that I mind, of course.'

'Quite clearly you do.'

'I do not!'

'I can see you do. Otherwise you wouldn't bring it up. It's a funny thing about women. They always want men to lust over them.'

Tilly put down the bread knife. 'That is absolute rubbish. For your information I genuinely do not care what you think of me.'

'Don't worry.' Graham gave her a kindly smile. 'I do think that, considering you're pregnant, you are not unattractive.'

'You've made my day. And you don't need to grate all that cheese.'

'Yes, I do. I'm very hungry.' He attacked the grater with renewed vigour and finally raised it with a flourish. 'There!' he said. 'Now that's enough!'

Tilly sniffed and put some bread in the toaster.

'Matilda,' Graham said, 'I've offended you.'

'Don't be silly.'

'You are attractive and I do not find you repulsive.'

'I don't care!'

'If someone told me I had to kiss you, I'd do it. Sleep with you: no, I'm sorry.'

'The problem with you,' Tilly said, 'well, one of the many

221

problems with you, is that I can't tell whether you're being serious or not.'

Graham grinned. 'Does it matter?'

'Not in the slightest. Though actually,' she sniffed again, 'in my present state of mind I can do without you telling me I'm unattractive.'

'Matilda, I was joking! Has something happened?'

'No. Nothing's happened. Nothing's happened at all. That's the problem. I'm just feeling rather low.'

'Why?'

Tilly laughed. 'Oh, no reason at all. I mean, why should I be miserable because my husband doesn't love me or find me interesting or fancy me even a little? Why should it concern me that I look in the mirror and feel so ugly? I feel like my life is over, that's all. It's all finished . . . everything: getting dressed up, going to the cinema, candlelit suppers. All I do is watch the news every night and watch my stomach growing bigger. So, I'm absolutely fine and have no right at all to be a touch oversensitive about my looks right now.'

'Listen,' Graham said, 'and I mean this quite seriously. If someone told me I had to sleep with you I wouldn't say no.'

'Thank you,' Tilly said, 'you don't know how much that means to me.'

'The trouble with you,' Graham said, 'is I don't know if you're serious or not.'

'I am definitely not serious.'

'All right. Can I have more than one slice of toast, please?'

'Are you ever not hungry?'

'No. And by the way, if someone told me I didn't have to sleep with you but it would be helpful if I did, I'd do it.'

Lucy appeared in the doorway. 'Mummy,' she said, 'the cartoon is over and we're ready for tea. Why are you laughing?'

'Because Graham's an idiot. Tell the others to come through.'

Tilly did most of the talking during the meal. Lucy was still preoccupied with the sundry injustices meted out to her by treacherous friends and Sam was intent on trying to lick the melted cheese from his toast. Jack's attitude to food was obviously like his father's: a serious business that should not be hampered by small talk. She watched the little boy dispatch his cheese on toast with remarkable speed and asked, 'Would you like a yogurt or some fruit?'

Jack studied the fruit bowl and let his hand hover over a banana before finally selecting an apple.

'Say thank you to Matilda,' Graham said.

Jack turned towards Tilly. 'Thank you, Matilda,' he said.

Lucy scowled. 'Everyone calls her Tilly, not Matilda,' she said.

Graham shrugged. 'I prefer Matilda.'

'Why?' demanded Lucy.

'Because,' Graham said, 'Tilly is a very silly name.'

Lucy's face broke into a wide grin. 'Tilly rhymes with silly!'

'Exactly,' Graham said. 'Tilly is a very silly name and your mother is not silly.'

Lucy nodded wisely. 'Jack's teacher has a silly name.'

Tilly looked at Jack. 'What's your teacher called, Jack?'

Jack blinked. 'Mrs Bendoh.'

'Mrs Bend-Over!' Lucy corrected. 'She's Mrs Bend-Over!' She looked expectantly at Jack and Jack looked back at her. Then he wrinkled his nose and put his hand over his mouth.

'Mrs Bend-Over!' Sam chanted. 'Mrs Bend-Over!'

Strange noises were emanating from Jack's mouth and Tilly realized with delight that he was laughing. In fact all three children began to laugh hysterically. Thank heavens for Mrs Bend-Over.

Lucy said, 'Can I get down and show Jack our toys?'

'If you've all had enough to eat,' Tilly said. 'Sam, are you going to eat that toast? It looks revolting now you've taken all the cheese off.'

'I'll eat it,' Graham said.

'You can eat the rest of my apple, if you like,' Lucy suggested, good humour fully restored.

Graham nodded. 'Pass it over.'

After the children had disappeared, Tilly watched in awe as Graham proceeded to hoover the remains of the tea table. 'You're incredible,' she said. 'You eat nearly as much as Horace did. How can you touch that toast after Sam's been at it?'

'It's all right,' Graham said. He pushed his plate away and licked his fingers. 'I'd better take Jack back to Carmen soon. He likes being here.'

'I like having him. He's done wonders for Lucy. Bring him over any time.'

'I will.' He stood up, stretched and opened the door into the garden. 'I need some fresh air,' he said and stepped out onto the lawn.

Tilly collected up the plates and took them over to the sink. Graham was performing his usual kung-fu kicks on the lawn. She could hear Lucy and the two boys chatting and laughing together in the sitting room.

Graham came back in and said abruptly, 'I'll take you out tomorrow evening.'

224

'Oh,' said Tilly, quite taken aback. 'It's very kind of you but . . .'

'We'll go to the cinema. You *shall* miss the news.'

'It's very kind of you but . . .'

'It's all right,' Graham assured her kindly, 'I don't make passes at pregnant women.'

Tilly blushed hotly. 'I wasn't worried about that!'

'Good! I'll come round about seven. They show foreign language films on Thursdays. Tomorrow, it's going to be *Hidden*; you probably haven't heard of it.'

'Actually,' said Tilly loftily, 'I know it by its French title, *Caché*.'

'Very complicated, apparently. Are you sure you can cope with it?'

'Do you know something, Graham?' Tilly said. 'You are probably the most annoying person in the world.'

A voice called out, 'Who's the most annoying person in the world?' Margot came in carrying a wedge of papers and a folder.

'He is!' Tilly said tersely. Then, reluctantly, she said, 'Mum, this is Graham. He's the one I told you about – you know, the dead man on White Sheet Hill.'

'Well!' Margot's eyes were dancing. 'I have heard so much about you!'

'Really?' Graham was pleased. 'Does she talk about me all the time?'

Tilly raised her eyebrows at Margot. 'You see what he's like?'

'I'm taking her out on a hot date tomorrow evening,' Graham said.

'Good!' Margot exclaimed. 'The hotter the better!'

'Mum!' Tilly shot a scandalized glance at her mother. 'Sometimes I really think I don't know you! Are you really exhorting your daughter to go out and behave badly?'

'Why not?' Margot said briskly. 'It's better than sitting at home and moping over your wretched husband!'

'Mum, you were the one to tell me I should do all I can to save my marriage!'

'I know and you have done. He hasn't! So go out and enjoy yourself.'

Tilly said primly, 'I will go to the cinema with you, Graham, but there will be nothing . . . nothing hot about it.'

'That,' Graham said, 'is a great relief.'

Tilly stared pointedly at the clock. 'Isn't it time you took Jack home?'

'A charming young man,' was Margot's verdict after the visitors had left and the children had been cleaned, read to and tucked up in bed. 'Of course the two of you were flirting outrageously.'

'Mum, Graham couldn't flirt to save his life. We spend the whole time being rude to each other!'

'Exactly. If he helps you forget your husband I shall be eternally grateful to him.'

'You'll regret speaking like this when . . . if . . . Robin and I get back together again.'

'I should take great pleasure in saying it all over again to him.'

'Well, that will entice him back!' Tilly glanced curiously at her mother. 'You're very sparky today!'

'Sparky?'

'Cheerful, confident, dogmatic, sparky! Something's happened!'

Margot said unconvincingly, 'Nothing important. In fact nothing at all!'

'What was the nothing?'

'Well . . . I've been offered a job! I can't believe it! I won't take it, of course, but it's nice to have someone want me. You know I went to tea with Bryony Lansdown? Her husband is a partner with Thringwell and Short in Frome. They need a new receptionist in a few weeks and he asked Bryony to sound me out.'

'Mum, how incredibly flattering! How many hours a week would it be?'

'Full-time. So of course I couldn't do it. It wouldn't be fair on you.'

Four seconds earlier Tilly might have agreed with her but she could hear the wistful note in Margot's voice and she recalled Charlotte's weary assumption that Tilly would always need their mother's help. 'Mum,' she said firmly, 'if you don't ring Bryony Lansdown right now and say you want it, I'll do it for you!'

Margot smiled. 'Don't be silly! You're about to have a baby, you'll need me more than ever.'

'No, I won't. I'm giving up my school job so I shan't need any child-minding.'

'Tilly . . .' Margot hesitated. 'Have you thought about what happens after the baby's born? I mean, have you thought about finances yet?'

Yes, Tilly had thought about finances, she had thought about them a lot, usually at two or three in the morning and every time she had reached the same conclusion: *she didn't know what to do.* 'I have all sorts of ideas,' she said airily. 'At the moment I'm thinking of going into child-minding with Rhona. Anyway, don't change the subject. Go and make that phone call. Take that job.'

Margot nodded. 'All right. Yes, I will.'

Tilly tried not to feel as if her safety net were being cut in pieces. She was sure it was time to stand on her own two feet. She just hoped she wouldn't collapse to the floor in the first five minutes. She thought of Charlotte and smiled. 'When you've rung Bryony,' she said, 'give Charlotte a ring too. And be sure to tell her I told you to take the job.'

'I will. Do you want to have a word with her?'

'No,' said Tilly, 'I am going to think about what to wear on my hot date tomorrow!'

The film was very good. Tilly thought it was the best film she'd ever seen. Much to Graham's disgust, she cried copiously and they emerged from the cinema, arguing hotly.

'How can you say you felt *sorry* for him?' Tilly demanded. 'He was *horrible*. He hardly ever visited his mother and he ruined that poor Algerian's *life*! The whole film is a metaphor—'

'Please,' said Graham, 'don't start talking about metaphors. I hate films that are metaphors.'

'Well, in that case,' Tilly said scornfully, 'you might as well . . .' The sentence died in her mouth.

Her parents-in-law saw her at precisely the same moment. Peter Taylor was the first to speak. 'Tilly!' he said. 'Fancy seeing you here! What a surprise! How are you? You're looking well.' He was clearly uncomfortable.

'I'm very well, thank you. Did you enjoy the film?'

'Yes, we did. Very much. Very moving.'

'I thought so.' Tilly searched around desperately for something to say. 'This is a friend of mine, Graham. Graham, this is Peter Taylor and this is Anne Taylor. They are Robin's parents.'

Graham stared at them and said very heavily, 'Oh dear.'

No one knew what to say after that. Anne stared at him in shocked surprise before reacting as if someone had plugged her into an electric socket. 'How are you, Tilly? We've been so worried about you. We've picked up the phone so many times but we felt it was, shall we say inappropriate, to contact you until everything's settled?'

'I quite understand,' Tilly said faintly.

'That's very sweet of you. I know my naughty boy has broken your heart and we are *so* sorry, aren't we, Peter? But once the dust is settled and the divorce is done, I hope we can all be friends again! I think you are so brave!' She put her arm through her husband's. 'Peter, darling, I'm very cold. Can we go home now, please?'

'Tilly,' Peter began, 'I wish we—'

'Peter.' Anne's voice remained calm and soft but Peter reacted instantly. 'Goodbye, Tilly.'

'Goodbye,' Tilly said. She watched them walk away and suddenly shut her eyes tight.

'Matilda,' Graham touched her arm. 'Are you all right?'

Tilly opened her eyes. 'I want you to take me in your arms,' she hissed, 'and kiss me passionately. And don't stop until I tell you!'

'If you insist,' Graham said. He lowered his face to meet her own and kissed her with a speed and a strength that almost took her breath away. At last she put her hand to his chest and he pulled away at once.

'There!' she said. 'They must have seen that!'

'What do you want to do next?' Graham asked. 'Make love in the car park?'

'All right,' said Tilly. 'But only if my parents-in-law are watching.'

CHAPTER EIGHTEEN

'If you don't get everything you want, think of the things you don't get that you don't want.'

OSCAR WILDE

It was funny how quickly one adapted to new situations. Already her life with Robin seemed unreal. Reality was her mother making scones and letting Lucy plunge her fingers in the splendidly malleable dough. Reality was Graham issuing sporadic shrieks on the lawn for no discernible reason or changing Tilly's furniture about with variable results. Reality was the edgily polite conversations she had with her husband when he arrived to collect or deposit offspring. Reality was the infant inside her, its limbs rippling the surface of her belly like a fish beneath the water.

Nothing was decided and the lack of resolution became a resolution in itself. As the days went by, Robin and Tilly studiously avoided all talk of their fractured future, Harry Treadwell continued to insist Margot was simply helping her abandoned daughter, Graham continued to maintain his wife would beg him to come home once her brother moved away. Indecision was safe.

Amy thought Tilly was mad. She insisted Tilly meet her for coffee at the Curved Wheel café so she could tell her so. 'Tilly, I'm sorry, but you're being utterly supine. Robin tells you he's

231

going away while he has his affair but to keep his bed warm just in case, and you say, all right, sweetie, that's fine. Two months later you are still politely waiting for him to make up his mind, you haven't instructed a solicitor, you have yet to make an ultimatum and Robin is probably having the time of his life. I don't understand. Has he left you or not?'

Tilly shifted her bottom in a vain attempt to find a position in which her back ceased to ache. 'Of course he has. I think.'

'Well, this might clarify things.' Amy reached into her carpet bag and pulled out a magazine. 'I bought it yesterday. Have a look.'

On the cover was the tree house in Cornwall that John and Robin had designed and built. The building looked like something out of a fairy tale, glinting in the sunlight through the leaves.

'It's a fabulous picture,' Tilly said. 'It's almost as good as a painting.'

'Never mind that,' Amy said. 'Look inside. Page thirty-seven.'

Tilly turned to page thirty-seven and was confronted by a photo of her husband and John, both grinning broadly, in front of a huge pile of wooden slats. On the facing page, she read *A Bit of Somerset Magic by Louise Honeytree*. Tilly read through the article, gave a short laugh and handed the magazine back to Amy. 'That should bring in some business,' she said.

'Is that all you can say?' Amy opened the magazine and returned to the offending page. 'Listen to this: "Just on the edge of Radstock, two young men are living the dream . . ."'

'I grant you it's a bit yucky but—'

'Listen! "Two young men are living the dream . . . Thirty-five-year-old Robin Taylor, tall, drop-dead gorgeous with dimpled chin, wickedly twinkling eyes and a deceptively soft voice" . . . blah, blah, blah . . . and thirty-eight-year-old John Strickland. . .That's it! That's all the description poor John Strickland gets! Robin is tall, Robin is gorgeous, Robin has sexy eyes, Robin has a sexy voice and John is . . .? John is thirty-eight! Tilly, that article is a love letter, pure and simple. That woman loves your husband and since Robin shows no sign of returning to the family home, it's at least possible that he's in love with her. What I'm saying is: shouldn't you begin to think through the implications of life as a single mother?'

Tilly raised her eyebrows and took a sip of her tea.

'Tilly?' Amy persisted. 'I don't mean to bully.'

Tilly said, 'You're not. Or if you are, I'm glad. I need it. I feel as though we're all swimming round and round a goldfish bowl and none of us dares stop in case we see how we're really living.' She stopped and smiled as a distant memory rose to the surface of her mind. 'I had a fish once, called Barney. He lived for six years. I got so bored with him. I kept hoping he'd die.'

Amy nodded in sympathy. 'I had a grandma like that. Every Christmas she came to stay and every year I'd think, please let her die this year, and every year she didn't. She lived to be one hundred and three.'

'That is old.'

'Yes, it is, but I don't want to talk about my grandma, in fact I don't even want to think about my grandma. Robin has left you. You agree with that?'

'Yes.'

'You're happy with that?'

'How can I be happy with that? My children miss their

daddy and the man I assumed I'd love for ever is currently uttering sweet nothings to a brilliant and beautiful woman. I had a great idea a few nights ago. I thought I'd send her a copy of "Jolene". Do you know the song I mean? It's sung by Dolly Parton.'

'Of course I know it. It's the one with the soppy woman begging Jolene not to take her husband from her. Please . . . *please* . . . tell me you did not consider doing that for even a moment.'

'No, I didn't really. It was one of those ideas that seem brilliant at four in the morning. I mean, I do think the lyrics are very moving.'

'The lyrics are maudlin and vomit-making. Anyway, I thought you'd decided you wouldn't want Robin to come back to you.'

'I wouldn't! I'm sure I wouldn't. I don't recognize him as the man I married.'

Amy cut her Curved Wheel flapjack in half and passed one piece to Tilly. 'He wasn't the man you married in the first place. No man is. When I fell in love with Derek I had no idea he was a hypochondriac who's scared of spiders.'

Tilly laughed. 'You're so horrid about Derek. You don't deserve him.'

'Yes, I do. I know all about him and I'm still prepared to live with him. That makes me extremely tolerant.'

Tilly narrowed her eyes and pointed her flapjack at Amy. 'Has it ever occurred to you that you aren't the woman Derek thought you were?'

'Of course I'm not! Derek thought I was sensitive and deep, with an unfathomable soul. Luckily for him I'm far more interesting. Will you really not have Robin back?'

Tilly shrugged. 'It's a pretty hypothetical question since Robin clearly has no intention of coming back. I feel so angry with him these days that I probably wouldn't.'

'Right,' said Amy. 'Prove it! Show you don't need him. Start to plan your life without him. Show him you don't need him! Show yourself you don't need him. Show the world you don't need him!'

Tilly froze, her flapjack in mid-air. Someone came up to have a word with Amy but Tilly was hardly aware of her. She was experiencing one of those moments when everything makes sense and all the jigsaw pieces fit together into one supremely comprehensible whole. There was Rhona who'd brought up Chloe with compassion and good humour and managed brilliantly until the arrival of Nigel. If Rhona could manage, why shouldn't she? It had to be better than her recent life with Robin, spent in the shadow of the twin Superwomen, Anne and Louise. If she had gone on like that, she would have become as empty-headed and useless as they no doubt thought her. Far better to cope on her own. Now was the time to reclaim her life and her self-respect, to show that she could survive on her own, that she could be content without depending on anyone else. She turned to Amy, waited for the other woman to go and then said, 'The first thing I'm going to do is get Mum to show me how to mend a fuse.'

The euphoria of her revelation acted like a starting pistol. In just a few months her third child would be born. Charlotte had given Tilly a selection of fridge magnets for Christmas. At the time Tilly, sensing a veiled hint in her sister's choice of gift, had thrust them into the kitchen drawer. Now she pulled them out and chose a small wine bottle with which to display her House List. This read: Finish Nursery, Get and Assemble Cot, Mend Pane of Glass, Get New Washer for Tap, Sort out Kitchen.

The nursery and the cot were very important. With Lucy and Sam she had been far too superstitious to prepare anything before the births, but this time she was anxious to make amends for all her negative feelings. Henceforth the baby's arrival would be trumpeted with full enthusiasm.

Then Tilly made an Independence List. This read: Change Fuses, Understand Boiler, Money. She found a bread-shaped magnet for that one. Lists were brilliant. She wished she'd used them more in the past. They cut huge, amorphous, pore-clogging problems into neatly parcelled directives. People might laugh at the apparent insignificance of some of her ambitions but the times when Tilly could triumphantly tick some of them off were moments of immense satisfaction.

It was only when Tilly stared at the word Money that her pen remained obstinately still. She would not be able to continue her three mornings at school and, besides, they could hardly provide a sufficient income if she were to ever free herself from Robin's financial purse strings. Besides, she had no wish to leave this baby with child-minder or mother if she could possibly help it.

It was Margot who spotted the advert for training courses in copy-editing and proofreading. Tilly instantly rang and a little breathlessly agreed to a place for just two weeks hence.

When Robin arrived to collect the children for the weekend, he was surprised to be greeted warmly by his estranged wife. He was even more surprised to be led to the shed where he was questioned closely about the boiler's workings and listened to with flattering attention. Finally, when Tilly had finished making a series of notes in her small blue notebook, she beamed and asked him if he'd care for some tea.

'Thank you,' said Robin. 'Are the children ready?'

Tilly switched on the kettle. 'I've packed their bag, it's there in the corner. They won't be a minute. They've gone with Mum to return the Sellars' drill. We've been doing some work upstairs.'

'You're making so many changes to the place, I hardly know what to expect these days.'

'We're working hard,' said Tilly. 'Of course I want to get everything finished before the baby's born. I'm so lucky. Graham's spent masses of time over here lately and the nursery is nearly finished, and Mum's been helping me to reorganize the kitchen.'

'Look.' Robin hesitated. 'If there's anything I can do . . .'

'Oh, that's all right,' Tilly said. 'I wouldn't dream of asking you.'

'Tilly,' said Robin heavily, 'I don't mind—'

'Oh,' Tilly interrupted, waving the teapot at him, 'remember to ask Lucy how she's done in her spelling test!'

'I will,' Robin said. 'I take it she's done brilliantly. You're looking very good. I like what you've done to your hair.'

'I'm growing it,' Tilly said. 'It saves on hairdressing bills. Would you like a biscuit?'

'No, thanks.' Robin sat down and looked about him. 'The dresser looks different.'

'I've polished it with lavender wax. It's funny. I'd always accepted the fact that I was a sluttish housewife and now I see I'm not. I just didn't seem to have the time before. My weekends are very productive these days. I don't have you or the children or . . .' her voice quavered for a moment, 'or Horace.'

'About Horace,' Robin began, 'I wanted to—'

'Did I tell you that Graham has mended the fence?' She put the tea pot on the table. 'I'll get you a cup.'

'Tilly, please sit down, I can get my own cup.'

'Actually,' Tilly said, 'I don't think you can. I've moved everything around.'

Robin watched her assemble a tray of milk and mugs. 'I was thinking,' he said and then stopped as Lucy and Sam burst through the door, both talking at once. He laughed, hauled Sam onto his knee and then stiffened as his mother-in-law followed her grandchildren into the kitchen. 'Margot,' he said, 'how nice to see you.'

Margot's response was a contemptuous glare. 'I wish I could say the same,' she said and turned her back on him. 'I saw Graham in town,' she told Tilly. 'He says thanks for the invite to lunch tomorrow and you're to give him a ring if you need any help with the nursery.' She glanced pointedly at her son-in-law. 'What a wonderful man Graham is! And so talented! He's transforming the house.'

Robin shifted Sam and stood up. 'I'll pass on the tea, if you don't mind. I'd better get going.' He picked up the children's bag and shouted out, 'Come on, kids!'

As Tilly waved them off, she realized she did not feel the usual searing pain. Along with making lists she had discovered there was a lot to be said for keeping busy.

Chloe arrived thirty minutes later and led her bike round to the back of the house. She was wearing paint-splattered sweat-shirt and tracksuit trousers but still managed to look gorgeous.

'Chloe,' Tilly said, 'this is so good of you. Are you sure you haven't had your arm twisted?'

Chloe smiled. In repose her face appeared naturally sullen but when she smiled she looked utterly different. 'I like painting,' she said.

'Cup of tea?'

Chloe nodded and dropped onto a chair. 'Two sugars, please.'

Tilly put the kettle on. 'Are you enjoying living with your Dad?'

Chloe shrugged. 'It's better than living with Nigel. He's creepy. And he's always touching Mum. It's gross. At least Dad hasn't got a girlfriend at the moment. Did Mum tell you about Tamzin?'

'Was she the one who chanted?'

Chloe gave a laugh that died as soon as it left her lips. 'She was weird. Nigel's worse.'

'Why?'

Chloe picked out a lock of hair and began to inspect it for loose ends. 'I dunno. He pretends to like me but I know he doesn't. He's a complete parsnip.'

Tilly's mouth quivered. 'What did you say?'

'He's a parsnip. And then they tell me Martin's not good enough for me! I *mean*!'

Tilly could think of no suitable response because actually Chloe was right. Given the mess that so-called grown-ups made of their love lives, did they have any right to pronounce on Martin? 'I suppose,' she said after a hefty pause, 'parents always want their children to be happier than they are.'

Chloe snorted and stood up. The conversation was obviously over. 'So, what is it you want me to do?'

'Right!' said Tilly. 'Follow me!'

In the spare room, Chloe looked about her and whistled. 'Wow!' she said. 'Did you do this?'

'I wish!' said Tilly. 'A friend . . . you'll see him at lunch tomorrow. He drew the designs. I wanted to make the room completely different and he suggested this. All we have to do is follow his instructions. It's painting by numbers, really.'

'Wow,' said Chloe again. She turned and looked directly at Tilly. 'Before we start, can I ask you something?'

'Of course.' Tilly smiled encouragingly.

'Do you mind if we have the radio on? It's my favourite programme at the moment.'

'Of course!' Tilly passed the radio to Chloe, who retuned it just in time to hear the DJ produce a huge, self-satisfied burp. Chloe giggled. Tilly felt very old.

Rhona rang about an hour later and Tilly said politely, 'I'll get Chloe for you.'

'Actually,' said Rhona, 'it's you I wanted. Can I scrounge an invite to lunch tomorrow?'

'Oh.' Tilly paused and said cautiously, 'Will that include Nigel?'

'He won't be here,' said Rhona quickly. 'His father's ill and he's gone down to see him this morning. He won't be back before tomorrow evening. It would be nice to see you.'

Tilly could have reminded Rhona that they had seen each other at school only yesterday, but she knew what Rhona meant. At work they had chatted about their children, as a result of which Chloe, a natural artist, was helping Tilly out now. They had only talked about children because neither could forget that Rhona had said Tilly's marriage had been an utter failure.

'It's only spaghetti Bolognese,' Tilly said, 'but I'd love you to come.' It was good to unhitch the wounded dignity from her back.

The relief in Rhona's voice was audible. 'I'll bring some wine! I haven't had any fun for ages!'

Tilly was flattered that Rhona thought she'd have fun. She couldn't remember the last time she'd presided over a successful social gathering. She wasn't sure that a lunch comprising an abandoned wife, a runaway wife, a battered wife and her sulky daughter, and an ejected husband and his bewildered son could be a recipe for fun but she was willing to try.

In the end it surpassed even Rhona's expectations. It started to gel when Tilly asked everyone to raise a glass to her soon-to-be brilliant career as a proofreader.

'What's a proofreader?' asked Jack.

'A proofreader,' said Graham, 'is a reader who proves writers can't write.'

'Rubbish!' Tilly said. 'A proofreader simply checks a writer's work for spelling mistakes and punctuation errors.'

'What I said,' mumbled Graham, thrusting a huge forkful of spaghetti into his mouth.

'My dad's a writer,' said Jack carelessly.

'Are you, Graham?' Margot asked. 'I thought you did decorating work with a friend?'

Graham nodded. 'I do.'

'He *is* a writer,' Jack persisted. 'He does stories with pictures. Lots of men and women kissing and hugging.'

There was a stunned silence broken only by a loud giggle from Chloe. 'You mean sex stuff?' she asked.

Everyone stared at Graham who looked affronted. 'I do not

do sex stuff. I do picture stories, boy and girl stuff for my sister's teenage magazine in Norway. I'm very big in Norway.'

'Wow!' said Chloe.

'Your father,' Tilly told Jack, 'is an extraordinary man!'

'When I was a girl,' Rhona said dreamily, 'I always wanted to be one of those women in the picture-strip stories with giant lips and Big Hair.'

Graham turned to Tilly. 'Have you any paper?' He leant forward and studied Rhona gravely. Rhona, unnerved by his scrutiny, laughed uncertainly.

Five minutes later Graham held up his creation: a definitely recognizable Rhona with surgically enhanced lips and bosom and a Pamela Anderson wig. The new Rhona was staring lovingly into the eyes of a man who bore more than a faint resemblance to Graham.

Rhona smiled shyly at Graham. 'Can I keep it?' she asked.

'Yes,' said Graham. 'I'll sign it for you. Tilly, is there any more food?'

'Yes,' said Tilly, 'but only if you do a romantic picture of me.'

'And me,' said Chloe.

Graham looked enquiringly at Margot, who said firmly, 'Don't you even consider doing one of me!'

'Pity!' Graham said. 'You have great bone structure.'

Robin and the children arrived back at four to find the kitchen in total disarray. The table was pushed back and the rest of the party was watching Tilly prowling around on all fours, growling ferociously while the cool and sultry Chloe was standing on a chair, screaming her head off.

'Mummy!' exclaimed Lucy. 'What are you doing?'

'She's the wolf!' Jack cried. 'You are the wolf, aren't you the wolf?'

'I am the wolf!' Tilly agreed. She stopped being the wolf and stood up. 'We're playing charades,' she said.

'Hello, Rhona,' Robin said.

'Hello, Robin,' Rhona said.

Lucy picked up a piece of paper from the table. 'Look, Daddy!' she said. 'It's a picture of you and Mummy!'

Robin came over and looked at a grotesquely pregnant Tilly standing with her foot on a prostrate Robin's stomach. 'So it is,' he said. He studied it more closely. 'Actually, it's a very good likeness.'

'Thank you,' Graham said. 'I accept commissions.'

Robin smiled blandly at him. 'I'll keep that in mind,' he said.

That was the moment when the party ended. Rhona cried suddenly, 'Heavens, just look at the time! Chloe, we must go. Graham, if you and Jack want a lift, you've got to come now!'

They were gone in a matter of minutes. Robin murmured, 'I hope I haven't frightened them away.'

'I wouldn't use the word frightened,' Tilly replied.

Robin rang later that evening. 'Tilly!' he said. 'How are you?'

'The same as I was this afternoon.'

'I didn't have a chance to talk to you properly today.'

'Robin,' Tilly said, 'when do you ever want to talk to me properly?'

'That's not fair.'

'It's perfectly true and you know it. And I know what you're going to say. You're cross because I had some people over.'

'Of course I'm not.'

'Of course you are. We had spaghetti Bolognese, economy mince without mushrooms. Graham and Rhona brought the alcohol, which I did not drink. We had a good time. Am I not allowed to do that?'

'Tilly, will you stop trying to make me out to be an ogre? I'm glad you had a good time and I don't care how much the meal cost.'

'As for that picture,' Tilly added, 'Graham did silly pictures of each of us. We weren't having a great anti-Robin bash, though I must say you deserve it.'

'I don't care about the picture,' Robin said, 'and I'm glad you had a good lunch party. I only rang to tell you I won't be around at Easter. I thought I'd better let you know in case you wanted to make any plans.'

'Oh,' said Tilly, 'will you be away for long?'

'A week,' Robin said. 'I'm not sure yet whether I'll be back in time to have the kids the following weekend. Can I let you know in a few days?'

'If you like. Am I allowed to know where you're going?'

'I'm going to Fontainebleau. An old friend's getting married and I promised I'd go.'

'What a lovely place to get married in. Who's the friend?'

There was a pause. 'It's Louise's brother. I got to know him very well when I was going out with Louise.'

'I see.' Tilly swallowed. 'I had no idea you kept up with him all these years.'

'I didn't,' Robin said, 'but he heard that—'

'Fine,' said Tilly and she hung up. She went out into the garden, blinked rapidly up at the stars and wondered if Robin would ever lose the power to hurt her.

CHAPTER NINETEEN

'Nothing in this world can take the place of persistence.'
CALVIN COOLIDGE

So that was it. The phoney war was over, the guns were out, the flag was hoisted and the marriage was finished. Tilly's first impulse was to find a solicitor with red braces and an anger that matched her own. Armed with a writ or whatever it was solicitors armed their clients with, she would march over to Radstock and fling it down on his desk before laughing scornfully and striding out again. She felt her baby give a hefty kick and knew she could never tell her unborn child she'd started divorce proceedings before its birth.

The trouble was, every time Tilly told herself to remain calm, an image of Robin and Louise in some romantic French chateau would consume her with fresh paroxysms of jealousy and rage. At night, she dreamt of the lovers in bed, on the floor, against a lamp post, in the bath, even – and Tilly thought this was very significant – on Anne Taylor's kitchen table. In the morning, exhausted and depressed, Tilly walked to the bathroom, took off her long grey nightshirt and stared dully at her body. It was horrible: a big white blob supported by spindle-thin legs.

This was what was so unfair. It would have been therapeutic to at least consider an affair of her own, a wonderfully

245

torrid and tempestuous affair in which Tilly would drown her misery in the delights of the flesh. Even she found it difficult to imagine herself lying seductively on a bed with a stomach that looked like a balloon about to pop. Amy had given her a novel about a pregnant woman who found cataclysmic sexual fulfilment with a man who found her belly irresistible. Tilly was unimpressed and told Amy that the lover must be seriously weird and the female author was probably a) pregnant, b) deluded and c) desperate at the time of writing.

She could never forgive Robin for this. She had done so well, she had come so far, and now with one brutal phone call he had kicked her right down to the bottom of the mountain all over again. She tried to cling on to that wonderful life-changing moment in the Curved Wheel but it was depressing to discover that transcendent moments of self-discovery were fragile phenomena and difficult to sustain. She talked to Amy, who told her Robin wasn't even worth thinking about. Tilly agreed but said she couldn't stop thinking about him while she was so angry with him, and since she didn't know how she could stop being angry she was stuck with having to think about him. She talked to Margot, who told her to come up with her to see Charlotte that weekend. The sisters, Margot suggested, could compare bumps. Tilly couldn't think of anything less appealing. She just knew that Charlotte's lump would be sleek and sophisticated. She pretended to consider the idea for a few moments. Actually, she said, she rather fancied having a quiet weekend on her own.

And then two very unlikely people came to her rescue. At school, Tilly had finally told Arthur she would not be returning to school after the end of term. He had taken the news very well, indeed he had taken it rather too well to suit Tilly's precarious self-esteem. As she walked towards the staffroom, the school secretary stopped her in the corridor with a message. Could Tilly ring her father before she went home? Tilly's heart sank. She had not visited him since her mother's defection, mainly because she didn't know how she should handle his reaction to it. Was it kinder to make him see the truth or let him cling to his fantasy? Tilly didn't know and at the moment she felt she couldn't honestly care.

She rang his office number and immediately adopted a brisk and chirpy tone. 'Hi, Dad,' she said easily, as if this were not the first time she'd ever rung him at work.

'Tilly,' he said, 'thank you for ringing back.'

'That's all right. Is anything wrong?'

'No, no, I'm fine. Very well.'

'Good,' Tilly said heartily.

'I didn't like to ring you at home in case . . . well, I thought it was better not to . . . in the circumstances.'

Tilly winced. It was the way he said those three words: *in the circumstances*. An admission of surrender and humiliation that was both touching and uncomfortable to hear.

'Well, it's lovely to speak to you,' Tilly said. 'I've been meaning to come and see you for ages.' If she were Pinocchio her nose would be stretching to the playing fields.

'That's why I rang,' her father said. 'Charlotte tells me Margot is coming up to see her at the weekend and I thought if you were on your own you might be lonely and might like to come to me.'

'I'll be fine, Dad, but that's very sweet of you.'

'Not at all, not at all. I don't like to think of you being on your own, that's all.'

'I don't mind being on my own.'

'Good, good. I don't seem to have got the hang of it myself. Well, I must let you get on. Goodbye, Tilly.'

'Dad! Wait!' Tilly couldn't bear it. 'I'd like to come and spend the weekend with you. I'll come at lunchtime on Saturday. Shall I bring anything?'

'Certainly not!' He sounded ridiculously pleased. 'You're my guest. Thank you. I shall go home this evening and plan the meals!'

He would too. Tilly could imagine him sitting down at the kitchen table, sharpening his pencil and making his shopping list. She couldn't bear the thinly veiled desperation in his voice. For the first time since Robin's phone call she found herself feeling sorry for someone other than Tilly Taylor. It was a diversion of sorts.

She received a second phone call that day, one that was hardly less surprising. Climbing over the barricades from the other side and waving her own little white flag, came Robin's marketing supremo and trusted friend, Josie.

'Are you busy at the moment?' Josie asked. 'Have you time for a chat?'

Tilly had been snoozing on the bed beside a recumbent Sam. She said warily, 'I can spare a few minutes.'

Josie was not one to waste time. 'It's Robin,' she said. 'Look, I'm probably out of order here but Robin's like a bear with two sore heads at the moment. I gather he told you about this trip to Fontainebleau?'

'Louise's brother's wedding? Yes, he did. It sounds as if it will be great fun.'

'The entire Honeytree clan is going to be there, apparently,' Josie said. 'I understand they're a very close family.'

'How nice for them. I'm sure they can't wait to welcome Robin into the fold.'

'That's why I'm ringing you. I can't be certain, of course . . .' Josie hesitated. 'But I don't think Robin really wants to go.'

'Why ever not? I'm sure they'll all be as wonderful as Louise.'

'Tilly, I know Robin and Louise have a history but I honestly believe Robin is not in love with her.'

'Has he said so?'

'No, he's very annoying; he won't talk to me about his private life at all and if he says anything to John, John doesn't tell me. But I get the feeling Louise is trying to set the agenda and—'

'Josie!' Tilly strove to keep her temper. 'If you're trying to tell me that Robin has been trapped into adultery, then that makes me despise him all the more. And don't tell me he's being forced to go to France against his will because I won't believe you!'

'Oh, come off it, Tilly, you know Robin!'

'I'm beginning to think I don't know him at all.'

'I've only met Louise once when she came into the office but she struck me as very confident and forceful. She's the one who's making the running in that relationship. Actually, she reminded me of Robin's mother: very decisive and used to getting her own way. That's not what Robin needs.'

'That's nice of you to say so but I don't think Robin would agree with you. He's made it very clear who he prefers.'

'I think you're wrong, I really do. And now . . . something he said . . . well, I think he thinks you don't give a damn about him.'

'He's right.'

'I see.' Josie's voice changed gear. 'Then I'm sorry I bothered you. Just so long as you know how significant this trip to France is. Goodbye, Tilly.'

'Wait!' Tilly took a deep breath. 'I'm sorry if I sounded ungracious. That was kind of you to ring me.'

Josie's voice softened. 'That's all right. If it means anything, John and I think Robin's behaved like a complete idiot in the last few months.'

'Thank you,' said Tilly. 'That does mean a lot actually.'

She replaced the receiver and blew out her cheeks. She pressed her hands to her forehead. She sat down, then she stood up and flung open the back door into the garden. She felt as if she'd been given an overdose of pure adrenalin. Her depression, already beginning to form a crust around her soul, was rudely booted into the ether to be replaced by a heady combination of anger, exhilaration and stomach-churning confusion.

She was angry that Robin, who had always seemed so strong, had proved to be so weak. She was angry that he was even thinking of swanning off to France when she was trying so hard to mind the pennies, and she was angry that he was dithering, if indeed he was dithering, about his feelings for Louise. It was heart-twisting to imagine him in the grips of an all-encompassing love but at least it provided a certain legitimacy to his actions. Now, if Josie was correct, then Robin was not only weak but indecisive, self-indulgent, self-centred, selfish, irresponsible and a complete slob. Why on earth would she even begin to want him back?

Tilly couldn't imagine and had no idea why she felt so wildly exhilarated by the possibility that Robin just might be having second thoughts about leaving her. That was where the confusion began. The children needed their father, their greatest wish was that he come home. For all her public defiance, that was what Tilly had wanted too. But if Josie was right, did she really want a man who could be so easily pushed by another woman into doing what he didn't want to? Come to that, did she really want a husband who could walk out on his pregnant wife and children in the first place?

Josie had as good as told her she had only three weeks in which to save her marriage. If Robin went to France he'd be eternally handcuffed to Louise. The weekends with the children would become more erratic, Louise would have babies of her own who would be brilliant at everything and Tilly knew she would never forgive herself let alone Robin for creating such confusion. He might have turned out to be a lousy husband but he was a good father. She picked up the phone and rang Robin's workshop.

She got Stuart, Robin's newest and youngest employee who had won her instant approval when he had distracted a tearful Sam with a quite superb imitation of an aeroplane. 'Hi, Stuart,' she said, 'it's Tilly Taylor. How are you?'

'Very well, Mrs Taylor. Our dog's had puppies and my sister's pregnant. Do you want me to get Robin?'

'Yes, please, and do say well done to your sister.'

'Well,' said Stuart, 'I don't think my sister thinks it's well done.'

Tilly went back into the kitchen and sat down at the table. She could hear Stuart shouting Robin's name. She cleared her throat.

'Tilly!' Robin said. 'Sorry to keep you waiting, I was in the yard. What's wrong?'

'I want to see you,' Tilly said, 'before you go away. And without the children.'

For a few moments she could hear only the sounds of his workshop and she wondered if he'd left the phone. Then he said, 'Work's a bit chaotic at present. It will have to be a weekend. How about Saturday?' He paused. 'I could take you out to dinner.'

He wanted to take her out to dinner! Of course she must go! Her father would understand. Even though he had made it plain to her how lonely he was, he would understand. Even though it had obviously taken courage for him to ask her to stay, he would understand. Damn it! Why had he invited her for *this* weekend?

'I can't,' she said. 'I'm staying with Dad. I haven't been to see him since Mum left and I don't want to mess him around.'

'How is Harry?'

'Lonely.'

'I'm sorry. I hope they work things out. I've always thought that underneath that macho image there's a rather sweet man. Your mother's far tougher than he is. Look, I have to go. If not this weekend, how about next? I'll take you out to dinner on your birthday and we can have a sensible talk. I was going to take the kids to Mum and Dad for the weekend anyway. They can babysit.'

'All right. That would be nice. Thank you.'

'No problem. Look, I have to rush. We're rather short-staffed at the moment. I'll see you soon. Goodbye, Tilly.'

Tilly put the phone down. It was impossible to tell if Robin had been glad or surprised or dismayed by the phone call. He wanted to take her out to dinner which was promising. He wanted to have a sensible talk which was not. He wanted to take her out on her birthday which *was*. Perhaps she would get some clue to his state of mind when he came to collect the children on Saturday morning. Perhaps she should ambush him when he arrived, offer him coffee and a chat.

Of course it didn't work out. As soon as he arrived, Lucy dragged him upstairs to see the nursery. Robin stood in the doorway and whistled. 'It's brilliant!'

'That's Aslan from *The Lion, The Witch and the Wardrobe*, that's Alice in Wonderland and over there on the hill are the Three Little Pigs and they're looking at Jack and Jill who are falling down the hill just behind Harry Potter, which Mum is reading to me at the moment.'

Sam tugged at Robin's sleeve. 'See? By the door? Thomas the Tank Engine. Me chose Thomas.'

Robin smiled. 'It's great. Who painted it all?'

'I did,' Tilly said carelessly. 'Chloe helped me.'

'Graham drew the pictures,' Lucy said. 'Graham can draw anything.'

'He's very talented,' Robin said.

'And look,' Lucy said, 'look at Thomas the Tank Engine. Can you see the passengers?'

Robin scrutinized it carefully. 'It's you and Sam and Mummy.'

'Yes,' Lucy nodded. 'We're waving to our baby.'

'Do you have time for some coffee?' Tilly asked.

'No,' said Robin, slowly taking his eyes off the train, adding as an afterthought, 'thank you.'

Lucy sat down on the bed. 'I don't want to go yet.'

'I'm sorry, sweetheart, but your mother's going to see Granddad Harry and we've got things to do at Nunney. Now, anyone who is in my car by the time I've counted to ten gets a sweet.'

'Bribery and corruption,' Tilly murmured as she watched the stampede down the stairs.

'It works,' Robin said shortly.

Tilly opened the front door of Robin's car and put the children's bag inside. 'I'll see you both tomorrow,' she said. 'Be good and have a wonderful time.'

Her son and daughter sat in their car seats with their coats on their laps. They looked very small. Lucy looked mournfully at her. 'Mummy,' she said slowly, 'I wish we could have Horace back.'

Tilly reached out to stroke her hair. 'I know,' she said softly, 'so do I.'

Robin put the key in the ignition. 'I think,' he said loudly, 'we'll go and find some lollies!'

Tilly watched the car drive away, her eyes fixed on the two little hands waving to her.

The house was different. Gone was the aroma of beeswax polish and home-made bread; now it smelt musty and unwashed. Harry had done his best to keep the place tidy but Tilly felt a strong desire to reach for a duster. She followed her father upstairs and he opened the spare-room door with a flourish and looked at her expectantly. She saw the tulips, jammed inexpertly into a thin glass vase. 'Thank you, Dad,' she said. 'What lovely flowers.'

He put her bag down on the floor and smoothed the bed cover. 'I'm glad you like them. I've bought one of those Chinese meals in a bag for lunch. You do like Chinese food, don't you?'

'I do.'

'We're having chicken Kievs for supper and a trifle and then tomorrow we're having chicken pie. I was going to make something myself but –' he paused to straighten a picture on the wall – 'it's finding the time, isn't it?' He was pathetically eager to please. It was frightening to see how quickly his self-assurance had faded.

Lunch was a curious affair. After the first flurry of exclamations about the food and jokes about chopsticks, the two of them eyed each other like acquaintances who wish to be friends but aren't sure how to go about it. Harry asked her if she was enjoying her job. Tilly told him she'd decided to leave. She mentioned her plans for the proofreading course. 'It's expensive,' she said, 'but I really want to give it a try. I don't want to depend on Mum. I don't want to depend on child-minders.'

'It sounds a good idea. You must let me pay for it.'

Tilly flushed. 'I didn't tell you because . . . I don't expect you to shell out for me. I've still got a bit of the money Grandpa left me. I can cope.'

'I know you can. I'd like to help, that's all. I am your father.'

'Thank you,' Tilly said, 'if you're sure. That's very kind of you.'

'Nonsense. I see it as an investment. When you're rich and famous, you can pay me back.'

'I'm hardly likely to be rich and famous from proofreading but I will pay you back.'

'If that's what you want.' He returned to his food, studying his plate with absurd gravity. Tilly, aware that she had overreacted, repeated somewhat lamely that the meal was marvellous.

'It makes a change from bread and cheese anyway!' Harry said. 'Charlotte tells me she's developed a craving for Chinese food, which is funny because she's always preferred Indian in the past.'

'I must give her a ring,' Tilly said. 'I haven't talked to her for ages.'

'She's doing very well. She's such a good girl. She rings me most nights.'

'I'm sorry I haven't been in touch more,' Tilly said stiffly. 'It's difficult with Mum . . . in the circumstances.'

'Good heavens, Tilly, I wasn't trying to imply criticism of you.' He looked at her with alarm, and pulling out a large white handkerchief wiped it heavily across his brow.

'No,' said Tilly, 'of course you weren't.'

After lunch Harry insisted she have a rest in the sitting room. 'Put your feet up,' he said, 'watch a film.' She agreed with very little protest, wondering which of them was the more relieved to have a break from the other.

Tilly awoke to find him snoring gently in the big armchair by the fire. She stretched and stared for a few moments at the television. Paul Henreid and Bette Davis were looking at the sky just before the credits came up. It was too bad! She'd missed *Now Voyager!* She'd missed seeing Paul Henreid light two cigarettes at once! She'd missed Bette Davis tell Paul they had the stars so not to worry about the moon. Perhaps she should try that on Robin: Let's be happy with the stars, Robin, you'll soon forget about the moon. Except Robin probably thought of her as a big, fat, clumsy meteorite rather than a star.

Tilly pulled herself up with an effort and went through to the kitchen to make some tea. Her father had taken to drawing a line through the days on the calendar. She could imagine him crossing out each yesterday as it slotted into the past: a small attempt to organize a life that had turned upside down. On the notice board he'd pinned a list of the week's menus. She opened the fridge door to take out the milk and was shocked by the frugality of its contents. He'd obviously lost enthusiasm for home-cooking.

She woke him up gently and passed him a mug of tea.

'Tilly,' he said, 'I'm sorry, you shouldn't be doing this for me. I don't know, I can't get to sleep when I'm on my own and I sleep like a baby when my daughter comes to visit!'

'Poor Dad!' Tilly sat down on the sofa and made a sudden decision. 'You miss Mum very much, don't you?'

'Oh, I'm all right! I mean, I get a bit lonely but there are a lot of people who live on their own and seem to like it so I'm sure I soon will. Evenings aren't easy. It's silly, really, because sometimes we hardly talked to each other but then it's nice to be with someone you don't have to talk to. Silly!'

'It's not silly at all.'

'I thought she'd see sense after a few days, I thought she'd come back and we needn't mention it. I've stopped ringing her, you know; it just seemed to make things worse. So now I don't know what to do! Any suggestions welcome!' He laughed but his eyes were sad and serious.

'I don't know what Mum wants to do,' Tilly said slowly. 'I'm not sure she does yet. I know she wants to be taken seriously and respected.'

'I've always respected your mother!'

'Dad, the number of times you told her she didn't know what she was talking about! You treated her like you treated me. You made us feel stupid!'

257

Harry set his mug down on the tray. 'I never meant to. I love you both, you know that!'

'I'm sure you do but it's a pretty rubbish sort of love if you make us feel worthless. And it didn't help that you always listened to Charlotte as if she were the fount of all wisdom!'

'So,' Harry sighed heavily. 'You think it's all my fault, then?'

'No, I don't think Mum helped either. She should have stood up to you ages ago. The trouble is, at the time it always seems easier to be a victim than to fight.'

Harry took off his glasses and rubbed his eyes. 'What can I do?'

'Well, you can't bully Mum into coming back, that's for sure. Why don't you take her out to dinner?'

'She wouldn't come.'

'She would if you make it clear you have no intention of trying to make her come back. Tell her you want to be friends, tell her you understand she needs her independence.'

'And then what? What do I say if she does come?'

'Nothing! Well, nothing serious anyway. Talk about Charlotte and me, talk about Lucy and Sam, ask her about her computer course. Don't be rude about her computer course. Chat. Make conversation. Be nice to her. Listen to her. Let her talk.'

'Suppose she doesn't?'

'Doesn't what?'

'Talk.'

'Then ask her questions so that she has to! And don't rush things. Don't even hint that you'd like her to come home to you. Don't expect her to fall into your arms after one glass of wine!'

'I don't expect anything,' Harry said. 'It all sounds very difficult.'

'Nobody ever said mending a marriage was easy. Nobody ever tells you how difficult it is to make a marriage work.'

Harry stood up and threw a log on the fire. He turned and cleared his throat. 'You're not stupid, Tilly. You're very wise. I mean it. Now Robin is stupid. Do you think he'll come to his senses?'

Tilly smiled. 'I'm working on it,' she said.

CHAPTER TWENTY

'Children sweeten labours but they make misfortunes more bitter.'
FRANCIS BACON

Margot came back from her weekend with Charlotte, tired and mildly irritable. It had been a very nice weekend, she said; they'd taken her to the theatre on Saturday night, given her wonderful food, spoilt her rotten in fact.

'So what's wrong?' asked Tilly.

'Nothing.' Margot slipped off her shoes and shut her eyes. 'I'm tired, that's all. I don't know why I find train journeys so exhausting. Did you have a good time with your father?'

'Very good.'

'Really?' Margot opened her eyes. 'That's good to hear. I take it he's not living in miserable squalor, then?'

'So that's what's wrong!' Tilly grinned. 'Charlotte's been having a go at you?'

Margot scratched at a slight speck of mud on her skirt. 'She did rather suggest Harry was incapable of opening a tin or washing his shirts. I mean, for goodness sake, anyone would think he was an idiot. He's not really unable to fend for himself, is he?'

'Of course not.'

'So how *is* he? Tell me the truth.'

'He's all right.'

'Is he eating properly?'

'Yes, mainly I think because he's stopped trying to cook for himself. The freezer's full of ready meals.'

'I suppose the house is a mess?'

'It's not too bad. Dad's doing his best to keep it tidy.'

'I'm sure he is.' Margot attempted a tight smile. 'You feel sorry for him too.'

'Well, of course I do, Mum. There's something very sad about a man of his age trying to cope with the mysteries of housework. That doesn't make you the baddie in all this. I know how much you've had to put up with. Dad's beginning to see that too.'

'That doesn't sound very like Harry.'

'He's had to do a lot of thinking lately. He accepts that you have left him. That's a pretty big admission in itself.'

Margot stood up. 'I'm glad about that at any rate.' She gave Tilly a light kiss on the forehead. 'It was good of you to stay with him. Are you coming up soon?'

'In a minute. I want to enjoy the fire a bit longer.'

'All right. By the way, Charlotte said to tell you that if you're serious about the proofreading she can—'

'If I'm serious? That is so typical of my sister! Why does she think I'm travelling all the way down to Exeter on Friday to spend six hours being taught how to proofread if I'm not serious?'

'Don't be so touchy. Charlotte genuinely wants to help. She says once you've trained and practised a bit you can do a small test for her company and if it goes well they'll put you on their list of proofreaders. She said you could get a lot of work from them if you want.'

'Oh,' Tilly said and felt justly chastised. 'Well, that is very kind of her. I must give her a ring.'

'Do that. She'd love to hear from you. She's very nervous about the birth. You could give her some advice.' Margot yawned. 'I'm off to bed. Goodnight, Tilly.'

'Goodnight, Mum, sleep well.' Tilly stretched her arms in front of her. The idea that Charlotte would listen to her words of wisdom made Tilly smile. But then who would have thought she'd be doling out advice to both of her parents? There was something very satisfying about giving advice to people who wanted to hear it. It must be terrific to be an agony aunt. Perhaps she could become an agony aunt after she'd become a brilliant proofreader. She could picture the column already: *Tilly to the Rescue*, with Tilly looking warm and sympathetic in the corner of the page. Anything was possible. If her father could try to change the habits of a lifetime, then so could she. (He'd even asked her with great deliberation over the Sunday papers whether she thought the Government was doing a good job. Tilly had nodded gravely and said she thought it probably was.)

The future, hitherto such a threatening cloud, now seemed infinitely exciting. There was the course on Friday and there was the fateful meeting with Robin on Saturday. She knew exactly how she was going to play it. She would suggest they go to the Italian restaurant in Frome. She would tell him about her course, show him she was determined to stand on her own two feet financially. She would ply him with questions about his work. She would be charming, confident and mature. She would ask him about Louise in a sweet, sympathetic manner and encourage him to tell her all about his doubts regarding the French trip. Robin would say in a bemused sort of way,

'Why did I ever leave you? What am I doing with Louise?' Tilly would turn away modestly and Robin would cry, 'I've been such a fool! Can you ever forgive me?'

The trouble was, Tilly wasn't quite sure whether she could forgive him, but perhaps if he begged her with sufficient desperation she might be able to. All right, she would say eventually, it would take time but she thought their marriage was worth a second chance, and he would say with wonder in his voice that she was far, far too good for him. Which was true as well.

Tilly stood up, put the guard over the fire and turned off the lights. It was going to be an interesting week.

Wednesday was Lucy's parents' evening. Tilly arrived at the school just as Amy was leaving.

'How was it?' Tilly asked.

Amy grimaced. 'Edward continues to be his teacher's nightmare and Luke seems to be happily following in every one of his brother's footsteps. The teachers complain they won't sit still and I told them: there's a simple solution. Make them run round the playground twenty times before lessons begin and they'll be too exhausted to move. It's obvious!'

Tilly grinned. 'What did they say?'

'Oh, it's *too* obvious for them. Derek's going to be furious. And he's already in a state because his finance director keeps bursting into tears.'

'Poor man. What's happened to him?'

'His wife has run off with one of the trainers at the gym. The man is utterly crushed. Derek thought you'd both have a lot in common. He said we should get the two of you over, it would do the man good.'

'Why? So we can be crushed together?'

'Something like that. Do you want to come to dinner? How about next Saturday?'

'For heaven's sake, Amy, let the poor man be crushed in peace. Besides, I'm hardly anyone's idea of a dream date at the moment.'

'No,' Amy agreed. She cast an eye over Tilly's bump. 'Are you sure you're not having twins?'

'My doctor assures me I'm not.'

'Good. Well, I must go and tell Derek he has to take the boys for a run every morning before breakfast. You have no idea how lucky you are to have a sweet, docile, clever daughter. I'm so glad I'll miss seeing you rise from your interview with your usual smug smile on your face.'

Not this time. Lucy had been discussed at the staff meeting, Mrs Dawes said her work had deteriorated badly. She was picking fights with the other children. 'Of course this behaviour is not at all uncommon in her circumstances,' Mrs Dawes said kindly. 'Children do tend to externalize their emotions. Lucy is confused and unhappy and she lashes out. It's only because she's always been so proud of her work that we're concerned. The trouble is, if a child slips too far behind it can be difficult to catch up.'

'Yes, of course,' said Tilly. 'Everything's been so up in the air. I do hope to resolve all our family problems soon.'

'That would be good for Lucy,' Mrs Dawes said. 'A child does need to understand what's happening.'

'Yes,' said Tilly, acutely uncomfortable. 'I'll talk to her.'

'Good,' said Mrs Dawes heartily. 'She needs a lot of love at the moment.'

Which she thinks I'm not giving, Tilly thought as she walked swiftly out of the building. That wasn't fair, though.

Mrs Dawes was simply stating the facts. Why did life do this? It was like a game of snakes and ladders. Every time you climb a ladder and feel good you go forward two places and slide down a rotten snake. The trick, she supposed, was to remain unsurprised by the proliferation of snakes and just wait for the next ladder that came along. If it did.

She did not need her mother to tell her Lucy was still awake. She took off her coat and went upstairs. Sam lay asleep in his bed with characteristic abandon, one arm thrown across the bedclothes, the other behind his head. She went over to Lucy's bed and sat down. 'Hello, you,' she whispered.

Lucy's head peeped out from under her duvet, her eyes anxiously fixed on Tilly's face. 'What did Mrs Dawes say?'

'She's obviously very fond of you. She says she's worried because you're not happy. She says she knows you're a clever girl and she understands you're having a difficult time at the moment. She says everything will be all right.'

'Did she tell you about Kylie?'

'No. What about Kylie?'

'Kylie said she didn't want to be my friend any more and she went off with Annabel so I took Kylie's Beanie and I didn't steal it, I was going to give it back and Kylie told Mrs Dawes I'd taken it and I said I hadn't and Annabel said she'd seen it in my drawer and Mrs Dawes asked me to get it and she said she was very disappointed and I said I didn't care and Kylie said she's never going to talk to me again and I hate school anyway and I don't want to go back because I haven't got any friends except for Katy Hudson and no one wants to be friends with Katy Hudson.' Lucy sniffed loudly and blinked rapidly. She was trying very hard not to cry and the trying not to cry made Tilly want to cry.

'Look,' she said, 'you may not know this but I promise you Kylie will be friends with you again. I see it all the time at work. Children stop being friends and think it's the end of the world and before I can say, "Don't worry", they're friends again. Shall I tell you why I *know* everything will be all right?'

'Why?'

'Because you are Lucy Taylor. You are a very special girl. You are very special because your mummy and your daddy and your brother think you are the most wonderful girl in the whole world.'

'Sam doesn't think I'm wonderful.'

'Yes, he does. He can't wait for you to get home from school. Whatever happens you have people who know you are really, really special. And nothing can ever change that. Whatever else happens there are people who care about you so much. And when you go to school tomorrow you will go knowing that your mummy and your daddy and your brother and all your grandparents love you more than anyone else in the whole school. If Kylie doesn't want to play with you tomorrow, play with someone else, even Katy Hudson. Kylie will come back.'

'What if she doesn't?'

'If she hasn't made friends with you in two weeks I'll do five cartwheels on the lawn.'

Lucy giggled. 'You can't do five cartwheels.'

Tilly smiled. 'I don't think I'll have to. Now go to sleep.' She kissed Lucy lightly on the forehead.

'Mummy?' Lucy pulled up the duvet so it could rest under her chin. 'Is Daddy *never* coming home?'

Tilly stood up. 'I don't know,' she said. 'I honestly don't know. Don't think about it now. Go to sleep.'

266

Downstairs Margot was laying the table. 'Supper in five minutes,' she said. 'How's Lucy?'

'Tired. Unhappy. Problems at school.'

'She'll be all right. She's a tough little girl.'

'She didn't look very tough just now.' Tilly sat down. 'Mum, you are great. If you weren't here I'd be eating a stale sandwich or something.'

'Nonsense. It's only shepherd's pie.'

'I love shepherd's pie. Did I tell you I'm going out with Robin on my birthday?'

Margot laughed. 'Not really? That's funny.'

'He's taking me out to dinner. Why is that funny?'

'Because we could all end up in the same restaurant. Harry invited me to dinner. I said I couldn't, but if you're going out . . .'

'Of course, go for it!' Tilly smiled. 'Should be interesting.'

Margot took the pie out from under the grill and glanced sharply at her daughter. 'Don't look like that, Tilly.'

'Like what?'

'Like the rainbow's just landed on the table. It's only a dinner. There's no point in not being civilized. Why on earth are you going out with Robin?'

'Same reason!' Tilly said. 'It's going to be a very civilized evening!'

Early on Friday morning Tilly stood on the platform waiting for the train to arrive. She was pleased with her appearance. She was wearing her old Laura Ashley dress with her mother's navy blue jacket. She had washed her hair and applied Golden Nectar lipstick to her mouth. In her bag she had a notepad and two pens. Today was a new beginning.

Two things happened to make the new beginning one of the rockiest launches since the *Titanic* set off.

First, Graham appeared out of nowhere and ran straight up to her, his face unshaven, his hair a mess. He looked so wild that he turned the heads of even the most soporific early morning commuters, and when he took her in his arms and said, 'I'm coming with you!' their eyes nearly left their sockets.

Secondly, when Tilly managed to disentangle herself from his embrace, she saw very clearly, on the other side of the platform, the goggle-eyed face of her elegantly-dressed mother in-law.

CHAPTER TWENTY-ONE

'A good indignation brings out all one's powers.'
RALPH WALDO EMERSON

Tilly struggled free. 'Graham,' she hissed, 'my mother-in-law is staring at us!'

'Of course she is,' Graham said smugly. 'I recognized her at once.'

'Will you lower your voice?' Tilly spoke through gritted teeth. 'I'm trying to pretend I haven't seen her.'

'Well, she's seen you,' Graham said. He waved his hand in the air and shouted, 'Hello there? Isn't your daughter-in-law beautiful?' He turned and gave Tilly an extravagant kiss on her mouth.

The train, like an angel from heaven, arrived in time to save Tilly from having to try to smile at her mother-in-law. She bounded onto the train, scarlet with embarrassment, and resolved to pay no attention to Graham. To compound his crime, he seemed to be quite oblivious to her fury. He sat down beside her but made no attempt at either apology or conversation. When she finally turned round, he was scribbling furiously on a piece of paper.

'Graham!' Tilly said, and then more sharply, 'Graham!'

He looked up from his paper as if he had just noticed her. 'What?'

269

'And don't look at me as if you have no idea what I'm talking about. You've just made me look a total idiot in front of my mother-in-law who already hates me anyway. She'll probably go straight home and ring Robin and tell him I was snogging a madman in public.'

'No, she won't.'

'Why not?'

'A woman like that would never use the word snogging. Too vulgar.'

'That's not funny. It's not funny at all. And you do not go round kissing people when the mood takes you.'

'I wasn't kissing people, I was kissing you.'

'Yes, and I know you were only trying to upset my mother-in-law but you might have thought about me. For all you know I might not want to be grabbed and violently kissed first thing in the morning.'

'Don't you?'

'Don't I what?'

'Don't you like me kissing you?'

'That's not the point. It's not something you should do.'

'I like kissing you. You don't like kissing me?'

'No, of course I don't . . . Oh, for goodness' sake, what are you doing here anyway? Don't tell me you've decided to be a proofreader.'

Graham frowned. 'Why the hell should I want to be a proofreader? I'm here to find my son.' He scratched his head vigorously. 'I'm so glad you're here. You can help me!'

'I don't want to help you,' Tilly said. 'Anyway what are you talking about?'

'I'm talking about my bloody wife!' Graham shouted. 'My wife has kidnapped my son!'

'You don't have to tell the entire carriage,' Tilly murmured furiously. 'And what do you mean, she's kidnapped him?'

'Exactly what I say,' Graham said. He started tapping his fingers on the table: one, two, *three*, one, two, *three*. 'I went round on Wednesday to see Jack and they weren't there. I went back again yesterday and the woman next door came out. She said they'd packed up and gone. She said Carmen told her to tell me she'd be in touch. She and her vile brother have taken my son!'

Tilly put a firm hand over Graham's tapping fingers. 'That is really irritating,' she said. She was aware that at least four strangers were following their conversation with open interest. 'And could you please keep your voice down?'

'I'm going to kill her,' Graham said. 'I really am going to kill her.'

'That's a good idea,' said Tilly. 'Jack can always visit you in prison if his foster home isn't too far away.'

'All right I won't kill her,' Graham said. 'At least, I'll try not to kill her.'

'That's an even better idea.' Tilly glanced at Graham. He was pressing his clenched fist against his forehead. She said more gently, 'So why are you coming to Exeter? Do you think that's where she's gone?'

'We used to live there. In Pennsylvania Road. She has some good friends there. I can think of at least four addresses we can try.'

'*We?* I'm sorry, Graham, I have a course to go to.'

'When does it finish?'

'Four thirty. And then I'm going home.'

'Fine. I'll go and find her on my own.'

'Good idea.'

'I'll kill her.'

'I don't care, I am not going with you! And if you do lose your temper you'll get nowhere. Poor Jack must be confused enough without seeing his father try to strangle his mother. For his sake you have to be calm and reasonable and understanding and patient.'

'I don't feel like being calm and reasonable and understanding and patient.'

'I know you don't, Graham, you never do. If you can't feel reasonable then you'll have to act reasonable. Pretend to be sensible.'

Graham waved a hand as if he were swatting a troublesome fly. 'I don't do all this hypocrisy stuff.'

'It isn't hypocrisy. Hypocrisy is saying one thing and doing another. You're going to do what you say even if you don't feel like it. I'll be home by seven. Give me a ring and tell me what's happened.' Tilly's attention was diverted by the arrival of the buffet trolley. The man who was pushing it smiled sadly at Tilly and asked, 'Any snacks or drinks?'

'A cup of tea, please,' she said.

Graham raised a hand. 'I want a black coffee, a bacon sandwich, salt and vinegar crisps and a packet of those biscuits. And I'll pay for her tea.'

'Thank you,' said Tilly. 'Are you sure you have enough to eat?'

Graham hesitated. 'You're right. I'll have another packet of biscuits.'

Tilly rolled her eyes and took a sip of her tea. Graham was now tearing into his bacon sandwich. She studied him critically. 'I've never met anyone who eats as much as you. Why don't you ever get fat?'

'I dunno,' Graham shrugged. He glanced at Tilly. 'You're only fat,' he explained kindly, 'because you're pregnant.'

'I'm not fat! Do you think I'm fat?'

'No.' He demolished the last piece of sandwich. 'Not very.'

Tilly scowled and turned her attention to the window.

'I saw your friend the other day,' Graham said.

'Which friend?'

'Rhona.'

'Why?'

'I saw her go into a house and I followed her and rang the bell. She'd mentioned at your lunch she might be going into child-minding. I thought it would be worth checking it out in case Carmen got fed up with playing mother.'

Tilly frowned. 'Did Rhona invite you in? Was her husband there?'

'He came in about five minutes later. Very quiet. Asked me where I'd met her and then shut up.'

Tilly stared anxiously at him. 'You didn't do your usual making-husband-jealous routine, did you?'

'Matilda,' Graham said. 'I'm not a complete idiot.'

'No,' said Tilly doubtfully.

Tilly emerged from her course with a carrier bag full of homework and a brain exhausted by all the information crammed into it. She took a bus to the station and wondered if Graham had found his family.

She soon found out. Graham was walking up and down the forecourt and as soon as he saw her, he called out, 'Matilda!' and ran straight to her.

'Have you found them?' Tilly asked. 'Are you coming back with me?'

'Matilda, I need you, I've been waiting for you for ages. Where've you been?'

'At my course. Which finished at four thirty, just as I said it would.'

'They're in Topsham. Carmen's staying with some mad friend who looks like a giant. I went there. I did calm and reasonable. You can't do calm and reasonable with Carmen. Her friend said she'd call the police if I didn't go. Jack wasn't there and they wouldn't tell me where he was. Matilda, you have to help me. Please.'

She had never heard Graham use that word before and it made her hesitate. 'I have a train to catch,' she told him.

'I'll get us a taxi and I'll get you a taxi back to the station afterwards. I just want you to talk to her, persuade her to let me see Jack.'

'Graham,' Tilly said gently, 'I'd like to help but that's crazy. I've never even talked to your wife, why on earth would she listen to me?'

'Because you look nice and normal and not threatening. Matilda, I'm desperate here.'

'This is ridiculous,' Tilly said. 'I'm tired and I want to go home.' She looked at him with mounting exasperation 'Will you stop staring at me like that? Oh, all right, I'll do it but don't expect me to perform miracles. And first I must ring Mum and find out when the later trains go.' She was rewarded with a fierce embrace and an envious smile from a pale-faced woman in a blue anorak. If you only knew, Tilly thought wearily.

They travelled to Topsham in silence. Graham sat tense and straight-backed while Tilly stared out of the window remembering happier times. She and Robin had walked along this road once. They had played I Spy. It all seemed a million years ago.

They drew up outside a large whitewashed cottage. Graham paid the fare and turned to Tilly. 'I'll be in the pub,' he said. 'Here's the number. You can ring or come and get me. Carmen's in the upstairs flat. Ring the bell marked Clayton. Make her see it's not fair. I know you'll manage it.'

He gave her arm an encouraging pat and walked away quickly. She wished he didn't have such confidence in her. She took a deep breath and walked up the path. She rang the doorbell, waited a couple of minutes and rang again. This time the door opened immediately.

'Yes?'

'Hello!' Tilly gave what she hoped looked like a friendly smile and tried not to betray any surprise at the sight of the six-foot-something woman with long blue hair. 'My name is Tilly Taylor.'

'Tilly Taylor?' The woman laughed, displaying a terrifying set of tombstone teeth. 'What sort of name is that?'

Tilly smiled lamely. 'I don't know. Umm . . . Could I have a word with Carmen?'

'Why?'

'I'm a friend of her husband, and please don't close the door, I promise he's not lurking behind the gate. I promised him I'd have a word with Carmen and I won't be very long because I have a train to catch.' She attempted another smile. 'Please?'

The woman shrugged and opened the door wide. 'Come on up.'

Tilly followed the giantess upstairs, through a white door, into a pink-carpeted corridor flanked by navy blue walls, and then left into a large room. The woman obviously liked navy blue but here at least the monotony of the colour was relieved by large film posters around the room.

'Oh,' said Tilly involuntarily, going straight up to one of them. '*It's a Wonderful Life*. That's one of my favourite films. Have you seen it?'

'Of course.'

'I love the bit at the end,' Tilly said, 'when the bell rings on the Christmas tree and James Stewart's daughter says, "Look, Daddy, another angel's got his wings." It always makes me cry.'

'That's not what she says. She says, "Look, Daddy, when a bell rings it means an angel has his wings." And then James Stewart says, "Good on you, Clarence."'

Tilly frowned. 'I don't think he says, "Good on you".'

'Whatever,' the woman said. 'It's a great scene.' She added carelessly, 'You can sit down if you like.'

'Thank you,' said Tilly.

The door opened and the stick insect walked in. She looked first at Tilly and then at the giantess, who said, 'She's a friend of Graham.'

Carmen took a cigarette from the packet on the mantelpiece and pointed it at Tilly's tummy. 'Who's the father?'

Tilly reddened. 'My husband.'

'Doesn't he mind you being with Graham?'

'My husband's left me.'

'Before or after you took up with Graham?'

'I haven't taken up with Graham. I've only known him for a short time. We're just friends.'

'So why's he sent you here? What do you want?'

Tilly shifted uncomfortably. The sofa was low and lumpy,

her back was killing her and she could hear her tummy rumbling. 'He loves his son,' she said. 'He really does love him and it's obvious that Jack adores Graham. A son needs his father.'

Carmen inhaled deeply and studied Tilly with an impassive face. 'You do know,' she said at last, 'that Graham is mad?'

Tilly blinked. 'Sorry?'

'Mad as a meat-axe, isn't he, Posy?' (Posy? Tilly thought: how could any parents make such a gross miscalculation? Perhaps Posy had once been a delicate little baby and perhaps she had grown so tall in order to punish her parents for trying to railroad her character at birth.) 'He charged in here, shouting Jack's name, opening every drawer. He even looked up the chimney, for God's sake. Like I'd put my son up the chimney!'

'He's very upset,' Tilly said.

'He's mad. Do you know what he did when I told him I was pregnant? He walked over to the window and put his hand through the glass.'

'Why?'

'He said it was because he was happy. There was blood everywhere. It cost nine pounds to replace the glass.'

'Well. . .' Tilly faltered. 'I know Graham feels quite strongly . . .' She rallied suddenly. 'But at least he only hurt his own hand. When I told my husband I was pregnant he walked out. That's far worse.'

Carmen considered this. 'Yeah, but leaving you was normal,' she said. 'Graham isn't normal.'

'That may be true,' Tilly conceded, and seeing the triumph in her opponent's eyes added quickly, 'but then who is? Most of the people I know seem to be acting very oddly these days.

I mean, if Graham had put *your* hand through the window then I'd have said you would be right to throw him out.'

'Yeah, right, I should be really pleased he broke the window with his own hand. What's your name?'

'Tilly,' Tilly began and then, fearing fresh laughter from the giantess, corrected herself quickly, 'Matilda Taylor.'

'Well, look here, Matilda Taylor, you come here poking your stupid, plain face into my business, talking about your mad friends and saying it doesn't matter if they *are* mad. You can't even keep your own husband, so don't try to lecture me about holding on to mine. What gives you the right to tell me what I ought to do?'

Tilly sat as straight as she could on the lumpy sofa. She no longer felt intimidated or dowdy or apologetic before these women. The rage was coursing through her veins like a shot of pure adrenalin and she embraced it like a lover. 'I may not know much about how to keep a husband,' she said, 'but I know what happens when he leaves. I know what happens when every father leaves, I know what happens when parents stop thinking about their children and start thinking about self-fulfilment, whatever that is. They chase after their own little rainbows and tell themselves that whatever makes them happy will make their children happy in the long run, and you know what? They're completely wrong. The children aren't happy at all. They miss their daddy and, God knows why, they think it's their fault he's gone. Because it can't be Mummy or Daddy's fault, can it, because Mummy and Daddy are grown-up and sensible so it must be their fault, and that makes them angry and mixed up and so they lash out at everyone else and then they're lonelier than ever because nobody likes a loser. And eventually the anger dies down and they carry around the pain in their stomach but it never goes away and they never quite trust anyone again, and meanwhile Daddy or Mummy or both are saying that the kids are fine, even though it's obvious they're not. It's all so hypocritical and selfish. People say they never mean to fall in love, it just happens, and it *never* just happens but it's so much more exciting to fall in love with someone new who thinks you're brilliant than to make concessions and compromises and bargains. And you need to make compromises if you're going to stay married because living with someone else is never easy but neither is bringing up children on your own. It's all so pathetic, this desperate search for perfect happiness with the perfect partner! And why in hell do people think they have a right to be happy all the time anyway? It can't be done, it isn't possible, and while all these stupid adults are finding that out, they're also doing a brilliant job of ensuring their kid has a miserable childhood. So I don't care if you think I'm a stupid, plain woman because I'm better than you because at least I'm trying to keep my kids' father in their lives.' She stopped abruptly, breathless and furious, her eyes darting from one woman to the other, daring them to laugh at her.

Carmen lit another cigarette. 'Shouldn't you be saying this to your husband?' she suggested mildly.

'I intend to,' said Tilly and she struggled to raise herself from the sofa.

'Don't get up,' the giantess said. 'I'll make some tea.' She glanced at Carmen and left the room.

Carmen picked up the box of cigarettes, shook it a few times and replaced it on the mantelpiece. 'I didn't mean to be rude,' she said.

Tilly stared at her. 'Yes, you did.'

'You're right, I did.' She smiled abruptly and dropped onto a large mottled-green floor cushion. 'Jack's coming home in the morning. He's with Tel, my twin. They've been to see my mother in Truro. We haven't decided where to go yet, we're looking at various options.'

'And Somerset isn't one of them?'

'No.' Carmen raised her face and exhaled a thin stream of smoke towards the ceiling. 'You might be right. Perhaps I am a lousy mother.'

'I didn't say that.'

'Yes, you did. You think I should come back and live with Graham again. Well, I won't.' She leant back and stubbed her cigarette out on the grate. 'They'll be back in the morning. You and Graham can take him out for lunch.'

'Thank you,' said Tilly. 'I'm going back tonight but I know Graham will be so pleased.'

'Oh, no.' Carmen shook her head violently. 'I'm not letting Graham take Jack out on his own. He would only take off with him. You stay with him or it's nothing. You can stay the night here. Graham can't.'

Tilly thought quickly. There was no need to rush home tonight and she could easily get home tomorrow in time to have a bath and wash her hair before Robin arrived. 'All right,' she said.

Posy popped her head round the door. 'Tea up,' she said.

Tilly was very tired. She had been up since six, she had spent the day learning a strange new language of symbols and squiggles and she had lost her temper, something she did so rarely that it left her feeling drained and shell-shocked. As she sat down in the small kitchen, eating baked beans on toast with the two women, she felt she wasn't really there, she was floating somewhere above, looking down at the three of them; the giantess, the insect and the blob.

Now the giantess was asking Tilly if she wanted her husband back and Tilly said yes and Posy asked why and Tilly said she wasn't sure. Posy told her she was in love with a man in Exeter who loved her too but had given her up because he only came up to her shoulder and he thought they looked silly together. Carmen said that was so typical, and after that Tilly lost touch with the conversation.

After tea Tilly rang Graham and then she rang her mother and then she asked Posy if she could go to bed. Posy led her to a small room at the end of the corridor and Tilly lay down on the bed and shut her eyes. Her last conscious thought was to wonder if she should start to call herself Matilda.

CHAPTER TWENTY-TWO

'Our greatest glory is not in never falling, but in rising every time we fall.'

CONFUCIUS

The sun streamed through the window and illuminated a million specks of dust. Tilly lay sleepily watching them. They were like miniature automatons, short-circuited by some malevolent scientist, speeding nowhere fast. Someone, probably Posy, had covered her with a rug. It was funny to think that here she was, lying in a crumpled dress on a strange bed in Devon, while tonight she would be sitting in a restaurant in Frome, looking as perfumed and pretty as she could manage with a tummy as big as a garage.

She heard voices and stumbled out of bed. Posy and Graham were sitting in the kitchen at either end of the small table. Posy was reading the *Daily Mirror* and Graham was constructing a house of cards, which disintegrated as soon as Tilly came in.

'Do you always sleep this much?' Graham asked. He began to gather up the cards. 'They'll be here in a minute. Carmen's gone to meet them from the bus stop.'

'I'll go and wash,' Tilly said. In the bathroom she cleaned her face with the grey shaving of what must have once been a bar of soap and then she squeezed some toothpaste onto her finger. She wished she could fast-forward today and be back in her own home and her own bathroom.

She felt better after tea and toast. Graham was walking to and fro, like a champion horse waiting for the race to start. Posy ignored them both. Suddenly, Graham yelled, 'They're here!' and raced along the corridor and down the stairs. Tilly went across to the sitting room and looked through the window. She saw the stick insects talking earnestly by the gate while Jack was frantically trying to lift the latch. He shouted, 'Dad!' and when Carmen opened the gate for him, the little boy flew into his father's arms.

Tilly picked up her bag and went down to meet them. Carmen and her brother came through the door as she was about to open it.

'I'll see you later,' Carmen said. 'Be back by three.' She did not introduce her brother and Tilly gave him a nervous smile before scurrying out to join Graham and his son.

They ate fish and chips for lunch. Tilly was worried about money but Graham said not to worry, he had enough. Tilly, feeling like his jailer, said, 'Graham, I promised . . . you won't try to . . . You're not thinking of . . .'

'I'll behave,' Graham said flatly. 'I'll get the train back with you.'

Jack, his mouth bulging with fish – he ate *just* like his father – said, 'I want to come with you.'

'Not this time,' Graham said and stabbed his ketchup with a chip.

After lunch they walked down to the sea. Tilly watched man and boy building a dam from the pebbles, both equally absorbed in their project. They were so alike, Tilly thought, it was a crime to separate them. She threw a stone into the sea and pondered the arguments she could have used to make Carmen understand that.

She checked her watch. If she were to catch the three o'clock from Exeter she needed to leave now, but there was no way she could break up their game yet. She studied the train timetable. If she caught the four thirty-two she would be back in Westbury by five thirty-seven. That was fine. She sat quietly in the pale sunlight, watching the way it danced on the water.

It was Graham who brought the afternoon to a close. 'We must get back,' he said to Jack. 'We've built a good dam. Let's go.'

Jack stuck out his bottom lip and kicked at the dam they had built. He kicked again and again until the water flooded the pebbles, making them glisten and twinkle like diamonds.

'Jack,' Graham said, 'you know I'll see you very soon.'

'No, you won't.'

'I will. I promise you I will.'

'I don't want you to go.'

'I know.' Graham stuck his hands in his pockets and began to walk quickly from the beach. Jack sniffed, wiped his nose with his hand and followed his father. Tilly stood up and walked behind them both. No one said a word.

When they reached the house, Carmen was waiting for them. 'Jack, your clothes are wet.' She looked accusingly at Tilly and Graham. 'You're late.'

Jack said, 'I don't want them to go.'

'Great!' Carmen muttered. She said to Graham, 'I think you and your friend had better go straight away. I'll let you know what we're doing.'

Graham bent down and tried to take Jack's hands. 'I'll see

you soon. I promise I will.' But Jack shrugged him off and turned his face away.

Graham stared helplessly at him for a moment, then stood up and said savagely to Tilly, 'Are you coming or not?' He made for the gate without a backward glance but was stopped in his tracks by an anguished yell from Jack.

It was horrible. He had to be prised from his father by Carmen, who was shouting, 'I knew this would happen! Bugger off, Graham, just bugger off!' Tilly almost had to run to keep up with Graham as he made for the bus stop, white-faced and grim. To make matters worse, when they arrived at the bus stop, Tilly realized she'd left her carrier bag with the proofreading homework inside.

Graham flung himself down onto the bench. 'I can't go back there,' he muttered. 'Can't you leave it?'

'No, I can't,' Tilly said. 'I'll get it, I won't be a moment.'

Tilly stumbled back along the road, supporting her tummy with her hands and cursing her ineptitude. Back at the house, she pressed the doorbell and waited. She wondered what she should do if they refused to answer.

The door was opened by Carmen, cigarette in hand, her face contorted with anger. 'Haven't you done enough damage already? What do you want?'

Jack appeared at the top of the stairs, his cheeks stained with tears, his eyes alight with hope. 'Dad?'

'No,' Tilly stammered, 'I'm sorry, it's only me. I left my green bag behind. It's on the bed, I think. I'm so sorry.'

Carmen turned on her heel and shooed Jack up with her. Two minutes later she came down the stairs and thrust Tilly's bag at her.

'Thank you,' Tilly said, 'I do apologize . . .' She hesitated and then spoke in a rush. 'You see how much they love each other. And then there's Jack's school, it's a good one and he seems so settled there and if you did decide to let Graham have him, I'd make sure he's all right, I'd collect him from school, I'd do anything to help, I'd . . .' She stopped and finished, lamely, 'I thought you should know.'

'I'm his mother,' Carmen said. 'Do you think that I don't love him? Or doesn't that matter?'

'I know, I . . . I know, I'm sorry.' Tilly turned and began to walk away.

'You're in love with him,' Carmen yelled after her. 'This is what it's all about. You're in love with him and you don't even see it! You poor, stupid cow!'

Tilly walked on, trying to ignore the stream of invective. There was no point in trying to answer such absurd accusations, the woman was impossible. As she turned the corner she could see the bus coming and lumbered heavily towards it. She could not see Graham anywhere and when the doors opened she stood, panting heavily, frozen by indecision.

The driver looked at her as if she were mad. Heaven knew, she probably looked mad. 'Are you getting on or not?' he demanded.

Tilly stared frantically about her. 'No,' she said, 'I'll get the next one.'

The driver rolled his eyes and drove off. Tilly sat down heavily on the bench. Where was Graham? Was he all right? It would be just like Graham to go and kill himself or something when he knew she had to catch a train. She saw him emerge from a newsagent's on the other side of the road. He was carrying a packet of crisps.

'Where were you?' he asked.

It was too much. 'Where were *you*? We've just missed the bus and I thought you'd killed yourself and I was worried sick and I've never walked so fast in my life and it's all your fault!' Tilly burst into tears. Graham sat down beside her and proceeded to pat her awkwardly on the back until she told him to stop, he was giving her hiccups. He offered her a cheese and bacon crisp and Tilly said she hated cheese and bacon, she only liked ready salted. So Graham said he'd go and buy her some ready salted, and that was why they missed the next bus too.

They arrived at Exeter fifteen minutes too late for the four thirty-two. The next train was due at five thirty-one.

'It gets in at six thirty-six,' Tilly said. 'That will do.'

Graham walked away abruptly. Tilly wandered along the platform and sat down. She had been a miserable failure. Jack was miserable, Carmen was furious and Graham was distraught. She had failed them all. She was aware that she was crying again but did not have the strength to wipe her eyes.

'Matilda?' Graham sat down beside her and thrust a glossy magazine and a box of chocolates in her lap.

'What's this for?'

'A thank you.' He put his arm round her and Tilly put her head on his shoulder and they stayed that way until the train arrived.

Thirty minutes after their train left Exeter, it came to a grinding halt. 'What's happened?' Tilly asked. 'Why did it stop?'

Graham shrugged. 'It will start in a minute.' Ten minutes later, he said, 'I'll go and find out.'

Tilly watched him thread his way through the carriage.

She pressed her nose to the window and forced herself not to look at her watch. Why was Fate so determined to stop her seeing Robin? She stiffened as a voice came onto the tannoy. 'Ladies and gentlemen, we are sorry that due to unforeseen circumstances there will be a thirty-minute delay. We are sorry for the inconvenience. The buffet car will be along shortly.'

Tilly yanked up her sleeve and tried to work out when she would be home. It was all hopeless, quite hopeless.

Graham came back. 'Apparently,' he said, 'a man threw himself in front of the train. Suicide. Very messy. Bits of body all over the track.'

Tilly snapped. 'I don't believe it! How unbelievably selfish! I hate people who kill themselves! Why couldn't he kill himself normally, take some pills and not bother anyone? He must have known he'd hold the train up! How stupid, how really, really stupid!'

'I expect,' Graham said, 'he had other things on his mind.'

'Typical! Suicide is so selfish!' Tilly took a deep breath and looked at her watch. 'Well, that's it! I shall miss Robin. It's all over!' She thought for a moment and plucked at Graham's sleeve. 'Can I borrow your phone?'

'I don't have one,' Graham said.

Tilly stared at him with disgust. 'How can you *not* have a mobile? Everyone has a mobile.'

'Do you have one?' Graham asked.

'No, of course not. I've never needed one until now.' Tilly bit her lip.

Graham stood up abruptly, cleared his throat and clapped his hands. 'May I have your attention?' he declared in ringing tones. 'My pregnant friend here is an abandoned wife. She was supposed to be meeting her husband tonight in an effort to persuade him to come home. If she can't tell him she is going to be late, it might ruin everything. Has anyone a mobile phone she can use?'

There was a stunned silence in the carriage and then suddenly the place was awash with mobile phones. An old lady in a tweed suit, two teenage girls, a young man in a leather jacket, all held forth their phones, eager to help.

'Thank you,' Tilly whispered, 'thank you very much.' The man in the leather jacket showed her which buttons to press and everyone watched silently as Tilly rang the number.

The voice on the other end, charming and friendly, said, 'Anne Taylor here. Hello?'

'Hello, Anne,' Tilly murmured, 'can I speak to Robin?'

'I'll see if I can find him.' The voice was as cold as ice, all warmth instantly erased.

Tilly, aware of the tension in the carriage, lowered the phone and said, 'That was my mother-in-law.' Everyone nodded sympathetically.

'Hello, Tilly.' Robin's tone was neutral and calm, impossible to read.

'Robin, I'm on my way back from Exeter and the train's been held up. I'm afraid I'll be late but—'

'That's all right. I'll see you tomorrow when I bring the children back.'

'Well, I was thinking,' Tilly said desperately, 'I could still see you tonight. I'll be ready by . . . is nine too late?'

There was a sudden jolt of the train and Graham grabbed Tilly's arm. 'Matilda,' he said. 'The train is moving!'

'I know,' Tilly hissed. 'So, Robin,' she asked again, 'can we meet at nine?'

There was a pause and then Robin said, 'I don't think that's a good idea. You'll be tired. I think perhaps,' he sounded almost gentle, 'we should call it a day.'

That was it, then. She was not going to argue or beg. She'd had quite enough spirit-crushing humiliation for one day. 'All right,' she said lightly. 'I expect you're right. I'm pretty tired. Goodbye, then.' She pressed the button and returned the phone to its owner.

'Any luck?' the man asked.

'He wants to call it a day,' Tilly said. She was aware she had deprived her audience of a happy ending and smiled apologetically.

No one knew what to say. There were a few murmured expressions of sympathy. Tilly returned to her seat, bit her lip hard and concentrated on the view from the window.

Graham did not speak until they had nearly reached Westbury. 'You know,' he said, 'getting Robin back isn't necessarily the answer. You can't just pretend that everything's the same after this.'

'I know.'

'No, you don't. Not yet. Matilda, neither your husband nor your mother-in-law is in the railway carriage so what I am about to do holds some significance. Look at me.'

Tilly turned to look at him. Graham took her face in his hands and kissed her very gently. 'That,' he said, 'is a practical demonstration of alternative possibilities.'

Tilly sighed. 'It's a nice kiss,' she said, 'but after the night and day I've had I would be crazy, completely crazy, to even think of getting involved with you. Your life is way too complicated.'

'And you want simple and straightforward?' Graham shook his head. 'Deadly dull, Matilda, deadly dull.'

They were arriving at Westbury now. Tilly picked up her bag and sighed again. 'At this particular moment,' she said, 'dull sounds just beautiful.'

CHAPTER TWENTY-THREE

'It takes two to make a marriage a success and only one to make it a failure.'

HERBERT SAMUAL

Tilly was in bed when she heard the front door slam. She glanced at her alarm clock: ten past eleven. For one insane moment she thought it might be Robin, desperate to see her – 'It's no use, Tilly, I can't leave it like this. We have to talk.' – but almost immediately she realized it must be Margot. She sat up and rearranged the pillows so that she could lean back in comfort. Oh, it was bliss to be clean and comfortable and warm again!

There was a polite knock on the door and Margot came in. She was wearing her wine-coloured dress and the pearls Tilly and Charlotte had given her on her fiftieth birthday.

She sat down beside Tilly and gave her a hug. 'Happy birthday! Robin is dropping the children promptly at four tomorrow, so we can have a good birthday tea and give you your presents.'

'Lovely,' Tilly said. She smiled. 'You look very nice.'

'Thank you. I wasn't sure you'd be back yet. Did you manage to see Robin?'

'No.' Tilly gave a short laugh. 'I've decided it wasn't meant to happen. I got bogged down with Graham's domestic battles

292

and spent too long trying to persuade his horrible wife to see sense. You should have seen poor little Jack when we left, it was terrible. Of course she couldn't believe I might be concerned with Jack's welfare. She even accused me of being in love with Graham!'

'Which of course you're not.'

'Mum, give me a break; of course I'm not. He's quite impossible!' Tilly stared indignantly at her mother. 'Why on earth would I be in love with him?'

'I can't imagine. So, what happens now with you and Robin?'

Tilly shrugged. 'It's over. I did my best, Mum, but he's not interested. I'm not sure I am any more.'

'He's a fool, Tilly. I'm sorry, but his behaviour is indefensible.'

'I've been thinking about that too,' Tilly said. 'I don't want my kids to go through what Jack had to endure today. The quicker Robin and I can start to be friends, the better for Lucy and Sam. I am going to try very hard not to be bitter about all this. Which means that, however enjoyable it is, we can't have any more slate sessions. I mean it, Mum, I am really going to try to think nice thoughts about him.'

'That's very commendable,' Margot said, 'so long as you don't expect me to join in.' She stood up. 'I was going to give it to you tomorrow but I think it would be nice for you to see it now. Wait a moment.'

She came back a few moments later with a large and clearly heavy package, wrapped in shiny pink paper. 'This is from your father and me,' she said. 'We thought it would be useful to you in your new career.'

'Wow!' Tilly sat forward, her weariness forgotten. She tore

open the paper and glanced up at her mother with mingled excitement and anxiety. 'A laptop! Mum, this is far too generous! You shouldn't have done this.'

'It's second-hand,' Margot said. 'Harry got it for a very good price. You can't do anything without a computer these days. He says he's happy to explain it all to you.'

'Mum,' Tilly breathed, 'it's fantastic! Thank you so much!'

'I'm glad you like it. And now you must get some sleep. I want to hear all about the course and everything else but you're looking tired. You must tell me all about it in the morning.'

'I promise you I'll bore you rigid! Did you have a good evening with Dad or was it terrible?'

Margot bent down to pick up Tilly's dressing gown. 'Oh, it wasn't nearly as difficult as I thought it would be. The meal was very good. I had a wonderful bean salad in anchovy sauce. I shall try to cook it myself one day.'

'Not when I'm with you, please. I never did like beans.' Tilly eyed her mother curiously. It was impossible to gauge her mood. 'Dad didn't spend the whole time insisting you came home?'

'No. No, he didn't.' Margot folded the dressing gown and laid it on the end of Tilly's bed. 'No, I was very relieved, he didn't ask me to go home at all. In fact,' she gave a little laugh that didn't sound wholly natural, 'he seemed to be very pleased I was living here with you. He's very concerned about you. We had a most enjoyable conversation about your husband's character. You wouldn't have approved.'

Tilly grinned. 'I'm sure I wouldn't. At least,' she amended honestly, 'I'd have tried not to approve. I'm glad it went well.

Perhaps, now Dad accepts that the marriage is over, you'll be able to be friends.'

'Yes,' said Margot. 'You think he does accept that?'

'Oh, yes,' said Tilly airily. 'He knows there's no point in trying to flog a dead horse and certainly not an angry wife.'

'Sometimes, Tilly,' Margot said irritably, 'you have a very peculiar way of expressing yourself.' She picked up the laptop and went to the door. 'I'm off to bed. Sleep well.'

'Goodnight, Mum.' Tilly threw Robin's pillows back to his side of the bed, switched out the light and grinned in the darkness. She hoped she hadn't overdone the bit about the dead horse. On the whole she thought she hadn't.

'You know,' Tilly said smugly to Rhona on Tuesday, 'I could solve most men's love problems in a trice. It is so easy and I can never see why so few men understand. The trick is never to appear keen, or rather it's to appear keen at first in order to catch the woman's attention and then to back off. That makes the woman go forward and so it goes on. Too many men ruin potentially brilliant love affairs by showing they're too keen too soon. I told Dad to be charming and attentive and interested and sympathetic and never to display any sign that he wanted her back.'

'But Margot doesn't want to go back to him.'

'No, but I think she doesn't want him not to not want her to go back to him. Especially now he's at last exhibiting signs of civilized behaviour. I could tell she was really annoyed but of course she couldn't admit that so she's been really short-tempered ever since. I've told Dad he is not to ring her for at least a week. I bet you fifty pence she rings him first.'

'You're on. Do you think she will go back to him?'

'If he does what I say.'

Rhona burst out laughing. 'You're really enjoying this, aren't you? I don't know who I feel sorrier for, your mother or your father!'

'Did you ever see *The Parent Trap* with Hayley Mills? I remember I saw it when I was a little girl and I so wished Mum and Dad would split up so I could get them back like Hayley Mills did.'

'And now you can. What a good daughter you are.'

'I am actually. I've been very spoilt lately. If Mum goes back to Dad, I really will be on my own, reduced to cooking my own meals, doing my own housework. Scary.'

'You never know,' said Rhona, 'perhaps you and Robin . . .'

'No. I know it's over. When he came back with the children on Sunday, he didn't even stop to say happy birthday. Mind you, I can't say I blame him. My mother has perfected the most terrifyingly glacial way of greeting him. No, it's just going to be me and the kids.'

'Well,' Rhona said, 'that doesn't sound too bad to me.' She smiled bleakly at Tilly and stood up. 'I must go. New lunchtime rota, I'm on homework club. By the way, am I right in thinking you wouldn't like one of Arthur's wife's pottery creations as a leaving present?'

'Absolutely not,' Tilly confirmed.

'I thought so,' Rhona murmured. 'Don't worry, I'll be very tactful.'

She would too. Tilly went to the cloakroom and collected her coat and bag. She wished she could help Rhona. Perhaps she should invite her and Nigel to supper, try to befriend him, make him see he had no reason to be jealous. 'Nigel,' she would say, 'you have to trust your partner. Marriage is all about trust.' She could imagine Nigel nodding his head thoughtfully as if suddenly struck by the wisdom of her remark. 'Perhaps you're right,' he would say. 'How is Robin these days?'

Reasons to be grateful, she thought quickly as she walked briskly out to the car park: I am not married to Nigel; I have a mother and a father who are both undergoing extremely constructive mid-life crises; I have Lucy and Sam; I am soon to stop being an inadequate special needs assistant and start becoming a brilliant proofreader.

Tilly climbed into her car and decided she needed a shot of Amy's bracing common sense. Moreover, as long as Sam wasn't there to break things, the gallery acted like balm to the weariest spirit.

She had forgotten that Amy was setting up a new exhibition called 'The Dark Side'. When she arrived at the Curved Wheel, Amy had just finished repositioning a huge oil painting. 'Hi, Tilly,' she said. 'What do you think of this? It's called *Despair*.'

Tilly dropped her bag on the floor and studied the canvas. An enormous grey hand, positioned like a claw against a black background was poised over a frail little candle. Tilly frowned. 'Why would anyone want to buy that?'

'Search me!' Amy said cheerfully. 'I think it's supposed to have some cathartic effect on the viewer. I must say, they're all a bit grim. There's *Envy* over there, that great red thing is *Hatred* and those four grouped together are different studies of *Death*.'

'Yuck!' said Tilly. 'How long do you have to live with these?'

'Three weeks. Actually, I find them quite inspirational for

my new project.' Amy went over to her desk and pulled out an exercise book from her drawer. 'I took your advice!'

'What advice?'

'You told me I should write a book. It was a brilliant idea. I mean, I spend half my time here just people-watching. You made me realize I could use all that. I shall dedicate my book to you!'

'Thank you!' Tilly was genuinely pleased. 'What's it about?'

'A murder. You remember the man in the suit? He's going to be my murderer. It will be very dark and very scary and have lashings of inappropriate sex.'

'So what happens when it's a best-seller? Will you give up the day job?'

'No. I love it here. Well, I love most of it. And now I'm writing, I love all of it. Every time someone new comes in I see a possible new character. You know, this is a very exciting time for both of us!'

'It is?'

'Of course it is! By the time I've finished my novel, you'll be an incredibly proficient proofreader.'

'Do you really think that?'

'Of course I do. And you'll be able to proofread my novel and you'll probably end up editing it as well, and you'll be brilliant at that. You see, Tilly, it's never too late to discover new challenges!'

'You're right!' said Tilly. She could feel another epiphany coming on. 'Thank you, Amy, you have fired me with new enthusiasm. Now I must go and rescue Mum from Sam.'

'All right. Come again soon.'

'I will.' Tilly picked up her bag and glanced around at

Despair, *Death*, *Hatred* and *Envy*. 'When did you say the exhibition ends?'

'Three weeks.'

'Right,' Tilly said. 'I'll come back here in three weeks.'

That evening she spread her homework out on the kitchen table. She had meant to start at seven but getting the children to bed had become a rather protracted affair owing to Lucy's compulsion to keep Tilly fully informed of the Kylie/Annabel/Lucy triangle. Apparently, Kylie's latest suggestion was to tell Lucy they could be friends whenever Annabel was unavailable. Stuff that, Tilly said rudely, you're better off with Katy Hudson. Katy Hudson wasn't bad, Lucy admitted graciously. She had brought her hamster to school and had let Lucy hold it and hadn't been cross when Lucy let it escape. Mrs Dawes had given up her lunch hour to helping them find it and she had been the one to spot it under the photocopier. Tilly asked rather anxiously if Mrs Dawes had been cross but Lucy said she had found it funny. Mrs Dawes, Tilly thought humbly, was a saint.

By the time Tilly finally emerged from Lucy's bedside, Margot had already gone off to her evening class. So Tilly had a perfect opportunity to do her homework. Her first assignment was to go through a long and very boring document on local housing policy. Tilly sat down and began to read it. Then she stood up and decided to make herself a cup of tea. She made her tea and sat down again, and after ten minutes went upstairs to find a cardigan. Then she came down and began to read again. She raised her head slowly. She had never been conscious before of all the noises a house can make. There was the hum of the refrigerator, the rattling of the windowpane, the rampant indigestion of the boiler. Perhaps she should get a dog to keep her company. She thought of Horace and her throat constricted. She shut her eyes firmly and opened them again. Concentrate, she told herself.

There was a loud knock at the door and Tilly jumped. It was only half past eight; it couldn't be her mother. Tilly walked cautiously towards the door, briefly entertaining the possibility that it might be an escaped convict. If it weren't an escaped convict she would definitely research the possibility of investing in one of those spyholes in the middle of the door. One could never be too safe.

She opened the door and took an involuntary intake of breath at the sight of her father-in-law.

'Hello, Tilly,' said Peter. 'Am I allowed to come in?' He was smiling but Tilly could tell his question was genuine.

She nodded stiffly and he followed her through to the kitchen. She had never seen him looking nervous like this and it gave her confidence. His eyes took in the papers on the table and he said, 'I hope I haven't called at an inconvenient time.'

'I'm doing my homework,' Tilly said. 'I'm training to become a proofreader. It's something I can do at home when the baby comes along.'

'Right. That sounds like a good idea.' He stood by the table, shifting his car keys from one hand to the other, looking so miserable that Tilly almost felt sorry for him. Almost.

'Do sit down,' she said. 'Can I get you some coffee?'

'Thank you. If it's no trouble.'

Tilly put the kettle on, unhooked a mug from the dresser, took milk from the fridge. She said nothing and they both knew her silence was more scathing than any words could be.

'You must be wondering,' he said, 'why it's taken me so long to come and see you.'

Tilly raised her eyebrows. 'I did at first. I don't any more.'

'Tilly—'

'Do you mind if it's instant?'

'What? No, of course not. Believe me, Tilly, I never wanted any of this to happen.'

'Really?' Tilly placed the sugar bowl carefully down on the table. 'You do surprise me.'

'You have every right to be angry. The number of times I've wanted to pick up the phone and come straight over . . .'

'But you managed to resist the temptation. Well done!' She poured the boiling water into the mug and brought it over to him. 'Milk? Sugar?'

'Just milk, please.'

She swept up the sugar bowl and returned it to the cupboard before passing him the jug of milk.

He waited for her to sit down and then he said, 'I would like to try to explain.' He sighed. 'You know, of course, that Anne has never liked you.'

Such a brutal statement to come from the mouth of her courteous father-in-law. Tilly blanched but made a valiant effort to disguise her surprise. 'I've sometimes suspected she disapproved of me.'

'She did,' Peter said baldly. 'It's not your fault. I often think that if only you had been given a different name . . .'

The conversation was becoming more surreal by the minute. Tilly scratched her head and said, 'I'm sorry, you've lost me. What's wrong with my name?'

'The first time we met you,' Peter said slowly, 'you told Anne your name was Matilda. That is her mother's name. We've never talked to Robin about his maternal grandmother. She was a deeply deranged woman. As a mother she must have been terrifying: unpredictable, unrestrained, good humour changing quite inexplicably to violent fury. We all have unhappy memories but Anne has more than most and they're all associated with Matilda.'

'I see.' Tilly frowned. 'I remember the first time I met you both. It was your silver wedding anniversary. She told me her mother had ruined her wedding day.'

'Yes, it was not pleasant. And I'm quite certain that it was your name that led Anne to take such an irrational dislike to you. She convinced herself that you were quite wrong for Robin . . . and she adores Louise.'

'Yes,' said Tilly, 'I've always known that I was a very poor substitute.'

Peter leant forward. 'I don't want you to hate Anne. She's always been terrified she might start to behave like her mother. She's been so careful all her life to be cool and calm and in control. It's ironic and very sad that it's only where Robin's concerned that she displays something of her mother's temperament. She's let Robin down as well as herself.'

'Peter,' Tilly said softly, 'it isn't Anne's fault that Robin left me.'

Peter cleared his throat and sighed. 'Do you remember,' he said at last, 'when you and Robin were living in Exeter and Robin's godfather gave him money to go travelling? Anne arranged that, she was the inspiration behind the letter that accompanied it. She suggested to her nephew that he travel to

India. She even paid half his fare and suggested he ask Robin to come along. She was sure that if he could only get away from you he would see the error of his ways and you would break up. She always thought you would break up. That's why she worked so hard at keeping in touch with Louise. And then we moved down here. We should never have moved, I should never have agreed to it. I told her she should stay out of Robin's affairs but it's difficult to talk sensibly to someone whose prejudice has no basis in sense. She invited Louise to stay. She could see you and Robin were hitting a difficult patch and she exploited those tensions whenever she could. I would love to believe that Anne had nothing to do with everything that's happened but I know that's not true. The night he left you, Anne told him it was the best decision he'd ever made.'

'Oh,' said Tilly. She tried to smile. 'I expect that was bliss to Robin's ears.'

'I told him I thought he was being weak and irresponsible, but of course words of sympathy are always more appealing than those of criticism.'

'But you never came to see me after Robin left.'

'No, I didn't.' Peter looked at her steadily. 'I think Anne is on the edge and I think she knows that too. She made me promise I would stay away from you. And became hysterical until I gave my word.'

'So why have you come round now?'

'Because I think Robin could be about to make the biggest mistake of his life. I don't believe he's in love with Louise but he's certainly very grateful to her. She's not only written articles about his business, she's spread the word among her circle and I know for a fact she's won him at least two new very lucrative commissions. I know she's in love with him and she's a very determined woman. I don't think you should let him go to France on Friday.'

'So what are you saying? That I should make another last-ditch attempt to save my marriage? Nothing you've said changes the plain and simple truth that Robin chose to leave me. He has never so much as hinted that he's regretted doing so. I even asked him to come out to dinner with me so we could talk, and when I rang to say I'd be late he told me not to bother.'

'Tilly.' Peter looked embarrassed. 'Anne told him she saw you kissing that man at the cinema and then again on the station platform.'

'Oh, right, so Robin instantly decides not to see me. Peter, your son has been sleeping with another woman virtually since the day he discovered he was going to be a father again. He's made me miserable, he's made his children miserable. If he wants to get in touch with me he knows where I am.'

'I do understand.' Peter rubbed his forehead with his hands and then stood up. 'I must let you get on with your work. It's silly, I keep expecting Horace to bound in. It doesn't seem right here without him.'

'No,' Tilly murmured. 'It hasn't been right here since he died.'

Peter took out his car keys and transferred them from one hand to the other. 'The man at the station,' he said. 'You're not in love with him?'

'Do you know something?' Tilly said. 'I am getting so fed up with people asking me that question. Goodbye, Peter, and thank you. You've helped me make one decision anyway.'

'What's that?'

'I was wondering whether to start calling myself Matilda. I think I'll stick with Tilly.'

Peter smiled. 'I think that's wise.' He went to the door and opened it. 'I also think you're worth ten of Louise.'

'So do I,' Tilly said. 'At least, I intend to convince myself of that. Goodbye, Peter.' She returned to the document on housing policy.

In bed that night she was reading the paper when her eyes fell on a picture of Jennifer Aniston. '*I Thought My Marriage to Brad was For Ever!*' ran the headline. So did I, thought Tilly. Perhaps Jennifer and I made the same mistake. Perhaps we were stupid enough to believe there could be such a thing as a perfect marriage.

The next day was Tilly's last at Hurstfield Middle School. She had expected to sail through the morning quite happily. She knew she was not the world's best classroom assistant and it was a relief to give up a job that constantly reflected her woeful shortcomings. So she was touched and more than a little humbled by the presents she received from the children she felt she had failed to help: a chipped wooden elephant from Kitty, a large bar of milk chocolate from Matthew, a box of Quality Street from Joseph with a card saying, 'Bonjour, Mrs Taylor!'

At lunchtime Arthur made a little speech in the staffroom and presented her with a vivid red fruit bowl. 'Goodbye is a very sad word,' he said, 'but in Tilly's case we hope it will be *au revoir*. We look forward to seeing the latest little Taylor and we all join in wishing you a happy and fulfilling future!'

Tilly stood up, to general applause and the cries of 'Speech!' Tilly wanted to say what she knew to be true: that

Hurstfield was a fantastic school, that from all her observations she knew that teaching was the hardest job in the world and that the teachers here deserved and received her boundless admiration. She cleared her throat and turned to Arthur. 'You're right,' she began. 'Goodbye is a horrible word . . .' A huge lump positioned itself in her throat and suddenly all she could manage was to whisper, 'Thank you. Thank you all so very much.'

CHAPTER TWENTY-FOUR

'Farewell! A word that must be, and hath been
A sound which makes us linger; yet – farewell!'
LORD BYRON

On Thursday evening, quite unexpectedly, Robin came round. Tilly was upstairs in her bedroom, reading a story to the children, when Margot appeared in the doorway with a face carefully devoid of expression. She spoke in sepulchral tones: 'Robin wishes to say goodbye to the children.'

The children yelled, 'Daddy!' and were out of bed in a moment. Margot said, 'I'll be in the kitchen,' and turned on her heel. Tilly moved quickly to disperse the thunder. 'Hello, Robin! How nice to see you! You can finish their story and tuck them in tonight!'

She went downstairs and found her mother decimating carrots with violent swings of her vegetable peeler. 'Really, Mum,' she scolded, 'you didn't have to bring Robin upstairs. He does know the way, you know. He must be terrified of you.'

'I very much hope so,' Margot said grimly.

'Would you like me to carry on with the carrots?'

'No, you've been tearing around all day. Sit down and rest those legs.' She glanced at her daughter and said, 'Why are you smiling like that?'

Tilly laughed. 'I'm sorry. It's you. You've changed so much!'

'Really?' Margot paused, her peeler suspended above its next victim. 'Why?'

Tilly pulled up two chairs and sat down on one while resting her legs on the other. 'You've always been so easy and quiet and so nice to everybody and now you're suddenly this strong, frightening woman!'

'Rubbish,' Margot said, sweeping up the peelings and tipping them into a bowl for the compost.

'It's true,' Tilly said, 'you have to admit you've changed.'

'I have a little. I find anger very liberating. I shall always think that politeness and courtesy are important but I'm sure it's bad for one's indigestion to be polite to people whose behaviour deserves contempt.'

'Perhaps you're right,' Tilly said. 'Don't eat your words for they'll give you tummy ache!'

'Very true. I can't help thinking, for example, that where you and Robin— That's the phone – I'll go.' Tilly watched her mother disappear with unusual speed. She heard her say a little stiffly, 'Hello?' before relaxing into, 'I'm very well. How lovely to hear you! How are you?' Fine, Tilly thought, it wasn't Dad. Whoever it was had saved her from a lecture on Telling Robin How it Was. What her mother didn't understand was that if she once started to tell Robin how she really felt she wouldn't be able to stop. Being honest with Robin would almost certainly lead to being hysterical with Robin.

She sat back in her chair and wondered why the presence of her husband in the house made her feel so tired. She yawned and allowed her lids to fall over her eyes. She was brought back to consciousness by the sound of her name being called. She went through to the sitting room. 'It's Charlotte,' Margot said. 'She wants to say hello. Come and sit here.'

'Tilly,' Charlotte said, 'is Mum still there?'

Tilly watched Margot settle on the sofa opposite her. 'Yes,' she said.

'I just want to say you've done wonders with you-know-who. He sounds far more positive about everything.'

'Good, I'm glad.'

'He said he had a lovely meal with you-know-who. It was rather sweet; he said they had a fascinating conversation about the new types of computer mouse.'

'Really? I can't say that would do a lot for me.'

'Do you think your tactics are working? Dad seems to think you're the expert.'

'Really? Yes, I think they might be.'

'If they do,' Charlotte said benevolently, 'you'll deserve a medal.'

'Thank you.'

'If they don't, I'll be furious with you for meddling.'

'Don't I know it!'

'I don't want to interfere with your plans.' Charlotte was whispering now. 'But I thought you should know we've had to change ours. Michael and I are going to his parents at the weekend. His mother has been ill. So we can't have Dad any more. Which means he will be on his own for Easter unless you can fix something.'

'I'll see what I can do.'

'Good. How's your bump coming along?'

'Very well. How about your own?'

'It's big! I can't wait to start maternity leave. By the way,

I've talked to Julia. She handles all the proofreaders with the company. She'll send you their test whenever you like.'

'Give me a couple of weeks so I can finish all my homework and then send it to me. I am grateful.'

'I'm glad I can help. I hope I'll see you soon. Michael is going away in June on some course and Dad suggested I stay with him. We'll have to get the babies together. They might even like each other.'

'I hope so,' Tilly said and meant it.

'I hear Robin's with you.'

'It would be more accurate to say he's with the children.'

'You can give him my regards if you like. With any luck he'll choke on them.'

'Charlotte!' Tilly said. 'That's not like you.'

'You can put it down to hormones. Have you made any decision yet?'

'I don't want to start divorce proceedings until after the baby's born.' Tilly paused and raised her eyes. She felt herself going very red. 'Charlotte, I'll pass you back to Mum. Robin's here.' She followed Robin through to the kitchen and said quickly, 'I didn't know you were there.'

'Obviously.'

'I was talking to Charlotte. She sent you her regards.'

'Laced with poison, I should think.'

Tilly smiled. 'Something like that. Would you like a drink before you go?'

'A small coffee would be very nice. Tilly . . .'

'Yes?'

Robin thrust his hands into his pockets. 'I've bought you all some Easter eggs,' he said abruptly. 'They're over there, by the dresser.'

Tilly wondered what it was he had decided not to say. 'How very nice of you,' she said. She switched the kettle on. 'So, you're off to France tomorrow. How exciting! What time are you going off?'

'We're . . . I'm . . . the train leaves in the afternoon.'

'I see.' Tilly nodded. She couldn't think of anything else to say. The sound of a car horn shattered the uncomfortable silence. 'Well,' she said, 'it will do you good to have a rest . . . though, I suppose,' she added, 'you won't be doing a lot of resting.'

Robin threw her a startled glance. 'Sorry?'

Tilly gave a twisted smile. 'I didn't mean that to sound the way it came out.' She heard her mother calling her and said, 'I won't be a moment.'

Margot was outside the front door, picking up an empty crisp packet. 'Tilly,' she said, 'Graham's in the lane. He wants to show you something.'

'I'm just making Robin some coffee.'

'I'll make his coffee. Go and see what Graham wants.'

A battered Ford Escort was parked in front of Robin's car and Graham stood with studied nonchalance by its bonnet. 'What do you think?' he asked carelessly.

Tilly grinned. 'So that was *your* car horn! Does it work?'

'It goes like a bomb. And it has a car radio, although I can't get it to work yet.'

'That might have something to do with the fact that the aerial's bent.'

'Good point.' Graham patted the aerial. 'I'll fix it.'

'When did you buy it?'

'Yesterday. You know that Norwegian magazine I do stories for? They're bringing out a facts of life book for teenagers and

I'm doing the illustrations for it. They've commissioned me, paid me something in advance. If you like,' he said magnanimously, 'you can be my model for the pregnancy section.'

'I'm overwhelmed.'

'That's all right,' Graham said cheerfully. 'But I didn't come here to tell you that. I'm going down to see Jack for a few days. I'm staying with a friend in Exeter. Carmen has given me permission to see my son on Easter Sunday. Very kind of her. Did I tell you she and Tel might be going to Brussels?'

'Brussels! Why Brussels?'

'Why not? They're either going to Brussels or they're coming back to Frome. I'm going down to try to persuade them that Frome would be best.'

'Remember, you won't get anything by losing your temper.'

'I know. I'm going to be the voice of sweet reason. I must go.' He stiffened suddenly and looked behind her. 'I'm sorry,' he murmured, 'I can't resist it.' He gave her a firm kiss on the mouth. 'Now, watch this thing go!' he said and leapt into the car. The effect was slightly marred by the fact that it took another thirty seconds for the car to start.

Tilly turned round to find her husband was standing by the gate. 'That was Graham,' she said unnecessarily. 'He's bought a car. You finished your coffee quickly.'

'Your mother,' Robin said, 'had put sugar in it.'

'Oh,' Tilly said.

Robin crossed the road, took out his keys, unlocked his car and opened the front passenger door. 'I've got a birthday present for you,' he said. 'I'm sorry it's late.' He reached into the car and brought out a cardboard box. 'If you don't want him, I'll take him back. You know Stuart's mother's dog had puppies? This one sleeps for England. He hasn't stirred since I collected him.'

Tilly looked into the box. A small, soft, King Charles Cavalier puppy, chocolate brown with splashes of black, lay curled up on an old towel.

Robin glanced anxiously at Tilly. 'Do you like him?' he asked. 'Stuart calls him Freddy but . . .'

'I think Freddy's lovely.' Tilly picked him up and covered him with her cardigan. 'I'll try not to kill this one.'

Robin said quietly, 'You didn't kill Horace.' He gave her a sudden, brief kiss on the cheek, walked round to his side of the car, got in and leant over to unwind the passenger window. 'Please tell Margot that if it's any consolation, I share her low opinion of me. I wish . . .' He paused. 'I wish things could have been different.'

He turned on the engine and she watched his car disappear down the road.

Margot was standing in the drive. 'Tilly, what exactly is going on? First, you kiss Graham, in full view of old Mrs Harris by the way – she nearly dropped her walking stick – and then you embrace your estranged husband, also in full view of Mrs Harris.'

'It's nothing, Mum,' Tilly said. 'Graham always kisses me when he sees Robin; it's a sort of Pavlovian reaction. And Robin was . . . Robin was just saying goodbye. He was very nice . . . he said he was sorry, I think. And he's bought me this.' She pushed back her cardigan. 'He's called Freddy.'

'He's given you a dog?' Margot looked at him in horror. 'For heaven's sake, that man is impossible! He may be going off with some amoral excuse for a woman, he may have abandoned a wife and two children and another one on the way, but it doesn't matter because he's bought you a puppy! Never mind that you're about to have a baby, never mind that you're trying to train for a new career, never mind that you are looking after his children all on your own. Never mind all that! Robin has given you a puppy! And to think I always thought he was a thoughtful, sensitive young man! I tell you something, if he comes near me again, I'll put more than sugar in his coffee and don't you dare to shed any tears for him, Tilly, or I'll go out and scream!'

'Mum,' Tilly said with complete sincerity, 'I wouldn't dare.'

CHAPTER TWENTY-FIVE

'Madness is to think of too many things in succession too fast, or of one thing too exclusively.'

VOLTAIRE

Reasons to be cheerful: no more dithering about whether to take Robin back; no more danger of committing Grandma's mistake of placing all happiness on shoulders of one man; no more tricky conversations with mother-in-law; satisfaction in having had mature and dignified exchange of words with husband yesterday.

That last was indeed a real achievement, the first test of her new life as a semi-official divorced spouse. True, there were huge mountains of horror lying in wait. She would have to be cool, calm and mature in all matters relating to her children and their soon-to-be stepmother. She could imagine it all. Lucy would return from weekends with her father and Louise, glowing with heroine-worship. 'Mum, you must start to use a blusher. Louise says it does wonders for cheekbones,' or 'Mum, you must start to go to the gym. Louise thinks you could look quite pretty if you tried.' Reasons to be cheerful, she thought desperately: Lucy is, as of now, not interested in blushers or exercise regimes.

Freddy had instantly elevated the holiday to a status worthy of Christmas. His original sleepiness had proved deceptive, or rather it had become fully comprehensible given his prodigious energy when he was *not* asleep. Tilly watched the children shriek with laughter as Freddy chased them round the garden, and felt her spirits lift. She was determined to create a terrific Easter. She had bought pizza, lemonade and ice cream for a Friday night celebratory supper. And there *was* something to celebrate. No more vacillation, no more indecision. The marriage was over and Tilly Taylor knew she could cope. Her man had been taken from her and she had been buffeted by storms of jealousy, inadequacy, bitterness and self-pity. But here she was: still sane, still able to laugh and armed with a new determination to fend for herself and her children. She'd recently been told a lovely Abraham Lincoln quote. 'Most people,' he'd said, 'are about as happy as they decide to be.' Well, Tilly thought grimly, from now on I'm deciding to be happy.

'Why are we having a party tea?' asked Lucy. 'We don't normally have party tea on Good Friday.' This was the difference between Sam and Lucy. Sam simply accepted any good luck that came his way. Of course that might simply be the difference between a three-year-old and a six-year-old but Tilly didn't think so. Sam had never asked why Daddy was no longer living with them. The bed-wetting had almost stopped now and the only visible sign of distress was the thumb that he kept tight in his mouth.

'We are celebrating,' Tilly said, 'the fact that you are here with me this weekend. And we're going to have one great Easter.'

'Daddy will miss us,' said Lucy.

'I wouldn't worry too much about Daddy,' Tilly said.

Lucy surveyed Tilly severely over her piece of pizza. 'Daddy said he would miss us very much.'

'Of course he will,' Tilly said, feeling correctly chastised, 'but it's nice for me because I have you instead.'

'Where's Granny?' Sam asked.

'She's gone to see Great-Grandma. She'll be back soon.' Tilly leant across to remove a sliver of onion from the side of Sam's mouth. 'So, what shall we do this weekend?'

'I know!' Lucy crowed. 'I've got Andrew Dale's birthday party tomorrow afternoon but you can take us for an Easter Egg hunt on Sunday!'

'I can,' Tilly said. 'We could go to the woods around King Alfred's Tower and then we could come back for Sunday lunch with Granny. How about that?'

Lucy nodded a benevolent approval. 'Can Granddad come?'

'You'd better ask Granny,' said Tilly. 'She'll be the one to cook the lunch.'

'I like Granddad,' Sam said.

'So do I!' said Tilly.

'Of course you do!' Lucy chortled. 'He's your dad!'

Weren't children wonderful? They bestowed on their parents a perfect, unconditional love, however undeserved, and they expected everyone else to feel the same. Perhaps that was why so many adult love affairs ended up on the scrapheap. Everyone was too busy trying to follow that treacherous childhood mirage of perfect, unquestioning love. Had Tilly expected too much of Robin? Yes. Had Robin expected too much of Tilly? Undoubtedly.

'Will you still love me,' Tilly asked her children, 'when I'm old and grey?'

Sam gave his mother a confident smile. 'You not get old,' he said.

Margot came home half an hour later, looking pale and weary.

'Cup of tea?' Tilly asked. 'I'll put the kettle on.'

'Thank you,' Margot said. She hung her coat and bag on the peg and pulled out a chair onto which she sat with a 'That's better!'

'You look tired. How was Grandma?'

'Fine,' Margot said. 'That's the trouble. She's quite happy.' She gave a long sigh. 'Dinah died in her sleep two nights ago.'

'Oh, no.' Tilly went straight over to her mother and enveloped her in a tight embrace. 'I'm so sorry. She was such fun.' She released Margot and scrutinized her earnestly. 'Are you all right?'

'Yes,' said Margot, 'I'm all right. I shall miss her very much and it upsets me that Mummy hasn't even noticed she's gone. For two years she's been Mummy's constant companion and Mummy probably can't even remember who she was. Tilly, if I ever get like that I want you to put me down. All right?'

'Absolutely. I'll keep a hypodermic needle with me at all times.'

'I hope you do. You know what's really sad? I remember Mum asking exactly the same of me and I probably gave the same answer you did. What are you cooking?'

'Spicy sausage casserole,' Tilly said proudly. 'And I don't need any help. I want you to take your tea into the sitting room and watch something very silly on television while I bath the kids.'

Lucy came in and said, 'Hello, Granny, can Granddad come to lunch on Sunday?'

Tilly turned her back on her mother and stirred the tea bags vigorously.

'I think,' Margot said, 'that's a very nice idea. But I expect he'll be going up to see Charlotte.'

'I don't think so,' Tilly said with finely judged carelessness. 'Charlotte told me they're going to Michael's parents.'

'Well, really, Tilly, you might have told me. We can't let Harry spend Easter Sunday on his own!'

'Can I ring him for you now?' Lucy asked.

'That's very kind of you,' said Margot. 'I'll come with you.'

'Have your tea first,' Tilly protested. She set a mug in front of her mother. 'There's no hurry.'

'I expect,' Lucy said, 'Granny wants to do it right away.'

'I expect,' Margot said, pushing back her chair, 'you're right.'

At half past three the next day Tilly took Lucy to her party and left after assuring Andrew's mother that Lucy and only Lucy had chosen his present. It was a violent-yellow lump of furry froth with purple eyes and it screamed every time it was thrown to the floor. Lucy knew that Andrew would love it.

Tilly climbed into her car and knew she did not want to go home. Margot had taken Sam and Freddy to see a friend whose ailing grandchild was in need of entertainment and Tilly knew that if she went home to the empty house she would start imagining Robin and Louise in some grand four-poster bed. In the old days she would have gone round to see Rhona but Rhona had Nigel and Nigel had done his best to seal her away from the outside world. Well, Tilly thought suddenly, perhaps she should play the Prince to Rhona's Sleeping

Beauty. She would venture in, armed with the simple sword of unthreatening female friendship, and make Nigel see he could not and should not isolate his wife. Tilly raised her chin, put her key in the ignition and set forth for Weymouth Road.

She parked the car after going backwards and forwards between two increasingly irritating cars and climbed out to study her handiwork. Her little white Fiat looked as if it were ready for flight, its front left wing straining to get away. It would have to do. Tilly's sword of friendship was beginning to wilt and if she didn't go now she would take fright and leave.

She straightened her jacket and walked towards Rhona's house. Then she walked back again because she'd forgotten to lock the car. Perhaps, she thought hopefully, Nigel wouldn't be there. Or perhaps Nigel would be there on his own. What would she say? As she walked up the path she rehearsed her greeting. 'Hello, Nigel, it's lovely to see you again/Hi, Nigel, I want to talk to you about Rhona/Hi, Nigel, I thought it was time I said hello/Hi, Nigel, please don't shut the door in my face.' She knocked on the door and heard steps. A voice, Rhona's voice, small and quavering, said, 'Who is it?'

'It's me, Tilly.'

The door was opened by an unseen hand. Tilly walked in out of the sun, blinked and said, 'Oh, my God!'

Rhona shut the door quickly. 'It's not as bad as it looks.' One side of her face was swollen and coloured with a violent-purple sheen. There was blood around her nose, blood on her hair, blood on her sweatshirt.

Tilly said, 'Where is he?'

'He's gone out to buy some wine.'

'He's gone to buy some wine! Rhona!' Tilly took a deep breath. 'You must see you can't stay here? Where's Chloe? Surely she's spending Easter with you?'

Rhona looked away. 'No. She wanted to be with her father.'

'Well, I'm not leaving you here with . . . with him. The man's either a brute or he's mad or more probably both. My car's outside. Get your coat and come with me.'

Rhona shook her head. 'I don't know. I don't know anything any more. I'm frightened.'

'Of course you are. It's going to be all right. But we need to go now before he comes back.'

Rhona bit her lip. 'I don't know. I don't know what to do.'

'I do,' said Tilly. 'You have to come home with me. You can stay as long as you like, until we sort all this business out. Rhona, suppose I'd been Chloe? What would she think if she saw her mother covered in blood? You can't live like this any more.'

'I don't think I can.' She sniffed. 'All right, then.' She bit her lip. 'I'll pack a few things together and I'll come with you. I will. I'll do that.'

Tilly struggled to keep the panic from her voice. 'What about Nigel? Shouldn't we just go now?'

'He won't be back for ages. He never comes back until he's calmed down. He hates himself for losing control. He can't help it, but he hates himself. I won't be very long.'

'All right,' Tilly said. 'I'll help you.' She followed Rhona up to her bedroom.

Rhona said listlessly, 'I ought to clean my face,' and disappeared into the bathroom. She seemed to have no idea of the need for speed and Tilly dared not hurry her in case she changed her mind. Tilly went into Rhona's bedroom and walked restlessly round the wrought-iron bed. She picked up a large Valentine card with a fat red heart sitting uncomfortably on a bouquet of red roses. Tilly opened it. 'To the love of my life from your devoted husband.' Tilly returned it to the mantelpiece with a shaking hand and walked over to the bay window. Outside, a woman was walking her dog, constantly pulling its lead and saying, 'Come *on*, Jasper,' every time it raised its hind leg.

Rhona came back with a washbag and towel. 'Don't worry,' she said, 'I won't be a minute.' She pulled out an overnight bag from her wardrobe and threw it on the bed. Her face crumpled. 'I don't know what to take,' she said. 'What shall I take?'

'Sit!' Tilly said. 'Sit down!' She pushed Rhona gently onto the bed and took the towel and washbag from her. Then she began opening drawers, taking out underwear, a jumper, a pair of trousers.

Rhona put her hands to her face. 'It's so silly,' she said. 'He found that picture Graham drew of me. I should have thrown it away but it made me laugh. I should have thrown it away.'

'Hush,' Tilly said. 'It doesn't matter now. Nothing matters.' She froze suddenly. 'Did you hear something?'

'I told him,' Rhona persisted, 'I told him Graham did pictures of all of us. I told him it was just a silly joke. How could he think it meant anything?' She stood up abruptly. 'I think I'm going to be sick.'

'All right,' Tilly said. 'Don't worry. You go to the bathroom.'

She followed Rhona onto the landing and when Rhona went into the bathroom she went to the top of the stairs. The house was so dark; how had she never noticed this before? She walked slowly down each stair, her ears straining to interpret the language of someone else's home. She stood in the hall and made herself walk towards the kitchen and open the door. It was empty, of course. This was stupid; there was no one there, she was making herself hysterical and, worse, she was wasting time. She turned and made her way back up to the bedroom as quickly as she could. She gathered up cosmetics, brush and comb from the dressing table and threw them all into the bag.

Rhona returned to the bedroom. Her face was deathly pale apart from the disfiguring purple lump below her eye. She shut the door and held up a tube of toothpaste. 'I can't find the top.'

'Never mind,' Tilly said. 'Leave it. I have gallons of toothpaste at home. Are you all right? Shall we go?'

Rhona glanced round the room. 'I should ring Chloe,' she murmured, 'and let her know where I am in case she wants to come round.'

'You can do that from my house.'

'All right, but—'

They both saw the door handle move. Instinctively, Tilly reached for Rhona's hand and pushed her back with her towards the window. They both watched the door and they both watched Nigel come through and shut the door behind him. He was so good-looking. Such a waste, Tilly thought, even as another part of her brain threw up desperate possibilities of charging past him. With a different character he could have been so attractive. If the muscle on the side of his face did not twitch in that funny way, if his eyes did not look as if they'd never understood a joke in his life, if he wasn't carrying that great big kitchen knife in his hand . . .

'Rhona,' he said quietly, 'what are you doing?' He came round the bed, past the mantelpiece with the Valentine card, and stood in front of the dressing table.

Tilly licked lips that had gone very dry. 'Hi,' she said. 'It's good to see you again, Nigel. I hope you don't mind but I've persuaded Rhona to come and stay with me for a few days.' Her voice was shaking. 'I'm afraid we really do have to go now.'

'Rhona.' Nigel's voice was low and flat. 'Tell your friend to go away and leave us alone.'

'Tilly,' Rhona whispered, 'perhaps you should leave.'

'I'm not going without you.' Tilly tried very hard to keep her eyes from staring at the knife in Nigel's hands. 'Look,' she tried to smile at him, 'why don't you put that knife down?'

Nigel glanced at Tilly for the first time. He moved forward a couple of paces until he was within spitting distance of her. He spoke very softly, almost politely. 'Why don't you leave before you get hurt?'

'Listen,' Tilly said quickly, 'can't we be sensible about this? Rhona just needs a little time away from you. She'll be back in no time. And I have to pick up my daughter from her party so we really must get going.'

'Shut up!' He hit her hard across the face.

Rhona shouted, 'Nigel! Don't! Please stop it! Tilly, go, go at once, please go!'

'All right, all right!' Tilly's voice rose. She was sick with fear and her face felt as though it was on fire, but she wouldn't let go of Rhona's wrist. 'I'm going, I really am . . .'

Nigel's face seemed to be swimming before her eyes. She heard him cry out, 'Rhona, I really loved you! I only wanted to love you!'

She saw him raise his knife and screamed, 'Don't! Stay away! Please, please don't! This is all so silly, Nigel, don't . . .'

She saw the flash of steel, tried to avoid it, heard someone screaming and fell.

CHAPTER TWENTY-SIX

'Words are physic to the distempered mind.'
AESCHYLUS

She was lying in the ambulance and a nice man was holding her hand and telling her everything was going to be all right. Fierce waves of pain were beating against her skull, trying to get out. Her arm was hurting, everywhere was hurting. She wished the pain would go away, it was making it difficult to concentrate on all the important things she had to tell the nice man. She opened her eyes and concentrated on his face.

'Lucy,' she said, 'my daughter. She's at Andrew's party. I have to pick her up at half past five.'

It was all so difficult. She had to remember Andrew's address and then she had to tell the man to ring Margot and if Margot was still not back she had to tell him to ring her father and if he weren't there . . .

'If he isn't there, I'll get someone else to go. Don't worry. We'll sort it out.'

'Will you ring now?'

'We'll ring right now.' He was talking to someone else. They were sorting it. Lucy would be fine, her baby would be fine. Everything was fine.

Now she was in hospital. A doctor was sewing up her arm.

326

He was a locum, he told her, he'd retired from general practice three years earlier but he liked to keep his hand in. It was
better to keep busy and the money was always useful, wasn't
it? Tilly said faintly it certainly was. The locum said he'd done
a good job on her arm and she'd be left with an interesting
scar. He told her she was a very lucky lady and Tilly said she
was sure she was.

Now someone was telling her she'd have to stay in hospital overnight so they could monitor the baby and keep an eye
on her blood pressure. Then a policeman appeared and told
her he'd have to ask her a few more questions. Her head was
still throbbing and she had to make a real effort to tell him
what had happened, not because she couldn't remember –
she knew she would never forget – but because it was difficult to speak without crying. Someone brought her a cup of
sweet tea and the policeman said he'd come again soon. She
said that would be nice and then apologized because she
realized her response was inappropriate, but he didn't seem
to mind.

Then at last she was in bed. Sleep. Blissful, pain-quenching
sleep. Consciousness seeped back slowly. The raging torrent
in her head had subsided, leaving a dull ache. She opened her
eyes and saw her father sitting on a chair beside her bed. He
had a Sainsbury's bag on his lap. She smiled sleepily, 'Hello,
Dad!'

Harry Treadwell visibly relaxed. 'Good girl!' he said. 'How
do you feel?'

'Not bad.' Tilly struggled to sit up and Harry was out of his
chair in a moment, rearranging pillows, levering Tilly gently
back against them. 'There! Are you comfortable now? Does
your arm hurt a lot?'

'No, it's all right, really. What about the children? Are they all right? Did someone get Lucy?'

'They're fine. I picked up Lucy from her party. I was only a little late and she was quite happy. I told her you'd had a slight accident. Sam was a bit upset at bedtime but when I left to come to you he was almost asleep. Your mother told me to give you these.' He held up the carrier bag. 'Face stuff, I think. I'll put them here, shall I?'

'Thank you.'

'Margot sends her love. She'll be along in the morning. She says she'll be with you at half past ten.'

'Oh, Dad, that's silly. She doesn't have to do that. The nurse says I can go home tomorrow afternoon.'

'I know, Margot rang the hospital, but she wants to come in anyway. I said I'd stay with the children. Lucy tells me I'm taking them on an Easter egg hunt.'

'Dad, that's truly noble of you. There's a large bag of little eggs in the back of the dresser. Mum knows where they are. You have to make the hiding places very easy and in Sam's case you have to have the hiding places virtually under his nose. I'm sorry to land this on you.'

'Nonsense, I'll enjoy it. Are you really feeling better? You've got a lump the size of an egg on your forehead.'

'It aches a bit. Everyone says I'm very lucky.'

Harry shook his head. 'I just can't believe this has happened . . . in Weymouth Road, of all places.'

Tilly smiled. For a moment her father's comment put a gloriously reassuring distance between her and the violence she had witnessed. Then she frowned. 'Dad, what's happened to Rhona? Do you know how she is?'

'She's staying with her daughter and her ex-husband.

What's his name? He did tell me.'

'Mark. He's called Mark.'

'That's it. He rang us just before I left. He said Rhona was quite hysterical. Understandable in the circumstances. I think she's under sedation at the moment. It's a very nasty business.'

'Will you ask Mum to ring her in the morning and say I am so, so sorry. Oh, God, Dad, it's all my fault. If I hadn't gone round . . .'

'You didn't put the knife in his hand, Tilly. That was his decision.'

'None of this would have happened if I hadn't been there. Rhona will never forgive me.'

'That's not true. I can tell you for a fact that's not true.' Harry took her hand in his. 'Her ex-husband – Mark – rang us to find out if you were all right. He said *you* were one of the reasons why Rhona was in such a state. She said she'd never forgive herself if your baby was . . . if . . .' Harry paused to clear his throat. 'Anyway, Margot was able to report that you were all right and that you would be coming home tomorrow. Mark was very relieved.'

'But if I hadn't been there—'

'If you hadn't been there,' Harry said, 'Nigel would have come home and been free to beat Rhona up again. I don't think you should waste any time feeling guilty about Nigel deciding to kill himself. You're all right. Your baby's all right. Rhona is *going* to be all right. Mark says Chloe is being marvellous. Apparently, she's already decided she's going to repaint Rhona's house so that they can start afresh.'

Tilly closed her eyes tight but the tears still came. 'I'm

sorry,' she whispered, 'I'm so sorry.' She felt her father's arms around her and she cried silently into his jacket. He held her for a long time, patting her arm awkwardly, saying over and over, 'There now, Tilly, there now . . .'

At last she raised her head and said, 'I've made your jacket wet.'

'Never mind that. Do you want to use my handkerchief?'

'I'll make that wet too.'

'I don't mind. Now blow your nose and promise me you won't blame yourself for what that madman did. I do know a little bit about human nature, you know.'

Tilly smiled again. 'I know you do.' She looked up as another visitor came towards her. Amy was holding a bouquet of lilies. 'I won't stay a minute,' she said. 'I bought you these but I suddenly remembered they're funeral flowers, which is either appropriate or incredibly tactless. Shall I come back tomorrow?'

'No,' Tilly said, 'stay a bit. And the lilies are beautiful. There's another chair somewhere.'

'Have mine,' Harry said. He stood up. 'It's time I got back.' He bent down and gave Tilly a quick kiss on the cheek. 'I'll see you tomorrow.'

Amy sat down and watched Harry escape. 'Oh, dear, did I drive him away?'

'I think he was glad of the excuse. He's rather overwhelmed by it all. How did you know I was here?'

'Mandy Roberts lives two down from Rhona. She saw the police and ambulance and rushed over to see if she could help. She rang Mark and Chloe and stayed with Rhona and the policewoman until they arrived. She rang me to see if I'd collect her boy from the party.'

'Did she say how Rhona was?'

'Pretty incoherent, apparently. She did say you saved her life.'

'That's rubbish. I did nothing of the sort. I just got in the way of Nigel. I don't think he meant to hurt me at all. Then I fell and knocked myself on the corner of that stupid bedstead.'

'Can you remember anything after that?'

Tilly's bottom lip quivered. 'I could only have blacked out for a few moments. Rhona was screaming, she was crouching in the corner of the room and she was screaming. Nigel lay on the floor. He'd killed himself with the knife. That was the worst bit. I didn't know if he was dead and at first I was too frightened to find out, but Rhona wouldn't stop screaming so I went over and he was dead, he was definitely dead. He'd been in the army so I suppose he knew how to do it properly. So then I got to the phone and I rang for help. And still Rhona screamed. It was horrible.' Tilly bit her lip. 'Oh, God, I'm going to start crying again.'

'You're allowed to do that. You're a heroine, Tilly.'

Tilly blew her nose. 'No, I'm not. Heroines don't cry.'

'Yes, they do. Mine do, anyway. You were very brave. Nigel was obviously a complete psycho. In fact,' Amy looked thoughtful for a moment, 'he'd make a brilliant villain.'

'Amy!'

'No, of course not. I'm sorry!'

'I should think so!' Tilly felt better. Amy's response, like Harry's, helped to distance the horror and reassure her that it was alien, foreign and nothing like the rest of her life.

A nurse appeared and said, 'I'll put these in water. And I'm afraid visiting hours are over.'

Amy stood up at once. 'Of course, I'm sorry.' She gave Tilly's hand a squeeze. 'I'll ring you very soon. I think you're fantastic! Now get a good night's sleep!'

Which Tilly did not get. Images of giant knives and gaping wounds haunted her dreams and once she woke up in a feverish panic until the sounds of the ward gradually soothed her into a state of calm. The woman in the bed next to her was snoring, in the bathroom someone was flushing the lavatory. Tilly lay back on her bed. She thought of Nigel and the way he'd looked at Rhona in the Indian restaurant. They'd been so happy then. He had such beautiful hands. Poor Nigel. Poor Rhona.

In the morning, the doctor came round and agreed that she could go home as long as she promised to rest. Tilly told the nurse that her mother was coming in at half past ten. The nurse looked at her watch. 'That gives you an hour and a half to get ready,' she said. 'That *should* be enough time.'

Tilly presumed the comment was a joke. She walked stiffly to the bathroom, armed with shampoo, soap, clothes and cosmetic bag. An hour later, she re-emerged, having discovered that bathing and dressing herself with an arm that had turned to wood was no easy task.

Back in the ward, she found a visitor was waiting for her. For a moment, her entire body felt as if it had stopped working. She gave herself a mental shake and walked slowly towards her bed. She was glad she had put on some make-up.

As always, her mother-in-law looked immaculate. Today, she wore a grey pinstriped trouser suit with a pale pink top that perfectly matched her lipstick. She stood up as Tilly approached the bed and watched gravely as Tilly heaved herself onto it. 'Tilly,' she breathed, 'you poor girl!'

Tilly winced slightly as she pushed herself back against the pillows. She wondered who had told Anne what had happened and she wondered why Anne was here now. Tilly wished she would go away.

Anne returned to her chair. 'I am horrified! What you must have gone through! What a terrifying experience! And your poor face! It looks absolutely ghastly!'

So much for the make-up, Tilly thought. She stared blankly at her mother-in-law. It was far easier to say nothing at all.

'You're very pale,' Anne said. 'I mustn't keep you long. I only came to see if you were all right. I wanted to bring you a present – flowers or chocolates – but in the end I decided that what you needed more than anything else was a sympathetic and understanding voice. Sometimes words are far more powerful than medicine, don't you think?'

Tilly moistened her lips and spoke at last. 'Yes,' she said, 'I think words are very powerful.'

'Before I leave you,' Anne said, 'I feel it would be . . . helpful . . . to say something about Robin.' She gazed earnestly at Tilly and when she received no response she glanced down at her trouser leg and proceeded to iron out an invisible crease. 'I may not know much,' she said, 'but I do know my son. Robin has always taken his responsibilities very seriously and I know he is racked with guilt about leaving you.'

'That's very sweet of him.'

'Yes, well, that's Robin. And knowing Robin as I do, I am pretty sure how he will react when he hears about your unfortunate experience. Even though he is desperately in love with Louise, I know that he will feel duty bound to return to his wife. Robin will say—'

'Robin will say,' said a voice, 'that his mother is talking a load of old crap.'

CHAPTER TWENTY-SEVEN

'Two mothers-in-law'
– LORD JOHN RUSSELL on being asked what he would
consider a proper punishment for bigamy.

Anne turned sharply. 'Darling!' she exclaimed. 'You look terrible!'

He did look terrible. His face looked as crumpled as his clothes, his complexion was grey and he needed a shave.

'You look,' Tilly said, 'like I feel.'

'I feel,' Robin responded, 'like you look.'

'This *is* a surprise!' Anne said brightly. 'I was trying to explain to Tilly that—'

'Mum,' Robin interrupted her wearily. 'Why don't you go away?'

Anne rose from her chair, her hands clamped tightly together, two pink circles forming on either side of her face. 'Robin,' she declared, 'you're tired and you're upset. You can't think rationally at the moment. Tilly is not right for you and this is no time to think about making rash promises.'

Yet another visitor had come into the ward. She positioned herself at the end of the bed and said, 'I couldn't agree more.'

There was a moment's silence while everyone looked at Margot.

'Thank God,' Anne said warmly, 'for a voice of sanity. I suspect I can speak for both of us when I say that we mothers have both of your interests at heart and if we think your marriage should end then you should take our advice seriously. At the moment—'

'At the moment,' Margot said firmly, 'Tilly needs peace and quiet. She's coming home this afternoon.'

'Mum,' Tilly said, 'they're letting me go home now. I'm ready to go.'

'In that case—' said Margot.

'In that case,' said Robin, 'I would like, if Tilly is willing, to take her down to my car and talk to her for twenty minutes. And then, after twenty minutes, you can take her home.'

Margot glanced at Tilly and pursed her lips before giving a stiff nod. 'You can have fifteen minutes,' she said, 'and not a moment longer.'

'In the meantime,' Robin suggested, 'you two can have a pleasant chat up here.' He helped Tilly off the bed and took her hand. 'All right?' he asked gently. 'You can manage this?'

Tilly smiled faintly. 'Just about,' she murmured.

They progressed slowly down the stairs with Robin keeping his hand on her good arm. 'I thought,' Tilly said, 'you were in France.'

'I was.'

'You can't have been there very long.'

'Long enough,' Robin said. 'Three hours.' He opened the door for her and they went down the steps of the hospital entrance.

'Three hours?' Tilly stopped and then shivered. The hospital had been as warm as a cocoon and there was a cold breeze that stung her eyes.

'Come along,' Robin said, 'let's get you into the car. I have a rug in the back.'

'I know you do,' Tilly said. 'It's very smelly.'

Robin helped her into the car and she allowed him to cover her legs with the rug, which was indeed smelly. He went round to the other side and sat down in the driving seat. 'Are you comfortable?' he asked.

'No,' Tilly said. 'My face hurts and my arm hurts. Why were you in France for only three hours?'

'I didn't go till yesterday. John was rushed to hospital on Friday morning.'

'*Why?* What happened? Is he all right?'

'He's fine,' Robin said dismissively. 'He had a burst appendix.'

'A burst appendix! Poor John! How terrible!'

'He'll live,' Robin said. 'But meanwhile I had to stay on and finish the order he was doing. So I went to France yesterday and I'd just got off the train at Fontainebleau when Harry rang.'

Tilly shook her head. 'Why did Dad ring you? I was all right. He knew I was all right.'

'I think,' Robin said gently, 'he thought I might like to know someone had nearly killed you.'

'That's rubbish,' Tilly said. 'Nigel didn't try to kill me.'

Robin's face hardened. 'I should have known he'd do something like this.'

'Don't be silly,' Tilly said. 'How could you possibly have known?'

Robin shrugged. 'He liked Oasis.'

Tilly shocked herself by laughing. She said, 'You shouldn't joke about Nigel.'

'If ever a man deserved to have bad jokes made about him,' Robin said, 'it is Nigel.'

Tilly bit her lip. 'I *thought* he was going to kill me. I thought I was going to lose the baby.'

'I know, but you didn't. You're all right. You're both all right. There's nothing to worry about.'

'I don't want to talk about it any more.'

'All right.'

'So tell me: what did you do then?'

'I crossed the platform and got the next train back to Paris. And then, when I got to Paris, I got the next train back to London.'

'Well,' said Tilly, 'it was very kind of you to be so concerned.'

'Look,' said Robin, 'in a few minutes your mother's going to appear and before she does, I need to say something and it might be too late but I have to try. The last few months . . . I don't know . . . everything seemed to get out of control and become big and weird and different and I didn't know how to stop it, but I need to tell you what happened and I need you to listen. Will you listen, Tilly?'

Tilly nodded. An old Renault Four drew up next to them and a young man in a tracksuit got out. He took from the back seat a huge bouquet of red roses, smoothed his hair and raced towards the hospital entrance.

'When I walked out ten weeks ago,' Robin said, 'it wasn't because I hated you. I hated myself. I didn't have the guts to admit you were right about Radstock. It was ridiculously premature, we should not have moved and we very nearly went under. I got more and more desperate and then when you said you were pregnant, I flipped. But I never, *ever*, thought our marriage was over.'

'Your mother said. . .'

'My mother has said lots of things and I'm pretty sure that most of them are untrue. I assumed – I believed – that once I'd sorted myself out, I'd be fit to live with you again. Louise rang a few days after I moved in with my parents. Anne had told her what had happened and she told me she had a friend who lived outside Radstock who would welcome a lodger. I've been working all hours since we got the van Duren order and it was great to have a place so near to the workshop. I was very grateful to Louise.'

Tilly kept her eyes fixed on the Renault Four. 'I'm sure you were.'

'Tilly,' Robin said, 'do you remember the first night we met? The day after that party, I was sitting outside Devonshire House on the balcony and Louise came up and joined me. She told me she'd made a mistake, she said she wanted us to get back together. And I looked up and saw your face in the window. You'd gone off without saying anything and I'd assumed you weren't interested, and then when I saw your face you looked so anxious and . . .'

'And what?'

'And I fell in love with you.'

'Oh.'

'In the last few months, I have seen Louise *once* and that was when she came down to do the interview. I haven't slept with her, I haven't kissed her.'

'Are you trying to tell me there is nothing between you? Are you telling me *she* doesn't want you?'

Robin sighed and put his hands on the steering wheel. He looked ill. He looked as if he hadn't slept at all. Given that last night he'd been in France and now he was here, he probably hadn't.

'No,' he said. 'We talked on the phone a lot. She's been very kind. She's gone out of her way to promote our business. She's got us some fantastic publicity and worked very hard. I owed her. And then, when everything started getting out of control, she told me that my mother had told her you were in love with Graham—'

'Excuse me?' Tilly exploded. 'Your mother said that? I've hardly exchanged two words with her since you left me.'

'Tilly,' Robin said, 'the man is nuts about you. I saw him kiss you.'

'That's what Graham does,' Tilly said. 'He likes to kiss me in front of my husband or my in-laws. He finds it amusing. He likes to make an impression.'

'I don't understand. I don't seem to understand much at the moment.'

'Join the club. So, basically, Louise told you I was having it off with Graham and therefore you could have it off with her.'

Robin's mouth twitched. 'She didn't put it quite like that.'

'I'm sure she didn't.'

'The thing was, I'd got myself into a corner. I'd walked out on you, I'd said terrible things to you, I'd behaved like a jerk and just as I was beginning to understand what I'd done, I found out that you had gone and fallen for someone else.'

'I hadn't.'

'And in the meantime, Louise was devoting huge chunks of time to furthering my career and telling me that she . . . that she . . .'

340

'. . . that she wanted to have it off with you.'

'It was difficult,' Robin said. 'I saw Graham doing all the things I should have been doing: putting up shelves, mending fences, preparing the nursery, and I knew very well that I was the idiot who opened the door and let him in.'

'If you were so keen to get back to me, why didn't you meet me for dinner when I spoke to you on the train?'

'I could hear Graham's voice. I thought you only wanted to see me to ask for a divorce or something. So I went off to France and I thought I'd lost you. And then Harry rang and all I could think of was that I had to get back to you.'

'My mother,' Tilly said, 'thinks I should go off with Graham.'

'My mother thinks I should go off with Louise. I bet the two of them are having a great time together, discussing ways of keeping us apart.'

'You were vile,' Tilly told him.

'I know.'

'What you did . . . it changed me. I'm a different person now. I want to earn my own money. I want to be a proofreader. I want to be a very good proofreader. And I'm having a baby. The house is going to be untidy again and it will probably go on being untidy for a long time. And I have to tell you, I'm not prepared to become a Stepford housewife in order to get you back. I'm not even sure I want you back.'

'I'm not surprised. I know my behaviour was appalling. But I'm different too. Do you remember when Clarence shows James Stewart in *It's a Wonderful Life* what his family and town would be like if he'd never lived? Well, I discovered what my life was like without you and the kids: flat and empty and no fun at all.'

341

'I'm flattered.'

'I'm not trying to flatter you. I'm telling you the truth.'

'Well, my truth is that I can't love you like I used to. I loved you so much. I probably loved you too much. I thought I couldn't live without you. Now, I know I can. And I'm not sure I can ever trust you again either. For all I know, there are hordes of ex-girlfriends waiting to tempt you away every time I fail to clean the floor.'

'I could never leave you again.'

'How can I be sure? I seem to remember you said that once before.'

'Tilly, I've learnt the biggest lesson ever. And I know I should have learnt it ages ago. I know everything you say is right. But there's something else. I know that ever since I stopped making you and the children the most important people in my life I've been miserable. I know I want to watch you feeding our baby in the middle of the night, I want to hold our baby in the middle of the night, I want to wake up in the morning and find Lucy and Sam trying to pull the bed-clothes off me. I want us all to go to the seaside in the summer, just like we did last year and the year before that. I want to hear Lucy telling me every endless detail of her entire school day, I want to watch Sam push all his fingers into his mouth, I want to kiss them both goodnight every evening. I want to be sitting in the car with you in twenty years' time listening to you singing out of tune to "Hey Jude". I know what's important in my life now and it's not my parents or my job, it's you – you, me and the children. I could never, I would never, risk that again.'

Tilly swallowed. 'I suppose . . .' she began and then stopped and said, 'Oh, my God!' Her mother-in-law was marching towards them, her small black handbag swinging crazily in her hand. Running a few steps behind, like an avenging angel, came Margot. In a moment she had caught Anne up and, with a swing of her arm, hit Anne's shoulder with her own much bigger bag.

'Oh, my God!' Tilly said. 'My mother's attacked your mother! Do something, Robin!'

Robin did something. He switched on the ignition, went into gear and drove up to the warring women. They both stopped to stare at him and Anne looked as if she was about to speak. Robin waved and drove out onto the road.

Tilly looked back and gasped. 'My mother's hit your mother *again*! You have to do something! What are you going to do?'

Robin looked at his wife. His hair was a mess, his face was white and unshaven, but his eyes were tender and loving and happy. 'I'm coming home,' he said.